BLIND DELUSION

BLIND DELUSION

A Novel

BOOK 2 OF THE DOROTHY PHAIRE ROMANTIC MYSTERY SERIES

Dorothy Phaire
Author of *Murder and The Masquerade*

iUniverse, Inc.
New York   Bloomington

Blind Delusion
A Novel

This is a work of fiction. All of the characters, names, incidents,
organizations, and dialogue in this novel are either the products
of the author's imagination or are used fictitiously.

iUniverse books may be ordered through booksellers or by contacting:

iUniverse
1663 Liberty Drive
Bloomington, IN 47403
www.iuniverse.com
1-800-Authors (1-800-288-4677)

Because of the dynamic nature of the Internet, any Web addresses or links
contained in this book may have changed since publication and may no longer be
valid. The views expressed in this work are solely those of the author and do not
necessarily reflect the views of the publisher, and the publisher hereby disclaims
any responsibility for them.

ISBN: 978-1-4401-6822-2 (sc)
ISBN: 978-1-4401-6824-6 (dj)
ISBN: 978-1-4401-6823-9 (ebk)

Printed in the United States of America

iUniverse rev. date: 09/30/2009

Dedication

This book is dedicated to my Dad, Paul Herring. Through the years he has taught me many valuable things that I needed to know to survive and be successful in life. The most important of these lessons is the meaning of unconditional love. By watching how my Dad responds with patience and love in good times as well as in times of crisis with support and encouragement to his family and friends—I have learned the meaning of unconditional love.

Acknowledgements

Planning and researching for this book traveled through many starts, stops, and restarts due to life's unplanned interruptions. I began researching for the sequel to my first book, **Murder and the Masquerade** several years prior to writing the first draft. In fact, at various phases over the course of four years I was working on revising **Murder and the Masquerade** and drafting the sequel, **Blind Delusion** simultaneously.

During this early research phase, numerous professionals and subject matter experts graciously gave of their time and granted me interviews. I am grateful to everyone who took the time to sit down with me for an interview. I would be remiss if I did not acknowledge a few specific representatives of organizations that early on shared their knowledge and expertise specifically for this book. I am indebted to the Washington, D. C. Fire and EMS Department for granting me a ride-along and to those individual firefighters and officers at Engine 16 and Truck 3. My special thanks go to Georgia K. Hilgeman, director of the Vanishing Children's Alliance and Kitty Dawson, social worker from Child and Family Services in Washington, D. C. Also, I am grateful to editor, Valerie Jean for helping to smooth out some of the rough edges during the early phase of drafting this novel.

Later in rewrite, many others accepted my request for their feedback and knowledge. For their invaluable contributions in helping me to get this book off the ground, I would like to thank my friend Charles Dean for reading sample chapters and asking smart questions that helped me to revise. My appreciation also goes to Professor Gerald Irvin for his feedback and for enthusiastically recommending my first book to his literature students, many of whom are now waiting to read this sequel. I would like to thank my friend and colleague, Dr. Mohamed El-Khawas for his unwavering encouragement and for listening to me hash out my plot scenarios. In the field of psychology I am grateful to longtime friend, Dr. Herbert Guggenheim for sharing his professional knowledge and responding to my questions about anxiety disorders. My special thanks go to those individuals who came through when I asked specific questions relevant to their areas of expertise; namely, Curtis Mosby, Mohammed "Jack" Khan, Professor Margaret Harris, and Darinka Clary. Thanks to the book club readers at Metro 9 Book Club; Reva Gambrell and her book club readers; and Beauty Within readers, for their support. I am also grateful to my friend, Charlene Ridley for being an avid reader who always gives me her honest opinion. To family members and friends who journeyed with me through a long period of revisions and total rewrites to see this book creation come to fruition, I am indebted to you all. If I left anyone out in expressing my appreciation, please charge it to my head and not to my heart.

PART ONE

Life's but a walking shadow, a poor player,
That struts and frets his hour upon the stage,
And then is heard no more.
　　From *Macbeth*, William Shakespeare *(1564 - 1616)*

PROLOGUE

October 6,

On this early Fall day in late afternoon, the alley behind 6th Street opened into a dark gray sky of low black clouds that looked heavy from the threat of rain. The only movement was the occasional rat running from one trash can to the next. The only sound was from the hissing of a cat stalking its prey and waiting for that perfect moment to pounce and make the rat his meal. But the cat scurried off when a figure appeared and walked down the alley behind the houses that faced 6th Street. The figure seemed nervous and cautious, much like the cat he had just deprived of its evening meal. He glanced backwards every so often. His shoulders were hunched and his face was concealed by an oversized, dark hooded jacket. The man carried a gasoline can in his right hand. When he arrived at the rear of 1236 6th Street he paused and took a quick snort of cocaine. A euphoric high rushed straight to his brain. Pumped up and adrenaline fed, the man set the gasoline can down on the back porch. Donning a pair of black gloves, he removed a screwdriver from an inside pocket of his jacket. One arm braced the screen door open while the other hand frantically chiseled at the back door lock. The door appeared to be double-bolted from the inside and would not budge. The gloved hand of the man trembled and beads of sweat trickled down his panicked stricken face. Frustrated by the dead bolt on the backdoor, he released the screen door and it slammed shut, startling the already nervous prowler.

His desperate eyes turned to the kitchen window next. Peeping through its filmy panes, the man could see that the upper inside window lock was damaged and had been secured with duck tape. The thick layers of duct tape lined the inside ledge and window frame in an attempt to hold the window latch in place. A sense of pleasure drifted across his face. With both palms, he pried, yanked, and pushed until the window began to yield. His heavy woolen gloves prevented him from reaching inside the window and grasping the edge of the duct tape to strip it off. Snatching off one sweat-soaked glove, he peeled away each layer of duct tape. Discarded pieces of ripped tape fell to the floor of the porch. With several more strong tugs, the window finally slid open. He picked up the gas can and pushed it through the open window, setting it down carefully on the floor just under the window. He climbed through the window and silently entered the house.

Jerome Antonio Johnson, the resident of 1236 6th Street, sniffed under his armpits then pulled off his undershirt and sweatpants. He placed a DMX CD in the Stereo System and cranked up the volume. As he turned toward the bathroom, he stopped to glance in the mirror at his naked, compact, muscled frame. The handsome, dark-skinned man in the mirror smiled a white-teeth grin back at himself. He ran his hand over his smooth, bald head then flexed his muscles. Brenda was right, he thought. He looked damn good. Any woman would be proud to step out on the town with him, but looking good wasn't paying the bills. Now that he was out of a job, they needed money and health insurance. He had to convince United Delivery Service (UDS) to rehire him. Even if he got that security job he had applied for at the mall, it wouldn't bring in enough money to feed his family and pay their bills. Jerome didn't argue with his wife because he knew she was right. It was his stupidity that had cost him his job and their family's security. Jerome fingered the engraved silver ID bracelet that Brenda had given him for their last anniversary. He never took it off. It had an inscription that read, *To Jerome. Forever Your Loving Wife, Brenda.* He felt the same way about her. These days if Brenda told him to stand in front of an oncoming train, he would. He had finally learned to appreciate the woman he married and he knew how lucky he was to have her and his baby son, in his life. Jerome's past drug habit and cheating with his ex-girlfriend had almost cost him his wife and his son. To keep this from ever happening again, he'd been attending rehab meetings in the evenings, and had cut-off all ties with Leenae Lewis for good. But Jerome would need his Uncle Ike's help to get his old job back at UDS. Jerome had been fired for failing a random drug test but he knew that test had to be bogus. He didn't understand why the test had shown a presence of drugs in his system. Odessa Dillon, Jerome's former supervisor, claimed she had other legitimate reasons for firing him such as using his UDS assigned truck for personal business. He knew other drivers had used their trucks to run personal errands and had only received a week off without pay, max. Odessa had made it clear that she wanted him for her new boy toy but he wasn't having any of it. He needed his Uncle Ike's financial support to hire a lawyer to file an EEO complaint against UDS for wrongful termination. Of course, Brenda didn't know anything about Odessa and her crazy self. If he won his case against her and the company, she would have to rehire him as feeder driver with back pay, like it or not. Then he'd request a transfer to another area, just like Hector Gonzales had to do in order to get away from her.

He and Brenda had no money in the bank and monthly bills to pay. The only protection they had from the unforeseen was a $50,000 term life insurance policy that they had opened up about a week after Baby Justin was born. Jerome recalled some of the telephone conversation with the sales agent who at first claimed to be calling to congratulate them on the birth of their son. Jerome didn't understand how these telemarketers seemed to find out personal information about people then use it to sucker people into buying things they hadn't even thought about buying. The sales agent had convinced them that for only a few cents a month they would each qualify for a $50,000 five-year term life policy in the unlikely event that something should happen to either of them. Thinking about it now, Jerome realized that he was worth more dead than alive to Brenda and his son now that he was out of a job and had no medical benefits.

But he didn't want to think about that now. He nodded approvingly at his reflection in the mirror, confident that things would eventually go his way—they always did. Jerome's self-adulation was interrupted by the telephone. Jerome hit the pause button on the CD player and glanced at the caller ID before picking up the phone. It was DL, the enforcer for the Jett Set Crew, the gang Jerome use to run with to make a little change on the side. That is, before he got hooked on the product and became one of their customers. He knew DL was calling to demand that he pay the two thousand dollars he owed the crew's leader, Drug Lord James Ian Mathias.

"Look here, DL, I can't pay you right now but I got me another gig, man. Starts on Monday," said Jerome, lying easily to his former friend. "It's a night security job at a mall."

"Hey, I ain't plannin' on waitin' 'til you collect social security, asshole," said DL.

Jerome responded, "I understand Baby but like my Grandmama says, you can't get blood outta a turnip."

"Maybe not but I can get blood outta your sorry ass," countered DL.

"Hold up, Man. Lemme, have some time to …" Jerome pleaded.

"Your time is up, chump. Consider yourself marked."

DL hung up. Jerome stood holding the phone to his ear for what seemed like 30 seconds or so listening to dead air until the silence was broken by the sound of the dial tone.

"Ah, DL just talkin' trash," said Jerome to himself and walked towards the bathroom, "Me and that fool go way back. I'll just borrow a coupla dollars from Uncle Ike tomorrow. That should hold him until I get the rest of their goddamn money."

Jerome hit play on the CD player, went into the bathroom, closed the door, and turned on the shower. He could no longer hear the rap lyrics to the song that was playing, just its thumping bass. Jerome hummed the rhythm of the familiar tune as he bathed his bronze muscular body. Although he knew the baby slept soundly in the nursery, Jerome didn't want to linger in the shower too long in case the little guy woke up. He knew he wouldn't be able to hear him crying through the pounding force of the shower's water flow and the bass playing in the background.

The intruder waited just inside the kitchen window for one minute as he had been instructed for an incoming call to his cell phone, which for obvious reasons was set to vibrate. This was the call that would have canceled the hit on Jerome Antonio Johnson. After exactly one minute of silence, the intruder quietly ascended the staircase and stepped over the threshold of the door to the first bedroom at the top of the stairs. The intruder could see steam seeping under the bathroom door and could hear Jerome singing in the shower. *He can carry a tune,* thought the intruder. *Too bad his singing days are over.* "I gotcha now, baby," whispered the intruder.

He doused the bed and floor with gasoline. Then, stood back just outside the bedroom door, and dug into his pocket for the matchbook. He ripped off a match and lit it. He hesitated, squeezing the lit match between thumb and index finger until both fingers were singed from the heat of the match. "Hell, too late to turn back now," he shrugged. He tossed the lit match on the gasoline soaked floor. The match ignited the gasoline and in seconds the fire rolled across the floor. The entire room roared, completely engulfed in smoke and flames. He picked up the gasoline can and threw the can into the fire. He stood transfixed at the bedroom door, watching yellow-white flames and black smoke drift upward. When the gasoline can exploded, the intruder turned to leave. He walked calmly down the hall much like a man leaving the office after a hard day's work.

Jerome's back and shoulders tingled from the shower's massage setting. Man, this shower feels good after my workout, he thought as the hot water beat against his back. He had been lifting weights downstairs in the basement and the forceful gush of hot water and stream soothed his muscles. Brenda didn't know it but he had more problems than just losing his job at UDS. He hadn't been able to pay back a past drug debt to the Crew on Wednesday night like he had promised Bombillo, the finance manager for the Crew. Bombillo had already talked DL into waiting until Wednesday but when the time came to meet that night, Jerome didn't show up. He had been concerned for his safety if he had shown up empty handed so he played it safe and stayed away. The other deal he had going to get the money fell through and now in addition to helping to get his job back, he had to depend on Uncle Ike for a loan to get from under the Crew. He didn't want to think about what might happen if he couldn't get the money from Uncle Ike. Jerome had explained to DL that all he needed was another week or so for his uncle to borrow against the equity in his home. He had begged DL to consider their friendship from the old days and give him some more time. But after the telephone conversation with DL just now, Jerome had an uneasy feeling that he was in deep trouble.

The way he figured it, in another month or so, he'd be set if only the Crew could wait a few more days for him to get the cash from his uncle and pay off his debt to them. Other than the debt he owed, Jerome had completely broken his ties to the Crew. He knew this had further fueled the Crew's anger with him since they had lost a regular customer.

The hot water beating against his body felt good. Baby Buddha should be waking up from his nap soon he figured. After he woke up, he'd take the little guy out for a walk in his stroller, maybe even swing by the park if it wasn't raining or too cold outside. He hadn't told Brenda that he'd decided to keep his son home today instead of taking him to the baby sitter. She had been running late this morning and asked him if he would drop Baby Buddha off for her. What Brenda didn't know wouldn't hurt her he figured. When he called the babysitter that morning to let her know she wouldn't be needed today, the sitter had made it clear they would still have to pay the full amount at the end of the week. Jerome didn't care about that. He wasn't ready to give up his role as full-time daddy yet. It had only been a week, but Jerome and the little guy had gotten into a routine before Brenda found their new babysitter. Jerome had the hang of it now and he thoroughly enjoyed taking care of his son. No more catastrophes with feeding and diapering.

Suddenly, Jerome detected a strong odor that mingled with the shower steam. It smelled so potent his nose cringed. It couldn't be gasoline, he thought, but that's exactly what it smelled like. As soon as Jerome turned off the shower, he heard the popping noise from a crackling fire outside the bathroom door. He couldn't hear it while the shower ran but now the sound grew louder. He felt the door and quickly pulled his hand away because of heat. With heart pounding and an unsteady hand, he opened the door enough to see that his bedroom was ablaze. He slammed the door shut. Panic swept across his face and his heart raced. Baby Buddha! Somehow, he had to get to the nursery to save his son. That's all that mattered. He grabbed the towel from the toilet seat and pulled down the shower curtain. He turned on the shower to drench the towel and curtain in water. He wrapped himself in the water-soaked curtain and threw the dripping wet towel over his head. He tried to open the door again but flames and black smoke pushed into the bathroom. Jerome slammed the door shut again. *I gotta get the hell outta here! Oh God, Help Me! I gotta get to my son!* Jerome threw open the door and leaped through the flames.

He yelled in agony as the fire burned his flesh. The heat was so intense Jerome only got a few feet from the bathroom door before he collapsed to the floor shrieking in pain, his body completely covered in flames. His howling screams echoed throughout the house until the thousand-degree heat and black smoke seized his last breath.

The intruder raced down the steps. Once back outside, he picked up a big rock lying beside the porch steps and hurled it at the rear kitchen window, shattering the glass and further feeding the fire with oxygen. The smell of burning, human flesh filled the air. The intruder turned to leave but stopped when he heard something else coming from inside the house. It was not the screams of a burning man but instead he heard the cries of a baby. "Damn!" he said under his breath, "they didn't tell me there was a baby in the house. I ain't no baby killer ..." Without hesitation he turned and ran back into the house. He stayed low just like a well trained fire fighter would and moved along the floor towards the stairwell and the sounds of the crying baby. He paused at the bottom of the stairs which were by now almost completely covered in flames. "Shit!! Shit!! Damn!! Hell!!" he cursed. He took a deep breath and ran through the flames up the stairs and down the hallway to the room at the end where the crying was coming from. He pushed the door open and saw the baby lying in a crib in the smoked filled room. He grabbed the baby and put it under his jacket. He turned and escaped back down the hall, back down the flaming stairs, across the kitchen floor and crawled through the broken window. He jumped to the ground and landed on his feet to keep from falling on the baby, which he held onto with one arm. The intruder ignored the sound of the crying baby in his arms. He ran down the alley in the same direction he had come from, firmly holding the baby under his jacket until he disappeared from the alley. The chilling screams of death emanated through his memory—sounds that would not go away long after he fled the burning house.

CHAPTER 1

A lonely French Colonial mansion sat atop a hill, spotlighted by the halo from a globe lamp and guarded by massive sycamores that hadn't yet shed their October leaves. The limbs spread out like hinged ribs on an umbrella—their brilliant yellow leaves now faded. It was now dark outside. Quietness enveloped this secluded Washington, D. C. enclave known as Foxhall Crescent Estates where the Hayes' mansion was the centerpiece on a sprawling landscape. Except for a rising wind that sounded like an old woman's raspy voice, all appeared peaceful.

Inside the mansion, Dr. Renee Hayes sat looking out at the moon from the breakfast window. She had delayed preparing dinner until 8 because she didn't want to eat alone again. Her husband had come home late for the past five evenings with no reasonable explanation. She knew he wasn't working late since he often complained that he hated his job as Senior Technical Instructor at EduTech Computer Training Center. She tugged at her wedding band until it finally slid over her knuckle. She tossed it onto the kitchen counter where it clanked against the marble. She washed her hands in lotion soap before preparing the appetizer, lemon-tarragon shrimp salad on a bed of romaine lettuce.

Removing her wedding ring a half dozen times or more for the simplest tasks, like hand washing or chopping onions, had become a habit. Mood lights brightened the French Provincial kitchen just enough for Renee to see the seasonings she sprinkled into the Alfredo sauce while the shrimp salad chilled in the fridge. The strong aroma of chicken tenderloins sautéed in onions and garlic drowned out the apple-cinnamon air spray. She had already set the table in their formal dining room. Two place settings of gold-rimmed china and a pair of wineglasses waited at each end of the elegant table that could easily accommodate 12 guests. A crystal lily-filled vase kissed by the flames of two white candles created a lustrous centerpiece while a saxophone jazz tune moaned soothingly in the background from the built-in CD player.

Renee heard the garage door open. When Bill entered the kitchen, glancing quickly at her, then away, all he said was, "Hi Babe."

She tried to sound cheerful but her voice fell flat. "Dinner should be ready by the time you wash up and change."

"No thanks, I grabbed something downtown."

Her insides tightened but she said nothing, too hurt to respond. It was a shame that after fourteen years of marriage, communication had deteriorated to a simple nod and a stiff greeting that could have easily come from a passing stranger on the street. Renee dumped the angel hair pasta down the drain. She had suddenly lost her appetite and in another ten minutes it would taste like paste anyway. Bill shrugged his shoulders, unfazed. Briefcase in hand, he walked down the hallway towards his office.

"You could have called before I went through all this trouble." Her voice sounding hard, rather than hurt. He disappeared down the hall as her voice trailed after him. She couldn't leave things like this. Renee followed him to his office where she found him leaning into the desk with his head buried in his hands.

"Bill, what's bothering you? Talk to me," she said leaning against the door and staring at him attentively.

He sighed and rested his head against the back of the leather chair, eyes closed. "Nothing. I mean, there's nothing you can do."

"Maybe not but I can listen." She moved towards him and gently touched his shoulder.

He lifted his eyelids slightly and stared at her through narrowed slits. "Yeah, I know. That's what they pay you the big bucks for."

"What's that supposed to mean?" Renee raised her eye brows and jerked her hand away from his shoulder.

"Forget it," he said, rubbing his temples, "I'm not in the mood for this."

"No, let's not forget it. Are you jealous because I make more money than you? Is that it?"

Bill grunted out a dry laugh. "Yeah that's it, Doctor. Once again you've psychoanalyzed correctly."

"Do you enjoy putting me down? It's obvious you don't respect my profession."

"Hey, I wasn't attacking your career. I'm just sick of being put under a microscope. I'm not one of those losers stupid enough to pay a week's wages for somebody to listen to their problems."

Renee folded her arms across her chest and ignored his sarcasm. "I want to know what's going on with you," she said firmly.

He turned away from her glare, and flipped open his laptop computer and booted it up. Then he glanced back at her, "Look Renee, do you mind? I have to work."

Renee felt like everything had spiraled out of control. All she wanted was a quiet, romantic evening for a change. What the hell had gone wrong? She'd been married to this man for 14 years and she still couldn't feel his love. As for her dream of becoming a mother someday, doctors had told her she'd never be able to conceive and carry a child to term. So far, they had been right. Her last attempt at motherhood was six years ago—an ectopic pregnancy that had to be aborted in order to save her life. That left adoption as their only option. An idea that Bill was vehemently against for his own selfish reasons, which she could not understand because he had refused to open up and share that part of himself no matter how many times she had relied on her years of textbook and clinical psychotherapeutic training to get him to open up. Meanwhile the clock continued to race forward towards a bleak and lonely midnight. On the eve of her forty-fifth birthday, Renee felt fearful of changing what she instinctively knew was wrong in her life. And, Bill became an easy target for her frustrations.

"For someone who claims to hate his job so much, you certainly devote a lot of time to it," she said in a bitter tone.

"This is not for EduTech," he said without looking up from the computer screen, "In fact, I may not be there much longer."

Renee couldn't believe this man was actually entertaining the idea of quitting his job. "What do you mean? Are you planning to quit?"

Bill said nothing. His fingers raced across the keyboard without looking away from the screen.

CHAPTER 2

The next morning the 'wake to music' alarm went off at 5 AM in Renee's bedroom, and she woke up to Lou Rawls's mentholated baritone voice crooning out soulful lyrics on 105.9 radio station's Thursday morning blues program. She closed her eyes and listened to the words that Lou Rawls sang.

> Around about the time the sun comes up
> Early Morning Love
> The kind of love you just can't get enough of
> As I slowly roll over …
> Early Morning Love.

After having lain in bed awake all night, alone—*Early Morning Love* was precisely what Renee was not getting and hadn't been getting for several months now.

The day folded uneventfully into the evening, and that night was no different from the previous night. She wondered, could Bill be having an affair? Punishing her for last summer? She didn't want to think about that. Finally, at half past nine Renee gave up waiting on Bill. She couldn't believe that he would come home tonight after 10 o'clock again. She swung open the French doors and strode into her bedroom, dimming the lights. Subdued bursts of accent lighting displayed a rich arrangement of artwork against mauve-painted walls. Modern art peacefully coexisted with traditional oils on canvas and impressionistic watercolors. One modern piece depicted a bare-breasted woman staring out from a triad of bulging eyeballs. Next to it, hung a sunset landscape in delicate watercolor. The bedroom's mellow hues calmed her. But Renee frowned when she spotted Bill's green-eyed, white Persian cat, curled up asleep on his side of the bed, taking ownership.

"Bill's got that cat spoiled worse than an only child," she uttered under her breath.

Despite her frequent pleas to get rid of that annoying cat, it was still there. Lately, she and Bill agreed on nothing and argued about everything.

Renee turned on the CD player then walked over by the window where she sank down on a Rococo Revival loveseat. She felt the whisper of billowy drapes against her neck. Moonlight pried through the floor-length, white linen curtains and illuminated the bedroom. Gladys Knight's mellow voice filled the room with one of Renee's favorite songs, an old 70s hit, 'Neither One of Us Wants to Be The First to Say Goodbye'. She listened closely to the lyrics.

It's sad to think
We're not gonna make it
And it's gotten to the point
Where we just can't fake it
Ooh, ooh, ooh, for some ungodly reason
We just won't let it die
I guess neither one of us
Wants to be the first to say goodbye …

Gladys was singing this song for her and Bill. He still hadn't shared what was bothering him, though she suspected it was something at work. Lately, he seemed more preoccupied than usual with his work. Or *was* there another woman involved? Though she didn't want to entertain the idea, she couldn't dismiss the possibility that Bill was cheating on her. The thought of answering the telephone in the middle of the night and hearing a woman's voice on the other end asking for her husband, put her stomach in knots. Perhaps he was trying to get back at her for falling in love with a younger man this past summer. She trembled and clutched at both arms, hugging herself tightly as she struggled to wipe away her memories of being with Deek. Her emotions were too fragile to think about Deek and how much she still missed him.

Renee got up and went to the built-in wine cabinet then poured herself a glass of burgundy. After only a few sips she placed the glass down and walked over to the Cheval mirror, the one gift from Bill that she cherished. Its hand-painted frame displayed a whimsical motif of winged cherubs that reminded her of babies and sweet innocence. She let her robe slip to the floor and stared at her naked reflection. The slightly plump figure before her still maintained a few vestiges of its former eighteen-year old, gazelle-ish self. Back then plum-size breasts that once stood at attention were fuller now. At 44, soon to be 45, years old she was grateful that they didn't sag. She loosened the chignon and let her thick, Egyptian sable hair fall to her tender brown shoulders. Still sexy. Still vibrant. Still alive. But the eyes gave her away. Sleepless and vapid, they marked her, as a woman unloved and untouched. Tomorrow was her birthday. Would Bill even remember?

At the jarring sound of car tires outside her bedroom window, she picked up her robe and wrapped it around her body. "It's about time, damn you," she voiced to herself. Then she shooed the cat off her bed and it scurried out the room. Renee shut the door so the cat couldn't get back in. She knew it had to be Bill finally getting home but she walked over to the window anyway, and pushed aside the curtains. She flinched at the sight of a brand new red sports car parked in their driveway. Even more disturbing was Bill sitting behind the wheel. Renee ran from the bedroom and raced barefoot down the stairs and out the front door. She approached Bill just as he slid his six-foot, muscular frame from the new car.

"Where the hell have you been?" she demanded, and then pointed to the new car, "What's this?"

Bill grinned and his white teeth contrasted against his ebony-hued face. "I bought it. You like it? It's top of the line, babe." He rubbed his palm over the shiny red hood and beamed, "It's a BMW M3 coupe."

Renee was still in shock and couldn't speak.

Bill opened the door and slid back into the driver's seat. "Check out these leather seats and all the bells and whistles she's got." He pointed at the dashboard while she rolled her eyes without showing interest. "It's got a high revving V8 engine with 414 horsepower that can hit sixty miles per hour in only 4.8 seconds. It'll eat up a quarter-mile in only 12.7 seconds."

Renee gave him a look that let him know she wasn't impressed. Bill sat ramrod straight and clutched both hands on the steering wheel as he grinned up at her icy expression. "Did I mention it's also got several state-of-the art features like drive by wire throttle bodies, dynamic stability control, dual clutch transmission, electronic damping control, and differential lock?"

"You still didn't answer my question. Where did you get this new car?"

Bill jumped out of the seat. "Good evening to you too, sweetness," he said as he tipped his head forward in a bow. His lips were set in a slight curve that Renee took for his weak attempt to smile. He glanced down at her bare breast peeking through a gap in her robe. "I can see you're glad to see me too."

He caught her by surprise when he suddenly pulled her into his arms and nuzzled her neck. She flinched as his mustache touched her skin and smelled his breath that reeked of alcohol.

"Come on, Renee, let's get in," he winked, opening the car door. "How 'bout a quickie in my new car? We'll break her in."

"Are you crazy?" She shoved him away, tightening the robe around her body and cut him an icy glare.

"What?" he looked at her through drooping, bloodshot eyes, "What did I do?"

Renee flipped up the collar of her robe without answering.

"I didn't know the woman I married would turn out to be so damn conservative and uptight," he snarled and slammed the car door shut.

"And I didn't know the man I married could be so childish." She folded her arms and glared at him sideways.

She could see through the windshield and to her the dashboard resembled an airplane cockpit panel. The interior sported red and black leather trim.

"Bill, we don't have the money for this car. Have you lost your mind? You already have a Range Rover parked in the garage. What do you need a race car for at your age? You're almost 52 years old for Chrissakes."

"I just wanted it, baby, and I had the money to get it. Another company bought out EduTech last week. They laid me off and all the old timers too. But who the hell cares?"

"You got laid off?" she said, incredulously, "You only hinted at the possibility of not working for EduTech. Nothing about them laying you off."

"It ain't no thing but a chicken wing, Baby," he shrugged with a loopy grin, "I'm in business for myself now. I took my severance package and bought this beauty with the money. My buddy and I launched our own software training and brokering business. I don't need EduTech. In this economy you can't count on anybody but yourself"

Bill seemed pleased with himself as he stroked the hood of his new car.

"What kind of rip-off deal have you gotten into this time?" she said, her voice now rising. She took a deep breath to calm herself. "And how are you going to pay for this business when you spent your severance on this car? Have you conveniently forgotten about the thirty thousand dollars you lost three years ago in that risky internet startup company? I carried you when that deal went sour, remember?"

"Get off my back." His playful mood had suddenly turned cold. "Money is the least of our problems. Anyway, you've got royalties coming in from those self-help books of yours. Then there's your practice. Why the hell are you hassling me about my investments?"

"Because what you do affects me. I'm tired of watching you act like a kid with too many toys to play with."

"Can't you for once think about what somebody else wants, Renee?" he said and slammed his palm against the hood of the car. "Instead of it always being about what you want. You're so damn self-centered and controlling."

Renee turned away. She didn't want to admit it but his words hit home and she couldn't meet his gaze. She didn't know how she was able to solve other people's relationship problems but still couldn't seem to follow her own advice.

"I don't know what you're talking about, Bill. I'm not self-centered or controlling," she said calmly.

"Oh, no? Then let me refresh your memory, sweetheart."

Bill proceeded to name times and dates when she had made major decisions without consulting him. "And what about this past summer when you met with that social worker behind my back and started adoption proceedings without telling me a damn thing!"

Renee stared at her painted toes while sifting through Bill's accusations. When all her excuses disintegrated, she realized he had a point. She had been self-centered and controlling at times. When she ran down the list of strategies that she advised her clients to follow, she admitted to herself that she had resisted following her own suggestions. No wonder her marriage was in trouble. She couldn't blame it all on him.

"You're right, Bill. Our problems aren't all your fault. And getting angry won't solve anything."

Bill unfurled his brow and reached out to her. "Come on, baby, let's go inside the house." He put his arms around her shoulders, "You're half naked out here and shivering."

Bill clicked the automatic door lock. They walked into the house and she allowed Bill to guide her inside as she tried to piece through these new, troubling events. Any stranger peering at them from the outside would see a well-off couple seemingly enjoying all the trappings of success, from the baroque statuettes perched atop Italian marble pedestals at the foyer to the flower-filled, crystal vases, and cloisonné-adorned tables. But Renee and Bill Hayes had long ago ceased to notice their fine paintings against the pale yellow walls, the mahogany antique furnishings, or the silk-threaded Persian rugs throughout their home that had been professionally decorated by Ambrose and Rockwell.

They entered the formal drawing room where a Steinway baby grand sat in a corner un-tuned and neglected. Bill slumped into a comfortable barrelback chair. He leaned back and closed his eyes. Renee sat beside him and when she touched him, his body instinctively jerked.

"What's wrong?" she asked.

He slowly opened his eyes and stared ahead. "Nothing. I was just thinking how today was my last day at EduTech after twelve years. I guess I'm feeling mixed emotions after all."

"That's understandable," she said, softening her voice.

His face contorted as he spoke, "They had the nerve to bring in some kids from Drake Beam to tell us how to write a damn resume. I told 'em to kiss my old, tired, Black ass. I might be a Neanderthal, but I was writing resumes when they were still in kindergarten."

"I'm sorry."

"You know how it is out there, Renee," he smoothed the gray hair at his temple, "We live in a youth-obsessed, self-centered culture. Everybody's out for himself. Why bother looking for another damn job only to hear some snot nose recruiter say, 'Sorry, Mr. Hayes but the client chose someone more qualified for that position.' Hell, what they really mean is, they found someone twenty years younger willing to work for less money." He pounded his fist on the arm of the chair. "To hell with all that bullshit. I got a new business partner and we're gonna make a whole lotta cash," he nodded and winked at her.

"Who is this new business partner?" Renee wanted to sound supportive but she was skeptical.

"You remember Clifton Corbin Shaw? One of the managing partners at Himes, Shaw, & Harrison? About three weeks ago I mentioned to Cliff that I was a senior technical instructor and moonlighted on the side in the computer business. Guess Ole Cliff was impressed 'cause he called right after that and said he wanted to give me the first shot at a partnership in this new company he had just started. Renee, you should hear this guy talk about his ideas for the future. He's a genius, another Bill Gates or Donald Trump."

Renee shrugged, "I don't recall meeting him."

"You know who I mean. We met at the Capital Tennis Challenge Auction last month. And I've been running into him at the gym every once in awhile. He's got a plan to set up a technical recruiting firm. Says he needs somebody like me to run the day to day operations."

Renee frowned as she suddenly recalled the evening she had met Clifton Shaw. Short and thickset with skin the color of wet mud, and small, close-together eyes. He had insisted that everyone join him for drinks at Blue Duck Tavern after the auction. It didn't take too many Jack Daniels™ for Shaw to unleash his obnoxious nature. It was bad enough that the man kept peering at her breasts whenever he spoke to her, but when she overheard him say, 'If a Brother plans to get ahead in life, he'd better marry a white woman. These sistahs out here are too damn angry all the time,' that did it for her. After hearing him say that, she had grabbed her purse and left the table.

"Oh, yes, unfortunately I do remember Clifton Shaw. Be careful that you don't buy into everything people tell you without investigating it first. I don't like that guy."

"Damnit, Renee! There you go again. Always criticizing everything

I do before it even gets off the ground. Let me handle my own business affairs and you handle yours."

He glanced at his watch. "Shit!" Bill shot out of the chair. "I gotta go, babe. I'm meeting Shaw downtown at his office tonight to go over a few final issues."

"Are you serious? It's after ten o'clock and you just got home. Did it ever occur to you that I might want some attention from you tonight? Who has a business meeting this late? I know you just lost your job but you're not the only one going through changes."

"What the hell do you want from me, Renee?"

"What do I want? I want a husband and a friend. Someone I can grow old with and know that I'm loved no matter what. I want to wake up in the morning and feel joy. Not feel like life is passing me by. I want to hold my own baby in my arms. A child may even bring us closer together. We could nurture him, love him, and watch him or her grow into a fine adult." Renee turned her face away and quickly wiped a tear. "I wish you'd try to understand what it's like wanting something so bad all your life and not being able to have it."

"You're wrong, Renee. I know exactly what that feels like." He stiffened, and then paused before continuing in a gentle tone. "Sweetheart, I understand you have this maternal need to take care of people. I guess that's why you became a psychologist. But I've told you before I'm too old to start being somebody's daddy." He approached her where she was seated. "Besides, my Pops wasn't the best role model to learn from. Who knows what kinda father I'd be? Why can't things just stay the way they are?"

He knelt down before her and took her hand. "Didn't you just promise to start seeing things from my perspective?"

"I want to—I mean, I will try but I need you to do the same."

Bill nodded and gave her hand a quick pat. "Okay, but right now I gotta get to this meeting. I just stopped in to pick up some papers we need to go over tonight. Shaw's a night owl and the only time he has to work on this deal is after hours since his law practice is so busy during the day. Don't wait up, babe."

Bill rose and started to walk away, but Renee grabbed his elbow. "You don't understand. I'm suffocating in this marriage and in case you haven't noticed, it's not working."

"I'm sorry babe but can we talk about this later?" He broke free of her grip and left the room without waiting for approval to end the conversation.

Suddenly, he turned on his heels and came back. "Trust me, Renee, I know exactly what I'm doing." Then he smiled. "Today's Thursday, right? I promise, we'll do something really special for your birthday tomorrow. If you can just be a little more patient, I'll make it up to you."

Renee blinked back her tears as Bill left the room, leaving her slumped in the chair. After a few minutes had passed she heard the front door slam shut. She wanted to scream, to throw or kick something, to hurt Bill. But she did nothing. "All right, honey," she mouthed the words silently in her head, "Go do what you think you have to do. And, I'll do the same." She inhaled deeply, then exhaled. Seven years of psychotherapeutic training, fifteen years of practice, and three years of emergency room nursing had conditioned her to stay calm under extreme pressure. This time would be no different. Renee had fought worse demons than Bill and had survived.

CHAPTER 3 - BRENDA

Brenda Johnson awoke suddenly when she thought she heard Justin, her three-month old son, crying in his nursery. Her ears were tuned into Justin's cries, even when she was in a deep sleep. But now fully awake, there was complete silence in the room, except for the sound of her husband, Jerome's breathing as he slept next to her. The only light came from an orange-yellow glow of a lit candle that Brenda had left burning on top the dresser. It emitted a spicy sweet fragrance of cinnamon and oranges that mingled with melting wax. She rolled over to face Jerome, tucking the spread under her chin. She pressed her body against him and softly massaged his back with her fingertips, yet he continued to sleep soundly. Her golden tan leg intertwined with his dark coffee-toned leg and their bodies blended into each other, a contrast of light and dark brown. As usual Jerome took up almost all of the space on their double bed. His muscular body from daily workouts was spread out across the rumpled sheets.

Brenda raised her head a little to glance at the clock on the nightstand next to Jerome, hoping she'd have a few more hours left to sleep. To her dismay it was almost 5 o'clock, and the alarm was due to go off in 5 minutes. She flung the covers back, then reached over to turn off the alarm. No sense waking up Sleeping Beauty, she thought, eyeing her husband with envy. He slept soundly on his stomach with his face buried in the pillow. With a sigh, she slowly rose from the bed. Every morning during the work week was the same. While they both had to leave the house by seven, Jerome only had to get himself out the door. She, on the other hand, had to prepare Justin's bottles, pack bag lunches as well as fix breakfast for Jerome and herself, get dressed, and get the baby fed and ready to take to the babysitter's. She stuffed her arms into her floral-print cotton robe without even bothering to tie the belt. *Why can't he get up at 5 o'clock once and awhile and let me sleep an extra 45 minutes? We're both working full-time.* But Brenda knew this was a rhetorical question because she already knew the answer to why she couldn't expect Jerome to do more. Just having him working steady for a change was a huge improvement over 18 months ago when he was still using drugs, unemployed, staying out all night, and messing around with his ex-girlfriend, Leenae. At least these days she knew where he was at night. Brenda braced herself with one hand on the edge of the bed as she bent down low to reach for her slippers with the other hand. She slid her feet into the well-worn slippers and sat on the edge of the bed, not yet ready to begin her morning routine. Things could be much worse, she thought. *Sure I'm dog tired and we don't have our own place yet, but at least Jerome's working steady now and not running the streets with his homeboys. That's exactly how he got into trouble in the first place.*

Jerome delivered packages for Union Delivery Service or UDS as he called it. She worked as an office assistant for Dr. Renee Hayes, a clinical psychologist in private practice in Washington, D. C. They were living temporarily with Mama Etta in a quiet Southeast Capitol Hill neighborhood. Until just two months ago Brenda and her husband had been living in subsidized housing in the Northeast Trinidad neighborhood. After little Justin was born, they moved in with Jerome's grandmother to save money and get on their feet. Brenda didn't want her newborn around flying bullets from drive-by shootings or drug deals gone bad. Mama Etta had left last week to stay with her sister in Ft. Lauderdale, Florida for about six months. She told them that cold weather made her arthritis act up and she hated wintertime in Washington, D. C. Brenda recalled Mama Etta saying, *you never know what you might wake up to in this city, a blizzard or a heat wave!* But Brenda suspected Jerome's grandmother really wanted to give the two young people some privacy so they could strengthen their marriage, especially after all the trouble that Jerome had gotten himself into in the past. Brenda desperately wanted a home of her own like Mama Etta's little house with its fenced in patch of grass and flower boxes on the steps. This tree-lined section of Southeast Washington, D. C in Capitol Hill felt safe and looked like a good place to raise a child. Staying at Mama Etta's for a while would help them fix their credit rating and save for their own house.

These days life was pretty good and she felt blessed. Brenda knew how quickly things could change. She got down on her knees and leaned over the edge of the bed, bowing her head into clasped hands, she said a silent prayer of thanks to the Lord for her husband's long clean spell and for giving them this lovely place to stay, no matter how temporary. She asked God to continue to keep Jerome from temptation. This was all she had ever asked God for. She wasn't praying for worldly goods like winning the Lottery—just to keep her family safe from all the evil out there in the world. When she wasn't too tired in the mornings to forget, this prayer was another part of her morning ritual. Still kneeling while resting her head in her hands, Brenda tried not to think about the way it was before, but she couldn't help it.

Before landing his current job six months ago as a driver for UDS, Jerome installed generators for the Washington Suburban Sanitary Commission (WSSC), where he was making good money and received excellent benefits. All that changed one Friday on payday when he neglected to show up for work three days in a row. Turns out he had used up his entire two-week paycheck on drugs. Before that relapse, he had kept a job for all of two months as a driver for a flower shop until he decided to use the company truck as bargaining collateral to buy drugs. Prior to joining UDS, Brenda couldn't recall a time when Jerome had worked anywhere for longer than six months. She knew she would have to keep praying, for Jerome as well as for herself.

Dear Lord, help me to forgive and to forget the past. Brenda tried to meditate on pleasant things as she recited prayers from her childhood. Yet, no matter how hard she tried to focus on her private prayers, bad memories about her husband's past drug abuse and infidelity crept through her thoughts. Brenda never understood what had led Jerome astray. He came from a church-going, middle-class family with an older brother and a younger sister, and grew up with both parents in the household. Even Jerome's father had tried to warn her before she married him. Mr. Johnson had explained to Brenda how hard it was as a father to use tough love and kick his son out for good despite his wife's protests that their son had no where else to go. Jerome's father said he would no longer enable his son's addiction. Brenda recalled the time that Jerome had once shared with her that he felt abandoned by his immediate family. The only two people that never turned him away were his Uncle Ike and his seventy-eight year old, maternal grandmother, Mama Etta, whose house they were now living in. So far, Thank God, everything was okay or was it? Brenda tried not to ask herself the questions, am I truly happy and content with my life? Or am I just kidding myself? Is this nothing more than blind delusion? Brenda didn't want to face the answers to these questions. She whispered 'Amen' and got up from her knees.

Brenda headed for the bathroom, turned on the light and picked up her toothbrush, avoiding looking at herself in the mirror that hung over the sink. She momentarily caught her reflection and saw the half-closed, sleepy eyes staring back at her. The longer she stared at herself the harder it was to block out the remarks from her girlfriends, saying she should never have taken Jerome back after the first time he got fired for drugs and for his many 'cheating with other women' incidents.

Brenda brushed her teeth vigorously, then bent over the sink to spit out the blob of toothpaste. She swished a handful of running faucet water into her mouth. She could hear her girlfriends' advice running through her mind. *A leopard never changes his spots. Girl, throw that loser out!* Cha-Cha Taylor, with her trademark 'know-it-all' attitude, had advised Brenda a long time ago to dump Jerome. Her other girlfriend from high school, Veda Simms, had agreed with Cha-Cha.

Brenda dabbed her lips with a towel and frowned defiantly into the mirror while finger-combing her soft, layered bangs and wisps of auburn-brown waves that tapered both cheeks. Cha-Cha was certainly no expert on how to recognize Mr. Right decided Brenda. These days Cha-Cha was always complaining about her love life. Brenda also couldn't forget that Cha-Cha and Jerome had once been an item back in high school. Whenever anybody brought that up Cha-Cha would say that was ancient history. Still, could Brenda really trust Cha-Cha to give her honest advice about an old fling? Veda was no better. Several months ago Veda had tried to punish her cheating boyfriend with a dose of rat poison in his drink. She was certainly nobody to take advice from. But it wasn't just her two best girlfriends who claimed Jerome was no good. Even her own mother hated Jerome. That had been enough right there to give the poor man another chance as far as Brenda was concerned. Brenda was determined to prove them all wrong, even if it broke her heart. Despite her husband's flaws and weaknesses, she felt Jerome could be saved. And, she knew deep down he loved her. She just couldn't be sure how she knew it—surely, not from his behavior. She turned out the bathroom light and quietly closed the door. She approached Jerome's side of the bed to better see the time on the clock that sat nearby on his nightstand.

Suddenly, he turned over on his back and yawned. With eyes still shut tight he stretched his arm across the bed and reached for her out of instinct. Brenda stood still and watched him. When he didn't feel her there, he opened his eyes and smiled when he saw her standing over him. He grabbed her elbow and pulled her down onto the bed. Despite her weak protests he freed her arms from the robe's sleeves and tossed it on the floor. She smiled and fell on top of him. He embraced her around the back of her waist, as they faced each other. Staring into his dark eyes, she outlined his thin mustache and his full, sensuous lips, and traced his smile with the tip of her index finger. At that moment, Brenda didn't think about how exhausted she felt every evening after picking up Justin from day care, preparing dinner every evening, getting the baby ready for bed, and laying out her own work outfit for the next day so she could get to Dr. Hayes' office by 8:30, an hour before the first patient was due to arrive. She rested her head on his shoulder and forgot that it was usually midnight before her head touched the pillow. She forgot about her dream to go back to college to get a degree with a double major in business and computer science, so that she could one day start her own computer consulting business and make enough money to have a huge house like Dr. Hayes, drive a new car, and vacation twice a year. Those dreams were too far away in the future, yet sometimes she worried just how fast the years passed by and she was still stuck at the same place, if not going backwards.

Although she was only twenty-eight years old, Brenda's body ached at the end of each day. Sometimes while sitting at a red light on her way home from work she'd let her eyelids drop and flutter for a few moments just to capture a brief semblance of sleep. But, Brenda forgot all about those complaints whenever she felt the warmth and hardness of Jerome's body against hers. When she lifted up her head to check the time again, she realized she was going to be late for work. Brenda quickly untangled herself from Jerome's arms and leaped out of the bed. He held out his hand to her to beckon her to come back to bed. "Where you goin' baby?" he said while squinting his eyes to look up at her.

"It's time to get up. You know I gotta make Justin's bottles, do our lunches, and fix breakfast," she said firmly, and picked up her robe from the floor and put it back on.

"Ten more minutes, baby," he pleaded, "Then I'll get up too and help you. Promise."

Brenda could see his erection under the covers as he lifted both outstretched arms toward her. She knew exactly where this would lead if she did what he asked. She shook her head, realizing that somebody in the family had to be responsible. "Naw, that's okay. I'll be half way done with my choirs by the time you get out the bathroom and stop looking at yourself in the mirror," she said playfully, while headed towards the bedroom door to leave. Just then the telephone ringing stopped her. Jerome quickly reached for the receiver before she could get to it. Brenda waited to find out who was calling.

"Yeah," he said in his still groggy voice. After a few moments of silence he placed the receiver back.

"Who was that?" she asked, cautiously.

"Hell if I know. They hung up. Maybe one of your boyfriends," he said teasingly and threw a pillow at her.

Brenda ducked, picked up the pillow, and threw it back at him. It landed on top of his head. "Yeah, right, Sleeping Beauty. Just don't get too comfortable. I'll be back to wake you up in twenty minutes."

Brenda left their bedroom and closed the door behind her. She walked down the hallway to the nursery to check on the baby before going downstairs to the kitchen. Justin or Baby Buddha as they called him, slept peacefully on his back. Everybody said Justin had the serious look, chunky cheeks and portly belly of a statue of Buddha that you often found sitting on a shelf in one of those Chinatown novelty shops. But, unlike those statues of a bald Buddha, Justin had a head full of soft, dark-brown curls and long eyelashes. He really should have been a girl, she thought, smiling down at him as he slept. After a while, the nickname Baby Buddha stuck. An empty bottle sat on the nightstand where Jerome had left it last night after feeding and rocking their son to sleep. Jerome may have his faults, but nobody could say that he wasn't a good daddy. She picked up the dirty bottle and bent over to kiss Justin, detecting the smell of milk and his own unique baby scent. His sweet smell permeated through the entire room as well as wafted through his baby clothes even after they had been washed, folded, and tucked away in the dresser. Brenda loved his baby smell. She watched his eyelids flutter as he slept. She didn't know what she'd do if anything ever happened to her sweet baby boy or to Jerome for that matter. Her priest had taught the parishioners during Sunday Mass that God gives his believers trials and tribulations in life to overcome, but God won't give his children more hardships than they could endure. Brenda believed what her priest had said, but she didn't want to be tested like Job in the Bible. Losing either her son, Justin or her husband, Jerome would be one tribulation that she would never be able to bear.

CHAPTER 4 - BRENDA

Brenda left Justin sleeping in his crib and went downstairs to the kitchen to start making Justin's bottles and to prepare bag lunches for work. She put a huge pan of water on top of the stove to boil. While she waited for the water to boil, she washed out the stack of dirty bottles in the sink with a bristled bottle cleaner. Next, she laid out slices of white bread on the counter top and spread the slices with mayonnaise and mustard, then layered extra pieces of deli ham and American yellow cheese on Jerome's sandwich, while only giving herself one thin slice of ham and Swiss cheese. When she heard the water boiling, she placed the bottles into the pan of boiling water to disinfect them. Only three more months left to do this, sighed Brenda. Then Justin would be six months old, and she'd no longer have to sterilize bottles and boil his drinking water for five minutes to kill any germs lurking in the tap water. She couldn't wait. That would be one less thing she'd have to do in the mornings.

She dropped the sandwiches into the two open lunch bags, along with a piece of fruit in each one and a handful of chocolate chip cookies in Jerome's bag. Jerome loved his sweets, she thought with a smile. In that regard and in many other ways, he was nothing but a big kid. He'd probably try to trade his apple at lunchtime for a Hostess Twinkie.

Although she didn't really mind her job as Dr. Hayes' office assistant, Brenda hated leaving her baby with a day care provider after her three month maternity leave ran out. She wanted to stay home and take care of Justin during his crucial first year. But staying home was a luxury she could not afford, and she had no trusted family member to look after her son while she worked. True, her mother was free during the day, but Irene Kenmore Adams had made it perfectly clear before Brenda even got pregnant that she had already performed her maternal duties by raising her and that was enough. As she told Brenda right from the start, her full-time babysitting days were over for good. With a documented age of 58 years old on her birth certificate and a fabricated age of 48, Brenda knew that her mother was not and never would be the grandmotherly type. In fact, she had told Brenda that she planned to teach Justin to call her Miss Irene whenever he started to talk. Grandma, Granny, Gran, Nana, not even Grandmother Adams suited her mother. According to Brenda's mother, she considered herself too young and vivacious to be a grandmother and she didn't want to be out with her grandson one day and have him mistakenly call her Grandma. Brenda recalled her mother's answer three months ago when out of desperation she had asked her to watch Justin when she went back to work.

"Sweetie, I'm not interested in going back to changing dirty diapers or making bottles. Honey, you know that's not my thing," said Irene. "You're a grown woman now. My maternal duties are over."

Brenda hadn't bothered to point out to her mother that, other than giving birth to her, she had performed very few 'maternal duties' as she called it. In fact, it was Bengi, their Philippino live-in nanny who had fed Brenda from the time she was two weeks old, clothed her, combed her hair, and took her to the playground while her mother stayed home and watched soap operas or ran out during the day on appointments. When it was time for Brenda to start kindergarten, it was Bengi, not her mother, who walked her to the bus stop everyday and was there to meet the school bus when it was time to come home in the afternoon. And, it was Bengi who prepared the family meals, cleaned the house, and taught Brenda how to say the rosary beads at night before she went to bed.

Brenda's mother had been baptized as an Episcopalian, but she did not practice any form of organized religious worship, and her father was simply indifferent to religion. So Brenda grew up under the influence of her nanny's religion of Catholicism. Guided by Bengi, a devout Catholic, Brenda went to Catechism Classes and to Mass on Sundays, and sometimes even during the week. Thanks to Bengi's arrangements with her priest, she was baptized as a baby. At seven years old she received the Eucharist during her First Communion. At eleven, she was anointed by the bishop with holy oil when receiving the Confirmation Sacrament. For the most part her mother was indifferent to having Brenda raised as a Catholic. The only admonishment that Brenda recalled hearing her mother tell Bengi, more than once was, "My little girl better not grow up to be a nun or I'll come find you and skin you alive, Bengi!" Whatever Brenda knew about being a good mother and a good Catholic, Brenda had learned from her nanny. Whatever she knew about what not to do and how not to behave, she had learned from watching her mother.

Brenda no longer bothered to update her mother about Justin's latest milestone or developments because she didn't seem the least bit interested in baby babbling. The discussion would usually veer into a negative, one-sided conversation about Jerome instead. In fact, Brenda recalled the day she announced her pregnancy to her parents. Her father was thrilled with her news just as she suspected he would be. But as for her mother, instead of congratulations, her mother's only reply in a dry voice was, "*Now you're stuck with him.*" Brenda didn't want to hear her mother's attacks of "*that man's not good enough for you*" and "*I don't trust him.*" She got enough of that from her girlfriends, Cha-Cha and Veda. The last telephone conversation with her mother was still fresh in her mind, where Irene had told her daughter, "*Darling you know your daddy and I would help you financially with the baby if you would just come to your senses and kick that loser to the curb. We'd even help you get your own apartment.*" Brenda knew the financial help would only materialize if she did exactly what her mother wanted.

During those stressful telephone conversations, Brenda never got a word in, so she learned not to even try to interject a comment. She held the phone to her ear and listened in silence as her mother continued her rant. "Sweetheart, I know you better than you know yourself. Ever since you were a little girl you always wanted to fix things. But baby girl, Jerome Antonio Johnson, is something that nobody, not even God Almighty himself, can fix."

Brenda would hear cosmetic jar tops being unscrewed and the clanking sound of bottles being placed on her mother's glass top vanity table. She could picture her mother pausing in mid-sentence just long enough to pluck a few stray hairs from her well-shaped, waxed eyebrows. "Honey, you deserve a man who'll treat you like a queen. Not like some third string fiddler in the back of the orchestra. You listen to your Mama, darlin'—that good-for-nothing man will never be satisfied with one woman, not even a good woman like you."

"Uhm um, yes Mama." Brenda had grunted, only half listening. But inattentiveness never deterred Brenda's mother from speaking her mind.

"Now, you take me for instance. I wouldn't have anything to do with any man unless he treated me like a queen on a pedestal. Your father has always been faithful and good to me. Though to be honest, I may not have always deserved it," she chuckled to herself before continuing, " …but that's what you call real love and not someone who's just using you. Darling, you know I don't mean to make you feel worse than you probably already do being married to the wrong man, but baby, I'd be negligent as a mother if I didn't help you see the obvious and share my *forty-nine* years of life's wisdom from surviving hardships."

Now that was a joke, thought Brenda. Her mother had never worked hard or had to survive anything in her life. After about ten minutes of this long-winded conversation, it would become too much for Brenda to listen to. She would say a brisk good-bye and hang up the phone. Brenda didn't want to think about her mother anymore. She reached under the cupboards and pulled out a large iron skillet. She pressed several slices of bacon close together into the pan. Once the grease from the bacon started to sizzle in the hot pan, she cracked open two eggs next to the bacon. Jerome liked his eggs cooked in the same pan with the bacon drippings. He said it was a waste of good bacon flavoring to use a different pan for cooking eggs. He told her that Mama Etta always saved the fat from her bacon drippings and the grease from frying chicken in a Crisco can. Brenda had to ignore all the healthy, low-fat cooking tips she had learned by watching the Food Network channel on television. Jerome wanted her to cook the old fashion way, like his grandmother cooked.

Jerome lumbered out of bed, stood up and stretched before getting down on the floor and doing 50 push-ups, just to get the blood flowing. He could smell the bacon cooking and the rich aroma of coffee brewing downstairs. He leaped up from the floor and headed for the bathroom to take a quick shower. He turned on the radio to his favorite rap and R & B station that Brenda never bothered to listen to. Standing in the shower with the hot water massaging his hairless chest and the music pumping, it felt good to have a job to go to in the morning and a good woman to come home to at night. Jerome realized how lucky he was to come right off the streets from being unemployed into a fulltime driver position with good benefits. That was rare. Again, he had his Uncle Ike to thank for it. Uncle Ike had been working at UDS for twenty years and had become a supervisor eight years ago. He had tried to get his nephew on at UDS last year but Jerome had been rejected.

While Jerome had easily passed the physical, the drug test was another matter. When the company's nurse asked him if he was drug-free he recalled what his uncle had once told him, always be honest with your doctor and your lawyer. The woman doing the drug testing looked like a nurse. That was close enough. So Jerome told the nurse that he had used drugs once around Christmas time. The holidays were always rough for him, especially when you don't have any money he explained. He assumed that he would pass a drug test because he knew it took 72 hours for drugs to dissipate out of your system. Jerome had not taken drugs for thirty days at the time of the test. What he didn't realize was that drug-free at UDS meant clean for one year. He did not get the job that time because of this technicality. But that was the past and Jerome didn't want to dwell on the past. Six months ago Uncle Ike had seen to it that he got another chance at UDS and this time he passed the screening. With Uncle Ike's connections, he got hired. This time he vowed it would be different. This time it was for keeps. Brenda was a forgiving woman but even he realized she was tired of his relapses and his lies.

Brenda heard the shower water running upstairs and smiled, glancing up briefly at the ceiling. Jerome had gotten up on his own without her having to come upstairs and wake him. Brenda worked hard to make sure the pressures of daily life didn't get too great for Jerome so he wouldn't succumb to temptation and slip back into the abyss of drugs. She and Jerome would be all right. They didn't need her mother's help, she thought to herself, scooping tablespoons of ground coffee into the coffee pot filter. Her mother didn't know a doggone thing about Jerome, and neither did Cha-Cha or Veda. They believed all the rumors and any negative piece of gossip they heard about him. While she set the kitchen table for two, Brenda reminded herself once again of the blessings to be thankful for. Jerome had been working steadily at UDS for the past six months. She didn't want to remind herself that the six month mark had always been his danger zone in the past. All she could do was pray that he wouldn't blow it again. She couldn't be with Jerome every minute of the day to keep tabs on him.

The hot water had begun to turn lukewarm. As the water rinsed away the suds from his body, Jerome felt good about being drug free for over a year now. He had managed to stay clean despite the pressure from being out of work for half of that year. Today, he was a driver with UDS, a company that paid good money, offered benefits and advancement potential. Being a driver gave him the freedom to be out on the road. Jerome knew he would never be happy stuck in some office all day. Winning Brenda's trust back and getting that job at UDS became his incentives to attend meetings every evening, to stop associating with his drug-using buddies and work the program. Jerome turned off the shower and stepped out, dripping water all over the floor. He grabbed a towel from the rack but instead of drying off he wiped the steam from the mirror with the towel so he could see himself clearly. He smiled at his nude reflection in the mirror.

The coffee plunked its last drop into the Mr. Coffee® pot and its aroma filled the kitchen. The lunches were made, Justin's bottles were refrigerated and ready to be packed, breakfast was ready and the table had been set. Brenda wiped her hands on her robe and headed upstairs towards the nursery to get the baby dressed for the day. The burdens didn't let up on her but she told herself she didn't mind if it meant keeping her family together. Jerome wasn't beating her or verbally abusing her. In fact, he had never been abusive. Sure, he had his problems, but despite what her mother and her girlfriends believed, he did treat her like a queen in his own way. He was going to work everyday and bringing home his paycheck. Maybe he didn't help around the house as much as she would have liked, but he had settled into fatherhood and was still drug-free after 18 months! Now that was something to be thankful for in anybody's book. Maybe things weren't always perfect, but all-in-all her life was pretty good. They had a healthy, beautiful baby boy. Jerome had a good job now. And, they had finally moved out of the Meadowland Gardens projects in their old Trinidad neighborhood in Northeast Washington. Brenda knew that could all change in a day, but she was not going to give up on Jerome just yet. She would never be like her manipulating mother and treat Jerome the way that her mother treated her father. All Jerome needed was love and understanding. Prayer, patience, and forgiveness were working. She would do her part to help her husband stay drug-free. Hadn't she done it for going on eighteen months now? She decided she was not going to let anybody give her unsolicited advice about her man, especially from people whose lives hadn't turned out any better than her own.

CHAPTER 5

Friday morning. Her birthday. Renee woke up with a headache. She glanced at Bill's sleeping frame. His broad back faced her like a stone wall. She got up slowly, not wanting to wake him, slipped on her robe and went into the anteroom. She pulled open the drawer of her French writing desk, barely noticing the gold and brass inlay as she retrieved a sheet of stationery and a sheet of red gift-wrap tissue. She removed her black, silk panties, enclosed them in tissue and placed them inside a small manila envelope so that nothing would show through. The last thing she needed was for the U. S. Postmaster to arrive at her door to have her arrested for sending indecent material through the mail. On the stationery she wrote:

'Bill, I wore these last night and dreamed of you. Meet me for dinner on Saturday at 7 in our formal dining room. I have a surprise for you, Darling.'

After dropping a few trickles of cologne on the note, she folded and sealed it inside the envelope. Renee addressed the envelope to Bill without placing a return label. She unlocked a side drawer and stuffed the envelope inside the desk temporarily for safekeeping. She would take it to the post office sometime later that day.

Before closing the drawer, she spotted her black and white speckled composition notebook that peeked out from its hiding place under a stack of papers and documents. Months had passed since Renee had last written in her diary. Journal writing was one of her recommendations to patients facing stressful life events and experiencing bouts of depression. Renee, however, rarely followed her own advice. But today was her birthday and she felt compelled to write down her thoughts.

I'm 45 today. Eligible for coverage on those 'burial costs' insurance policies that I keep seeing on commercials—age 45 to 65, no physical required. In five more years AARP will be hounding me to join them. Is this all there is? Live a meaningless life then you die? Does God really exist? Then where's he been for the last 39 years? Bill and I were briefly separated a few months ago then got back together. Why, I have no idea because nothing has changed. Like Gladys Knight's song, Neither One of Us … wants to go to the courthouse and file for legal separation. I know what I want but can't seem to get it. I want a baby. I want a man who loves me and who's not afraid to show it. That, sure as hell is *not* Bill! But do I end a 14-year marriage and risk facing 50 alone? Nobody's perfect, certainly not yours truly. So here I sit in this hopeless state of limbo. Living a lie. I've been purposely avoiding Deek. He's called my office a few times and left messages just to say hello but I never return his calls. Lately, I only think of him a couple of times a day instead of every hour like I used to. I guess that's progress.

Renee put down her pen, shut the notebook and locked her diary back inside the drawer. Writing down her feelings hadn't really helped. She hoped her birthday celebration and the follow-up evening she planned for Bill on Saturday, would rekindle their relationship.

When she returned to the bedroom, she heard the green-eyed monster scratching and purring at the bedroom door to get inside. Renee ignored the cat's pleas as she stood in front of the mirror and brushed her hair. New grayish growth was coming in and the hair felt crinkled at the roots. It was a good thing she had an appointment with Cha-Cha at Good Looks that afternoon. The stylist would undoubtedly work her usual miracles. As 45 stared back at her, Renee understood that her sadness had little to do with the puffy circles under her dark brown eyes from lack of sleep and the reality of growing another year older. The emptiness stemmed from losses—the loss of her mother at six, of a father who preferred traipsing around the country in search of musical fame, and the loss of her unborn child. Renee no longer remembered what it was like to feel normal, to wake up and feel joy about facing a new day. Instead, she felt a heaviness weighing her down as if she needed to be pulled along in order to advance through each hour of the day.

The cat's loud purring continued to echo behind the closed door. Buying Angel had been Bill's idea of a sweetheart gift during their one-month trial separation. After inviting Renee to see one of her favorite Washington Ballet performances, *Romeo and Juliet* at the Kennedy Center, Bill had shown up that evening handsomely dressed in a black tuxedo. He'd ruined the entire date by surprising her with this tiny ball of white fluff that nestled in the crook of his arm. Its large green eyes glowed in the dark without blinking. Even as a kitten, it had hissed at her and Renee swore the thing was possessed. Bill stationed the creature in its carrying case on the kitchen floor and spent a good fifteen minutes bent down smiling and talking to the kitten through the plastic bars. They had been late for the ballet and Renee had spent the entire evening picking white cat fur off his sleeve. If she had any guts at all she would put Angel in her carrying case after Bill left for work this morning and deposit her at the nearest animal shelter. Surely somebody would be duped by those big, sad, green eyes and adopt her. The cat's purring and scratching eventually woke up Bill.

He got out of bed and opened the door then gently scooped up the cat that had become more his than hers. Angel in turn greeted her master with purrs and rubbed her side against his hand. Whenever Bill was around, she circled his ankles or curled on top his lap. This cat definitely had a split personality. With Bill she was gentle and affectionate. With Renee she'd arch her back and turn into a snarling, scratching, toe-biting vixen. Renee knew she could forget about getting any peace, now that Bill had let that damn cat into the bedroom.

"How did your meeting go last night? I didn't hear you come in," she said with an unmistakable edge in her voice. Though, if Bill caught the irritation in her tone, he ignored it.

"Great," he said, still playing with Angel, "Shaw's well-connected politically and that's important in this city. I know you're not interested in our business details. Pick out one of your best dresses, babe. I'm taking you some place special tonight."

He gently lowered the cat. It jumped from his arms to the floor.

"Where?" she asked, her eyes glistening like a child's.

"It's a surprise, Renee. Don't be so nosey." He playfully tossed a chair pillow at her, purposely missing.

"Did it occur to you that I might need to know how to dress, dear?" She emphasized 'dear' as she threw the pillow back at him, making contact with the back of his head.

"Oh, all right. It's black tie. And I know how you are so I'm warning you now, be ready by 6:30 sharp. We need to be on time, cocktails start at 7 and dinner's at 8."

He disappeared into his bathroom and Renee heard the shower running. As soon as Bill had left the room, Angel snipped at Renee's feet with sharp, angry teeth. Renee kicked her but she came right back with a vengeance and continued to bite and nip Renee's toes. When Renee wildly swung her arms at the cat, Angel took flight and leaped on top of a silk-skirted table next to the bed. She knocked over a stack of books, and a silver-framed photo of Renee's parents, but the plush alabaster white carpet cushioned the frame and kept it from breaking.

"Damn you," Renee whispered under her breath, "You better hope I don't catch your furry little behind." She chased the cat and tried to grab it by the neck but Angel quickly jumped down and hid in Renee's closet. Running on a bad attitude, a hangover from too much wine last night, and no morning coffee, Renee didn't have the stamina to box with a cat this morning. She slammed the closet door shut and locked the cat inside, knowing that Angel's punishment would be short-lived once Bill heard her cries.

Water gushing from Bill's shower drowned out Angel's moans until the water stopped. Renee swung open the closet door to release her just in time. The cat hissed at her then raced down the hallway. Bill came out of the bathroom and dressed quickly in silence. He appeared to be lost in his own private thoughts. But he had obviously planned a wonderful evening tonight for her birthday, which seemed out of character for him. Renee looked forward to dressing up and looking fabulous. The evening might turn out to be fun. It would help take the sting out of aging another year.

"See ya later, Babe." Bill bent down and planted a swift peck on her check. "I gotta go make some money. Don't forget now. I need you ready by 6:30 tonight." He hadn't even wished her happy birthday.

The reconciliation with Bill was speeding down a slippery runway to an inevitable collision. She knew they needed more marriage counseling but every time she brought up the subject he avoided it. When she did schedule appointments, he neglected to show up. Although Renee was trained to help others with their relationship problems, she couldn't seem to repair her own. She hoped her plans for a sensual evening on Saturday would work. Renee was more than willing to meet Bill's needs and desires. But who would meet her needs?

CHAPTER 6

Renee sat at the kitchen counter and absently picked at her chicken salad and sipped green tea, while reading her latest issue of Mental Health Weekly magazine. She still didn't have much of an appetite even after having skipped breakfast that morning. An article on post traumatic stress syndrome wasn't holding her interest as the article said nothing that she didn't already know. Glancing at her watch, she saw that it was almost time to leave for her 12:30 PM appointment with Kim at the nail salon for a pedicure and French manicure. The telephone rang just as she rose to put away the rest of her salad. The callerid showed it was Bill calling from his cell phone. Renee smiled and picked up the receiver. He hadn't forgotten to wish her happy birthday after all. "Hi Honey, I'm so glad you called," she said, "I'm really looking forward to this evening. I bet you ..."

Bill interrupted before she could finish her sentence. "Babe, I can't talk long. I'm in the lobby at the Courthouse and I need to get right back to Shaw before his next docket number comes up. Sorry, I had to rush outta there so fast this morning. Did you feed Angel for me? I didn't have time to feed her this morning."

"Of course, I fed her. Bill, I thought ..."

"Great. Thanks babe," he said, cutting her off. "I'll be home on time so be ready to go, okay? Love you," he blurted out in one anxious breath.

She heard a quick airwave kiss followed by a brisk hang-up then the dial tone. So he hadn't called to wish her a happy birthday. It was that damn cat again. She held the receiver to her ear, listening to the flat, reverberation for several seconds longer.

"Jerk." She muttered when she finally slammed the dead phone down. "Okay. I'm going to force myself to act calm and sweet, even if I have to turn schizophrenic to do it," she said to herself. She was determined to not let anything spoil her 45th birthday, not even Bill. Renee grabbed her jacket and purse and headed towards her first stop at Kim's, her manicurist. On the way to Kim's she made a quick detour to the Post Office to mail the letter containing her silk underwear to Bill. If that didn't get his attention nothing would. Kim was fast, as usual, and in less than an hour, Renee was out of the nail salon. Next, she maneuvered through congested streets in stop and go traffic to get to her two o'clock with Cha-Cha, her long-time hair stylist. Good Looks Beauty Shop was located in the multi-ethnic part of Adams Morgan. Renee had been going to Good Looks ever since her office assistant had recommended Cha-Cha over a year ago. The two young ladies had known each other since high school. Remarkably, Renee found a parking space close by the shop. The door chimed as Renee entered the salon.

Poster size headshots of models with complexions ranging from ivory to deep mahogany, and wearing a variety of hairstyles dyed in vibrant colors, lined the beauty shop walls. Renee wrote her name on the client sign-in sheet, put Cha-Cha's name down as her stylist and marked her arrival time as 2:05 PM. She sat down to wait and silently fumed. Typical Cha-Cha behavior, she thought, always late. Renee didn't know why she had risked getting into an accident to get there on time. Obviously Renee needed her stylist more than Cha-Cha needed the money. As much as she wanted to get up and leave, Renee couldn't get another appointment with someone else this late. Besides, whom else but to Cha-Cha could she trust her hair? Bill was taking her someplace special tonight for her birthday. She needed a fresh application of Egyptian sable rinse to conceal the few sprouting gray roots, a touch-up to lay down the new growth, and a fancy 'up-do' for the evening. After leaving there, she'd stop by Saks for some Bobby Brown lipstick and matching eye shadow and buy that 'Flatter Me' bra for her Dolce & Gabbana gown she planned to wear tonight. If Cha-Cha didn't show up soon, she might not have time to run all her errands. Cha-Cha's tip was dwindling with each passing minute.

Renee was well aware that for years Cha-Cha had paid her station fees to a string of shop owners in order to serve her loyal clients as Cha-Cha claimed. Just recently, Cha-Cha had bought out Good Looks Beauty Salon's previous owner, and now ran her own establishment. But to Renee it seemed that becoming a new owner hadn't changed Cha-Cha's old habits. Her stylist had still not arrived on time. While she waited, Renee observed the activity around her. On this Friday afternoon, the art deco adorned salon was packed. Clients sat reading under dryers, leaning back into wash bowls, or sitting in styling chairs, getting their hair creamed, coifed, or cut by one of the other three stylists. Laughter and idle chatter mingled with a concert of popular tunes coming from the too loud CD player. Every five minutes the telephone rang and the teenager at the desk answered it, repeating variations of the same message, "Sorry, Ma'am. Cha-Cha's not in yet. Her appointment book is full all day today and tomorrow. Try calling back to see if she can fit you in."

You would have thought Cha-Cha was the personal stylist for a string of Hollywood celebrities as much as she was in demand. Renee scanned the customers still waiting and hoped none were there for Cha-Cha. A forty-something brownskin woman wearing a black leather jacket and clutching a Louis Vitton handbag sat on one of the cushioned chairs opposite Renee and rested a tired head in the palm of her hand. Next to her sat a plump woman in a Washington Redskins jacket who hid all her hair under a maroon knit cap.

The door chime rang and a middle-aged, stout, liverish-colored man of average height lumbered through the door and immediately made his presence known. "Did anybody request a handsome Black man?" he grinned, with outstretched arms. "Here I am, Ladies." He then greeted everyone in the shop with a loud, "How y'all doin'?" Renee had seen him at the shop many times before. Today he sported some mustard-yellow gabardine slacks and a matching yellow, silky shirt from his 'seventies era' Cavalier wardrobe. Always the flamboyant dresser, Renee had never once seen him wearing jeans or looking scruffy. He stroked his clean-shaven chin, looked around and finally sat down in the only empty chair left. Whittni, his stylist, told him she'd be ready to cut his hair in a few more minutes.

"Okay, baby. Take your time, Sugah," he said, and smoothed his gray-tinged mustache before settling down for some social and relaxation time.

Renee knew all the girls at the shop who worked with Cha-Cha—Whittni, Takara, and Nadine. She had also become familiar with some of the regular customers, including this gentleman. Whittni called him Mr. Woods but he said his name was Alonzo Woods or Al to all his friends. He always got Whittni to shampoo and cut his hair and would wait however long it took for her to get to him. Renee suspected he preferred the beauty parlor to the barbershop down the street because he wanted to be in the company of the ladies. On a number of occasions Renee heard him brag that he drove an 18-wheel tractor-trailer as a top feeder driver for United Delivery Service (UDS). She found him overly friendly to the point of being sickening. He made her uncomfortable with his flirtations and sexual overtones. Renee was glad that Whittni chatted with him as she worked on her other customer's hair. His heavy-lidded eyes closed at times as he spoke. Alonzo Woods always looked like he needed a nap.

Whittni had a pleasant face and usually wore long braids. Today's style was a handful of braids pulled at the crown in a ponytail while the bottom half of her braids touched her shoulder blades. She rarely made her customers wait more than ten minutes, so Renee figured she wouldn't have to put up with Mr. Woods' endless prattle for much longer.

"Lawd, there must be some ugly women out there 'cause God gave you all they looks, Sistuh," he grinned at Renee, revealing brownish yellow stains on his teeth, no doubt from years of heavy smoking in his younger days.

Renee tried to conceal her dislike for him and politely said thank you and picked up a magazine to skim through. Mr. Woods turned his attention to the plump woman wearing the Redskins jacket and struck up a conversation with her. Not having anything else to do but wait for Cha-Cha, Renee eavesdropped on their conversation while pretending to read the magazine. She rarely participated in conversations going on at the beauty shop. She preferred to sit quietly and remain as invisible as possible. You could learn a lot about people just by listening to them talk.

"I see you still a fan," Mr. Woods said, pointing to the woman's Redskins jacket.

"Yeah, we Redskins fans don't give up. It's not over for 'em yet. We're only a month into the season."

Nadine led her customer over to a hair dryer next to the waiting area and set the timer for thirty minutes. Nadine had a pleasant face, tinted the flavor of rich cocoa and got along with everybody. She asked the Redskins' fan to go sit in her chair while she made a quick telephone call. As soon as the Redskins' fan left, Mr. Woods made his move on the lady in black leather.

"Who you waitin' for, Sistuh?" he asked her and licked his dry, chapped lips.

"Takara. Looks like she's finishing up her customer. Shouldn't be much longer, thank God! I am beat. Worked the nightshift last night. I thought about sleeping in but I had to get my hair done."

Both Takara and Whittni summoned their clients. The woman wearing the leather jacket jumped up when Takara called her.

"Mr. Woods, I'm ready for you," said Whittni.

"Mr. Woods? Who the hell's that?" He snarled at the formal name, "Baby, how many times I got to tell you to call me Al."

He smiled at Whittni and bounced towards her chair in what he probably considered a cool, hip-hop strut. "I ain't that old, girl. I could show you a thing or two," he winked then squeezed himself into her chair.

Renee then sat alone. She checked the clock again. Twenty-five minutes had passed but it seemed like she had been waiting forever. At 2:30, Cha-Cha strutted through the door, head held high, and lips rigid with attitude. Only 5'4" in bare feet, the platform boots lifted her to a statuesque 5'7." Renee was too angry to say anything to her and pretended to be absorbed in the magazine. Cha-Cha walked in like Queen Sheba, hips curvy in a pair of butt-hugging FrankieB Jeans. A leopard print nylon top peeked through her leather jacket to reveal other God-given assets. Cha-Cha sported a short, tapered Halle Berry cut that showed off high cheekbones on a golden tan complexion, arched eyebrows, dark eyes, and perfectly formed lips painted glossy berry by MAC™. She nodded a greeting at Renee but did not apologize or explain why she was so late.

"Hey girl," she greeted the teenager at the desk in a sultry, drawling voice, "Any calls?"

"Just the usual. Mrs. Gordan wants a touch-up, color, and trim. Janice got her hair wet and needs another press-n-curl. And your cousin, Tamika wants you to squeeze her in tomorrow before 5. She said to tell you she finally got a date."

Cha-Cha rolled her eyes and sucked her teeth. "That girl's always trying to get her hair done for free. Like I don't have bills to pay," she said, pointing to herself as she held a defiant stance.

Renee suppressed the urge to say out loud; *You don't act like you have bills to pay. You're thirty minutes late for my appointment.* But her anger subsided since she knew Cha-Cha would transform her into a glamorous femme-fatale and Bill wouldn't know what hit him tonight.

"Oh yeah and a Jillian Brock left a number for you to call her," said the young assistant as she handed Cha-Cha a slip of paper, "This lady's desperate. Says she hasn't been to you in ten months because she could never get an appointment. She's been going to somebody her girlfriend recommended and they messed her hair all up. She'll pay anything and can come any time if you'll fix the disaster this other hairdresser 'inflicted on her head'. Her words exactly."

"Oh, well," said Cha-Cha in a nonchalant voice, "That's what you get when you go to unprofessionals. Clients have to make a commitment and keep trying to get me. I don't have time to call her right now. Thanks for taking the messages, Sherrelle."

Cha-Cha appeared to be in no rush putting her things away. She sauntered over to the supply closet and retrieved her hair relaxing crème, colors, sprays, and setting lotions. She arranged the curling irons, pressing combs, and handheld dryer at her station. She yawned then continued chit-chatting with the young receptionist. "Sherrelle, tell your triflin' mama she don't have to call nobody," said Cha-Cha with a sly smile.

The young girl with the bobbed hairdo, cropped just below her ears, spoke up to explain, "Mama's been sort of busy lately. She just got a new job." Sherrelle closed the appointment book then glanced up at the wall clock. "She should be here soon to pick me up. You said I could get off at 3 today, right Miss Cha-Cha? That's what I told Mama."

"Sure, baby. That's fine. Just make sure you get all the towels out the dryer and folded and straighten up that back room before you leave," said Cha-Cha. "Um hum, I can't wait to hear what my girl Veda's been up to these days."

Suddenly, Renee realized that Sherrelle was Veda Simms's fifteen-year-old daughter. Veda was a former patient that she had treated several months ago. Like Cha-Cha, Renee was also interested in finding out how her former patient was faring after a trying ordeal of getting caught embezzling funds from her old job to give her ex-boyfriend a loan and later being falsely arrested for murdering him. She had eventually been released when the police apprehended the real killer, but it had been an awful time for Veda. The only good that came out of it was Veda's reconnection with her once estranged teenage daughter. Veda had first come into treatment six months ago as an outpatient referral from Washington Hospital Center's psychiatric ward when she had swallowed half a bottle of sleeping pills. After only a few sessions with her, Renee discovered that Veda's tough exterior disguised an insecure, lonely woman on the inside. On the surface her problem appeared to be a five-year love obsession for a man who did not love her and never would. Like most patients, Veda came in with one problem but the bigger problem emerged as they peeled back the layers and worked through her issues. Veda's biggest problem had been low self-esteem, which stemmed from a childhood marred by a distant relationship with her mother, and the sexual and emotional abuse at the hands of someone she had once trusted.

At that moment the door chime rang and Veda herself sailed through the door! Renee didn't want to be recognized. She didn't want to catch Veda off guard and possibly dredge up painful memories that were still too recent to have healed completely. She picked up a fashion magazine and hid behind its pages, pretending to read it. From this vantage point, Renee could still hear everything and catch glimpses of what was going on. It was obvious to Renee that Veda was wearing a wig because instead of her naturally-thick nut-brown hair that had only reached below her ears a few months ago, today Veda sported a jet black silky mane that reached the middle of her back, even when pulled up into a ponytail. Renee thought her sky-blue sweat suit complimented her cocoa-tinted skin tone. Renee was also relieved to see that the brief stint in jail had not altered Veda's usual easygoing manner.

Veda's narrow field of vision focused only on her daughter seated behind the reception desk. Veda smiled and glanced at her wrist watch, "'bout ready to go, Baby?"

Close to forty years old, Veda had no delusions about her waning youth, and unlike her girlfriend, Cha-Cha, she was past trying to look 'cute.' Veda was not the type of woman who spent much time on her hair, makeup, or her wardrobe. While Cha-Cha was one of her best friends, Veda couldn't understand why people spent half their day in a beauty parlor—first, waiting for Cha-Cha to show up and then, waiting as Cha-Cha took her sweet time to do their hair. Manicure and pedicures were rare treats for her—not regular rituals, which is why her cuticle-chewed nails were often brittle and unpolished. But she didn't care. Veda thought of herself as more the 'wash and go' type.

Before Sherrelle could answer, Cha-Cha walked up to the desk and put her arms around Veda in a warm hug. "Hey girl, how you been doing?"

"Better than I was this time a few months ago," said Veda, and winked at her daughter who then disappeared into the back room to fold the towels and straighten up the supply/laundry room so they could leave. Sherrelle called out to Veda from the laundry room, "I'll be finished my work soon, Mama. I won't be too long."

Cha-Cha wasn't going to let Veda out of her sight so quickly without grilling her with questions first. Cha-Cha leaned across the reception desk and planted her elbows so that her chin rested atop clasped hands as she gazed inquisitively at Veda. "So, tell me Girl. What you been up to these days?" asked Cha-Cha.

Renee strained her ears to listen in on Veda and Cha-Cha's conversation. This was more interesting to her than anything in that fashion magazine she was pretending to read.

Veda clutched the strap of her shoulder bag and muttered with a half smile, "I found another job. I'm a secretary now for United Delivery Service or UDS as it's called. Been there for about three weeks now."

At hearing the name UDS, Alonzo jerked up his head from the shampoo bowl where Whittni had been massaging his scalp. "I thought you looked familiar, Sweet Thing," he said, pointing up at Veda. Renee noticed that Veda gave him a half second disinterested glance then turned back to Cha-Cha.

Alonzo wasn't ready to give up. "You know I'm one of the top drivers for UDS," he said to Veda. "What did you say your name was again?"

"I didn't," Veda quipped and continued to ignore him.

Whittni gently pushed his shoulders back to stop him from interjecting himself into Cha-Cha and Veda's conversation. "Please be still Mr. Woods so I can give this head a good scrubbing," she said.

"Yes, Ma'am." Alonzo beamed up at Whittni and obediently sank his head back down over the rim of the bowl.

After rolling her eyes one more time at Alonzo, Cha-Cha lowered her voice as she spoke, "Girl, that's great about the new job. It's good your old boss didn't give you no hassle about … well, you know."

"Yeah. I was pretty lucky," Veda nodded. "Brenda told me about the opening at UDS right after I got released. I guess you know Jerome works there? He told her that apparently their secretary got fired for some reason. I didn't hesitate to put my application in as soon as Brenda told me that."

"I hear ya, Girl. It's not like you haven't worked around creeps before. Speakin' of creeps how's things going with Jerome these days? Brenda say anything about that?"

"Don't ask me. That's their business. Cha-Cha, you're worse than a bunch of old church ladies. Trying to get into everybody's business so you can go back and talk about 'em."

"I'm just asking. I don't want her calling me cryin' at two in the morning 'cause she don't know where her husband's at. You know it's only a matter of time before he screws up."

Veda shrugged and folded her arms. "To tell you the truth, I don't see much of Jerome. He's a driver and I'm in the office all day. Lord knows I'm just thankful to have this job. I'm not trying to cause trouble and I don't have time to get into people's business. Mr. Davis, my old boss, said he wouldn't press charges if I kept up my payments on the installment plan he worked out for me. So you see, I'm off the hook as long as I can keep this job and pay back the money I owe the firm."

"Humph. Just make sure you stay outta trouble this time," said Cha-Cha.

"Don't worry. And, as soon as I pay the firm back, I plan to take the LSATs so I can get into law school. That's always been a dream of mine. But in the meantime, I'm going to take an online class in criminology."

"Criminology? You should ace that course, Veda. In fact, you could probably teach it," laughed Cha-Cha. Veda gave her girlfriend an evil look.

"Girl, you know I'm just playing," said Cha-Cha, waving her hand at Veda. Veda shrugged and started laughing with Cha-Cha at her own expense.

Renee sat quietly in the far corner of the waiting area, with her face buried in the magazine that she was not actually reading. She felt a tinge of guilt for eavesdropping in on Veda and Cha-Cha's casual banter, but it gave her personal satisfaction to hear her former patient's progress and to see how Veda had gotten past her emotional insecurities. Renee was also a little envious. It must be nice to have girlfriends to joke around with when things were going good and to confide in when things were not so great. If only she herself could advance towards self-discovery and learn from her mistakes the way Veda apparently had. Renee was proud of her former patient. She'd come a long way.

Cha-Cha reached out and examined Veda's real hair under the wig and saw that she was clearly in need of a touch-up and trim in Cha-Cha's opinion. "If you want me to hook up your hairdo for the club tonight I can fix you up if you don't mind waiting a little bit."

Veda raised her eyebrows in a look of disbelief. "Cha-Cha you must be crazy if you think I'm giving you my whole paycheck *and* waiting around here all day for you with your slow self."

Veda stuffed her loose hair back in place, "Besides, my little bottle of Dark & Lovely at home'll work just fine. I'm just here to pick up my daughter. Speaking of which, … Sherrelle?" she called out, "you 'bout finished with your work, baby? We gotta go."

"Suit yourself, Veda. My customers know I make them look good. They don't mind waiting for me."

"Humph, that's what you think. News flash Cha-Cha—people have better things to do than sit around here all damn day."

Veda continued with a chuckle. "Anyway Cha, I'm not trying to look too good on the job these days. I've already been warned by one of the girls in shipping and receiving not to come in to work looking too cute."

"What?" said Cha-Cha, "What's that supposed to mean? Why can't you come to work looking fabulous? I know I couldn't deal with that."

Veda glanced over at Alonzo at the shampoo bowl before whispering to Cha-Cha. "One of the girls who works at UDS said 'looking too cute' is exactly what got the last secretary fired. Apparently, this girl came to work everyday like she thought she was starring in an MTV rap video. They say our boss is some kind of nutcase and feels threatened by attractive women. I don't know if any of this is true but my coworker said Boss Lady doesn't want any female coming to the office looking better than she does. The only problem is, that's gonna be hard to prevent," said Veda with an amused look on her face.

Cha-Cha laughed and waved her hand at Veda. "Oh, I get it. Your new lady boss is a mud duck." At that, Veda couldn't help laughing too. "Well maybe not that bad. A little thick around the middle and too much facial hair above her lip. It's nothing that a personal trainer and a good waxing job couldn't fix."

Veda's smile faded as she turned serious, "Cha-Cha, you know how some people like to gossip. Who knows why the last secretary got fired.

All I know is, I'm glad I got a chance to take her spot. I don't intend to mess up. Lord knows I need this job."

"I know that's right," Cha-Cha mused, wearing a slight smirk. "Who knows. She could've stolen money from the company account and gotten herself fired." Veda's face turned stone cold. Cha-Cha stopped grinning when she saw the serious look on Veda's face. Cha-Cha cleared her throat. "Like I said, Veda. Stay outta trouble, Girl."

"Don't worry about me, Cha. I learn from my mistakes."

Just then Sherrelle walked up and grabbed her purse from behind the desk. "I'm ready to go now Mama. Is it okay, Miss Cha-Cha? I'm finished everything."

"Sure baby." Cha-Cha smiled at Sherrelle and opened her arms wide. "Where's my hug good-bye, young lady?" Sherrelle hugged her briefly then started towards the door. Cha-Cha nodded her approval to Veda. "You got yourself a good girl right there Veda. Looks like you did something right. So Sherrelle, what're your plans after you finish high school?"

Sherrelle stopped and looked back, smiling with excitement. "I'm going to cosmetology school next year to get my license. And, one day I'm going to have my own shop."

"Well, well. This little diva's got ambition, Veda," said Cha-Cha, "Just like her Mama. Ya'll be careful out there." Cha-Cha sighed, "Enough socializing for me. Guess I better get back to work."

"Get back to work?" Veda said, mockingly, "Girl, looks to me like you haven't even started yet." Before Cha-Cha could react, Veda leaned in and gave Cha-Cha a hug good-bye. "Good seeing you, Cha. Take it easy."

Cha-Cha nodded and returned the hug. "You too, girl." She gave Veda and Sherrelle a wave as they went out the door. After Veda and Sherrelle had gone, Renee put down the magazine that she had been using as a shield and gave Cha-Cha direct eye contact while visibly checking her watch. Cha-Cha glanced at the client sign-in sheet on the desk and saw Renee's name written next to hers as stylist. "Come on back, Honey," Cha-Cha motioned for Renee to come sit in her chair. She kept up her non-stop talking to the other stylists as she worked. It did not escape Renee's notice that Cha-Cha still had not apologized for making her wait so long.

"Nadine, can we please listen to something a little less nerve-racking?" asked Cha-Cha as she began applying the creamy mixture to Renee's hair, "all that yelling and screaming is giving me a daggone headache."

"Girl, that's my new Ludicrous CD and this jam right here is tight. Besides, when it's your week to pick the music, you can play Barry Manilow for all I care," said Nadine, tartly.

Whittni cleared her throat and chimed in, "I'm with Cha-Cha, girl. My last client's at 7 so I'm gonna be on my feet all day. Can we save the pumpin' Club jams for later?"

There was an awkward moment of silence between the women, while the music blared. Nadine, a plump thirty-ish looking woman in a short, natural Afro marched over to the CD player and popped in a soft love ballad by Mariah Carey.

"Thanks, girl. I didn't get to bed 'til three this morning," said Cha-Cha.

"Up all night again with some 'Yo boy', huh?" teased the petite, willowy one they called Takara. Dressed in tight, black knit pants and a V-neck top, Takara's creamy complexion accented her highlighted chestnut hair that was cut in a short, layered style.

"Yo boy? What the hell's that?" asked Nadine.

"You know, one of them gansta wannabes, always saying 'Yo man, what's up or Yo Ma, come here,' explained Takara, "Every third word out of their mouth is Yo. A wannabe thug who failed eighth grade English."

"Nah, Takara. That's your type," said Cha-Cha as she sashayed over to the shampoo bowl, motioning for Renee to follow, "Y'all can just kiss my big, black luscious behind."

"So what's your excuse for keeping your client waiting for almost an hour?" said Nadine as she set the flat iron down and put her hand on her hip, "Just who do you think you are—struttin' in here like Queen Makeda? Then taking your sweet time to start working."

There it was, out in the open. Nadine had voiced the same sentiments that Renee had been feeling and had wanted to say to Cha-Cha herself but couldn't bring herself to do it. Renee felt her head tingle from Cha-Cha's strong nails, scratching and massaging the shampoo into her scalp. Nadine's accusations must have hit a nerve.

"Girl, you better watch the time on your own customer's relaxer and mind your own damn business," said Cha-Cha to Nadine over her shoulder.

A moment later she switched to her sweet, seductive voice and offered an explanation.

"Well, I did meet me a real cutie pie last night in the Helix lounge at Club 2K9," said Cha-Cha, "Of course, I didn't need a VIP pass 'cause I was looking fly in my red spandex sequined halter. The dude at the door just let me right on in. Anyway, that Brother I met is one fine specimen of a man. We played some pool, drank some Cristal. And got to know each other better, if you know what I mean." Cha-Cha paused, as if recalling a dream.

"James Ian Mathias," Cha-Cha went on to say, "His friends call him Ian. He's got dark, dreamy, bedroom eyes. He's 29 years old and he's a Scorpio like me. The Brother drives a midnight-blue Jag—an XK8. He graduated from Georgetown U four years ago with an MBA and now runs his own Marketing Consulting business downtown. And by the way, he owns a lavish condo in Georgetown. I didn't want to say anything about him in front of my girlfriend, Veda. I didn't want her to be jealous seeing as how she's all alone right now."

"Oh, how thoughtful of you," said Takara, sarcastically, "What did you do, girl? Have the man investigated? You got his whole damn dossier. Anyway, no need for your girl to be jealous of you. This dude sounds like a drug dealer to me. One of them executive thugs, you know what I'm sayin'?" The other stylists started laughing in agreement with Takara.

"Y'all just jealous 'cause you ain't getting no play," Cha-Cha taunted the other girls over the running water.

"Umhum. Ian right? Where's this dude from?" said Nadine.

"He was born in D. C. but his mama's people are from Jamaica and his daddy's American—Black. Ian said I was like champagne in a Dixie cup and he'd make sure that from now on I'd always be poured from a crystal glass."

"What? What kinda sorry bullshit line is that?" laughed Nadine out loud.

"Girl, you getting ready to get in trouble again," said Whittni as she shook her head.

"That's right," said Nadine, "Y'all know she stay stuck on stupid. We ain't forgot about that married man you keep going back and forth with. I don't know who the hell you think would be jealous of you."

"Shoot, that's ancient history, girl. I'm all through with that. Anyway, Ian ain't nobody's 'Yo boy' and he's too refined and educated to be a drug dealer. And he is S-I-N-G-L-E. You'll see for yourselves soon enough. I gave him my card and he's coming in for a haircut today."

"Umhum. Yeah, okay. Right," they all said in unison, "We don't believe a word of your Cinderella bullshit, Cha-Cha."

At that moment the chimes on the door sang as it opened. Everybody looked towards the door. His eyes were deep-set, dark brown and piercing. Caramel-colored complexion on a clean-cut baby face and dark softly waved hair radiated a Fortune 500 image. He removed his sunglasses slowly and scanned the shop, squinting at the room full of people through the blinding overhead lights. Renee's eyes locked onto his at the same time that his gaze struck her. A sinister eerie feeling washed over Renee from his three-second gaze.

Everyone stopped what they were doing and conversations ceased in mid sentence. Even Mr. Woods stopped talking. If Cha-Cha had walked in earlier like the Queen then this man arrived like the King. Tall, slender and muscular without bulkiness, his height reached almost

6'4." He carried himself majestically and had them all mesmerized. Renee noticed he wore one small diamond earring that had baguettes encased in white gold. He had on a pair of loose-fitting, cocoa-brown, soft leather Versace pants, zip-side biker boots, and a brown leather aviator jacket.

He held a clear champagne bottle in one hand and two lead-crystal flutes in the other. He walked over to Cha-Cha without saying a word, bent down and kissed her on the neck. Then again on her exposed chest. Everyone in the shop stood motionless with their mouths hung open and jaws dropped to their chins. Even Cha-Cha seemed dazed and had allowed a glob of hair color to linger on Renee's head and ooze down her client's forehead.

"How are you Charis?" he said in a sexy, soft-spoken voice, "I brought you some more Cristal, Baby."

There was something about this man that Renee did not like. And she had good instincts about people. He was like a spider encircling Cha-Cha and enclosing her into his web. Renee didn't trust the quiet, innocent-looking, clean-cut façade. She believed he would not hesitate to give an order to have someone killed if they got in his way. But Cha-Cha, or Charis as he had re-christened her, was completely taken in. He poured the champagne and offered Cha-Cha a glass. They both took a sip then Cha-Cha sat her glass down at her station.

"What're you wearing, Ian?" said Cha-Cha and nuzzled her nose close to his neck.

"Yves Saint Laurent. Like it Baby?" he said and took another drink of champagne.

"Umhum. Very nice."

"Do you have time to give me a shape-up, Baby?" he asked.

"Uh huh," she answered in a trance-like state.

They acted like no one else was in the shop. Finally, Nadine broke the spell.

"Cha-Cha, um ... I mean, Charis, your customer's color is drippin'."

"Damn," said Cha-Cha as she grabbed a damp towel and blotted Renee's neck and face.

Cha-Cha dipped her fingers in a pot of ashes sitting on her counter and scrubbed along the hairline to remove the color stains from Renee's skin. She rubbed Renee's forehead so hard, Renee thought her skin was peeling off right along with the color.

"C'mon, over to the bowl, honey, so I can rinse out your color." Renee followed Cha-Cha quickly to the shampoo bowl and leaned her head back, welcoming the rush of warm water on her scalp.

"Ian, just let me get my client under the dryer to pre-dry then I can take care of you, Baby," said Cha-Cha.

Ian took a seat in the waiting area and poured himself another glass of champagne. He offered the girls some but said he only brought two glasses. Takara rushed into the back room and came out with a coffee mug. Ian looked at her strangely but she didn't seem to care. She held out her mug for him to fill.

Ian finished his drink before Cha-Cha had barely taken a few sips. Renee didn't say anything, but she hoped Cha-Cha would wait until she finished her 'up do' before drinking any more of that champagne. Cha-Cha combed out Renee's wet hair then positioned her under one of the dryers. She made sure Renee was comfortable under the dryer then set the timer for twenty minutes and handed her a magazine. She looked over at Ian and turned on her seductive voice, beckoning him to come forward. She invited Ian to sit at her station and meticulously shaped and trimmed his naturally soft hair. The back and forth teasing that had been going on between the four stylists before Ian arrived had stopped. Even the customers kept silent and watched how the two lovers interacted. It was easy to see the sexual tension and chemistry between Cha-Cha and Ian.

"I hope you don't mind me calling you by your given name, Charis," he said turning around to admire her, "Charis is actually the name of a beautiful Greek goddess who carried herself with grace and purity.

Cha-Cha sounds ghetto and you're too sophisticated and classy a lady to be called that."

"Umph," snorted Nadine and stomped over to the CD player to change the music and turn the volume up.

"Keep still Baby," said Cha-Cha sweetly then turned to cast a sharp glare at Nadine.

Ian's cell phone rang. He whipped the phone out of his pants pocket and checked the caller-id display before answering. "What's up B?" said Ian to the caller and held up his hand for Cha-Cha to stop cutting and give him a second.

"Re-up, ten to twenty. Cool, that's a M.C."

Ian hung up and apologized for making her stop so he could take a business call. "Sorry. That was important, Baby. I'm closing a major investment deal and those fools at my office can't handle shit without me."

Twenty minutes seemed like an eternity but finally, Renee heard the timer on the hairdryer go off. She pushed the hood up abruptly to let Cha-Cha know that the drying cycle had completed. This guy, James Ian Mathias had just walked in and didn't even have an appointment. Not only had her stylist kept her waiting for forty minutes between arriving late and carrying on personal conversations, she was making Renee wait even longer while she took extra time on her new boyfriend's hair. Renee slammed down the magazine and stared straight at Cha-Cha. She was getting dangerously close to losing her temper and that's something she didn't want to do in public. Cha-Cha didn't look up because she was absorbed in a heavy, intimate conversation with the handsome young man in her chair. Renee felt a tap on her arm and saw Nadine's smiling face.

"What you getting today, honey?" said Nadine in an understanding voice, "My customer's been wet set and needs to stay under the dryer for 45 minutes. I can finish up your blow dry and curl in about fifteen minutes."

There was an unspoken rule among stylists that they didn't try to steal each other's customers, especially not in front of their face. Cha-Cha must have taken her eyes off Ian long enough to realize what Nadine was up to. She slammed down the clippers and marched over to Nadine. Cha-Cha glared at Nadine without uttering a word. If looks were bullets, Nadine would be dead.

"I know you've lost your damn mind, Nadine."

"No, you the one lost *your* damn mind," said Nadine raising her voice, "We've all seen you goin' through changes. Now that you own the place, you're late all the time. You expect Whittni and Takara to take your messages when Sherrelle's not here—'cause I sure as hell ain't your secretary. Your license's been expired for two weeks. What if the inspector drops in and sees you operating with an expired license? The shop closes and we all lose money. I don't wanna get in your business but…girl, you need to get your priorities straight."

"I plan to get my license renewed tomorrow morning so y'all don't have to worry about that. And anything else I do is none of your damn business."

"All I know is some people don't sell their butt to get what they want," said Nadine eyeing Ian.

"Look y'all need to just stop this mess right now," said Takara, "We have customers in here."

"I could say a lot about you, Nadine, but I've got too much class to stoop to your level. You and everybody in here know I can slice you up with my tongue anytime I feel like it. I don't need no other weapon to bring you down, girl."

Nadine stormed out the back door to cool off. Cha-Cha finished up Ian's hair in silence.

"Baby, do you have plans tonight?" Ian asked and lifted Cha-Cha's mood. She brushed the loose hair from his back and answered him in a sexy voice. "I do now. What do you have in mind, Baby?"

"I wanna take you to a black tie political fundraiser tonight. I know it sounds lame but there'll be some important people there I need to get friendly with for business reasons," he said. "If you came with me, I could stand it for a little while."

Ian held out a fist full of hundred dollar bills and told her to buy a new outfit, shoes, and all the accessories she needed for the evening. Cha-Cha always dressed stylishly in designer clothes and kept up with her manicures and pedicures. She insisted she already had several gowns in her closet, bragging aloud that her outfits and shoes fit into a separate room. Ian shoved the money into her hand anyway and said he wanted his woman to buy something new.

"I'll pick you up at eight. So we can fall in the joint fashionably late and make our grand entrance."

Cha-Cha shouldn't have any problem being fashionably late, thought Renee. Cha-Cha and Ian kissed good-bye at the door and Cha-Cha was finally ready to turn her full attention to Renee's hair. When Renee sat down in her stylist's chair, she sensed that Cha-Cha was pre-occupied and still fuming from the argument she had with Nadine. Now that Ian had left the shop there was nothing to keep her distracted. She barely spoke a word as her fingers tucked, pulled and pinned Renee's hair. Cha-Cha didn't need to add a synthetic hairpiece because Renee's own hair was thick enough to provide volume. She swept up Renee's hair in the back into a graceful French twist. A few remaining strands of hair cascaded downwards in feathery, loose ringlets. Although, Cha-Cha worked quickly, the finished effect was exactly what Renee had envisioned. Her stylist had created an elegant evening up-do. Cha-Cha sprayed the final creation with a mist of oil sheen. The end result: elegant and sophisticated. As usual, the wait had been worth it.

"You did it again, Cha-Cha. Performed another miracle," Renee beamed as she raised the hand mirror to admire her hairstyle, "I love it!"

"I'm glad you're pleased," said Cha-Cha, fingering a stubborn wisp of Renee's hair into place. Cha-Cha turned around and gave the other stylists an 'I told you so' look of satisfaction.

Renee now felt ready to celebrate her birthday tonight. Nothing was going to stop her show—not even Bill quitting his job or buying a new car he didn't need. She had something special in store for her husband. Something he'd never forget.

CHAPTER 7

Renee pulled into the garage around 5:30 PM and panicked when she saw that Bill had arrived home before her. Both of his cars were parked in the garage. He had told her to be ready by 6:30. She rushed to her bedroom but fortunately he wasn't there. Probably somewhere in his office, she thought. She began quickly stripping out of her clothes. After a quick bath, she slipped on a burgundy satin robe and lingered in front of the mirror touching up her makeup.

Bill was dressed and ready to go. To ease his impatience, he waited in the study and watched the evening news as he sipped on a glass of Courvoisier. While he hoped he'd be wrong this time, he didn't expect Renee to be ready on time as he'd requested.

Renee removed her robe and snapped on the new 'Flatter Me' bra to push up, tuck in, and pad where needed. Not only did this miracle bra enlarge her breast size an extra cup but its corset wiring sucked in her slightly soft middle as well. She put on a pair of kidskin gloves and slipped her legs through ultra sheer, flesh-toned hose. Black slingback shoes lifted her 5'4" height another few inches. Then she stepped into a floor length, blue-black gown with plunging neckline. She added the finishing touch, a pair of diamond drop earrings and matching teardrop necklace that settled close to the crevice of her enhanced bosom. Renee admired herself in the full-length mirror and practiced a sexy, slow-strutting Mae West walk.

But within moments, the under wire of the push-up bra began to pinch her breastbone. She discovered if she stood straight with shoulders back and breast protruded, it didn't hurt as much. Her swept up hairdo with side tendrils framed her face and the shimmering makeup transformed her from attractive to dropdead gorgeous. Renee smiled at her reflection in the mirror and twirled around like a schoolgirl dressed for the prom. Forty-five ain't so bad after all. More of an intellectual type, the role of beautiful uninhibited sex goddess was not a typical part for Renee to assume. It might be fun playing that role tonight, she thought. Then she remembered the private dinner invitation for Saturday that she had mailed to Bill that morning. The new Renee would be in just the right mood for Bill's surprise on Saturday night. Suddenly, her husband's restless voice calling upstairs interrupted her thoughts.

"Jesus Christ, Renee, aren't you ready yet? It's past 6:30!"

"Five more minutes, dear," she called back, sweetly.

After rinsing the eye-shadow stains from her fingers, she discovered the water wouldn't turn off. The faucet felt loose so she kept turning and turning the knob to the off position but water continued to pour out. Just then the cap popped off and a gush of water shot up into her perfectly made up face and hair.

"Damnit." Renee slammed the cap back on the faucet to plug up the spray of water and quickly turned the knob in the opposite direction. Eventually, the water stopped. She cursed her own stupidity as well as Bill's laziness for not fixing the faucet. He had promised over a week ago to replace the O ring or get a new fixture for her sink after she told him repeatedly that the water in her bathroom faucet dripped. Of course, he hadn't done it. Just one more example of the many things he promised to take care of but didn't. She dabbed her face lightly with a towel, not wanting to smudge her makeup and plugged in the electric curlers to mend her drooping side tendrils. Well, he would just have to cool his heels and wait. Renee reapplied rouge on her cheeks and dusted her face again with translucent powder while waiting for the curlers to heat.

She realized that half the day had passed and he still hadn't wished her happy birthday, or presented her with a gift, let alone a card. But, obviously he had given this evening some thought. Perhaps he planned to give her the gift at dinner tonight. Renee quickly repaired the last curl and unplugged the curling iron. She graciously stepped down the spiral staircase, one hand on the banister and the other clutching a black evening bag. Bill stood speechless at the foot of the stairs. As she descended, his wide-eyed gaze zoned in on her enhanced bosom.

"I'm ready, dear."

"Nice dress," is all he could think to say without taking his eyes off her swelling décolletage.

"Thank you, darling. You look rather dashing yourself this evening," she said and patted the lapel of his jacket.

Bill presented the image of a sophisticated gentleman in his classic three-button tuxedo complete with a wing-collared shirt and cravat. His gray-flecked hair and graying mustache looked quite distinguished. He helped her with her coat and they left through the front door after he activated the security alarm. As soon as she eased into his sporty BMW and sank down into the leather seat, the 'Flatter-Me' bra's stiff under wirings cut into her breastbone mercilessly. Her chest and breathing felt tight and constricted. Bill turned on the ignition and the car pulled out of the driveway. They got as far as half way down the block when she screamed in a panic, "Stop the car!"

"What's wrong?" he frowned, "Don't tell me. You forget something."

"No," she panted, "I can't breath in this ... bra."

"What the hell ... what're you gonna do about it now? We're already twenty minutes late."

"Let me out. I have to get out of this bra."

"Jesus Christ of Nazareth!" he said, and made an abrupt turn around, "Are we ever gonna get the hell outta here tonight?"

"Must you use the Lord's name that way?"

"Since when did you become religious?" he said, "I always took you for an agnostic like myself. I didn't think you'd turn into one of those religious fanatics on me." He made an abrupt stop in the driveway and glanced annoyingly at his watch.

"Can you please unlock the door and come help me out of this batmobile before I pass out?" she said.

Bill sighed heavily and got out of the car, slamming the driver side door. With his help, she lifted her constricted body out of the sports car. Renee ran back into the house and raced upstairs, nearly tripping in her high heels.

Bill stood at the bottom of the stairs and shook his head. Then, he went to go sit down in the living room to wait. Every few minutes, he glanced at his watch, annoyed.

Renee frantically tore off her gown and struggled to release the bra's death grip. When getting dressed she had taken her time to hook and snap each loop but now her torso felt so restricted she could barely breath. Her fingers grappled at the seemingly endless row of miniature hooks. Cheeks now flushed and forehead wet with perspiration, Renee breathed rapidly as her newly manicured nails worked against her now that she was in a hurry. All the while she was cursing Bill under her breath. Why hadn't he come upstairs to help her out of this damn bra? Or to at least make sure she hadn't passed out from lack of oxygen! Wouldn't that have been the gentlemanly thing to do? If she didn't get out of that contraption soon Bill would have to call paramedics to revive her. That is, if he ever bothered to come upstairs and check! Rationally, she knew it was wrong to blame Bill. Still, he was an easy target to blame. He and this damn bra were responsible for her misery. A death bra that she had only bought to try to look good for him!

"To hell with it," she said and snatched the scissors from the dresser. She cut a seam through the nylon-lycra corset, snipping carefully to avoid accidentally stabbing herself. Finally, she was free of this expensive torture device and could breath again. Bare-breasted, she stepped into her walk-in closet for a quick inventory to select something more comfortable to wear. She did not have another evening bra that would accommodate the plunging neckline on her gown. She changed into one of her everyday bras and chose a black, silk Donna Karan pants suit and beaded stretch nylon camisole. It didn't matter if her bra strap showed through the camisole because she planned to keep the suit jacket on. She replaced the stiletto slingbacks with a lower heeled pump. Now, not only could she breathe freely, she wouldn't have to worry about falling down a flight of stairs and breaking her neck. It's amazing what pain women subjected themselves to for the sake of beauty, she thought. Renee glanced at her new look in the mirror and felt relieved that her desperate effort to get out of the 'Flatter-Me' bra hadn't ruined her makeup or hair. She ditched the five-inch evening bag and selected a more practical purse that was big enough to hold her wallet and cell phone.

Renee returned downstairs this time looking more like her old self, a psychologist, rather than an enticing femme-fatal.

Bill stood up and noticed immediately that her bulging cleavage and tiny, pinched in waist had vanished. "What happened?" he asked with a frown and pointed to her chest.

"It was the bra, Bill. Not me. This is me. Let's go," she said, passing in front of him. "I'm ready now."

Renee could never be glamorous the way Bill liked. If he couldn't accept her without the fakeness and pretense, then that was his problem. It felt good to accept herself just as she was, imperfections and all.

Bill grumbled while speeding out of the driveway. "Damnit. I just knew we'd be late for this thing. Even though I asked you to be on time for once," he said without bothering to hide his anger. She decided to ignore Bill's chilly mood. To her, it seemed like he was trying hard to ruin her birthday. When he turned on the CD player it blared out some loud repetitive beat that Renee immediately found annoying. She studied the rows of buttons, dials, and symbols on the console but couldn't identify the volume control. Her irritation was evident when she finally gave up and spoke to him in a clipped voice. "Do you mind turning that noise down? Or better yet … off?"

Without a word of protest, Bill obliged by switching the button to Off position. "Was that so hard for you to do?" he said sarcastically. Renee's reply to him was her silence and a prolonged glare at his profile. The early niceties from the evening's romantic beginnings had evaporated. During the rest of the drive downtown they spoke intermittently and only when necessary. While it seemed their night out for her birthday had turned unpleasant, she was hopeful that things would improve once they both had a chance to relax and remember why they were there—to celebrate her 45th birthday. Bill stopped at curbside on 13th and Pennsylvania Avenue behind a succession of limousines. Exquisitely dressed, jeweled women in furs with perfectly coifed hair and men dressed in tuxedos wearing shiny, black shoes emerged from stretch limos, M-class Mercedes, Beamers, jags and other luxury vehicles. A valet appeared and opened Renee's door just as another valet accepted the car keys from Bill on the driver's side.

"Careful parking her in the garage, buddy. And be sure to leave plenty of room between cars."

"Yes, sir," the valet nodded and got behind the wheel.

"Where are we?" asked Renee, staring ahead at the massive building in front of her.

Like many native Washingtonians, Renee had lived in Washington, D. C. all her life but still couldn't identify all the magnificent, neoclassical, and Greek Revival architectural structures situated throughout the city. The nation's capital represented a masterpiece of artistic monuments, buildings, parks and statues that most D. C. residents took for granted. Its streets were efficiently arranged in a symmetrical grid of circles and right angles that only confused an illogical mind.

"That's the Ronald Reagan Building. We're practically in President Barkley's backyard. The White House is just two blocks away."

"Then my next question is, why are we here?"

"You'll see. Just come on." He took her by the elbow, leading the way up the numerous rows of white concrete steps.

The lobby buzzed with downtown high-rollers and power brokers. Renee hoped that Bill had reserved a more intimate setting in one of the private dining rooms for her birthday. After checking their coats, he led her down a packed hallway to the elevators. They stopped at the concourse level floor and entered the Atrium. A row of stately columns divided the ballroom and the Atrium Hall. Overhead a long glass skylight revealed the onset of dusk through a cloudless, slate-gray sky. Natural light from high-filter accent lights bathed the room in shimmering iridescence. A centerpiece, overflowing with reddish pink amaryllis and long dancing stalks of full-bloomed paperwhites, sat on a covered table in front of a mirrored wall. Burning tea lights encircled the floral arrangement and bestowed a magnificent, glowing effect when reflected off the mirror.

Beautiful woman escorted by formally-dressed gentlemen glided down a grand staircase. The reception area was packed with black-tie attired Washington symbols of power and money—bankers, lawyers, real estate tycoons, high-powered political figures and lobbyists. They all assumed the familiar 'grin' and 'grip' position. Renee realized the evening to celebrate her birthday would not be the intimate atmosphere she had envisioned. Why would Bill bring her to this type of affair for her birthday, she wondered.

Renee recognized the mayor and a few sports figures from the

Washington Wizards basketball team. Bill pointed out some of the players from the Capitals hockey, Nationals baseball and Redskins football teams that were also present, accompanied by their entourages. Just as Renee was about to ask Bill what all this was about, a dramatic visual appeared on a large monitor and displayed words of welcome to sponsors and supporters of this year's fundraiser dinner for Boys & Girls Clubs of Greater Washington (BGCGW).

The program's host stood on stage in front of the wall-sized screen and rattled off impressive statistics. He told guests that the Washington Boys and Girls Clubs operated 17 clubs and 7 group homes in the District of Columbia, Suburban Maryland and Northern Virginia. BGCGW was the second largest affiliate of Boys & Girls Clubs of America where over 25,000 youth participated, and it had served youth in the community for over 114 years. Their goal tonight was to raise one million dollars. The host reported that the President of the United States volunteered for the Washington Boys and Girls Club whenever his busy schedule permitted. He wanted to be there today but prior commitments prevented him from joining them.

"However," continued the host as he waved a sealed letter in the air, "President Barkley sent this letter expressing his support which I'd like to take a moment to read to you now."

A wave of applause preceded complete silence. Then the host read the president's letter that commended the organization for saving youth's lives. President Barkley congratulated this year's BGCGW Youth of the Year and indicated his pledge for a generous donation. Renee started to feel guilty about not wanting to be there among all these strangers on her birthday. The black-tie fundraiser of more than 1,000 guests represented a worthy event where old and new money mingled for a common cause. Education, recreation and mentorship for underprivileged children were easy goals to support, but it was completely out of character for Bill. He cared about children as much as he cared about giving money to any charities, virtually nil. She was the one who volunteered on alternate Saturdays for the Court Appointed Special Advocate (CASA) program where she worked with abused, neglected or seriously ill children. She was the one who sent in pledges and donations to charities whereas Bill would toss the unopened envelopes in the trash if he got to the mail first. So why did this particular Boys and Girls Club fundraiser dinner hold such interest for him?

There was no need to ponder her question any further because the answer walked up wearing a five-button tuxedo and silver tie—Clifton Corbin Shaw, her husband's new business partner. Clinging on Shaw's arm like an accessory, stood a mocha complexioned, twenty-something beauty in an emerald green Oscar de la Renta bustier gown. Next to Shaw's choice of eye candy for the evening, Renee suddenly felt plain and matronly. Shaw turned to Renee with a fake grin that looked like he had grabbed a smile out of his pocket and pasted it on his face. He introduced his date merely as LaToya and led her and Bill to his private table where other political and business people from Washington were already seated. Renee seethed internally. This was one time she regretted her years of practicing how to maintain composure and not make a scene. Her muscles tightened and she walked robotically behind Shaw, who led the way to the table, with LaToya close to his side. Renee didn't trust herself to look at Bill.

CHAPTER 8

The conversation at the table centered on Shaw and his many accomplishments. He held his audience captive while answering questions about himself. He clearly relished the attention.

"Well, Shaw, you look like future presidential candidate material to me," said a gray-whiskered man as he gulped his Merlot, "A rising star. Got the brains, the youth, and the charisma. The elderly gentleman raised his glass to Shaw, "Hell, if a former beauty queen turned soccer mom can be a serious contender for the White House, why not you?"

Shaw sat up straight and squared his shoulders proudly, "Give me another eight years, George, before I take over the presidency. At forty-six, I'm still a young man for politics. But you're right about one thing. In Washington it ain't *what* you know, but *who* you know. Anyway, I got my eye on an ambassadorship to a Caribbean country or a cabinet appointment first." Shaw went on talking about himself. "Before I'm though greasing the right palms, it'll be a slam dunk. Yeah, a Presidential Appointment with a senate confirmation or a PAC should last me for about a year and a half, tops. Oh, and for those of you unfamiliar with Washington-speak," he explained, looking directly at Renee, "a PAC stands for Political Action Committee. Or, I could make due with something on the level of cabinet, secretary, department, or a deputy cabinet level position. Any of those positions would work just fine for me as a launching off pad. Since I'm not the favored son of somebody important, I gotta do whatever it takes to get my political ducks lined up. And that translates into a lotta loot, my friends. If you expect favors, you gotta pay for 'em. Ain't nothing free in this land of milk and honey, my friends."

"Well, you've got what it takes, son." George raised his wine glass to Shaw once again, before gulping down a swallow.

"I hope so, George. In politics you need money and an influential political mentor. It's all about power and money. Money talks and bullshit walks. Nobody's your friend in Washington. If you want a friend in this town, go out and get yourself a pit bull," Clifton Shaw quipped.

Everyone at the table laughed at Shaw's worn-out jokes and overused clichés except Renee. She had heard Bill's speech about this man's political aspirations so often she had practically memorized it. *'A Princeton graduate with a double-major in political science and history. While in grad school he landed an internship with a prominent Republican senator. During that year working for the senator he met many powerful people who helped him get established in Washington. After graduation Shaw did a stint on Capitol Hill, followed by several Republican appointments.'* According to Bill, Shaw was on his way to becoming one of the top minority business owners in Washington D. C. The only thing Bill said he wasn't too keen on was that his new friend still held strong political ties to the "Grand Ole Party" or the GOP Republican Party as it's more commonly known. But Bill had made it perfectly clear that he would have no problem switching teams if need be in order to get connected. This was not the same man she had married 14 years ago. Ever since being forced to retire from his job at EDUTECH, it seemed to her that Bill was acting like he would be willing to sleep with the Devil if he thought it would help him get ahead in his new career. She also realized something else troubling. Shaw clearly had ambitions towards one day taking up residency on 1600 Pennsylvania Avenue. Renee cringed at the possibility of seeing Shaw in the White House and being able to push the button in a time of national crisis. It didn't take her long to diagnose Shaw as suffering from Narcissistic Personality Disorder. She closed her eyes briefly and shuddered to remove the scary thought of someone like that running the country.

"Yeah, I'll donate what I have to for this type of plate fundraiser," said Shaw, "I get invited to these things automatically. But in an election year, you better believe I'm an Eagle donor. I'll plop down five grand a pop at a fundraiser just so I can get right in and see the important people in town." Shaw took a sip of his drink before continuing. He glanced around at his audience to make sure everyone was still listening. "Yeah, you know when you call for an interview the first thing they do is put you on hold. That's because they're checking the list to see what you gave. When I call up, I always hear, '*Oh yes, Mr. Shaw, what can we do for you?*'" he said, mimicking the receptionist. "And, do you know why? It's because I always give significant donations. That's my ticket right in the door." He nodded, pleased with himself.

Renee sighed in boredom. A smooth-sounding band called NuJeau played an assortment of jazz and R&B oldies, but even their mellow music didn't help her to relax and have fun. She tapped her fingers on the table absentmindedly. It was now obvious beyond doubt that Bill had forgotten her birthday. He attended this elegant affair at Clifton Shaw's last-minute invitation only to schmooze and network. Renee debated whether she should remind him that it was her birthday, suffer in silence, or just get up and leave. Not able to decide which option to take, she sat there, fuming.

The waiter kept Bill and Clifton's drinks—Jack Daniel's with cranberry juice and Vodka martinis—refilled while they talked endlessly about business and politics with whomever listened or even pretended to listen to them. LaToya, Shaw's wide-eyed young date, accepted another glass of Champagne and nibbled at the shrimp-filled pastry puffs on her plate. The woman seated next to LaToya was named Maggie Dymond, a Legislative Assistant to Senator Monroe on the

Hill—big bosomed and middle-aged, she wore a drapery top that only made her huge chest appear larger.

"So what's this latest venture of yours all about Cliff?"

"Well, Maggie, my new business partner and I," he patted Bill on the arm, "have been in meetings all week with our attorneys along with a silent partner who put up a hundred grand in seed money to help launch my startup, Techands Inc."

"Oh?" said Maggie, feigning interest while she sipped a whiskey and tonic.

Without much prodding, Shaw continued. "Our venture capitalist friend recently cashed in some stocks and said he wanted somewhere to park his money as long as he could remain anonymous. I was able to work out the details to his satisfaction. As a matter of fact, he liked my prospectus so much he agreed to make future investments towards my new company's growth. If any of you want in at the ground level while the price is still cheap, it's an incredible investment opportunity."

"Is it legal?" asked Maggie.

"Of course, it's legit. Shit, Maggie, how can you ask me that? My startup is based on innovative technology and I've rounded up the best brains to lead the troops to victory."

Shaw slapped Bill on the back and grinned, "Yeah, old Bill's one of my book boys. He's in charge of the day to day operations on the IT side of the business."

"Looks like you're still winning at the races, Shaw," smiled the elderly, bearded gentleman named George. "Tell me, what makes your idea so damn attractive to this secret investor?"

"A nice, fat guaranteed return. It works for us too," said Shaw, pointing to himself and Bill, "The key to good business is to use other people's money. Our primary investor rakes in over eight mil a year from his other investments. You know, stuff like real estate and retail. He's not hurting for coins and can afford to take a risk on us. Though, there's virtually no risk of failure involved here. A

100% guaranteed sweet return. Like I said, I'm a pit bull when it comes to business and politics. And with this business plan, I'll pull in enough cash to fund my ass right into the presidency or damn close to it." He chuckled.

"What's your mission statement?" asked Aaron Kaufman, a skeptical accountant-type with piercing blue eyes behind thick, black-rimmed bifocals.

Shaw had a quick answer to give. "Techands Inc is a H1-B sponsor that'll host and train foreign nationals to work in this country using the hottest new technology. In fact, the name stands for 'technical hands'. Sort of like ranch hands on the farm. But instead of herding cattle our guys are herding software code. We find 'em, clean 'em up, train 'em, and move 'em out," grinned Shaw. "They get the job done for our clients in half the time and for half the cost."

"You're quite the altruist, Shaw," said Maggie in a sarcastic tone.

"That's right," Bill interjected, "We provide fast, cheap, and accurate software support to American companies. Eventually, we'll expand into the international market. With this sluggish economy we're in, the trend is towards outsourcing, where companies farm out their Information Technology services to Third Party Vendors."

Everyone at the table looked at Bill as he spoke. Renee noticed that Shaw frowned when the spotlight had momentarily shifted away from him. With added confidence, Bill continued to explain their company's strategy. "Businesses have eliminated entire IT departments so they can focus only on operations, marketing, sales and customer fulfillment. Techands Inc specializes in the design and development of solutions using the hottest languages out there today. Languages like Java, Oracle, DotNet, C and C++, you name it."

"Listen buddy, I think you're going a bit over their heads with the techno babble," smiled Shaw, "these good folks talk politics, my man—not bits and bytes."

"Speak for yourself, Shaw," said Maggie, "I can keep up. I design and maintain my own website. So Bill is it? How does Techands Inc use these field hands, as you fellas call them, to turn a profit?"

"It's pretty simple, Maggie. Companies send us their assignments and specs and we send them back the executable code for a fair price. If they want the source version too then they can buy it for an additional fee," Bill explained. "Otherwise, they'll have to come back to us for changes and future enhancements—which means more money for Techands. The concept is nothing new but our approach is different."

"Got it, but what I meant to say was, where are you getting these folks?" asked Maggie, "By the time you pay the going rate for your Silicon Valley types, you'll end up losing money. Not to mention how fast the techies dump you nowadays for bigger bucks at Northern Virginia software companies. After you train them, they're gone in three months."

Shaw spoke up in response to Maggie's point. While Bill's head bobbed up and down in agreement to everything that Shaw said. "That's the beauty of it, Maggie, we're using only cheap, foreign labor and training them ourselves through a rigorous, boot-camp program. I've leased a training facility out in McLean with some of our investment money. Bill's already got brand new computers wired, networked, and ready to go. We're in the last stages of our trainees' H1-B visa applications. We're on a roll, aren't we, buddy?" said Shaw, turning to flash a wide grin at his new business partner.

"That's not a new concept in the IT world, you know. Anyway Shaw, what's in it for the worker bees?"

"I'm not saying it's an original idea, Maggie," said Shaw in a defensive tone. "Look, if you already got a wheel, roll with it. Why invent a new one? And as far as what my guys get out of it, for starters, they get free technical training and a damn good salary to boot. The contract stipulates they only owe Techands three years of service. Like I said, training and operations are Bill's responsibility, but Techands was all my idea from soup to nuts," beamed Shaw, polishing off the last of his drink, "so that makes me the HNIC."

"The what?" said Aaron Kaufman, squinting as he positioned his glasses up from the tip of his nose.

"The HNIC. That's like your CEO, Aaron," laughed Shaw. When Kaufman continued to stare at Shaw with a confused look, Shaw slapped Bill on the back to give him the go ahead to explain. "Go on translate for the white boy, Bill. Some of ya'll know what I'm talking about." Shaw laughed loudly, clearly amused with himself. When Bill failed to comment, Shaw offered the translation. "Aaron, that's what we call the Head Nigga In Charge," said Shaw, motioning for the waiter to return and re-fill his drink.

After a brief awkward silence, Kaufman spoke up, wearing a look of skepticism. "Your plan may sound okay in theory but I still don't get how it will actually work."

LaToya shook Clifton Shaw's elbow and pouted, "Cliff baby, I'm aging over here like a dried-up prune. Let's go to the ballroom and dance."

"Be cool, baby, let me finish my conversation." Shaw turned his back to LaToya and addressed Kaufman's doubting glance. "Look Aaron, let me explain it to you like you were a two year old." Then, he chuckled to himself, "Ya'll remember that was Denzel's line in that Philadelphia movie about the gay guy. Anyway, man, it's like this. Bill here put up a website and we've been soliciting our services over the web. Right now we've targeted Bangalore, India for the first wave of trainees because that's the technological center in that subcontinent. So, initially our entire development team will be made up of these guys from Bangalore. They'll undergo employment screening at the U. S. Embassy next week as part of the visa application but we don't expect any problems with their visas being issued. Do we, Bill?" Bill immediately shook his head in agreement and motioned for Shaw to continue.

"The initial pay is $40,000 to $50,000 per year. Believe me, that's a fortune to these guys and they'll work without complaining. Unlike American workers. These people are focused on one thing—

programming," said Shaw, "There's no leaving work early to go run errands or watch a kid's soccer game or ballet recital. Our U. S. clients get their code written by highly skilled workers at a cheaper price. It's win-win for everybody."

"So they won't be with their families for three years?" asked Maggie.

"That's right. We explained to them that their families will have to remain in India until they can save enough money to bring them over. I think that's fair."

"Well ya know what this sounds like to me?" That was a rhetorical question because Maggie didn't wait for Shaw's response before continuing. "Sounds like when African slaves, European immigrants, and Native Americans were used for cheap labor as indentured servants in the 17th century. Granted, nothing was as awful as The Middle Passage when Africans were forcibly brought over here on slave ships then hosed off and 'cleaned up' before being displayed on the auction block and sold away from their families. This plan of yours sounds too much like these foreign workers might be at risk of being taken advantage of. I hope this isn't a case where History repeats itself in the 21st century."

"Maggie, you've got too much imagination. This isn't anything like that," quipped Shaw.

"I'm afraid I have to agree with Maggie, but for different reasons. It sounds to me like you're taking advantage of cheap foreign labor when our workers here are in desperate need of jobs," said Kaufman.

"What the hell are you talking about? All businesses these days rely on cheap foreign labor if they want to stay competitive," said Bill with a sharp edge in his voice.

"Shaw, I'm with you and Bill," nodded George, "Case in point. When I lived in Atlanta a few years ago, illegal Mexican immigrants dominated construction work down there. If the INS forced all illegal immigrants out of Atlanta, construction work would come to a standstill. These immigrants worked for $7.00 an hour and kept their whole family in one small apartment. And they wouldn't ask the boss to be off on weekends either. Nobody else was willing to do this work for that price. I get your point."

"What about the effect on American skilled programmers?" asked Maggie, "Some groups believe that importing foreign labor lowers wages for American employees and makes it more difficult for citizens in this country to be considered for career opportunities in technology. And, you're planning to train foreigners to do high-paying jobs that American workers could be trained to do."

Shaw slammed his glass down and scoffed. "I don't buy that argument, Maggie. Anyway, it's not my problem. If somebody is highly qualified or willing to learn, they can always find work no matter if they're black, white, yellow, or brown. In America the opportunity is there for anyone willing to work hard like our foreign recruits at Techands are eager to do. It's the mediocre folks standing around the water cooler and taking two-hour lunch breaks who have to worry about their goddamn jobs, not the dedicated workers."

Bill frowned at Shaw's last statement but he did not challenge him and Shaw continued talking in a boisterous, 'know-it-all' tone.

"Why should a company keep dead weight on the payroll if they can't produce when businesses can come to a company like mine and get their code out the door quicker and for half the price? This is business Maggie, not a popularity contest and certainly not a handout."

"If I'm not mistaken Shaw, you're one of those people who's always out on two-hour lunch breaks whenever I call your secretary to try to setup an appointment," said Maggie with a wicked grin and raised her glass to him as a truce.

"Hey, I'm no average worker. I'm a goddamn lawyer—pardon me ladies, Maggie excluded—and a partner at that. I conduct better business over a fine meal and a few drinks. Being in a nice restaurant puts my clients at ease."

"Pay no attention to Maggie. I think it's a damn brilliant idea, Shaw," said George, after polishing off the last of his third glass of Merlot, "wish I'd thought of it myself and was young enough to pull it off."

Even though Bill had given Renee the impression that the business was still in the planning phase, he'd obviously been working on this deal for months without even bothering to consult with her. It wasn't too difficult for her to figure out why he had kept his plans secret. He knew she would not be supportive of this scheme hatched by Shaw and he would be absolutely correct. Renee didn't like it at all.

Finally, she excused herself to go to the ladies room. If she had stayed a moment longer she might throw up. Shaw's date popped out of her seat and announced she wanted to go with her to powder her nose. Renee cringed but couldn't diplomatically say she preferred to be alone. As she maneuvered around the dinner tables in the dining area to get to the main hall with LaToya in tow, Renee heard LaToya's girlish voice chirping away without actually listening to a word of the nonsense that the young woman said. The pitch of her voice sounded flighty, but listening to LaToya was less grating on her nerves than remaining at the table and listening to Shaw.

As she worked her way out of the room, a few tables away Renee spotted someone who from a distance looked uncannily like Deek. She ceased walking in mid-step and her heart seemed to suddenly stop as well. She stared at the handsome man who had not yet noticed her. She hadn't seen or spoken to Deek since August. "What's the matter," asked LaToya who had also stopped in her tracks. Without answering, Renee took a deep breath and continued forward. As she got closer she realized it was him—Detective Degas (Deek) Hamilton, D. C. Metropolitan Police, homicide. The man who had intruded on her private thoughts for the past several days and now here he was in the flesh at the very same Boys and Girls Club fundraiser dinner.

CHAPTER 9

Renee was relieved he didn't see her. Deek appeared to be engaged in a conversation with a lovely, dark-haired, young woman in a red sequined gown and matching satin shoes. Renee turned abruptly to leave before he spotted her. She bumped into a waiter balancing a tray in one hand and a coffeepot in the other. The waiter dropped the tray and some of its contents spilled on her jacket.

"Oh my Gracious!" said the waiter, "I'm terribly sorry, Ma'am. Let me get that." He dabbed at the stain with a cloth napkin.

"It's okay, really. I was on my way to the ladies room. I'll take care of it. Don't bother."

At the sound of crashing plates, Deek along with everyone else close enough to hear, had looked up. A broad smile crossed his face when he saw Renee—a smile punctuated by dimpled cheeks and straight, white teeth. Renee wanted to become invisible when she realized he had noticed her. She watched as he excused himself from the table and walked towards her. His athletic, 6'2" physique owned the black tone-on-tone tuxedo with its nearly invisible vertical stripes and vintage tuxedo shirt.

"What a gorgeous hunk," shrieked LaToya and nudged Renee. She had forgotten that Shaw's date was still standing beside her, but in her private thoughts she agreed with LaToya on that assessment. She had never seen a more perfect face on a man. Bronze-toned features created from an artist's paintbrush had sought perfection and found it. Nicely arched eyebrows defined his dark, serious eyes and his lips—simply luscious. She knew this firsthand because she had already tasted their warm, sweet, moistness this summer. The black hairs of his well-groomed mustache lay in neatly trimmed layers. Deek had grown a hint of a goatee since she'd last seen him. He wore a stylish haircut that revealed the soft, texture of his jet-black hair. Far from the look of the typical disheveled and overworked cop, Deek could have splashed the covers of Code Magazine, a popular style publication for men of color, any day.

Deek once told Renee that his grandmother, Katia Dessalines had immigrated to New York City from Martinique when his mother, Aurelie, was sixteen, and had named him Degas after the French impressionist painter whose work she admired. Thanks to Grann Katia, as he called her, even his name sounded exotic and romantic. But his friends and coworkers simply called him Deek.

"You know that tasty treat?" asked LaToya, "From the way he's eyeing you, looks like he'd sop you up like gravy on a biscuit if given half a chance."

Renee didn't even want to try to respond to that comment. Despite her hip city pretense, LaToya had just revealed her down-home, Southern roots. Deek gave Renee a brief, friendly embrace, brushing his lips against her cheek as he held her hands.

"It's good to see you. You look beautiful as always. What are you doing here tonight?"

His soothing baritone voice that she had become addicted to from the moment they met several months ago, held her captive and she couldn't answer him for a moment. When she could speak her voice betrayed a hint of nervousness.

"I … I mean we … were invited by someone. And you? I see you're still involved with youth. Are you also a mentor for the Boys and Girls Club in addition to your many other endeavors?" Deek nodded and gave Renee one of his dazzling smiles, "Umhum, I'm a volunteer for the Metropolitan Police Boys and Girls Club."

"The way you kickin' it in that tux, my Brother, you must be a mentor with some deep pockets," gushed LaToya and thrust out her hand for him to shake, "I'm LaToya Perry and my date tonight is Clifton Corbin Shaw, the prominent Washington attorney. You probably heard of him if you live in this city. Cliff told me the tickets to this fancy shindig were $500 a plate. So what else do you do besides mentoring, Mr …?"

"Hamilton," said Deek and shook her outstretched hand briefly," Detective Lieutenant Degas Hamilton, D. C. Homicide. I work for the city so my pockets are hardly deep, Ms. Perry."

Renee knew that Deek was smart enough not to reveal his financial status to her. She knew the fact was that, Deek didn't need to rely on his income from the city. He simply enjoyed tracking down criminals and bringing them to justice. He had once told Renee that he had sold the rights to a complicated encryption program that he developed while working as a systems engineer at IBM before joining the police force. As a result, he lived quite well from his investment dividends. If LaToya knew Deek was not only handsome but financially secure, she'd probably beat Renee down to get to him.

"It's LaToya to you, handsome," she said in a seductive voice and moved closer.

Deek took a step backwards. "It was nice meeting you, Ms. Perry. Renee, may I speak to you in private for a moment?" he asked and without waiting for a reply took her arm and led her towards the stairway leading to the Atrium Hall.

LaToya stood there for a shocked moment with her mouth open and one hand on her hip. Renee could feel her staring at their backs as they walked away.

"Thank you," whispered Renee, latching onto Deek's arm.

"Don't mention it. You looked like you needed a quick rescue."

"Seems like you're becoming good at that, Detective Hamilton. Rescuing me, that is."

They slipped into a private room upstairs that appeared deserted. The walls were painted hunter green and radiated a soft light. Instinctively, they chose a corner far away from the door and hidden from any passerby who might happen to peep into the room. They sat facing each other in plush, velvet green upholstered chairs. Although the conversation did not cross the boundaries of friendship, the familiar intimate dance between them began nonetheless. Renee stared out the window at the blackened sky lit by stars and streetlights. She tried without success to avoid gazing directly into his eyes.

"By the way, congratulations on your promotion to lieutenant. I saw your picture and write-up in the Washington Post's Metro section a few months ago."

"Thanks. Taking that bullet this summer did me some good I guess. Got a promotion out of it and a new assignment at least. I'm working on a task force with the FBI and MPD called the DC Joint SOS Task Force. SOS stands for Save Our Streets. It's gotten a lot of support from the Mayor."

"Yes, I've heard about it on the news. Sounds dangerous though," she frowned.

"Comes with the territory, Doc. Anyway, you know I like danger. As soon as Medical released me from desk duty, I was back on the streets."

"I'm not surprised."

"For the last three weeks I've been reporting to FBI headquarters downtown. The FBI's been conducting a long-term probe on this drug kingpin we've been after for drug trafficking, gang related homicides, and a laundry list of other federal violations."

"That must mean you're finally free of your old partner, Lieutenant Melvin Bradford," Renee said, crossing her legs, "What an obnoxious man."

"Mel's not so bad. He's retiring at the end of the year anyway and he actually wished me well on my new assignment. I still have other cases I'm working on so half my time's still at police headquarters, and he's still my partner."

"I never cared for that man." A momentary awkward silence rose between them.

"Renee, do you mind if I ask you a personal question?" Deek whispered, out of the blue.

"Sure. But I can't promise I'll answer it." Renee folded her hands in her lap. She felt she knew where this might be headed.

"Are you happy with your decision to go back to your husband?"

Renee looked away. Although she'd suspected he would ask her something like that, she was not prepared to answer.

Deek touched her cheek and cupped it in the palm of his hand. "I know it's not my place but you just don't look happy. Today's your birthday and this is not the face of a woman who's loved the way she deserves to be."

"How did you know it was my birthday?"

"Why wouldn't I know? I remember every single detail you ever told me. It's permanently locked in my memory bank. Unfortunately, I remember too much about this past summer. That's why I miss you so much." He stopped abruptly. Then went on, "I'm sorry, I shouldn't be saying these things to you."

Renee abruptly stood up and walked in front of the huge window. She spoke without facing him. "I can't go through that again Deek. This summer with you was like an escape for me but I'm not the kind of woman who can have an affair and still feel good about myself. Besides you seem to be doing all right without me. You've apparently met someone. I saw that pretty young woman in red that you're with tonight. I'm much too old for you anyway and ..."

"Wait a minute." Deek stood up and turned to face her. "First of all, Special Agent Santos is my new partner on the SOS task force. She's here for the same reason I am, to support the Boys and Girls Club and to case out the target of our investigation. We received a tip that he might be here tonight."

"A gang leader dealing in drugs and ordering murders—here at this fundraiser?" Renee was incredulous.

"Yeah, this guy's real slick. He leads a double life. I suspect not even his own wealthy, upper-crust parents know what he's involved in. He poses as a legitimate businessman but looks for deals and buys up property in other people's names so he can launder his ill-gained drug money. We estimate he's pulling in several million a year. He's cagey, the type of guy who'll one minute help an old lady across the street or carry her groceries, then the next minute shoot someone in cold blood because they missed a payment."

"And as for you being too old for me, ..." he stopped as if gathering his thoughts, "Look Doc, your age does not compute with me. That's your hang-up, not mine. When I see you and talk to you, I see a young, beautiful, vibrant woman with so much untapped passion that if it ever fully erupted ... Well, you get what I'm saying, don't you?"

"I do want to be appreciated, Deek," she said, "but you're so young and handsome. I'm afraid that if we did get together, one day you wouldn't want me anymore and ..."

"Well, you're wrong, Doc. Dead wrong. Whenever you're ready for me to show you, I'll spend a lifetime proving it to you." He instinctively grasped her hand, but her look of discomfort caused him to release it.

"I think we'd better go back now," she whispered and retrieved her evening bag from the chair. "I suppose Bill will be wondering what happened to me."

"Okay but come with me to my table first. I'd like to introduce you to Agent Santos and a few of my friends, including my brother's girlfriend, Sasha. She's a lovely girl from Peru. Sasha rode here with Agent Santos and me since my brother Luke's away in Atlanta on a training assignment."

"Your brother?"

"Yep, Luke's my only sibling. Our grandmother had the final say in his given name as well. If you think Degas is bad, Grann Katia named my big brother JeanLuc but he calls himself Luke for obvious reasons."

"So he's the oldest?"

"Only by a few years. He's a lieutenant for the D. C. Fire Department. He's attending an intensive seven-month training program in Georgia in fire investigation and defusing bombs. He's still got another three months left to go in the program. When he gets back to Washington, he and Sasha are to be married and I'm to be the Best Man. I really miss him."

"Your brother sounds like a great guy, Deek."

"Luke's amazing. I've always looked up to him. If everything goes as planned, early next year he and I will be working together with the FBI and other law enforcement agencies on an anti-terrorism task force. Luke will have the bomb skills and I have investigative experience. This SOS task force mission I'm working on now is like a trial run for me."

"Well, I hope you get your man, Detective."

"I always do, Doc. It's my women I seem to be having trouble with." Deek smiled lightheartedly and Renee returned his playful glance.

Deek and Renee continued talking about nothing in particular as they walked through the green room on their way back to the dining area. Upon passing a French silk screen that concealed an obscure hideaway, they heard the unmistakable sounds of moaning. Deek pressed a finger to his lips to signal silence. They stepped behind the screen and flashed a brief, mortified look at each other. Propriety dictated that they exit the room quietly but they were mesmerized and could not move.

Amidst the muted shades of olive green walls trimmed in gold leaf, on a tufted back sofa, a man and woman groped each other feverishly. Plush, velvet pillows lay strewn on the floor, along with a black lace slip dress. A late Victorian wall fixture emitted a thin beam of light to the otherwise pitch-black room. It spotlighted the couple like a camera recording a soft-porn movie.

The young woman, clad only in her black, satin, corset bustier, satin thongs, garter-belt and ultra-sheer black stockings, lay underneath the man. One stiletto-heeled foot was draped across the plunging back of the velvet-covered sofa. His still fully dressed body straddled hers. From the look on her face and the continuous moans of pleasure, she appeared to wallow in a state of ecstasy. His fingers explored her breasts and his tongue reached for deep-throated kisses.

She began to slowly unbutton his silk shirt. He slipped his arms out of the tuxedo jacket. It landed on the floor, crumpled up next to her evening gown. With eyes closed and mouth parted in bliss, his hands brushed up and down her thigh. He lowered his head to kiss the inside of her smooth, tan-tinted thighs. After bringing her to another heightened level of pleasure, he raised himself up to meet her eyes and smiled.

"You've made this easy for me, baby," he said and reached down to unfasten his trousers, "No panty hose to struggle with."

"I hate 'em too, baby," she agreed, "Just like chastity belts. Impossible to get in and out of."

"My kinda woman," the man whispered and kissed her neck.

It was Deek who interrupted them. "Hey, man. You and the lady need to take this home. This is not the time or the place." The couple stopped kissing and looked up. At that moment Renee recognized them. She knew the young lady well and had just met the man earlier that day. The woman was her stylist at Good Looks Beauty Salon, Cha-Cha or Charis Taylor as her new boyfriend preferred. She also recognized the man as the same one who had come into the shop earlier that afternoon for a haircut—James Ian Mathias. Who could forget that name with Cha-Cha reverently repeating it all afternoon?

Ian leaped from the sofa and adjusted his trousers. Cha-Cha frantically slipped back into her gown and smoothed down her hair while Ian stood before them fully composed in his Giorgio Armani one-button tuxedo. Deek and Ian glared at each other. Cha-Cha's once perfectly made up face turned crimson red from embarrassment. Her glossy red lipstick and smoky-lidded eyes were smudged. She whipped out a mirror from her tiny bag and repaired the damage with a spit-wet finger.

"Mathias, I'm not surprised that you'd put the young lady in this compromising situation just to satisfy your own selfish desires," said Deek.

"Why am I not surprised to find you here, sniffing around?" said Ian Mathias, "You need to be out solving real crimes, Detective, instead of spying on innocent people just out for a little fun."

"Innocent, huh? We both know despite that clean-cut, baby face of yours, Mathias, you're nothing but a criminal in a three-piece suit."

"Why don't you get a life Detective? You're just envious because I've got it all and you ain't got jack. You and your clumsy Fed buddies need to back the fuck off. You ain't got shit on me."

"If nothing else, you can both catch a charge for indecent exposure," Deek threatened calmly.

"Criminal? Not me, Detective. I'm a businessman. A real estate investor to be exact."

Mathias reached in his jacket and Deek instinctively positioned his hand on the gun tucked under his waistband.

"Chill Brother. It's just a couple of C-notes," said Mathias, holding out a handful of one hundred-dollar bills, "Why don't you go buy your lady something nice on me."

Deek pushed away Mathias's outstretched hand, "You disgust me. If it's the last thing I do I'm gonna be sitting in that courtroom when the DA puts you away for life. I should write you up for trying to bribe an officer even if it means I'll be at the precinct all night filling out paperwork."

Renee pulled his arm and shook her head, "No, Deek. Let's go. Please."

"Consider yourself lucky that I don't feel like doing the paperwork on you Mathias. Get the hell outta here."

"C'mon baby, let's roll," Ian said to Cha-Cha, holding his shoulders back and signaling for her to follow. Mathias, then offered his arm to Cha-Cha and as they walked away he turned around to face Deek.

"Maybe I can't grease your palms with my loot Detective but everybody has their weak spot. Even a straight up cop like you. Give me some time and I'll figure out what your angle is."

He gave Renee a sly grin and stared at her for a few menacing seconds then left. She placed her hand on Deek's chest to hold him back and could feel his anger swell from his heartbeat. Deek hugged her waist protectively as he walked alongside her. Watching Cha-Cha and Ian in the throngs of passionate lovemaking reminded Renee how much she missed being with Deek. She couldn't repeat that torrid summer romance with him under the same terms—married to Bill and sneaking around laden with guilt afterwards. She had hoped that her birthday would end in a romantic evening with Bill but she knew that was out of the question now. She would spend her birthday night at home like every other night, frustrated and lonely.

When Deek and Renee returned to his table, they walked up on animated voices and laughter. Deek introduced her to Special Agent Ana Santos and Luke's fiancée, Sasha Rojas. Both young women were striking in their own way. Agent Santos had the lean and buff physique of someone who worked out in the gym regularly. Her outfit was definitely not FBI issued, Renee noted. Agent Santos wore iridescent topaz earrings and matching necklace that set off her red form-fitting dress with spaghetti straps. Her warm brown hair fell in casual waves around her shoulders. She had pulled out her chair and sat casually with her crossed legs in ankle-strapped heels and ultra sheer stockings. A gold mesh shawl had been draped across the back of her chair. After having met Agent Santos, Renee's comfort level about Deek's new partner on the special task force, quickly plummeted. "Pleased to meet you, Dr. Hayes," said Agent Santos with a slight Spanish accent and a sincere smile. Agent Santos reached out her honey-colored hand for Renee to shake.

Renee's eyes then drifted to the other Latin beauty, Sasha Rojas who was equally lovely, but in a more innocent and girlish way. Sasha wore a pink satin gown that showed off her tiny waist. She had a heart-shaped face with a small button nose and large expression brown eyes. Her thin pink-tinted lips formed a pleasant smile as she greeted Renee. Sasha was going to be a beautiful bride, thought Renee. Both of Deek's companions for the evening made her feel welcome, along with everyone else at his table whose names she did not remember as soon as they had been introduced. Renee sat down sandwiched between Deek and Sasha while Agent Santos sat next to Deek. Renee enjoyed the jokes and upbeat camaraderie at Deek's table. On a few occasions she felt uneasy when Agent Santos and Sasha leaned past her and spoke to each other in Spanish. While Deek did not actively join in their conversation, he clearly understood the language. This made her feel isolated. He must have been able to sense her discomfort because when he said something to them in rapid Spanish, both women nodded and resumed speaking only in English. Other than this one unpleasant episode Renee enjoyed being around these friendly fun-loving people. That is, until she looked across the room and spotted Bill coming in their direction. He hadn't seen her yet and she didn't want him to find her with Deek.

"If you folks will excuse me," said Renee suddenly getting up to leave, "It's been a pleasure meeting all of you but I must get back to my own table."

Deek rose as well and kissed her on the cheek as she stood up to leave. At first, she headed in the direction of her table then detoured towards the ladies room. As she ascended the long, winding staircase, she felt someone's close presence. She thought it might be Bill sneaking up behind her. At the top of the stairs she turned to look and collided into Clifton Corbin Shaw. She caught him stretching his neck to admire her rear end, then he shook his head.

"Damn, baby. All that backyard and ain't nobody playing in it," he said as if talking to himself, "My boy Bill must be a damn fool to ignore a woman as fine as you."

Renee bristled at his comment and cut a stern look his way. When she tried to pass by he touched her arm and gently pulled her back.

"If you let me, I know how to treat a woman right. I can tell you're not having much fun tonight, are you Sweetie?"

"It's Dr. Hayes," she said coldly.

His actions and words just confirmed her suspicions that he was a sleazy creep. Here he was trying to hit on her, his new business partner's wife. Shaw stood too close and for an uncomfortably long time. Renee winced at the strong scent of his heavy-handed cologne and alcohol-laden breath.

"By the way, *Dr. Hayes*, have you seen LaToya?" he asked, "She left with you to go to the little girls room over an hour ago."

"It's not my turn to watch her. Though she does look like she could use a babysitter."

"Touché, Dr. Hayes. You might not believe it but I like older, intelligent women like yourself. LaToya can get on my damn nerves after awhile. Are you by any chance free for lunch tomorrow or dinner if you prefer?"

Renee wiggled past him without touching his body and without dignifying that stupid question with an answer. She thought her open disdain would be enough for him to get the message, but obviously not because he blocked her pathway once more. It was not in Renee's nature to say what she really wanted to tell him, but the words played out silently in her head as he stood leering at her. '*I don't like you Shaw and I didn't like you the moment I first saw you at the Capital Tennis Challenge. If it's the last thing I do, I will get my husband to come to his senses. Then you'll have to find yourself another flunky to use.*' Instead, she simply said, "Excuse me." Then, she took a detour in another direction.

Renee could feel him staring at her backside as she disappeared down the hall. Why was it that every man in this place was coming on to her tonight except her own husband? Was she wearing a sign with the words, 'Desperate and Lonely' on the back of her jacket? When Renee walked through the door of the ladies room, she spotted Cha-Cha in front of the mirror with a damp hand cloth pressed to her face. When Cha-Cha removed the cloth she noticed Renee's reflection in the mirror.

"I'm sorry about what happened in the VIP room back there, Dr. Renee. How long were you and that good-looking detective watching us?"

"Too long, I'm afraid."

"Just for the record. That's the first time something like that ever happened to me. I guess Ian and I got carried away."

"I'm in no position to judge you, Cha-Cha. You're a grown woman of legal age. Just be careful."

"Yeah, I know but … I bet you'd never be caught doing something like that in a fancy place like this."

"Who knows, Cha-Cha. Maybe I should," Renee sighed and studied herself in the mirror as if the years were ticking by too rapidly. "It looked like you two were having a good time before Detective Hamilton and I interrupted. Perhaps, I'm the one who should be apologizing to you."

"No, Dr. Renee. Ian and I can always finish up where we left off later tonight at my place or his."

"Well, I envy you then. Today is my 45th birthday and it hasn't turned out at all the way I expected."

"Something tells me that handsome Detective is not your husband."

"No, my husband's been schmoozing all evening with his new business partner, a real sleaze. Judging by the way Bill's been acting this evening, I don't even think he remembered it was my birthday today."

"I'm sorry, Dr. Renee. That must feel awful. Well, I sure as hell know what I'd do. I'd leave right now with Mr. GQ and not tell what's his face a damn thing. I'd let him wonder where the hell I was all night long. And if he didn't bring me one of those little blue, velvet boxes and a dozen roses to apologize, I'd kick his sorry ass right out."

"That's just it, Cha-Cha," said Renee, "I'm not you. You have the nerve to pull that off and get away with it."

"Look girl, I know we're not girlfriends but I'm gonna give it to you straight. Honey, you'd better get some nerve and go take what you want in this short life. Before you know it, you'll look up and another year will have flown by and you'll still be stuck in the same place. Me, I'm gonna live 'til I die."

"Be careful, Cha-Cha. Make sure you find out more about your new boyfriend before you get in too deep. I'm worried about you, Dear."

"Don't worry about me, Dr. Renee. I can take care of myself. Ciao," she said and gave Renee an air kiss before walking out of the ladies lounge.

'Live until you die.' Cha-Cha's advice made good sense. Perhaps her stylist should be the one getting paid to listen to other people's problems. Renee went back downstairs to find Bill. She couldn't take it anymore. Her head hurt and she wanted to go home. Renee didn't even bother to sit down at the table but leaned over Bill's shoulder and whispered to him that she was ready to go. His brows furrowed together when he squinted up at her, eyes now red from too many drinks.

"Damnit, Renee. We're still talking business. Cliff'll be back in a minute. He went looking for LaToya. Jesus Christ, I don't even know why I brought you. Can't you entertain yourself for another hour or so?"

Yes, she could find some way to entertain herself while he discussed business, as she thought of Cha-Cha and Ian in the VIP room upstairs. But, instead of telling him what was on her mind the way Cha-Cha would have, tears welled in her eyes and burned her cheeks. She tasted their saltiness at the corners of her mouth. Her entire body felt hot from rage. She sensed everyone's eyes on her. The only thing she trusted herself to say was that she was leaving and would see him at home later.

Renee almost ran up the stairs. She anxiously waited for the elevator to take her up to the main lobby. Once in the lobby she retreated to a corner, dried her eyes and retrieved the cell phone from her purse. She pressed the programmed code to Remy's Sedan Service and hoped her driver could run her home on such short notice. Otherwise, she'd ask the front desk to call her a taxi. Remy picked up on the first ring and from the background traffic noise she could tell he was on the road. Luckily, he was between pickups and said he could be there anywhere from 5 to 10 minutes. She asked the concierge to let her know when her driver arrived. Then she sank down in a carved wooden chair to wait. Lost in her thoughts, she didn't see Deek walk up.

"Are you okay, Renee?" he asked and sat down in a chair beside her.

"I noticed you looked upset so I followed you. Was it stumbling in on the premiere of 'Deep Throat I' that bothered you?" He looked genuinely concerned. "I'm sorry, I should have insisted on leaving right away instead of getting into it with Mathias back there."

She looked away so he wouldn't see fresh tears forming. "No, that's not it, Deek."

"What is it then? What can I do to help?"

"Shouldn't you be getting back to your friends?" she said, avoiding eye contact, "Don't bother about me." Before he could respond, Bill appeared.

Deek stood up to face him.

"What the hell are you doing here Detective?" asked Bill.

"Same as you, I assume. Supporting the Boys and Girls Club."

The muscles in Bill's face tensed as he spoke, "I warned you over the summer to stay away from my wife."

"Look man, Renee and I are just friends. Anyway, she seemed upset so I wanted to find out if she was alright."

Bill lowered his voice to a whisper as he glared directly into Deek's eyes. "Understand this, Hamilton. Any fool trying to take what's mine will find his punk-ass stretched out on a slab with somebody trying to match his dental records. I got connections. You just might not recover from your next bullet wound."

"You're the fool. Who would be stupid enough to threaten a police officer and one whose been assigned to an FBI task force at that. You're not the only one with connections, Buddy."

"Let me clue you in on a few things, Detective. Renee and I may be having our problems but she's still my wife."

While the two men argued back and forth, neither noticed that the concierge had summoned Renee to tell her that her driver had arrived. When they stopped bickering long enough to look for her, the black Lincoln town car was pulling away.

"Where is she?" asked Bill.

"You just missed her," said Deek, pointing outside, "She had her driver take her home and if I were you, I'd go after her."

"Well, you're not me. And don't worry about my marriage. Renee's just moody this evening for some reason. Not that it's any of your fucking business, but our marriage is stronger than ever."

"Whatever you say, man." Deek turned and walked away.

CHAPTER 10

Renee woke from a fitful sleep when she heard the garage door downstairs slam shut. It took a few groggy moments for her to recognize the guestroom's periwinkle blue walls and antique white sleigh bed. Suddenly, she replayed what had happened at the ball that night and remembered why she didn't want to wake up next to Bill. Bill had been emotionally distant for weeks. Now she understood why. He had been too busy plotting and scheming with his new partner, Clifton Shaw, to remember her birthday. Despite her disappointment with how things had turned out on an evening that she had mistakenly thought was intended to celebrate her birthday, Renee fought against the urge to phone Deek for comfort. She couldn't deny how good it felt running into him at the fundraiser dinner. Still, it wouldn't solve anything to get entangled again in a romantic relationship outside her marriage with a much younger man. Been there, done that, she thought and all it produced was guilt-ridden, sleepless nights.

She heard Bill's heavy footsteps lumber up the stairs. She tossed the covers aside and ran out to confront him just as he reached the top of the landing.

"It's two thirty in the morning. Where've you been all night?" she said in a voice that made her wince. She sounded too much like those whining wives in therapy that she dreaded listening to every week.

"I have a headache and I'm tired. Can we talk about this tomorrow?" He reached for the door handle for the master bedroom.

"It is tomorrow, and yesterday was my birthday!"

"Oh, shit," Bill dropped his head in his hands. "Baby, I'm so sorry. You know how hectic things have been lately trying to get this company off the ground. Shaw leans on my cell phone 24-7. Please forgive me. Let me make it up to you, Sweetie."

Bill reached for her but she backed away. "Don't bother. I can't believe you actually forgot my birthday and we just talked about it the other day."

"I know but …"

"What's the matter, forget to take your Ginseng? Or is there someone else on your mind these days?" she eyed him suspiciously.

"Hell no. I don't even remember my own goddamn birthday. That's just how little birthdays matter to me."

"Well, they matter to me. The years are flying by and I'm not getting what I need out of this marriage, emotionally or physically."

"Neither am I, quiet as it's kept. But you don't hear me complaining," Bill answered. Then he paused before continuing. "Guess I may as well tell you now since you're up," he said. "I'm leaving for Bangalore, India later this afternoon for about a week. I've got to bring back our new recruits and make sure they get settled. Their first training class starts Monday after next. Shaw wants to get things rolling now that our investor has laid down so much cash."

"What? You're not serious?"

"Listen, Renee, I'm finally well on my way to becoming one of the black elite business owners in this town. This is probably my last chance to make it big. I'm damn near 52 years old. My PC customization company turned out to be nothing but a sinkhole and a huge headache. Another opportunity like this might not come around for me again at my age. You'll see. Before long I'll be calling the shots."

She rolled her eyes towards the ceiling. "If you say so."

"Look, I gotta get some sleep, babe. The limo driver's picking me up at 4:00 PM," Bill checked his watch. "I've got to be at Dulles two hours before my 6:40 flight."

"There's a million things I need to do before I leave: get my currency exchanged, check on the guys' work visas, touch base with Cliff, stuff like that," he said, "I'll only be gone six days, Sweetness. Just an in and out trip. I'll make all this up to you when I get back next Thursday, promise."

Renee threw up her hands. "I must be the stupidest woman alive to put up with your bullshit. I talk to women in denial every day. I show them why they should leave an intolerable, hopeless situation but they just keep coming back for more. Then I have to hear about it again and again and again. Guess I'm no better off than my patients since I, too, seem to be exhibiting the same type of cognitive dissonance."

"Look Renee, I'm really beat. Can we not have a therapy session tonight? It's almost time for me to get up and I haven't even slept yet."

"Whose fault is that?" Renee stormed off without waiting for his response. She returned to the guestroom where she promptly locked the door. She wished there was some way to retrieve her silk underwear and the letter she mailed yesterday inviting him to a romantic dinner tomorrow night. As it turns out, he wouldn't even be home. She crawled back into bed then tossed and turned for several more hours before drifting in and out of sleep. Renee wondered if it was really worth the effort to try to repair her marriage. How would she ever convince Bill to adopt a baby as long as neither of them felt satisfied in their marriage? And was it fair to bring a child into their unhappy home? She felt her time running out. If she didn't become a mother soon, it would be too late.

At 7 o'clock Friday morning, the skies threatened rain but Renee decided she needed a morning jog to help relieve the tension from her argument with Bill last night. She changed into a jogging suit and zipped a small bottle of Evian water inside a fanny pack belted across her hips. Fortunately, Bill had already left the house to run errands and prepare for his trip, so she managed to avoid seeing him. Renee stepped out into a hazy, blue-gray morning. The air felt cool as she jogged along the winding, neighborhood roads. Roads flanked by tall trees, their branches wrapped in misty clouds. Renee quickened her pace and after about twenty minutes of running, she had worked up a sweat. Suddenly, a car appeared out of nowhere. A mass of black metal raced by at a speed well over the residential ten miles per hour. Her balance wobbled and she fell hard to the gritty pavement. *Damn you, moron!* The car had come dangerously close to hitting her but whizzed by too fast for her to get a tag number. She brushed off her knees and started to limp back home.

She labored up the long winding driveway's sharp incline that led to her house. Dense thicket and a grove of evergreen trees populated the grounds and bordered the driveway. The excessive foliage was designed not only for its landscaping beauty but also to hide the front and rear entranceways. It gave the Hayes couple a false sense of privacy from voyeurs who drove through their neighborhood just to gaze and drool over the sprawling estates of others.

Upon approaching the narrow, red brick path leading to the rear entrance of her office, Renee suddenly stopped and listened. She thought she heard rustling coming from a tangled patch of bushes near the doorway. She scanned the entire area for any sound or movement. There was nothing but stillness. Must have been falling leaves or a squirrel, she thought and continued up the path. Just before sticking the key in the door and unlocking it, she turned to look behind her. Renee blinked a few times to focus—not sure if her mind had conjured up this vision or if the figure standing behind the bushes was real. A mosaic of thick, multi-colored leaves shielded what appeared to be a motionless shadow.

Renee quickly unlocked her door and opened it just enough to squeeze inside; then slammed the door shut, locked, and bolted it. She leaned against the door for a second, and took a deep breath. After gaining her composure, she ran to the front foyer and turned the security alarm on. Usually she was diligent about activating it. But this morning she had forgotten to turn it on when she left for her run. Renee recalled her terror this past summer upon finding a burglar in their home before the security system had been installed. She'd been lucky once only because the person wasn't interested in harming her. She might not be so lucky the next time. Whether the vision outside was real or imagined, it was a wakeup call for her to be more careful.

Renee glanced at her watch. In an hour her secretary, Brenda would be arriving to setup for the day's appointments. She gulped down several sips of Evian water and grabbed a ripe pear from the kitchen table's arrangement of apples, pears, oranges, bananas, and grapes. That was just about all the breakfast she could tolerate after last night's ordeal at the fundraiser ball. The only good thing about it was running into Deek. She noticed that her stomach had been feeling queasy over the past several days. She attributed her waning appetite to depression and stress. Renee dragged herself upstairs to shower and get ready to face another morning of listening to her client's problems and complaints. Could she be facing career burnout? Lately, she dreaded listening to the same stories over and over and in some cases zoned out during a therapy session. Or was it simply that her own personal problems were becoming too great to allow her to focus on someone else's troubles?

CHAPTER 11

D r. Renee Hayes descended the stairs to her basement office, wearing her typical workday uniform—comfortable black slacks and cardigan with a white shell. The soothing melody of Mozart's piano concerto in A major and the aroma of fresh-brewed coffee greeted her at the door. Her secretary, Brenda Johnson had made a good choice of music selections this morning. She heard the steady clicking of fingertips on computer keyboard coming from the waiting room area. Renee popped her head into the reception area to see Brenda who in turn gave her boss a friendly good morning and a happy birthday greeting.

Brenda had arrived early enough to perk Renee's favorite Gevalia® coffee and fill up the pewter pot and tea set. Next to the coffeepot sat a vase overflowing with white phlox and lavender. Renee's Japanese housekeeper, Chizuko Tanaka, had come yesterday. Every Thursday she arranged fresh-cut flowers and their bouquet always smelled aromatic. Renee retrieved a porcelain teacup and saucer from the credenza. She chose the strong coffee over tea to combat morning drowsiness from yet another sleep interrupted night. She took a huge swallow and the hot liquid burned her throat, but the jolt revived her.

Sunlight from the window bathed the buff-colored walls of her office with a warm, golden luster. A carved wooden shelf, full of books and statuettes, stood over the credenza. The credenza had been her Aunt Clara's family heirloom years ago before she passed away. Degrees and professional certifications were positioned above her chair for patients to easily view. Two floral, chintz wing back chairs surrounded a cream-colored sofa that blended with the copper and beige needlepoint rug underneath it. Renee's office was decorated as a safe refuge for both herself and her patients who came to share their stories and reveal their pain.

Since it was ten minutes to nine, she figured Brenda must have been working diligently for twenty minutes. Renee felt lucky to have Brenda as her secretary. At first she wasn't sure things would work out. Even though she came highly recommended by Cha-Cha, Brenda didn't have office experience, plus she had gotten pregnant just two months into the position. Brenda had begged Renee not to replace her because she needed the job and intended to return to work six weeks after her baby was born. Brenda worked right up to her delivery date and proved to be a fast learner just as Cha-Cha had promised. Despite Cha-Cha and Brenda's on-again, off-again friendship through the years, Cha-Cha said Brenda was honest and reliable. Renee took a chance and hired her. Instead of paying for six weeks maternity leave as was the employer standard, Renee paid for twelve weeks. She understood the importance of early bonding between mother and newborn. Nothing, especially a job, should interfere with that maternal connection.

Now Brenda showed her appreciation by being dependable and arriving before office visits to make sure Renee had time to relax and review patient records. She had also taken on the time-consuming task of inputting all the manual files into the computer and coding them for easy retrieval. Renee found out about a program that would handle the management of patient records. Brenda followed the tutorial, read the user's guide, and was now a pro at using the software. Even with a new baby and all the demands of running a home, Renee was impressed to learn that Brenda had recently enrolled in a weekend computer course at a nearby community college that offered adult continuing education classes. She told Renee she wanted to get more technical training and improve her job skills.

Renee glanced at the stack of files on her desk that she needed to review before the first patient arrived at 9:30. It could wait a few more minutes she decided. There was also a large pink envelope on top of the patient files. From the flowery handwriting Renee guessed it was a birthday card from Brenda. Since she was out yesterday, she probably had left the card on Renee's desk this morning. While the music lifted her spirits and the coffee stimulated her, Renee gazed out the window at the multi-colored, October leaves. A deer posed among the trees for a split second before vaulting from sight. Renee thought about how deer roamed through the suburban neighborhoods in Maryland and Virginia, as well as throughout the outlying residential areas of Washington, D. C. Rapid housing development had bulldozed nearly every inch of their habitat so there was nowhere else for them to go.

Renee then settled down in the leather burgundy chair behind her desk and flipped through the stack of files to see what lay ahead for next week: major depressive disorders, identity confusions, attempted suicides, bereavement, histrionic personality disorders, and marital counseling, as well as a prospective new patient for today. Those sessions covered only some of her full patient caseload. She felt her life had become too complicated. Just then Brenda's voice came through on the intercom.

"Excuse me, Dr. Renee. Your first patient and her parents are outside in the waiting area. They arrived a little early so I got them started on the new patient forms."

"Please ask them to wait until I've read their daughter's file." Dr. Renee drank a few more sips of coffee and reviewed her notes. The case involved a family in crisis that needed immediate intervention. The situation was discovered when the student's ninth-grade teacher reported her suspicions to a school guidance counselor. The Office of School Administration for Montgomery County high schools then referred the student and her family to Renee. The student's guidance counselor had met with Dr. Renee last week and gave her a detailed report on the case.

As a therapist, Dr. Renee had seen this scenario played out many times before. A family in turmoil because of an unwanted teenage pregnancy. Many middle-class to well-off parents gave their children material possessions but were too busy with their own lives to monitor the teenagers in their home. In this case, the mother, Mrs. Hope Hollingsworth worked full-time as a Marketing vice-president for a telecommunications company and Mr. Hollingsworth, the father, was a senior accountant at a large investment firm. The parents recently learned from the guidance counselor that their 15 year-old daughter, Heather, was already four months pregnant. Renee studied the case notes but as she read her mind began to wander back to the summer of 1972 when she herself became pregnant at 16.

Nothing before had ever triggered the long-forgotten memories of that summer and released her pent-up emotions. The psychoanalytical word for her memory lapses was disassociation and apparently that is what she had done. Her aunt's harsh words, the empty feelings had all been blocked out, but there was something about the words used in the report, the description of the domineering mother, the feeling of lost control and manipulation that brought this particular family's problems too close to home for Renee.

When her Aunt Clara had found out that sixteen-year old Renee was pregnant, she'd immediately taken charge of the situation. Everything happened so quickly. The very next day after Renee's admission of guilt, she was on a train headed to a remote cottage tucked away in the countryside of York, Pennsylvania. Renee didn't realize what the doctor intended to do to her. Hours later when she woke up from the anesthesia, Aunt Clara said the 'problem' had been resolved. Aunt Clara warned her never to speak of the incident again. Renee's fear, confusion, and guilt had sealed the memory far back into the deep recesses of her mind. When she read the report on her new patient, 15 year-old Heather Hollingsworth, that day in June 1972 slowly began to resurface despite her efforts to stop the memories from flooding her thoughts.

Dr. Renee closed her eyes and massaged her temple. She couldn't fight off her mental screen's projection of the broad-shouldered, ample figure of her long deceased Aunt Clara. Aunt Clara stood rigidly, clothed in the same outfit she always wore, even in the summer—black, cotton shirtwaist dress with a high-neck, rounded white collar. Far safer to stare at the foreboding figure's garment than the turned down corners of her mouth, the sagging jawline, and dark, vacant eyes sunk into a hardened, brown face that glared down at her. Dr. Renee snapped open her eyes and Aunt Clara's form suddenly vanished. She took several deep breathes to calm down and tried to prepare herself emotionally for the Hollingsworth's first visit as best she could.

At precisely 9:30, she pressed the intercom for Brenda to allow the Hollingsworth family to enter her office. Dr. Renee greeted the solemn-faced trio and invited them to sit down. Mr. and Mrs. John and Hope Hollingsworth, both dressed in expensive-looking clothing, sat on the double chintz wingbacks in front of her desk. Their daughter, Heather slouched her heavy frame on the sofa at the far end, as far away from everyone as she could get. The round, innocent, apple-cheeked face looked younger than its 15 years. Lank, mouse-colored brown hair hung about her face and almost reached the small of her back. The mane of flowing hair shaded her ivory-complexioned face. Dr. Renee noticed that she hid behind a shield of hair.

The lost and frightened young girl appeared exactly as the counselor had depicted her. Heather was a big girl who according to her school counselor usually wore baggy, oversized clothes. Her parents apparently had not noticed she was pregnant. She had been missing school and sleeping in class. The guidance counselor discovered that Heather was already 16 weeks pregnant when she finally got the girl to open up to her. The counselor tried to reach the parents for several weeks until finally the mother's secretary returned the counselor's calls, and then the counselor had been able to set up this appointment with Dr. Renee. Mrs. Hollingsworth sat stone-faced with her legs crossed and hands folded rigidly in her lap. She did all the talking, spilling out a frenzied, thirty-minute commentary on what needed to be done immediately to correct this deplorable situation.

To make matters worse, Renee found out that Heather was pregnant by her first cousin. For the past several months, Mrs. Hollingsworth's 17 year-old nephew had been staying with them in their Potomac, Maryland home while he completed his senior year at Heather's high school. According to Mrs. Hollingsworth, her nephew had always been a problem kid whose parents were worthless drifters, so she eventually got stuck with taking him in because no other relative wanted to be bothered with him anymore. Both her nephew and daughter were minors and blood relatives. This presented a major complication for the family, in addition to the teenage pregnancy. When Mrs. Hollingsworth found out about her daughter's pregnancy and who was responsible, she immediately kicked her nephew out of her house. She told Renee that at this point she really didn't care what became of her nephew.

Mrs. Hollingsworth insisted that a decision had to be made soon about the 'problem' before Heather reached her sixth month when it would be too late to end the pregnancy. None of the clinics she contacted in the Washington, D. C. Metropolitan area would perform late term abortions after 24 weeks, the third trimester.

"Dr. Hayes, I need your help in convincing this stubborn child to see reason. She's only 15 for godsakes! If she doesn't agree to go through with the procedure soon, we'll end up spending more time and money flying out to another state where they can do late-term abortions."

"Money can't fix everything, Hope," said Mr. Hollingsworth in an exasperated tone.

"Maybe not but it can sure fix this mess," snapped Mrs. Hollingsworth.

After that one outburst, her husband stumbled back into his seemingly well-rehearsed silence while his wife continued to dominate the session. If she couldn't get her daughter to agree to have the abortion in time, they would have to go out of state to a place that approved them. Mrs. Hollingsworth said she felt this would be even more traumatic for Heather. She feared it might be too late if they didn't act within the next few weeks. More than once she emphasized that the problem needed to be solved immediately.

"What do *you* want to do Heather?" asked Renee gently when she could finally squeeze a full sentence into the conversation. After a brief silence the girl replied.

"Don't know," she mumbled while shrugging her shoulders.

Heather had been quiet throughout the session. She had kept her chin pressed to her chest and her blue eyes cast downward. Renee proposed to the parents that if they agreed to subsequent private sessions after this initial meeting, Renee could focus on Heather in order to find out what the child's true feelings were and what she wanted to do. Then based on what Heather wanted she would try to get her to think about how it would all work if she decided to give birth. For instance, if she wanted to have her baby and keep it, how did she see herself being able to care for a baby and what support avenues would she have? In preparation for their first session, Renee had researched several support organizations that Heather could turn to. She discovered that Adopt A Child helped young, teenage girls with babies to stay in school. The organization taught the young mothers sexual responsibility, counseling, and parenting skills. During their weekly sessions, Renee would plan to include the parents periodically to strengthen the family's communication. Then parents and daughter could decide what to do and what the consequences of their choice would be. This approach would take much longer than what she feared Mrs. Hollingsworth expected.

"What difference does it make what she wants?" said Mrs. Hollingsworth, "I'm her mother and I know what's best for her. Besides," she continued, "she and my nephew are cousins so marriage is not an option. I just can't see the sense in ruining two people's lives."

"What two people do you mean, Mrs. Hollingsworth?" asked Renee, wondering if she meant Heather's and her nephew's future.

"Why Heather's and mine, of course," said Mrs. Hollingsworth.

"There's just no other choice for her, Dr. Hayes. Adoption is out of the question because nobody wants to adopt a possibly retarded baby whose parents are first cousins!"

Mrs. Hollingsworth began to produce tearless sobs. Heather shifted in her seat and gave her mother a darting glare. While Mr. Hollingsworth patted his wife's hand and reached for a tissue out of the box that Renee held out to his wife. Mrs. Hollingsworth snatched the tissue from her husband's hand and began carefully dabbing at her eyes without smudging her eyeliner.

"I've been under a lot of pressure at work lately. I might lose my $20,000 year-end bonus because our department hasn't met its quotas. Having Heather pregnant at 15, by *her cousin* no less, is just too much for me to deal with right now."

Mrs. Hollingsworth startled everyone when she jumped up from the chair and confronted her daughter, pointing a finger in her daughter's face as she ranted, "Can't you see how you're ruining your life!"

At that moment, Renee's breathing became shallow as she struggled to catch her breath. She placed a hand to her heart and felt her heart beating rapidly. No one noticed her obvious discomfort because all eyes were focused on Mrs. Hollingsworth as she continued to chastise her daughter. Instead of hearing Mrs. Hollingsworth's high-pitched, annoying voice, Renee's mind played back the angry, authoritative voice of Aunt Clara who had spoken those very same words to Renee, "Can't you see how you're ruining your life!" This had never happened to Renee before. She had always been able to focus completely on her patients during a session. Suddenly, she found herself thrown back in time. Back twenty-nine years ago where vivid scenes from her own life at sixteen intruded on her consciousness. She felt as if she were going to pass out, and clutched the edges of her desk. She knew she had to hold it together. She could not allow herself to breakdown in front of her clients. These people expected her to tell *them* how to feel better. But how could she do that when her entire world was falling apart?

Instead of hearing Mrs. Hollingsworth, Renee heard Aunt Clara's voice. *"You'd better do as you're told Missy and keep your mouth shut. God'll punish you for your sinful ways sure as I breath. Mark my words. When I was growing up they had names for fast girls like you but I'm too much of a decent, church-going lady to say it out loud."*

Dr. Renee jerked her attention back to the present and picked up in the middle of Mrs. Hollingsworth's dialogue.

"There can't be a marriage or an adoption because they're first cousins!" she shrieked at her husband, "Why is this so difficult for everybody here to get? It's a no brainer, for chrissakes. Heather has to be convinced to end this pregnancy now before it's too late."

"That's not necessarily true, Dear," said Mr. Hollingsworth, "the baby would be adoptable as long as it's healthy because the biological relationship between cousins is not as close as bother and sister." Mrs. Hollingsworth glared at her husband and folded her arms.

Renee felt herself slipping out of control again as her mind drifted off and her breathing accelerated. She had been listening but not listening. She slowly rose from her chair, barely able to stand. The Hollingsworths' turned and gave her a startled look. It was Mr. Hollingsworth who showed the most concern as he rushed behind the desk to grab her arm. "Are you all right, Dr. Hayes? You don't look well. Should we reschedule?"

At that suggestion, Mrs. Hollingsworth bristled, "Reschedule? Are you mad, John? How much time do you think that girl has left? Just look at her belly for god's sake!" she said, pointing at Heather.

"I'm sorry," said Renee, massaging her forehead, "Please excuse me for a moment. I won't be long. Please help yourself to a cup of coffee or tea."

Renee gently released herself from Mr. Hollingsworth's support and gave him a smile. "Thank you, Mr. Hollingsworth. I'll be fine." Before Mrs. Hollingsworth could launch any further complaints, Renee disappeared through a door marked 'Private', which led to her own bathroom. The restrooms for patients were located just outside the reception area and Renee was glad that she had installed a private powder room of her own.

Once inside she locked the bathroom door. Then, Renee immediately sank to the white and black tiled floor, balled herself in a knot and buried her face in both hands as she sobbed. Through the years she had learned how to self-heal, ever since she lost her mother at age 6 in a tragic bus accident and fell under the guardianship of her bitter and controlling Aunt Clara. Renee wrapped her arms tightly around her torso as if feeling the comforting arms of a mother's embrace. She knew she could not allow herself to collapse now, but the haunting memories from her past when she was only 16 years old came flooding back.

Renee recalled that this particular day at Calvin Coolidge High School had started out like any other school day but it didn't end the same way it normally did for sixteen-year old Renee Janette Curtis and Randolph DeWitt. Typically, Randolph would walk her home from the bus stop and carry her books and wouldn't be allowed to see her again until the next day at school. They had been inseparable for the first nine months of their junior year at Coolidge High. This was the first time they had decided to skip classes. It was the last day of school before the summer break began and the last time they would be able to hang out together. Renee knew that Aunt Clara would keep tight reigns on her all summer. And, Randolph would be leaving next week to stay with his grandparents for two months in North Carolina. A summer swim in the lake, a picnic lunch, listening to Randolph's poetry, and holding each other's hand—that's all they had planned to do on the day they skipped school. Losing her virginity and becoming pregnant was not in her plan.

Renee willed herself to put these memories aside for now. She wiped her eyes with the back of her hand and sat still on the floor with her eyes closed. She listened to the sound of her controlled breathing. Between sets of deep inhalations of air and slow exhalations, she counted by two's until reaching the number ten. While focusing on her counting and breathing she pictured herself in a peaceful meadow, with a running stream, singing birds, and a warm breeze on her neck. Time seemed to stand still as a wave of relaxation and calmness washed over her. Once she felt back in control, she grabbed hold of the sides of the sink and lifted herself from the floor. Leaning over the porcelain bowl, she splashed cold water on her face several times until her cheeks tingled, and then she patted her face dry. Renee stared at her reflection in the bathroom mirror to make sure she would appear okay to the outside world. Only then did she reappear at the doorway of her office, slightly red-eyed and with flushed cheeks. She glanced at the clock on the wall, relieved that she had only been in the bathroom for five minutes though it seemed longer during her relaxation exercise.

"Are you all right, Doctor?" asked Mr. Hollingsworth, rising from his chair to come to her aid if necessary. He didn't notice his wife glaring at him, but Renee saw it.

"Yes, thank you," said Renee, returning to her desk and reaching for an appointment book, "But would you both mind if we ended our session a little early today? I can see everyone tomorrow at the same time."

Mrs. Hollingsworth shot Renee an angry look as she tapped the face of her wristwatch. "I paid for an hour's session, Dr. Hayes. We still have ten minutes. What do you plan to do for my daughter, Doctor?

I want to know before I leave here. I've already given up a morning's worth of work to be here."

Nothing surprised Renee anymore, not even this woman's callous reaction to her daughter's situation and how she managed to turn it around to be all about her.

Renee took a deep breathe and folded her hands on her desk before answering. "First of all you should know that I'm not here to tell any of you what to do, but only to try to get you all to talk to each other and decide the best thing for Heather," said Renee, feeling very much in control again. "She's still a child herself and like any child, she needs love, attention, and guidance, not constant criticism," said Renee, looking directly at Mrs. Hollingsworth.

"I'm sorry that I can't wrap things up neat and tidy for you today, Mrs. Hollingsworth. I feel I'll need another five or six sessions of private counseling with Heather to get to what she wants first before I can advise you about what decision you need to make as a family."

"That's almost two more months!" shouted Mrs. Hollingsworth, "What the hell are we supposed to do in the meantime? Heather will still be pregnant and the problem won't be resolved. I'm all about problem resolution. That's what I do for a living and that's what I'm good at. This is a bunch of bull crap."

Mr. Hollingsworth held his wife's arm to calm her down, "Please, Hope, Dear. Let the doctor speak."

"I don't give a damn what she has to say," said Mrs. Hollingsworth, "I'm the one in charge here, not Heather and not this ... outsider! Nobody seems to care how I feel."

"You may not want to hear it, but this really is Heather's decision, Mr. and Mrs. Hollingsworth," said Renee gently, "Legally, no one can be forced or pressured into having an abortion, not even a minor. She needs your help and guidance in making the right decision and understanding what the impact of that decision will be. But in the end, it is up to her to decide." Renee paused for her words to sink in. "I'd like to see Heather alone next Monday if I have your permission. Is that all right with you, Heather?" asked Renee, smiling.

The girl looked at Renee for the first time and nodded. She straightened up in her seat a little. Renee felt she had achieved some degree of trust from her new patient.

"And what about you, Parents? Do you agree to allow me to counsel your daughter?"

"Yes, Dr. Hayes," Mr. Hollingsworth spoke up, "Thank you for your concern."

Mrs. Hollingsworth let out a defeated sigh and rolled her eyes towards the ceiling.

"Heather, I want you to understand that your parents love you and only want what's best for you," said Renee, "I'm not excluding them and they will be with you during some of our meetings. Ultimately, you and your parents will decide what's best for you, not me. Though I will offer advice."

"Dr. Hayes, what can my wife and I do in the meantime to help?"

Renee asked Heather to wait outside in the reception area while she talked to her parents alone. After Heather left, Renee gave the Hollingsworths her candid analysis of the situation based on their initial meeting and studying the school's background report. She told the parents the two main problems she saw within the family were that there was no communication and Heather had exhibited signs of self-esteem issues. Their child needed attention and guidance. Heather's cousin had given her attention but for all the wrong reasons, to take advantage of her vulnerability and the parents had been oblivious. Now, Mrs. Hollingsworth wanted to erase the problem away and start with a clean slate as if nothing had ever happened, but that wasn't possible. Mrs. Hollingsworth looked indignant when she spoke up.

"What about all those outside activities I had her involved in? Tennis, swimming, soccer, you name it," wailed Mrs. Hollingsworth, "I paid our maid extra to make sure she got to practice and events. But

Heather never excelled in sports like I did when I was her age because all she does is eat junk food, lay around all day and watch TV. She's so much like her father. I tell her about this all the time but nobody can get through to that thick-headed, stubborn kid."

"Mrs. Hollingsworth these activities would be great if Heather enjoyed doing them. But they're just fillers. Things to keep her busy so you don't have to spend time with her yourself."

Mrs. Hollingsworth nearly jumped from her seat upon hearing Renee's interpretation of her motives. Instead, she clinched her jaw tightly and kept silent for a change. She didn't like hearing what Renee had to say, but finally Renee was able to get both parents to admit they'd been too busy with their own lives to supervise the two teenagers and spend quality time with them. Mr. Hollingsworth traveled frequently on business and Mrs. Hollingsworth was usually out and about, concerned with making more money and achieving more power and prestige in her career. Just like the pattern they had assumed with Heather, when her cousin came to stay with them, they focused on other priorities and left the boy to his own devices. Like Heather, he didn't make friends in the new high school. Heather didn't have friends either so the two of them clung to each other for attention and acceptance.

Renee told the parents that just from this initial visit she could tell their entire family existed in a disconnected household. She gave them suggestions on how to improve communication. Everything Renee explained was common knowledge to parenting experts and child psychologists. Basically, they needed to spend quality time with their child, not just the time spent taking her to and from events or activities. And the passive activity of watching TV together should not be considered quality time. Renee urged each of the parents to focus on their daughter. She described how they could create a ritual of family night. Even if all they could spare was 15-minutes, it would be time Heather would learn to expect. During their family time, no one should answer phones or pagers, logon to the computer, or think about other things they had to do. Also, it would be counterproductive to use family quality time to criticize Heather or tell her what she should or should not be doing. Criticism would just undermine their few minutes of quality time together. A good family night might consist of talking, playing board games, cooking together or anything that they all enjoyed doing as a family. Family quality time would have also helped her nephew feel like part of the family. After hearing Renee's observations, the parents sat mute with guilt-ridden faces.

"Please understand me, Mr. and Mrs. Hollingsworth, I'm not blaming you for what happened to Heather and your nephew," said Renee gently, "It's useless to sit around assigning blame. I just want you to be aware of how the pregnancy could have happened, and to help you adopt ways to prevent it from ever happening again."

"I know, Doctor," said Mr. Hollingsworth, looking down at his folded hands.

"During the next private session with your daughter, I hope to find out what Heather's needs are, and where her head is, so to speak," explained Renee, "Later, I want her to begin to understand the implications of any decision she may make. That's where I'd like you both to be involved in helping her break down the logic in her reasoning and choices."

"That's all fine doctor, but how are we going to solve the problem now?" asked Mrs. Hollingsworth, "That's what we're here for today, isn't it?"

"Basically, the choices come down to either she will have the baby or not. If she decides to have it, the next decision will be to keep it or not," said Renee, "These are important decisions that ultimately Heather and you, her parents must make."

"But why on earth would she want to keep it?" asked Mrs. Hollingsworth.

"I can't answer that. My primary objective is to get your family communicating as quickly as possible. I'd like to help you both as parents to build a bond with Heather so she no longer feels like she's alone whenever there's a crisis in her life. Then mother, father, and daughter can work things out together and decide what's best for Heather."

"So you don't intend to make her see reason during your private sessions with her?"

Renee sighed. "I don't think you're hearing me, Mrs. Hollingsworth. That's not my job. I'm not going to make the decision for Heather," said Renee. "I wouldn't want someone else to do that to me."

Finally, the session was over and the Hollingsworths left. Thank God they were gone. She asked Brenda to hold her calls for the next fifteen minutes and take a message if anyone called. She stumbled over to the coach and collapsed, then buried her head within folded arms. She tried to listen to the cheerful melody of Mozart's flute concerto in D major that played softly from piped in speakers, but it was no use. She leaned back and lay down on the couch with her eyes closed. The whirring noise of the ceiling fan above her head reminded her of the sound the equipment had made in the doctor's back room. When the disturbing images in her head started to reappear, her breathing became constricted once again and her heart beat accelerated. Renee recognized her symptoms as an anxiety attack and knew she was not actually having a heart attack though a non-medical person might think that, so she didn't want to worry Brenda who she knew would dial 911. Renee did not want to call 911 because the licensing board, at worst, could revoke her license to treat patients. At best she could be put on probation or get suspended. She knew just what she needed in order to stop these anxiety attacks and drive away the bad memories. She retrieved her cell phone from her jacket pocket and called her mentor and psychiatrist, Dr. Helen Stone. Dr. Stone picked up on the first ring.

"Helen, I need to talk to someone professionally. Do you have anyone that you can recommend?"

"Are you all right, Dear?" Helen asked.

"No. Actually, I'm not," said Renee, fighting back her tears.

"You can talk to me, Renee. We've known each other for years, professionally and personally. Are you feeling depressed or overwhelmed by something?"

"Not exactly. Well, I'm not really sure."

"This sounds serious. I have an opening this morning at 11:30. Does that sound good for you?"

"Yes. Thank You, Helen."

"Okay, then, Honey. Here's my new address. I've recently relocated to a new office downtown on K Street," said Helen and read off the address.

"I'll be there," said Renee, solemnly.

"All right, Dear, I'll see you at eleven thirty."

"Right. Good-bye Helen and thanks again for seeing me on such short notice."

Renee opened the door that led into the reception area and instructed Brenda to reschedule all of her afternoon appointments. She didn't know what time she would return to the office and probably would not feel like seeing clients. She told Brenda she could lock up and leave for the day once all the afternoon appointments had been rescheduled. Renee felt bad about being distracted throughout the Hollingsworths' visit that morning, but she was in no position to help anyone today. Typically, she focused entirely on the patient by raising her eyes to the speaker and not withdrawing her attention until he or she finished speaking. But after suddenly remembering what Aunt Clara did to her when she was sixteen, she couldn't concentrate. She grabbed her navy London Fog trench coat from the closet and went upstairs to exit out the front door of the main house, avoiding Brenda's questions and the look of worry on her secretary's face.

CHAPTER 12

As Renee drove towards downtown K Street, she saw that a late morning drizzle had left a smoky-colored mist over the sky that made it difficult to see clearly. Rain brought out even more than Washington's usual road-raged drivers locked in bumper-to-bumper traffic. As a psychologist trained in the Jungian school of thought, Renee had been taught to cure herself first before treating others. She had suffered from bouts of depression before but nothing had triggered the memory of the traumatic time in her life before the session with Heather and her parents. There was something about that woman, Mrs. Hollingsworth, that had reminded her of Aunt Clara's reaction to news of her own teenage pregnancy. Suddenly, everything had come flooding back to her. Physician heal thyself. She knew the familiar maxim all too well. Her mentor and now colleague, Dr. Helen Stone, had agreed to see her right away this morning. If Helen urged her to dig deeper, would Renee like what she found underneath the superficial surface that she presented to the world? Would she be able to accept the truth about herself? Would she be able to slay her own dragons? Face her own demons? How else would she be able to begin healing and start living a life she wanted and not one that had been mapped out for her—programmed into her subconscious?

Renee parked her car in the only spot available several blocks away from Helen's office and walked briskly through the light rain as the wind swept through her trench coat. As she walked, she tried not to think about that doctor's house located in a backwoods country town where her aunt had taken her to have an abortion without her knowledge. She focused on her breathing, inhaling deep breaths then letting each breath out slowly to try to forget. It didn't work. Renee blinked several times to clear away the onset of tears that had begun to blend in with the rain's light drizzle falling on her cheeks. She couldn't shake her feelings of helplessness amidst so many disturbing thoughts that she found difficult to handle on her own right now. She glanced down at her watch and saw she was early for her appointment with Helen.

Renee entered the security-guarded building fifteen minutes early and took the elevator to the 5th floor. She walked into Dr. Helen Stone's office feeling even worse than before. Fortunately, the waiting lounge was empty when she arrived and she had a few minutes alone to collect herself before the receptionist returned from her break or wherever she was at the moment.

After several minutes of waiting alone in the reception area, Helen herself appeared to invite Renee into her counseling chamber. Helen explained that she was lacking a receptionist at the moment. Her secretary had not been able to make the move to the new location and had resigned. Renee stammered an apology for making this last minute appointment, but Helen's smile and warm, amber eyes immediately put her at ease. Helen was dressed in a tweed, calf-length skirt and maroon turtleneck sweater that give a bit of color to her pale complexion. Renee draped her raincoat across a nearby chair and sat down. While Helen poured them both a cup of herbal tea, Renee studied her colleague's new office. Potted, floor plants bursting with healthy foliage filled the room. A row of hanging plants lined the window and more potted greenery competed with books for shelf space on the floor-to-ceiling case. Renee almost felt like she was in a tropical rain forest. Pastel pink walls, impressionist paintings, and ocean sea breeze music playing in the background further added to the room's tranquil effect. Renee closed her eyes for a moment as her nose delighted in a pleasant aroma of potpourri and relaxing tea blends. Did she really want to be here and face the truth—reveal old wounds that she had shut out years ago? Renee experienced a brief tightness in her chest. She gripped the arms of the chair and thought about getting up and fleeing the session.

Helen sipped her tea in silence as she watched Renee. Renee understood the doctor/patient dance well enough and knew that Helen was waiting patiently for Renee to open up. That morning's session with the family of a pregnant teen had unlocked Renee's memory of an unpleasant event that she had long forgotten as a self-protection mechanism. Now she remembered more and more details of that particular time in her past. She gradually began to feel comfortable sharing those details with her psychiatrist. Renee told Helen what happened to her that summer in high school when she was sixteen. Everything came out in a jumbled blur.

"For the first time I remembered my high school boyfriend, Randolph. He and I were walking hand-in-hand to Memco Department store to buy our unborn baby's first outfit, yellow knit booties, matching sweater and cap," said Renee, gazing into her folded hands, "I fear that was my last chance to be a mother."

"How does that make you feel?"

"I feel like I'm being punished," said Renee, "I should have been able to stop Aunt Clara somehow." Renee began to sob into her hands. She accepted the tissue that Helen handed her. She heard Helen pouring a glass of water from the pitcher and place the glass on the edge of the desk in front of her, but she didn't look up. Suddenly, in Renee's mind it was July 1972 again. Aunt Clara's voice permeated her thoughts.

"There's no need in involving your worthless father. I'll take care of this myself." She'd just returned from the doctor's isolated cottage tucked away in a York, Pennsylvania countryside, and Renee was staring at the

rosebud border encircling her pale pink bedroom walls and crying. She jumped at the sound of Aunt Clara bursting through her bedroom. *"Stop this foolishness right now, Renee Janette Curtis! No sense in you lying around here moping. The whole bucket of milk is spilled and you want to put it back."*

At 16 she hadn't understood what Aunt Clara meant about the spilled milk but now she did. They had snatched her unborn baby from her body twenty-nine years ago while she slept in an anesthetic coma. Like spilled milk, her baby couldn't be put back. The churchgoing Aunt Clara had looked Mr. and Mrs. DeWitt in the eyes and lied. She had told Randolph's parents that Renee started hemorrhaging in the middle of the night and had to be rushed to the hospital where she lost the baby. It was best for all concerned if Renee and Randolph stopped seeing each other. The DeWitts agreed with her and promised to keep their son away from Renee. Like everyone else in their middle-class Northeast neighborhood, Renee feared Aunt Clara. She'd kept quiet about their family secret just as her aunt ordered. Over the years, she'd completely erased it from her memory until now.

"I've wrestled with an unknown guilt for years but didn't understand why. Now it's all come crashing down on me. I don't deserve to be happy."

"You've been suffering from a type of post-traumatic stress, Renee. That's how you were able to lock away the trauma of losing your baby. It's been deep within your subconscious for so many years."

"Perhaps, this is the reason you tried to adopt a baby without your husband's agreement," Helen continued, "You saw adoption as another chance at motherhood."

"Yes. I know how Bill feels about being a father but I thought I could get him to change his mind. I suppose I have to accept the fact that motherhood is just one more part of my life that will have to go unfulfilled."

"How are things at home between you and your husband?"

Renee hesitated for a moment and then opened up to her therapist. She was surprised at her candidness in confiding to Helen the intimate details of her marriage. Although, she respected her as a colleague and mentor and even considered her a friend, Renee never had any close girlfriends to call on when things became emotionally rough. Her entire childhood and now adult life had involved keeping her true feelings hidden. Years of psychotherapeutic training had taught her how to be evasive while compelling others to face the truth. Add to that, Aunt Clara's constant admonitions to always present a respectable and private demeanor. But this time, Renee didn't mince words when she answered Helen's personal questions about her relationship with Bill.

"My husband competes with me and resents my success. Right now, he's occupied with some joint venture he's involved in and he's not concerned about how I feel about anything including adoption. He doesn't have time to listen to me. I'm nothing more than a warm body to him. We haven't made love in over a month and when we did I was just an outlet for his built-up, sexual tension."

"What about your own built-up, sexual tension?" said Helen, "Are you doing anything about that?"

"Like everything else in my life, I've learned how to block it out," said Renee, "Sex with Bill is predictable. I know what he'll say, which is nothing. I know what he looks like, feels like. I know how long it'll last and exactly what happens afterwards. He'll go back to sleep. I don't feel special to him. I don't feel loved or cherished."

"Honestly Helen, I'd rather get up early and watch the sun come up and sip a good, hot cup of coffee than linger in bed with him. I'm afraid he probably feels the same about me."

"Well, Renee, you're still a young, attractive woman. What are you prepared to do about this situation? Are you going to demand changes in your marriage or are you going to end it and seek happiness elsewhere?"

"I'm not sure I follow what you mean?"

"Happiness comes to those willing to fight for it. Are you up to the battle, Renee? Or do you intend to just stay numb the rest of your life? These are questions that only you can answer."

Renee told Helen how she tried to do something completely out of the ordinary. She described her preparations in arranging a surprise, intimate evening with Bill. But the plans blew up in her face. Now she didn't have the desire after he brushed her aside on her birthday.

"It's time you discovered who Renee Hayes really is, what she wants, and how to get it," said Helen. "Two negative emotions will try to stand in your way, fear and guilt. Don't let them. Release your fears of not ever being truly loved and not experiencing motherhood. Then get rid of the anger and guilt from things that happened to you in the past."

"This may sound cliché, but that's easier said than done," said Renee, trying to hold back her tears.

"Renee, I believe you're experiencing the long-term effect of losing both your parents at a young age" said Helen, as she continued, "I believe this has affected all of your adult relationships from what you've told me over the years. Your mother died when you were seven and your father simply wasn't there for you. To me, you appear to be manifesting symptoms similar to children of divorced parents. Then, there's your recent memory of a teen pregnancy that ended without your consent or knowledge. You do realize that you're suffering from anxiety because of all this?"

"Yes, I know Helen. But, I thought I had it under control."

Helen rested her clasped hands on top of her desk as she looked Renee straight in the eye. "Honestly Renee, what would you tell your patients in this situation?"

"I would first suggest the behavioral approach. I'd teach them breathing desensitization and relaxation techniques to ease their anxiety."

"Well, there you have it! Have you tried these exercises that you would advise your patients to follow?"

"Yes, I've tried that. It's not working for me. I need you to prescribe something."

"I can prescribe an anti-depressant. Zanax or perhaps Ativan. Do you have a preference for any particular type of the common benzodiazapiens?"

"You and I both know those will take 3-4 weeks to work! Why don't you give me some Lexapro? That will work much faster."

"Of course, you're right. I can prescribe Lexapro for you, but you know that medication is addictive."

"I know, but it won't be a problem. I won't be on it that long. I just need something to get me through this. I need something to stop these horrible intrusive memories. I'm actually afraid to go to sleep."

"Very well," sighed Helen as she unlocked her desk drawer and removed a prescription pad. "Listen to me, Renee. You must free yourself from all those fears—fear of loss, of change, and of being hurt. It's a liberating sensation when you do." Helen ripped the filled out prescription from the pad and held it up, away from Renee. "Don't be afraid to change."

"I'll work on it, Helen," said Renee, holding out her hand for the prescription. "You know, a friend said something to me last night and I've been thinking about it ever since. She said live until you die. Up until now, I haven't really been living at all."

"Your friend's right. I'd like you to come back early next week. If you can get your husband to come with you, that would be helpful to your progress and to his. You will need a lot more help than this one session to get through this, Renee. You don't have to do it alone, you know."

Renee nodded, but she knew it would be a cold day in hell before Bill would come with her to see a psychiatrist. It was about one thirty when Renee arrived home after her session with Helen and after getting her Lexapro prescription filled at the pharmacy. What was left of today's stack of mail sat on the pier table in the foyer. Bill had already picked out his mail but she knew he was not home because his sports car was missing. That's the only thing he drove these days. Renee wondered if he received her scented, mysterious envelope. She grabbed her mail and headed downstairs to her office.

Before unlocking the door to her office, she turned back and started towards the stairs leading to the first floor landing. A dark-pined, hidden alcove under the stairway caught her eye and she stopped. Renee had passed by this alcove hundreds of times when coming down to her office without giving it a thought. Now she couldn't ignore it. *Pull yourself together, Renee. For God's sake, you're a trained psychologist,* she tried demanding of herself. The narrow, 26-inch staircase snaked around a column that reached to the attic floor. The sun emitted a shaft of light through a small window above the alcove. Renee passed through the swirling dust gnats that bounced off the light as she slowly climbed the uncertain stairs. She approached the staircase in a trance-like state as if some spirit hovered about, warning her to go back. When Renee almost reached the top landing, she lost her footing and nearly tumbled down the rickety stairs. She grabbed hold of the banister and continued forward.

The attic housed a tower of cardboard boxes and a chest full of her high school and college graduation gowns, yearbooks and memorabilia. Aunt Clara's cedar chest stood in the middle of the floor, and had not been opened since college. Whatever had been tucked way in its cedar chipped linings had moved with her from house to house, untouched and buried. Renee looked around and flinched upon seeing her mother's full-length, mink coat draped around a life-like mannequin. She dropped the handful of mail on the attic floor. Then, walked over to the mannequin and stroked the coat's fur collar, and thought of her long-deceased mother. Renee recalled how thrilled her mother had been to receive it from her jazz musician lover, who was Renee's father, after one of his more profitable gigs when he performed onstage with Lena Horne in the early fifties. Her parents had never married, but no one who saw them together ever doubted their love and commitment to each other.

Renee wiped a tear from her eye as she thought about how much she still missed her parents. Her mother, Tina Joye, beautiful, willful, and smart, would have been more than a loving mother had she been alive today. She would have been Renee's best friend and confidant. Renee remembered her mother as she was just before her death, a petite caramel-colored, twenty-five year old beauty with silky, black hair. A true free spirit who had been a singer and showgirl until a tragic accident took her life. Renee's mother had been killed instantly in a bus accident on March 5th, 1959 while traveling with her tour group when Renee was only seven years old. Her father, LeRoy Curtis, an alto saxophonist and composer never made it big in the music business but toured all over the United States and Europe, thirty-five to forty weeks a year. Growing up, Renee rarely saw him. With her father on the road most of the time and her mother dead, Aunt Clara begrudgingly took on the responsibility of raising her.

Renee put on her mother's mink coat and suddenly felt a bit flirtatious and carefree just as if she had taken on the persona of her feisty, showgirl mother. Here was a woman who managed to slay her own dragons—the biggest one of them being Aunt Clara. If only she could be more like Tina Joye, she wouldn't be afraid to fight for her own happiness. Renee twirled around in a half circle then bumped her ankle on the large cedar chest.

"Damn," she cursed aloud rubbing her ankle. Renee took off the coat and gently laid it down. She knelt in front of the chest, and brushed away its thin blanket of dust and spider webs. She struggled to open it. Eventually, it gave way and creaked as she pushed the lid up. She pulled out her black high school graduation cap and gown. Next came her yearbook, and piles of cards. A stack of bound letters stuck out from under an indigo blue, satin prom dress, poi de silk pumps, and elbow-length evening gloves. She remembered hating that dress, which her aunt had bought for her senior prom, but Aunt Clara said she was too dark-skinned to wear pastel colors that light-skinned girls could easily wear.

She took out one of the letters from the chest and examined the return address. She could tell from the return address that the letter was from her old boyfriend, Randolph DeWitt. It had not been opened. Renee surmised that Aunt Clara had kept it from her and after awhile it had been long forgotten. He wrote it when he was staying with his grandparents in Greensboro, North Carolina the summer she got pregnant. Renee's hands shook as she opened the folded letter. Randolph had been her first and only love at Coolidge High School when they were both sixteen years old. Her palms felt sweaty as she played with the paper's folded edges. Renee closed her eyes, and the memories rushed back in panoramic color.

Renee held Randolph's unread letter as the scenes from the past replayed before her like a bad movie. Sitting on the attic floor before the cedar chest with her legs tucked under her, Renee opened Randolph's nearly thirty-year old letter, written on lined school paper and stained yellow from age and she cried. She recognized his handwriting, even after all these years. Reading it now she struggled to make out his immature handwriting, through her tears.

Dear Renee,

I got your letter on 8/13/72 and mailed mine on 8/13/72. Excuse my sloppy writing but I've been nervous lately. I still wish we could seek our future together but I know it's out of the question. I was very hurt when my folks told me you lost our baby and I felt that life wasn't hitting on nothing. It's okay down here in Greensboro with my grandparents but I wish I was still up there in DC with you and the gang. When my Pops told me that your Aunt, came to see them and wanted me to stay away from you for good, it hurt me to my heart. I'm sorry our little baby didn't make it, Renee. But does that mean you and me have to break up? I know I promised my Pops never to talk about it to you and I hope this doesn't make you cry but I still love you and I don't know why your Aunt hates me. My Pops said I should leave you alone for awhile like she wants. They don't want no more trouble for her or for you. I heard she transferred you to that school for girls in Northwest Washington, Maret, starting in the Fall. We start school September 4 back at Coolidge and my folks said I will have to stay down here until the end of August. So I guess that means I won't get to see you much anymore. I plan to go into the Army after I graduate high school next year. I guess you will go on to college like your Aunt wants. I remember you saying that you wanted to be in show business like you Mama was. I really liked you in our school play about Romeo and Juliet. I could never get up in front of all my friends, teachers, and parents like you did last year. I was proud to tell everybody, that's my girl!

I put your picture in my wallet, so when I open it up your picture is the first thing I see. Hey! I got good news, Pops gave me the Wildcat and we drove it down here. I guess he felt sorry for me. It's a nice car but it's eating up my savings. I'm going to give it back to him when I get my Volkswagen. A V.W. is much cheaper to operate. Well I would send you a picture of me too but I don't have any, plus I have gone from bad to worse. When Mother Nature was giving out faces she left me out. (smile) Other than that I'm OK I guess and my brain is still the same, increase No! Decrease, Yes! Well, I guess I better go before I bore you to death. Plus Grandma is on my back, she wants me to go into town to the store. Now I wish I couldn't drive at times but if I couldn't drive she'd probably make me walk the five miles. Take care of yourself and I hope you find peace of mind.

Yours Forever,
Randy DeWitt

P. S. I liked the pink paper and perfume in your letter. It smelled like the roses in my Mama's garden. (I dig it). I miss you a lot and think of you all the time.

Renee's tears spotted the frayed letter so much that she had trouble re-reading it. She went back over the part of Randolph's letter that said she had once wanted to be in show business. She had completely forgotten about her childhood dream to perform on stage just like her mother. But as with so many other things she wanted, Aunt Clara had squashed that idea. Aunt Clara told Renee that acting, singing and dancing were all useless ways to earn a living. *"Look at where your parents ended up. Besides, what talent do you have? You're lucky my church lets anybody join the children's choir."* These were words she recalled hearing over and over again.

Renee put everything away in the cedar chest, picked up her mother's fur cost, and swung it over her arm. She carefully maneuvered the steps going back down with one hand on the banister and the other holding onto the mail and the coat. She decided to send the coat to the furrier's for cleaning. Then, she'd keep it in her closet as a reminder of her mother.

After returning from the attic, she hung her mother's coat upstairs in her closet and then headed towards Bill's study to see if he had come home yet before leaving on his trip. Perhaps, Helen was right. She needed to fight for happiness. Bill didn't appear to notice her come into his study. The smell of leather and polished mahogany dominated the air in his office. A glass-covered cabinet contained a wall-size case of ancient classics, textbooks and software manuals. Bill's notebook PC sat flipped open on top the desk and his eyes studied the screen. Just then his cell phone rang and when he picked it up to answer it, he spotted Renee standing in the doorway. He waved her in and pointed to a chair, while talking and nodding into the phone.

"Hey, man. Yeah, it's about that time, Cliff," he said, with a quick glance of his watch.

While he talked Renee noticed a wastebasket filled with ripped open envelopes and lots of unopened junk mail. She saw her manila envelope sticking out of the trashcan unopened.

"Umhum, that's right, buddy. The driver should be here in about an hour. I'm taking Air France's flight 27 out of Dulles at 6:40 this evening and switching planes in Paris at Charles de Gaulle Airport," he said, studying the passenger itinerary ticket. "I land in Paris at 8:10 in the morning their time. Right," said Bill, nodding. "Then from Paris I hop on Indian Airlines at 10:30 AM and arrive in Delhi at 10:15 PM." He paused. "Yeah, there's a layover. I'll have to stay overnight in Delhi and take a 6:35 AM flight straight to Bangalore. That'll put me in Bangalore at 9:10 AM on Sunday."

The whole time Bill talked to Clifton Shaw on his cell phone, he typed rapidly on his laptop. Her husband was great at multitasking, thought Renee. It's just that he couldn't seem to find the time to fit her into his multiple task plan. "Yeah, 18 ½ hours just to get there, man. You're right, India's almost eleven hours ahead of us. Jet lag'll be a bitch," he chuckled. "I've got a reservation at the Maurya Hotel, something like our Hyatt here in D. C. so it should be pretty nice." Bill nodded with the phone to his ear, "Yeah, I'll call when I get there after I check in. You too, buddy. Later." He disconnected and looked up at Renee.

"How are you, baby?" he said smiling at her. "Sweetie, I don't want us to be mad at each other before I leave for India."

"I can see you're busy and you don't have much time left. I don't want to be mad either, Darling. Why didn't you open all your mail?" she said and pointed directly at the manila envelope.

"Oh, that's all junk. One of 'em had a strong perfume smell so that was probably a free sample of some cologne I don't need," he said. "I'm sure the rest of it's from charities and solicitors begging for donations. I've got too many important things to take care of right now. I can't waste time wading through that pile of junk mail." Renee didn't try to hide the disappointment on her face, but he seemed not to notice anyway.

She decided now was not the time to bring up her therapy session with Helen and what she remembered from her past. She'd wait until he came back from India when she had his full attention.

"I meant to ask you earlier, but I haven't been able to catch up with you for five minutes," said Renee.

"Ask me what?" he said, stuffing papers into a briefcase.

"My secretary is studying for her MCSE certification to become a Microsoft Certified Systems Engineer. I'm sure you know what that is even if I don't. Anyway, she wanted me to ask you if it was okay to practice setting up a network and connecting our two PC's."

"I guess so," he said in a distracted manner as he responded to email while she spoke, "She'll need to know my administrator's id and password to do that."

Bill wrote his id and password on a post-it note and handed it to Renee.

"I keep my system backed up regularly so I can easily restore if she screws it up."

"Thank you, dear. She won't mess up. Brenda's amazingly savvy with computers, just like you," said Renee, trying a little flattery on him.

"Hum, maybe I should recruit her into my boot camp," he smiled and came from behind the desk to embrace her. "Now, give me a good-bye kiss so I know I'm out of the doghouse."

"I wish you didn't have to go. There's so much I need to tell you."

"I know, baby. But keep it on ice 'til I get back. I won't be gone long."

CHAPTER 13

Several days had past since Bill left for India. Renee was taking the Lexapro that Helen had prescribed for her to ease her anxiety attacks. She got through each day as if on autopilot. Everyday she wrote down her thoughts and feelings in a diary just as she advised her patients to do. She stared at the pill in the palm of her hand for several seconds, trying to decide if she should skip this one and lower the dosage. The pills allowed her to function somewhat normally. But at times her mind went blank during therapy sessions with her patients. She felt tired and listless throughout the day, which was another unwelcome side effect. Renee heard voices outside her office in the waiting room and knew that her last patient had arrived. She folded the pill inside a tissue and placed it inside her front desk drawer. Then, she straightened up in her chair and buzzed Brenda on the intercom to allow the client into her office

Thankfully, this one was a regular. She had heard him relate the same self-loathing issues many times before and didn't have to listen too closely. She pretended to write lengthy notes as he spoke and kept her eyes glued to the yellow notepad on her lap, only glancing up at him periodically to feign concern. He talked freely without the need for prompting questions, which made it easier. Today, she was grateful for his nonstop, asthmatic-sounding voice. Her strategy to get through this last session—sit there and appear interested until his fifty minutes were up.

After her last patient left, Renee retreated upstairs to her bedroom's anteroom and sat down at her writing desk to go through a stack of mail. She flipped through the mail haphazardly until she caught sight of a thick envelope, stamped with a foreign return address. La prison de Luynes, France was marked in bold, black ink. Immediately, she knew it was a letter from her father, Leroy Curtis. Renee could hardly contain herself from the excitement. She ripped open the envelope and a photo slipped free. It was a picture of her father, clutching his saxophone and standing next to another gentleman in front of a cafe. Renee flipped the picture over and recognized her Dad's cursory, handwriting on the back. *1961 at Haynes Restaurant, Montmartre, France with owner, Mr. Haynes.* Leroy Curtis would have been thirty years old in that photo and looked as dapper as she remembered him to be in those days. He sported his trademark, pencil-thin, Clark Gable mustache; wavy, promade-slicked hair, and a double-breasted, pinstripe suit.

In his letter, her father told Renee that he loved her and how good it had been to see her this summer in August after so many years of thinking that she hated him. Prior to visiting him a few months ago in prison, Renee hadn't heard from her father in 18 months when she had received his last letter from Frankfurt, Germany. Tears stained her cheek as she read his heartfelt apology for not being a real father to her. Leroy said he realized how much he had sacrificed for his music. He now realized that touring throughout the States and Europe ten months out the year had cost him his daughter's childhood, as well as, her young adult years. He knew now that was the time in her life when she needed a father, especially after her mother died in that freak bus accident. Those were difficult times for a seven-year-old to deal with. He understood that now, but he had been selfish.

Her father was right. As a child, Renee didn't understand why her mother would never come home again and why her father left so abruptly right after the funeral. Aunt Clara's harsh words only make it worse. No amount of Lexapro could erase the memory of what Aunt Clara said to her after they returned home from her mother's funeral. *"It's your fault your Mama's dead. You're a disobedient child and your room's always a pigsty. That's why the good Lord took your Mama to glory—to punish you. Now I'm stuck with you for good since that no-account daddy of yours has gone off again, traipsing all over the world."*

Aunt Clara had warned Renee then that if she didn't change her devilish ways, more punishments from the Almighty would follow. Renee had never understood what awful crimes she had committed as a child that deserved the wrath of God like Aunt Clara said—unless it was not reacting fast enough to her aunt's daily list of orders. Her aunt reserved Saturdays for cleaning. That meant everything, including garbage cans, had to be scrubbed until they gleamed. Throughout the week another strictly enforced rule demanded that everything be put away in its proper place when not in use. On Sundays they observed sunrise service at St. Augustine's Catholic Church in Washington, D. C. Aunt Clara's daily praises and devotions to the Lord and testifying about God's goodness to all within earshot made others think she was a good woman but Renee knew her cruel side. On Thursday and Friday evenings, Renee attended catechism class as well as devotion and prayers instead of running wild in the streets like other people's kids who had no home training, according to Aunt Clara. In her many years of counseling youth, Renee knew that children required discipline, structure, and love in order to thrive. Growing up, Aunt Clara did provide her with two out of three of those necessities in extreme quantities, discipline and structure. But Renee never felt truly loved by the woman who she came to understand raised her only out of duty. The sudden death of her mother, and losing her own baby at sixteen were the two worst times in her life. That's when she felt completely alone and powerless. Yes, she had needed her father as a child, but even now as a grown, married woman of 45, she still needed him.

Leroy wrote that he felt like he had let her down and abandoned his parental responsibility. At that moment Renee longed to hug her father the way she always did when she was a little girl. She wanted to recapture the excitement as he rushed through the door after arriving home from a lengthy tour. She now understood that Leroy Curtis was a free spirit, just like her fancy, showgirl mother had been. They were both happiest when performing before an audience. Leroy wrote that he had never stopped writing music or playing his sax even in prison. Though he was grateful for his daughter's forgiveness, Leroy said he wanted her to see only the debonair man he used to be in the picture—not a beaten-down convict in wrinkled prison garb.

"Please daughter, I beg you not to come back to this horrible place again. Have faith and be patient. I will be home by Christmas," he ended his letter.

Renee's hands trembled as she reread that last line. How could her father be home by Christmas? He had only served one year of a three-year prison term for manslaughter. But as she read on, her doubts were answered in the letter. Leroy explained that Detective Hamilton had been working to finalize arrangements with the Parisian police department for his release. He went on to say it was a godsend that her detective friend had taken it upon himself to discover his whereabouts. Otherwise, he would be languishing in la Prison de Luynes for another two years for something he didn't do. Renee would never forget that day during the summer when Deek told her he had found her missing father. *"Renee, I tracked down your father using one of the department's on-line investigative International data bases. For the last year, he's been serving time for manslaughter in a Parisian prison."*

She would never forget those words and how she felt when she heard them for the first time. Deek had renewed her hope then, and now he was doing it again. Renee read through her father's entire letter once more. She just couldn't believe it.

Dear Daughter,

How have you been? As for me I am quite well under these circumstances beyond my control. I have missed you even more since your visit this summer. For the past few years before my arrest, I had felt like the creative freedom and tolerance that Black Americans had enjoyed in Paris, during the 50's and 60's, were all but gone. Paris no longer meant the City of Light to me and I had grown weary of traveling around the world. To be honest Renee, I was actually ready to come home and then I got arrested.

When you were here, I didn't want to spoil your visit by going into details about my arrest. But I want you to know that I am not guilty of manslaughter. I want to explain now what happened last year that got me in this mess. One night after finishing my final set at a jazz club where I played regularly every Thursday through Saturday night, one of the band's backup singers and I were sitting at the bar having a drink. I could tell she was stalling and was not looking forward to going home. At some point the woman's drunken husband came into the club looking for her. We didn't know he had a knife. When he saw us laughing and talking, he got the wrong impression that I was fooling around with his wife. I tried to reason with the man but as I said he was drunk. When he lunged at me with the knife, we struggled. I was only trying to get the knife away from him, but I accidentally stabbed him during the scuffle. He later died at the hospital.

At the trial, I explained that I was only trying to be a friend and to lend a sympathetic ear. This woman said her husband had been an abusive drunk throughout most of their marriage. I guess no one believed me even though the woman testified on my behalf. The singer and her husband were both French and I was a Black foreigner. The jury found me guilty and I received the maximum penalty for manslaughter.

Renee, your friend Detective Degas Hamilton went above and beyond after he found out about my case. He promised me he would do everything he could to get me off with time already served. At first I didn't get my hopes up. But eventually I saw that he was sincere. He asked the French inspector to send him a copy of my file so he could learn all the details of the city's case against me. He then petitioned the American embassy in Paris to intervene and use their clout to get the case re-opened. Due to the questionable circumstances surrounding the case, the embassy agreed. Detective Hamilton also asked a criminal attorney friend of his to file the necessary motions and act on my behalf pro bono. This is one young man that I look forward to thanking personally when I return home to Washington, D. C.

So, Please daughter, I beg you not to come back to this horrible prison again. Have faith and be patient. I will be home by Christmas. Take good care of yourself. I just have to hold on a little longer until I see you again.

Love Always, Dad

Renee wanted to leap out of her chair. Leroy ended his letter by saying he owed his impending freedom all to her friend, Detective Degas Hamilton. Renee had to agree with her father. It was typical of Deek to keep his good deeds undercover. Had she known all the behind the scenes effort he undertook to gain her father's release, she would have thanked him last night at the fundraiser. She could never adequately repay him for all he had done to obtain justice for her father. But the least she could do was to say thank you. Renee picked up the telephone and dialed his mobile number instead of calling him at FBI headquarters or the police station. She wanted to speak to him directly, not leave a message on his voicemail at work. Deek picked up on the first ring. Street traffic and voices echoed in the background.

"Yeah," he answered with an edginess in his voice.

"Deek? This is Renee. Did I catch you in the middle of something?"

"Yeah, you could say that. I'm in the middle of hell. There's been another gang related shooting and witnesses are scared and tight-lipped as usual. But luckily, the suspects missed their target this time, and no one was killed."

"Oh, … will you be able to get everything under control?"

"Trust me, Renee, you don't wanna know what's going on down here. Anyway, what's up with you?" he said in a softer, more relaxed tone.

"I received a long letter from my father today. He says he'll be home by Christmas and he owes it all to you. Deek, I just wanted to thank you for everything you've done for him," she blurted out. "But you sound busy so I'll let you get back to your work. I'm sorry if I bothered you, but I had to call and thank you personally. If I had known when I ran into you at the fundraiser I would have thanked you then."

"No need to thank me, Doc. Hearing from you has been the highlight of my day. Renee, I know this is short notice but are you free for dinner tonight? We never did get a chance to celebrate your birthday and you left the fundraiser rather suddenly."

Renee took a deep breathe before answering. "Thank you Deek, but I'm not sure that's a good idea."

"Please Renee, don't turn me down. Not today."

"Bill's out of town and I feel funny about going out with you," she said, and rubbed her forehead to relieve the tension that was suddenly building.

"I understand, but listen. It's Friday night and I can't take another day dealing with these knuckleheads who wanna shoot each other over nothing."

"It's just that, I don't think we should …"

"I just want to treat you to a birthday dinner that's all. I swear if you say no, I'll pay one of these thugs to put me out of my misery. I'm sure they'd do a drive-by on me for free," he said in a humorous tone.

"Don't even joke about that, Deek," she said.

"Who's joking? I really need to see you."

"I guess you're not going to give up easily, are you?" she sighed.

"Nope. Especially when it's something I really want. Just give me a couple of hours to write up this report and change clothes. Do you want to meet me at my place or should I pick you up at home around six?"

Renee analyzed how she had gone from a range of emotions over the past few weeks—from depression and loneliness to a renewed acceptance of herself as a woman who needed to be appreciated. What could it hurt to have dinner with someone who made her feel special and whose company she enjoyed? She just wouldn't let things get out of hand like the last time. Since Bill was gone until Thursday, Deek could actually come to her house to pick her up as long as he got no further than the front foyer.

"Well, I'm waiting. What's it gonna be, Doc?" Renee could hear the impatience in his voice as he waited for her reply.

"I suppose it's okay as long as we're just talking about dinner. If you want to pick me up at my house, I can be ready at six. I'm really in no mood to drive this evening anyway."

Despite trying to remain calm and detached, a light giddiness came over her after she hung up the phone. Now, she was glad she had decided not to take that last dose of Lexapro. She certainly did not want to appear lethargic and distracted around Deek. The forecast called for chilly weather that evening so she wanted to wear comfortable clothing. She riffled through her wardrobe and finally selected a black stretch velvet skirt, black cashmere V-neck sweater and leather boots. She clasped an amethyst drop necklace around her neck and clipped on matching teardrop earrings. The jewelry helped dress up the casual outfit. Knowing Deek, he'd probably take her downtown to some place really nice for dinner. The closer the clock approached six, the greater her anticipation and excitement grew. No matter how hard she tried, she couldn't brush off that wild, happy feeling of a romantic schoolgirl. "Or more like some romantic fool," she said out loud to herself.

Ever since running into Deek at the Boys and Girls Club fundraiser last night, from time to time she had found herself imagining all sorts of crazy circumstances that she knew could never be. At one point, she actually pictured herself married to Deek. In her fantasy, they lived in a small country cottage just outside the city, and she was holding a newborn in her arms. When she was at her lowest point, she would try to replace her bad memories with good visualizations. Her good images and memories were ones that typically included Deek. Renee realized that if she ever found herself alone with him, it would take all her strength and willpower to resist making love to him again. Dinner downtown in a public restaurant was about the only safe place she trusted herself to be with him. Renee could not keep lying to herself. Her feelings for Deek were too strong to be considered innocent. She knew the safest thing for her to do was avoid tempting situations.

At exactly six o'clock, Renee heard the doorbell. When she opened the door, Deek stood before her dressed in hip, causal gear of buff Timberlands, stonewashed, and loose-fitting jeans. His muscular torso stretched a ribbed cocoa sweater under a sporty, fur lined jacket, and his smile mesmerized her into total speechlessness until he spoke and broke the awkward silence.

"Well, can I come in?"

"Yes. I'm sorry, Deek," she said and stepped aside, "please come in. You're not exactly dressed for dinner downtown. Where are we going, Detective Hamilton?"

"Let me worry about that, Doc," he smiled, "But you look even more beautiful than I expected. So are we all set to go?"

"Yes, I'm ready," she said, hoping he couldn't detect her school-girl excitement as she retrieved her coat from the closet. "Now, you're sure you won't need a jacket and tie to get into the restaurant?"

Deek helped Renee with her coat as she slipped her arms through the sleeves. "Like I said Doc, everything's under control," he smiled mischievously and brushed her cheek lightly with a kiss, "I have a surprise for you, Birthday Girl."

CHAPTER 14

Deek slid a CD in the disc player of his black, two-seater vintage Mercedes convertible. He turned the volume up and sped down New York Avenue away from the city. Renee didn't care that he drove over the speed limit or that on this particular evening he liked his music loud with a decidedly youthful rhythm and beat. Perhaps they were both from two different worlds, with little in common, but at that moment she felt exhilarated—like a teenager defying the rules. She'd always lived life as if playing a chess game—every move was made in a logical fashion with a definite purpose. Moves made haphazardly caused problems later on. Tonight she didn't even want to analyze the consequence of this move. She just enjoyed sitting next to Deek, full of sexual tension, and heading straight towards the unknown. She glanced over at him and felt a wild abandonment. The Capital and Washington Monument disappeared in the distance, veiled in a foggy mist. She dismissed her twinges of guilt by reasoning that she was just going out for an evening of innocent fun and relaxation with an old friend. Nothing more. This was something she really needed after her stressful encounters with Bill over the last several days.

"I thought we were going downtown for dinner. Just where are you taking me, Lieutenant Hamilton?" said Renee with an impish smile.

"I told you, it's a surprise, Doc. You didn't look like you were having much fun the other night. So I intend to make up for it tonight."

Renee clasped her hands together in her lap in order to resist the strong urge to touch his thigh. For most of the ride, she stared out the window rather than risk being tempted by one of the features she loved most about him—his boyish dimples whenever he smiled. After racing along Route 50, they reached the Bay Bridge in less than forty minutes. Renee looked out into the waters off the Chesapeake Bay.

"Now I must insist that you tell me, Deek, where are we headed?" She crossed her arms and stared at his handsome profile, waiting for an answer.

"Okay, Doc, I confess. I'm taking you to Hemingway's Restaurant on Kent Island just across the bridge," he said, "The seafood's as great as the view of the Bay. If we hurry we can catch the sunset's reflection off the water."

"I had no idea a D. C. homicide detective could be so romantic," she said in a teasing voice.

"Forget about my job, Renee. I have. We're on my time now, not the department's or the FBI's." He looked away from the road just long enough to give her a wicked smile.

"You're right. I'm sorry."

"Actually, I'll let you in on a little secret. Several weeks ago, I bought a getaway cottage in Bay City. Someplace I can escape to on weekends or whenever I get a chance. When I can't use the cottage myself, I plan to rent it out."

Renee pushed aside a lock of hair from her eyes and turned to him in surprise. "You did what?"

"Yeah, you heard right, Doc. I bought another house. It's in a small, historic town called Stevensville, not too far from the restaurant. If you'd like to see it after dinner, I'll take you there and give you my five minute tour."

Renee shook her head in disbelief, but inside she felt her anticipation growing. "You're always full of surprises. But I think we should stick with the original plan and just have dinner at the restaurant."

Hemingway's sat on a marina with a 180-degree view of the Chesapeake Bay. The Annapolis skyline peaked out over the water further off in the distance. The waitress led them to a table by the window and Deek ordered a bottle of Chandon wine while they studied the menu. They started off their meal with crusty bread and house salad smothered in raspberry vinaigrette. A few sips of wine took care of the chill in the air. Deek warmed her hands in his as they both watched the sun disappear behind the skyline. The sun left reddish, orange accents on the rippling water. As the sun set, the sky changed into multiple shades of pinks, oranges, reds, and yellows. Waves flapped on the water. The setting was so beautiful and calm, Renee felt herself falling for Deek all over again—not that she'd ever stopped loving him.

She was glad when their shrimp and crab cakes arrived so she could focus on the food instead of his dark intense eyes. Throughout dinner live music played, and laughter floated upward from Lola's Tropical Bar & Grill, a beach club that was basically a tent under Hemingway's. After finishing dinner, Deek suggested they go downstairs and check out the club. At Lola's they danced, told each other funny anecdotes, and shared their worst workday moments over the loud conversations around them. At 11 o'clock, a steady downpour of hard rain began to beat against the club's tent-like enclosure while the wind bellowed outside.

"Perhaps we'd better wait out this storm before driving back across the bridge," said Deek, "My cottage is no more than ten minutes away. Would you like to wait the storm out at my place?"

Renee frowned and feigned a serious look on her face. "Your place? And be swallowed up in the belly of the whale?"

"Huh?" He looked at her questioningly, his eyebrows knitted in confusion.

She smiled. "Ignore my biblical symbolism. What I mean is, I don't think that's wise to go to your place."

"Why not Doc? I have a case of Moet and my frig is stocked. It sounds like a good plan to me."

Renee finally conceded that Deek was probably right. The storm appeared to be getting stronger instead of subsiding. The beach club tent offered little protection. There was no way to make it back over the Bay Bridge until the storm died down. They ran out to the car and headed for his cottage. Even at full force, Deek's windshield wipers couldn't clear the rain from the windows fast enough. Ten minutes later, he parked in front of his new ranch-style cottage with its wrap-around porch. Although it was dark, Renee envisioned a nicely landscaped, scenic setting from the surrounding looming trees and perennial gardens. Deek pushed aside the screen and unlocked the front door. He turned on the wall switch in the hallway and Renee's eyes adjusted to the dim light. The hardwood floors were covered with area rugs and oak wood furnishings. A large, stone fireplace dominated one wall in the living room. Ethnic prints mingled with tartan plaids on chair covers and pillows gave the décor a rustic appearance. He lit candles on the mantelpiece and started a fire.

"This is nice Deek, but I never knew you had a penchant for the country look."

"I don't. I prefer leather and a modern style but the house came fully furnished so it'll work for now."

"Actually, I love it. It's very peaceful out here. Kind of remote though."

"Yeah, that's why I like it. I needed a place to get away," he said, "Would you like a drink while we wait for the storm to pass? I have something I'd like you to try."

Renee followed him to the modest-sized kitchen and in route was given a quick tour. She sat down at the bar stool in the kitchen. She rested her chin on the back of her hand and watched as he retrieved two tall glasses from the cabinet and plopped in several cubes of ice into each one. "What are you making?" she asked.

He retrieved a bottle of Gosling's® Black Seal Bermuda Black Rum from the pantry and set the bottle on the countertop. "It's a drink called 'Dark and Stormy.' Kind of appropriate with the weather outside," he smiled and measured out 2 ounces of the rum for each ice-filled glass.

Renee watched as he poured the rum into their glasses and pulled out a bottle of what looked like beer from the refrigerator and a fresh lime. Renee wondered if he was really planning to drive her home tonight. Next, he added 4 ounces of the other substance to each glass. "What's that you're putting in the rum?" she asked.

Deek held up the bottle so she could see the label, "This is Jamaican Ginger Beer. I don't have Bermuda Ginger Beer, but the Jamaican brand will do. This drink has history," he said and proceeded to slice the lime. "When the Royal Navy ships came over to Bermuda from England in the 17th century they would add a little Ginger Beer to make the alcohol last longer during the long voyage."

He squeezed in a little lime, stirred the mixture a few times, and handed her the drink to sample, "Whaddya think?"

"Um," she said, taking a small sip, "It's good." Not accustomed to liquor, Renee thought the drink was a little strong for her. She figured she'd better drink it slowly, especially after having consumed wine with dinner. They carried their drinks back to the living room. Deek put on a jazz CD and a melodic blend of bass and drum accompaniment melded with the sound of soothing piano ballads. They sat next to each other on the pillow-backed sofa, covered in indigo blue and crimson plaid. Deek entertained her with stories of when he and his brother, Luke were growing up. His grandmother lived with them and would only speak French or Creole, alternating between the two.

"Do you speak French fluently?" Renee asked.

"Yes, I do, as well as, Martinican Creole. Luke and I didn't learn English until we started kindergarten."

"Really? You wouldn't know it. What kind of language is Martinican Creole?"

"Well, it has French syntax but it's a mixture of French and African dialects, with a little English, Spanish and Portuguese thrown in. They speak a similar type of Creole in Louisiana and French-speaking islands like Haiti and Guadeloupe as well as in English-speaking islands of Saint Lucia and Dominica that are close to Martinique. Perhaps one day I can take you there," he smiled.

"Are French and Creole the only languages you speak besides English?" she asked, and took another sip of Dark and Stormy.

"I can hold my own in Spanish pretty well when I need to," he said. "What about you?"

She shook her head. "Not really. I studied Latin in college and how practical is that?" She said with a sarcastic smile, "I've since forgotten most of it anyway." Deek agreed that there was probably not much demand for Latin these days.

Renee slipped off her shoes and curled her legs up on the couch, feeling completely relaxed from the drink and the jazz music. "That CD you're playing is really nice," she said.

"It sure is," said Deek, nodding. "That's Bill Evans Trio playing, from the album *Everybody Digs Bill Evans*. It's a classic collection and I managed to get my hands on two copies of it. I keep one copy here at the cottage and one back in the city. When I've had a really rough day, I come home and listen to this number playing right now called 'Peace Piece' until it puts me to sleep."

Even after talking for over an hour, the storm still hadn't let up. Renee felt light-headed from the drink and from the wine at dinner.

"It's getting late, Doc. Why don't you just stay overnight in the guest room?" he suggested, "and I'll take you home in the morning."

Renee hesitated then shook her head, "Deek, I don't …"

He held up his hands as a harmless gesture. "Whoa, Doc. I don't have any ulterior motives here. You're perfectly safe with me. I don't want you to do anything that you don't want to do."

"That's the problem, Deek," she whispered, laughing to herself, "But I guess you're right. I can barely keep my eyes open." She yawned.

"I'll get you a towel and one of my pajama shirts to sleep in," he said, "It's not Victoria Secrets but it'll be comfortable for one night."

When Deek returned, he handed her the folded bundle. "The guest room's right there and the bathroom's at the end of the hallway if you want to freshen up. There's also an extra toothbrush in the cabinet."

"Thanks. You've thought of everything," smiled Renee.

"I try to. If you need anything else I'll be in the room next door. Good-night," he said, then kissed her briefly before going to his room and closing the door behind him.

Renee showered and rubbed her body with the French perfumed lotion called Saphir by Boucheron that she carried in her bag. She slipped Deek's cotton nightshirt over her head and hoped the perfume's enticing scent lingered in his shirt long after she left tomorrow. That way he would have no choice but to think of her. She already knew that no matter how hard she tried, she wouldn't be able to stop thinking about him. The bedroom walls were thin and she detected his jazz music playing next door. She heard Deek moving around in his bedroom. Renee couldn't sleep either, not knowing whether it was her excitement at being alone with him again or the crashing noises coming from the storm outside.

She laid awake in bed for what seemed like an hour when suddenly, the wind flurried and a blast of lightening split a tree in back of the house. The small single-floor dwelling vibrated when a large tree limb smashed against Renee's bedroom window. She leaped from the bed. At the very instant she flung open her door, Deek stood in front of the doorway and caught her in his arms. Her pajama top brushed against his bare chest. He wore only the matching drawstring bottoms. His familiar, spicy scent comforted, as well as, excited her. She felt him getting erect and quickly pulled away.

"I can't hide it, I want you," he said, drawing her close again.

"Deek, I can't. It's not right. The guilt afterwards is too much."

"I understand, sweetheart. I don't want you to do anything you'll regret later." He kissed her forehead and gently pushed her away at arm's length.

"Try to get some sleep and I'll take you home first thing in the morning. If you get frightened again, don't worry. You know I won't let anything happen to you."

"I know that," she said, staring down at her bare feet, avoiding his irresistible eyes.

Deek walked over to the window to see if there was any damage from the tree limb. "I don't think there's any harm done. I'll look at it tomorrow. Goodnight then," he said.

"Goodnight, Deek. Thanks for coming to check on me."

He nodded and closed her door behind him.

Renee crawled back into bed and lay awake in the dark staring up at the ceiling for hours. The wind ebbed and peaked throughout the night as it whipped against her window, but she felt safe inside with Deek in the next bedroom. The last thought on her mind before falling asleep was of him.

CHAPTER 15 - BRENDA

Around midnight that Friday, Baby Buddha woke up crying to be changed. Brenda had hoped he would sleep through the night, but no such luck. She knew there were no more diapers left in the diaper bag that she had packed earlier that morning. She opened the closet in the nursery room where she kept the supply of disposable diapers and found no diapers! Brenda threw up her arms in frustration. She had asked Jerome to bring home more Pampers when he went out to get his cigarettes earlier that afternoon, but now she realized that he hadn't done it. He was out on a 14-hour run for UDS and wouldn't get in until six that morning. The only all-night 7-Eleven Brenda knew of was in her old Trinidad neighborhood in Northeast where she and Jerome used to live before moving in with Jerome's grandmother in her Southeast Capitol Hill neighborhood. Only a first-class A-1 fool would go into Trinidad after midnight toting a three-month old in her arms, she thought.

She grabbed a pair of large blue diaper pins and retrieved a folded cloth diaper from the top dresser drawer. Brenda didn't think she'd ever use those cloth diapers and rubber pants that her environmentally conscious aunt had given her to use. Her aunt had tried to talk her out of using disposable diapers because they weren't biodegradable. Brenda recalled her aunt saying at the baby shower, "*Honey, those Pampers will be sitting in landfills long after Baby Justin starts collecting social security and beyond.* "But her aunt was childless and pushing sixty. She'd never have to rinse out, soak, and wash a load of dirty cloth diapers every day. It certainly didn't help that Jerome was on the night shift now. Brenda cared about the environment too but realistically she wouldn't have time or the energy to use cloth diapers for the next three years. But tonight she was glad to have them available in an emergency.

Brenda couldn't shake the feeling that something wasn't right. She played back in her mind what had happened earlier in the day when she had come home from work early and found Jerome there at 4 o'clock in the afternoon when he usually didn't get home from work until 7 in the evening. Surprisingly, the loud music coming from behind her closed bedroom door didn't wake up Baby Buddha as she climbed the stairs with him sleeping in her arms. She had placed the baby in his crib and walked back down the hallway to confront Jerome and find out what he was doing home so early. She recalled shaking him on the shoulder to wake him up and asking him point blank, "Why aren't you still at work, Jerome? It's only 4 o'clock." Brenda had braced herself for his answer.

"Oh, you're home," he yawned, and lifted himself from the bed. He had been napping and hadn't heard her come in. "Big Cooper just got back this morning from a worker's comp injury. He's one of the senior guys so my supervisor bumped me from my day shift. My new run starts at 8 tonight and ends at 6 in the morning." He walked over to the dresser and began grooming his mustache in the mirror. Brenda felt relieved that her first suspicion of him getting fired wasn't the case, but she still didn't like his new hours.

"Isn't there anything you can do to get back on the day shift?" she said, and sat on the edge of the bed, trying to ignore how tired she was. "I need more help with Justin in the evenings. You know I started that online computer class last week and I have to study. Now you won't even be here until just before I leave in the mornings." Brenda sighed.

"Well, I ain't the boss," said Jerome, slipping on a clean shirt. "I gotta play by their rules."

"I know, Baby," she said and leaned back on the bed and closed her eyes. Jerome walked over and kissed her lightly on the forehead.

"Wassup, Girl? You sick or somethin'? What are you doin' home this early?"

"Dr. Renee closed up shop early," said Brenda, then sat up and rested her head on one hand. "She's been acting kind of strange lately. She seems a little confused at times, but maybe she just has a lot on her mind." Brenda could tell that Jerome wasn't really interested in her boss as he recovered his shoes from under the bed. He appeared to be preparing to go out. She asked him to bring back some diapers before he returned home to change into his uniform for work. He had said he would, but of course now she saw that he hadn't brought back any Pampers.

Brenda pinned the cloth diaper snuggly and slipped on the rubber pants. "This'll have to do Little Guy until I can get hold of your daddy. He can pick up more Pampers on his way home."

Baby Buddha wiggled his toes and gave Brenda a toothless grin, obviously content now that his diaper had been changed. She settled in the rocking chair and cuddled him close to her breast as she fed him his bottle. After drinking the last of his formula, Baby Buddha fell asleep with droplets of milk on his bottom lip. Brenda kissed her baby's milk-soaked lips and set the empty bottle on the nightstand. It was almost 12:30 AM. She knew that he would sleep through the night now that he was dry and fed. She laid him down in the crib on his back without waking him up and gave him another kiss goodnight.

Once inside her bedroom, she paged her husband, keying in their agreed upon emergency code of '911.' This code meant to call back immediately. She sat down in Grandmama Etta's favorite high-back cushioned chair at the foot of the bed and waited for the telephone to ring. Twenty minutes passed without receiving a callback. Brenda knew something had to be wrong when he hadn't responded to her emergency page. Jerome had once told her that drivers have CB's in their cabs, so a dispatcher could contact a driver at any time in an emergency. She hoped dispatch would make the effort to get a message to him. Brenda recalled how Jerome had complained to her about dispatch. "*Those A-holes hate to interrupt a run so don't call unless the damn house is on fire,*" Jerome had said.

Brenda dialed Union Delivery Service's emergency contact number to request that their dispatch unit radio her husband. She waited for what seemed like an eternity before a human answered. She told the dispatcher it was crucial that she get in touch with her husband. She didn't want to reveal that her emergency was to bring home more Pampers. Dispatch put her on hold and she waited even longer before the next voice answered—a woman with a sugary sweet mid-western accent. The woman identified herself as Odessa Dillon, Jerome's supervisor. Jerome must have been right about UDS not wanting to prevent a driver from completing his run. Dispatch had retrieved the supervisor before putting through the call to Jerome at her request. Brenda assumed they wanted to first assess the nature of the emergency.

"Mrs. Johnson, I am so sorry to be the one to tell you this, Honey, but our dispatchers can't get in touch with your husband, Darlin'," said Ms. Dillon in a cloying voice that didn't sound genuine to Brenda.

Brenda took a deep breath and exhaled. "Why not, Ms. Dillon? Jerome told me your dispatchers don't ever want to interrupt work but this is a real emergency. I need to speak to my husband and it's really nobody's business why."

"Calm down, Honey. I don't have a clue where your husband is at. I wish I did, I mean for your sake and all. But the fact is ... well, Jerome shoulda been the one to tell you this ... but ... he was let go 'bout a week ago."

"Let go!" said Brenda, "Why? What happened?"

"Uh, it's really not my place to be tellin' it. Sugah, ya need to talk to your huz-band."

"Tell me what!" Brenda demanded.

"Fact of the matter is, I gave Jerome every chance I could. Customers kept complainin' about his attitude. More'n a coupla times he strolled in here late as you please and didn't wanna follow my orders."

"Ms. Dillon, I beg you to give Jerome another chance. I know he flies off the handle at times," said Brenda, slumping down in the chair, "And, yes, sometimes he does have a problem with authority, but please let me straighten it out with him."

"Well, Sugah, 'course if that's all it was to it I'd be happy to oblige. I understand a woman tryin' to keep her family together and all. But unfortunately it's a little bit more complicated I'm sorry to say."

"Sorry to say what?" said Brenda, "Please Ms. Dillon, just be straight with me."

"Well, when you put it like that …" she paused. "Last week, your huz-band … Jerome, … Uh, … tested positive for drugs on a random drug test."

"What? I don't believe it," cried Brenda, "He's been clean for over 18 months. Why would he do something like that now?"

"I wish I could tell ya, Sugah," said Odessa Dillon in a saccharine drawl, "All I know is, our health practitioner's report showed Jerome's urine contained traces of drugs. So, 'course I had to terminate him. I had no choice. We have a no tolerance policy here at UDS. There was nothing else I could do, Darlin'."

"Couldn't the test be wrong?" Brenda sobbed.

"No, Sugah. I'm afraid not. For what it's worth, you have my sympathy, Mrs. Johnson."

"Thanks for letting me know the truth," said Brenda and hung up the phone.

Brenda cried for thirty minutes before her head cleared enough to be able to think about what to do next. She needed to talk to someone she trusted. Brenda dialed Dr. Renee's emergency number and after four rings, her boss's recorded message came on. *If this is an emergency dial*

911 or go to your nearest emergency room. Otherwise, to leave a message for Dr. Renee Hayes, press 1 or stay on the line. Brenda didn't want to leave a message so she hung up. She didn't get any answer when she tried Dr. Renee's home number either. Where could Dr. Renee be after 1:30 in the morning with her husband out of town? Out of desperation she decided to try to reach one of her girlfriends, Cha-Cha or Veda. Brenda didn't want to reveal any trouble in her marriage, especially when she had told them that things were going well, but under the circumstances she didn't have any choice. Who can you rely on if not your closest girlfriends? Brenda dialed Cha-Cha's number first and prayed that she'd be home. Cha-Cha picked up on the first ring.

"Baby, where are you?" said Cha-Cha in an anxious voice. "You're almost an hour late!" Her girlfriend had obviously expected someone else to call. Brenda hated to disappoint her. "Cha-Cha, it's me, Brenda."

"What? Brenda? Girl, what're you doing calling me so late. What's the matter?"

"Are you busy right now, Cha?" Brenda asked cautiously.

"Sweetie, I stay busy," said Cha-Cha in her sultry voice, "Got on my fly D&G's, my matching thongs and I'm a be kickin' it at a private VIP party with my man tonight. Hold up, I think I hear the bell. That's probably him now with his late self." She chuckled into the phone and told Brenda to hold on. But, Brenda hung up before Cha-Cha could return to the phone. She knew Cha-Cha would probably send her boyfriend away and come to her aid, but Brenda didn't want to impose knowing how madly in love Cha-Cha was for the first time in months. These days all Cha-Cha ever talked about was this fine Brother she'd been seeing. When they weren't spending time together they were text-ing each other little love messages all day long. It's a wonder either of them got any work done, thought Brenda and tried hard not to feel envious.

Next she tried calling Veda, but didn't have any luck in contacting her either. Brenda figured Veda could be anywhere, doing just about anything so there was no point leaving a message for her. Finally, there was no one else for Brenda to turn to except her last and worst resort—her mother, Irene Adams. She didn't want to call her mother because she knew her mother would start right in on Jerome. *"Where is he and why isn't he ever around when you and the baby need him?"* Whenever Brenda relied on her mother to help or to give her advice, it proved to be more trouble than it was worth. Brenda dialed her mother anyway and braced herself for the tongue-lashing 'I told you so' to come.

Brenda's parents lived on Primrose Street just off the 16th Street Gold Coast as it was called in the old days and even today. She figured it would take her mother at least twenty-five minutes to get there. But she was wrong. Irene was at her front door in fifteen minutes. Her mother never drove within the speed limit so Brenda should not have been surprised at her lightening speed arrival. Brenda couldn't help noticing when she opened the door that her mother arrived looking fabulous. Even in a crisis, Irene Kenmore Adams had to look good. Irene breezed through the door wearing a black pencil skirt that came just above her knees, high-heel black shoes, and an emerald-green cashmere sweater that matched her green contact-lenses and honey-beige skin tone.

Brenda gave her mother a tear-soaked and lingering hug. Having her mother there to hold onto felt comforting. Even a mother who was not very motherly was better than no mother at all, thought Brenda. Not having anyone else to turn to, Brenda sat down and confided everything to her mother—Jerome getting fired for failing a random drug test and pretending to go to work everyday when God only knows where he really was. Brenda had no idea where he really was since he had lied and said his shift wouldn't end until six in the morning.

Brenda stood up and began pacing the living room floor. "Mama, wherever my husband is, he planned to be there all night," she said. "Or maybe Jerome's hurt or something terrible has happened to him."

Irene pushed aside wisps of blond-feathered hair so that Brenda could visibly detect her obvious 'eye rolling' towards the ceiling.

Then, she let out a deep groan before addressing her daughter. "Baby Girl, don't be so gullible. Your first mistake was trusting that no good husband of yours. Sweetie, I'm worried about you and little Justin. I think you both should come home with me."

"I appreciate your concern Mama, but I just can't leave my home and uproot Justin. Besides, you're too far from my job," said Brenda. "No, I need to wait here until Jerome comes home and explains all this. Running away is not going to solve anything."

"Too far? I got here in 15 minutes," said Irene, frowning, "But go ahead and suit yourself. I know what I'd do. Where do you think he is right now anyway?"

Brenda shook her head and wiped away a tear with the back of her hand. She sat down and massaged the throbbing temples of her forehead while Irene gently rubbed her back.

"Humph, I've got a pretty good idea, if you don't," said Irene, wearing a look of disgust on her face. "Once a hussy always a hussy."

Brenda knew her mother was implying that Jerome was with his ex-girlfriend, Leenae Lewis, who both he and Brenda had known since high school. She didn't want to believe that but what other explanation could there be?

Irene got up and walked over to the window and drew back the curtains to look out into the darkness. Both of them knew Jerome probably wasn't coming home any time soon. After a brief moment of silence, Irene spoke up. "Honey, you better get on over to that slut's house and catch him in the act. You'll need evidence for your divorce."

Irene walked back over to the couch, plopped herself down, removed her heels and crossed her feet on top of the coffee table. "You've got ample grounds for divorce, Baby Girl."

"Divorce! Mama, you just can't break up a marriage at the first sign of trouble." Brenda shot up out of the chair and began pacing the floor again.

Irene folded her arms under her chest, "Honey, you need a man, not another baby to take care of. While you're out working everyday, taking care of Justin, cooking, cleaning, and whatnot, his ass is over there right now Livin' La Vida de Loca with that ghetto tramp."

Brenda stopped pacing and looked at her mother. "Mama, we don't know for sure that's where he is."

Irene sucked her teeth and rolled her eyes again. "Listen to me, Honey. Your marriage to Jerome was a big mistake from the get go. Despite what your Doctor Boss and all those other self-help gurus have to say, not *every* marriage should be saved."

"Mama, you just don't get it. Marriage means for better or worse. I know you think I'm a fool, but I still love Jerome. I'm not going to be like one of those drama queens and go over to Leenae's and create a scene. I'll hear Jerome's story when he comes home. Then we'll work things out together."

"You got that right, *his* story," Irene sneered. "Look, Brenda Jewel Adams, I didn't raise no fool. Just get your tail on over there, girl and see what's going on for yourself. Why are you gonna sit here and wait for him to come home and tell you a bunch of damn lies? I'll stay here with the baby until you get back."

Brenda slumped down at the opposite end of the couch and buried her head in her hands. Irene scooted closer to her daughter and patted her back.

"Mama, I don't know what to do." Brenda looked up with a faraway gaze in her eyes, "Would you mind leaving me alone now? I'll be fine. Don't worry, Mama. I need to be alone to pray on it."

"Pray on it! What the hell is praying gonna solve?" said Irene, throwing up her hands, "You've been praying to Jesus all your life thanks to that fanatic nanny your father hired to take care of you. Bengi, I think her name was if I recall." Irene turned up her face in a scowl. "I swear I'm surprised she didn't brainwash you into joining a convent or some cult. Come to think of it, that might have been better than marrying that loser you married."

"Mama please," said Brenda, with a frustrated sigh, "I do appreciate you coming over here but will you please leave! I'm sure Daddy's worried about you being out this late."

Irene shook her head, playfully. "Not hardly. He should be used to it by now. Besides I've got my overnight bag in the car." Brenda's face turned ashen gray at the thought of her mother spending the night and continuing with her tirade against Jerome. She didn't know if she would be able to stand it.

"Don't worry, Baby Girl," said Irene, grabbing her purse. "I don't wanna be here when he finally does come home. I don't trust myself to be in the same room with him. No telling what I might do."

"Call me when you get home, Mama," said Brenda, not able to hide the relief on her face as her mother headed towards the door, "So I know you got home safe."

Irene nodded as she reached for the doorknob. She turned back to look at her daughter. "You know Brenda I just don't get it. You've been carrying the full weight of the family ever since you and Jerome got married. This isn't even his house. It's his grandmama's house," said Irene, shaking her head and holding onto the doorknob. "As your mother I feel it's my job to protect you, but I don't know what else to do if you won't open your eyes and face the obvious. This man is never gonna make you happy. No matter what you try to do to fix it."

Irene left and closed the door behind her, leaving Brenda to her own thoughts and misery.

CHAPTER 16

After last night's storm had cleared up, sunlight glittered between the trees and pushed through clouds. It was 7:00 AM when Deek and Renee set out to return home to Washington, D. C. On the way back they enjoyed the beauty of a clear Saturday morning. Deek wanted to take her on a tour of Kent Island before they left the Eastern Shore, but Renee told him she needed to get home to see about her cat. That wasn't really the reason. She had left Angel enough extra food and water to last until early evening. The truth was that in case Bill called she didn't want to lie about where she'd been all night. Even though nothing really happened, she couldn't deny the sexual tension between her and Deek. Renee was glad she resisted acting on it. While music from 102.3 FM's Oldies but Goodies station crooned from the radio, Renee remained silent on the ride home in spite of Deek's efforts to draw her out.

Once they reached the gates of Foxhall Crescent Estates, Renee gave him the passcode to lift the security gate. Deek punched in the code on the keypad and drove through.

In his rearview mirror he noticed that the gate took several minutes to lower. He drove along the neighborhood's winding, tree-flanked streets, and periodically took his eyes off the road to sneak a glance at her profile. When Deek reached her house, he parked in the driveway. Before Renee could grab the car door handle, he gently turned her chin so their eyes met. "I'm sorry for putting you in an awkward situation last night. If you want me to keep my distance, I will. Is that what you want, Renee?" While he hoped it wasn't, he needed to hear the truth from her.

Renee looked away in silence. She had strong feelings for Deek, but didn't know what to do about it. She wasn't ready to make drastic, permanent changes in her life. Not even for him. She needed more time. Time to think. Time to find out if there was anything salvageable left in her marriage.

"Don't bother answering, Doc. But just so you know, it's not the end of my wanting you no matter how you feel about me."

"Deek ... I ... Our friendship means the world to me. I wouldn't want anything to ruin that."

"Uh oh, the 'Let's be friends' speech—the kiss of death. The last thing I want is to cause you misery," he said in a serious tone, "Just do me a favor, don't ask me not to care because I can't ever do that."

Before driving off, Deek leaned out the car window. "By the way, call your security management firm and tell them the gate is defective. It's coming down too slowly. Anybody could piggy-back and drive right through behind you."

"All right. I'll call them," she said with sadness in her voice. Renee stood there, not wanting to leave.

He got out of the car and walked over to her. When he kissed her goodbye his trim mustache brushed against her lips. She let her gaze follow him as he got back in his car and drove away. Renee went inside the house and headed straight for the kitchen to check on Angel. All of a sudden her vision blurred and her feet gave way from under her. She knew this sudden unsteadiness could not be the effects of the Lexapro that Helen had prescribed for her because she had not taken it for the past two days. She grabbed the arm of a nearby chair just in time and fell into it, letting her head drop between her knees so the blood could rush to her brain. Perhaps she was anemic. A year had passed since her last physical when she was diagnosed with borderline iron deficiency. And then she wasn't getting any younger. Perhaps, this was the first stages of menopause creeping up on her. Renee shuddered at the thought of how quickly time was running out.

Renee staggered to the kitchen cabinet and gulped down an iron tablet. Soon after swallowing, her stomach convulsed and she ran to the powder room toilet to throw up. Once she had composed herself, she retrieved her phone book and dialed her general practitioner's emergency number. The weekend answering service noted her symptoms and paged the physician on duty. Within twenty minutes, the doctor on duty called. After asking a battery of questions that Renee quickly responded 'no' to, the physician asked, "When was your last menstrual cycle, Mrs. Hayes?" The question took Renee by surprise. She had no idea.

"I'd like you to come into the office for an exam and pregnancy test. If you call on Monday morning at nine, the receptionist will give you an appointment. In the meantime, if you feel nauseous again eat some dry crackers and try a little ginger in your tea. Avoid dairy products and fatty foods for now until one of the OB/GYN's can examine you."

Renee covered her hand over her mouth after hanging up the phone. Pregnancy test? And here she thought her delayed periods were from the onset of menopause. No way would she wait until Monday to make an appointment and then wait even longer to find out if her prayers had been answered. She grabbed her coat and rushed out to the drug store to buy a home pregnancy kit.

Once back home, she sat down to study the instructions in the kit, not wanting her nervous enthusiasm to cause her to skip a crucial step and affect the results. She was sure she followed each step correctly. There was no mistake about the results. The green line meant the test results were positive. Renee couldn't believe it. Her heart raced, but this time it was from joy and not an anxiety attack. A smile stretched across her face as she sat up on the bed with her arms folded about her knees. She found herself chuckling aloud with excitement. She couldn't wait to tell Bill when he returned home from India. She had needed a purpose in life and this was it. She couldn't remember exactly when it happened, but obviously it had happened at least a month ago. Becoming a mother would give her life meaning. She'd been cheated out of motherhood at sixteen and now at 45 years old, this was her last chance.

She and Bill would have to try harder to save their marriage. She didn't feel the type of passion for him as she now knew she was capable of feeling, but that didn't matter any more. She would forego passion so that her baby would grow up with both parents. She had counseled enough adult children of divorced parents to witness the far-reaching emotional scars later in life. Always in a psychoanalytical frame of mind, Renee raced through the implications of how a divorce might effect her baby later in life. Many of her own patients who had grown up with divorced parents feared loss, change, and betrayal in their own adult relationships. They could appear fine on the outside, but once they tried to have relationships of their own, these fears that were created when their parents divorced often manifested. From her training in psychology, Renee compared children of divorce to what happened in her childhood and saw striking similarities. Divorce resulted in many of the same abandonment emotional scars that occur when a parent is absent due to death. Her mother had left when she was 7 years old, and when a parent is just not there, as in her father's case …

"Stop it Renee," she admonished herself out loud. "You haven't even given birth yet but you're already projecting your fears into the baby's future. Now is the time to celebrate and be thankful for this blessing!"

But she couldn't control the onslaught of negative, anxious feelings. She worried about how Bill would react to the news. He had been perfectly clear about his feelings on fatherhood. Adopted or natural, Bill did not want children. To make matters worse, Renee recalled her last obstetrician's warning six years ago when she had suffered an abnormal gestation from an ectopic pregnancy that had to be aborted in order to save her life. The doctors said even if she were fortunate enough to conceive, in all likelihood the fetus would spontaneously abort within the first three months because of possible birth defects or would have to be terminated to avoid a health risk as was the case the last time she got pregnant. According to the best medical experts Renee would never deliver a normal, full-term, healthy baby without putting her own life in jeopardy.

She would refuse to accept their doom and gloom predications. She would believe the baby growing in her womb was a gift from God, and only God could save him. Renee put on her coat and rushed back out the front door. Even though it was a Saturday late in the afternoon, something compelled her towards the church that Brenda attended, the Nativity Catholic Church on Georgia Avenue. She arrived a few minutes after the 3:30 Mass had begun. Renee entered the vestibule, dipped her fingers in holy water and made the sign of the cross. Before slipping into the back pew she genuflected in the red-carpeted aisle before the Virgin Mary. The cathedral ceilings, imposing statutes, candles, dim lighting, and beautiful stained glass windows gave the church a surreal atmosphere. The melodious voice of the monsignor echoed throughout the sanctuary. Renee knelt and prayed, making a fervent plea to God to see her pregnancy through to full-term with the delivery of a healthy baby. After mass the congregation filed out. Renee approached the altar and lit a candle for her unborn child. She knelt down and prayed that he or she would survive the next nine months. As she rose to leave, she heard someone whisper her name.

"Dr. Renee?"

Renee turned around and saw Brenda holding her son, Justin.

"I'm glad you came to visit my church, Dr. Renee. I hope you enjoyed this afternoon's Mass. It always brings me peace to come here," said Brenda, struggling to support her wiggling baby with both arms.

"Oh, yes, Brenda. I needed to be here today."

"Is something wrong?" her secretary asked, touching her sleeve, momentarily. Brenda hesitated before continuing, "To be honest, I've been worried about you. You seem to be a little unsteady and preoccupied at times, as if your mind is a hundred miles away. Actually, I tried to reach you last night. When I didn't hear from you I didn't know what to think."

Renee frowned, "I'm sorry, Brenda, I haven't checked my messages yet. I'm all right but why were you calling?"

"Do you have time for a cup of coffee? There's a café called La Baguettes not too far from here."

"Of course, I need to talk to you as well." Renee said, needing to take control.

"Follow me then. I'll show you where it is. I'm warning you though," said Brenda, smiling, "La Baguettes sell the most irresistible fattening pastries and breads."

The café was less than ten minutes away. Renee carried Brenda's decaf coffee, a cup of herbal tea for herself, and two blueberry sconces to an isolated corner where Brenda waited with her son. Brenda's baby sat content in his carrier seat and then fell asleep almost immediately. Renee could tell that something was troubling Brenda.

"Is anything wrong?" Renee asked, with an intense look.

"I shouldn't bother you with my problems, Dr. Renee," said Brenda, staring down at her cup of coffee.

"Don't be silly," Renee said with a wave of her hand, "I'm sorry you couldn't get in touch with me last night when you needed me. I suppose you were shocked to see me at Mass today. I haven't been a practicing Catholic since childhood."

"God sees our hearts, not what particular doctrine or religion we follow."

"I'm glad I went to mass this afternoon," said Renee and took a sip of tea. "The monsignor's words uplifted me and he sang like an angel. I could actually feel the presence of a higher power in the midst. I hope this time God answers my prayer."

Brenda nodded, "Me too."

"I finally realize what you've been saying all along, Brenda. I need more than my psychotherapeutic textbook training to get me through problems in life."

"Yes, prayer is powerful. We all need the Lord's unconditional love, his guidance and protection, especially during these uncertain times. If we pray and believe, he'll see us through anything … in His time though, not ours. He's the one in control, you know."

"So they say," said Renee, nodding in agreement as if she finally understood. "One thing's for sure, I'm certainly not in control."

"Has something happened to make you renew your faith, Dr. Renee?"

Renee smiled down into her cup and encircled it with both hands as the heat warmed her palms. "Yes, Brenda. Something wonderful has happened." Renee looked up and met Brenda's curious eyes, "Believe it or not, at 45 years old," she stopped, filled up with tears. She suddenly realized Brenda would be the first person she told. This would seal a bond between them. "…Brenda, I'm pregnant. I can hardly believe it myself after all these years of wishing for it to happen again." Renee's face lit up upon sharing her news.

Brenda leaped from her chair and gave Renee a tight embrace. "I'm so happy for you. Don't worry about anything," beamed Brenda, "I'll be there to help you. I can even be your LaMaze coach if you need one, but I guess your husband will want that privilege."

"I don't expect any special treatment. You have your own family to take care of." Renee glanced down at the sleeping baby in the carrier seat and smiled. "I'll be just fine. As for my husband, he doesn't know yet."

"Well, I'm sure he'll be thrilled to hear your news when he gets back from India."

"I hope so but I pray that I can carry this pregnancy to term. I'm not as young as I used to be and I've had problems in the past. I don't think I could stand it if I lost this baby."

"Don't worry Dr. Renee, God won't put more on us than we can handle. You deserve to be happy. I couldn't survive losing my baby either," said Brenda smiling down at her fat-cheeked son, "For me, having Justin is my biggest joy."

"Enough about my news, Brenda. Forgive me for rambling on about myself when you obviously wanted to talk to me about something. I'm sorry I wasn't there when you called last night. What can I help you with dear?"

Brenda stared down at her folded hands resting on top the table and hesitated. Renee put down her cup then spoke to Brenda in a comforting voice. "You can trust me, Brenda. Just tell me what's on your mind."

After a few moments Brenda's eyes clouded as she told Renee the whole ugly story about her husband, Jerome—about how she found out from talking to Jerome's boss last night that he got fired from his job—about how she later discovered that he was at Leenae's, his ex-girlfriend's apartment, not at work where she expected him to be.

"Dr. Renee, I really thought things were going pretty good for us. You know Veda works at UDS too, right?" Brenda felt encouraged by Dr. Renee's nod and the caring look in her eyes. "Well, I had asked Veda to keep an eye on him at work and let me know if she noticed any sign of trouble. I know I shouldn't have been spying on my husband, but I wanted to make sure he stayed on the straight and narrow."

While confiding her troubles to Dr. Renee, Brenda suddenly realized how desperate she must sound. Still, she couldn't seem to stop herself from revealing all the ugly details. Fortunately, Dr. Renee remained silent and non-judgmental. Somehow it made Brenda feel better to get it all out. Brenda recited the lie that Jerome had first told her when he finally came home at six o'clock that morning—that he'd been assigned to an overnight run. When Brenda let him know that she had already spoken to his boss, Jerome confessed about being let go.

"Naturally, I confronted him about where he'd really been all night," said Brenda, getting teary-eyed. "He didn't deny where he'd been, but he claimed he was an innocent victim. Said his supervisor hated him—that's why she fired him. He said he never had problems when he reported to his uncle." Brenda sighed and dabbed at her eyes with the napkin.

"Of course, he didn't mention anything about failing a random drug test until I let him know that I already knew the truth about why his boss had fired him."

"Did he admit to taking drugs?" asked Dr. Renee.

Brenda shook her head. "I love my husband, Dr. Renee, but he is a habitual liar. I don't know what to believe."

"What did Jerome say happened?"

Brenda shrugged then looked downward as she spoke. "He kept insisting that the so-called random drug test had to be wrong. He said his boss had it in for him from the start. He was angry and stressed out about getting fired and that's why he gave in to his ex-girlfriend, only once, he claims—to the free drugs that Leenae offered to him." Even as she relayed her husband's excuse for his actions, Brenda knew it sounded feeble and lame. "Jerome begged me to give him another chance and to help him be strong."

"I see," said Dr. Renee, circling the rim of her cup with her finger. "Do you know what you're going to do now?"

Brenda looked up. "Honestly, I don't know what to do, Dr. Renee. This isn't the first time Jerome has screwed up. But like a fool I really believed all our problems were over and that he'd truly changed. Apparently, I was wrong." Brenda avoided Dr. Renee's stare once more so she wouldn't have to see the pity in her employer's eyes. "Maybe you could give me the name of a good marriage counselor. I know Jerome would be too embarrassed to talk to you about what he's done, Dr. Renee," said Brenda.

Renee had listened quietly without interjecting her opinion. Other than a few questions now and then, the only sound she made was from stirring her tea as the spoon scraped against her tea cup. Brenda wept softly, and Renee took her hand, still without speaking. Renee wasn't surprised when Brenda asked her to recommend a marriage counselor. She understood why Brenda would want to see someone neutral since Jerome might feel like he was outnumbered if she counseled the couple, being Brenda's employer. Renee felt relieved that Brenda asked for a referral.

She resisted the urge to explain to her secretary that she was in denial. Better to let another professional do that, Renee thought. She would recommend someone well qualified and let that other therapist help Brenda see what was obvious to everyone else. Brenda's story sounded like so many other women she had counseled in the past who described their parasitic and selfish mates. These women stayed in relationships stemmed in neglect, lies or serious abuse. It always turned out the same. Like Brenda, they waited, prayed, and hoped for miraculous personality changes in their men. Instead, they got mistreated or disappointed time and time again. As Renee let these observations about Brenda stew around in her head, she quickly dismissed the question that arose from her intellectual mind. How was she any different in expecting Bill to change and become someone he clearly was not? Wasn't she too, in denial?

Renee closed her eyes momentarily and willed herself to remain focused on Brenda without making comparisons to herself. Yes, she would let another psychologist help Brenda realize the inevitable truth about her husband, Jerome—that he was probably the type of guy who would always shoot holes in her lifeboat. Brenda was smart, pretty, and ambitious. She worked hard, studied computer technology to improve her career opportunities and took care of her son with almost no help. Renee didn't understand why she kept going back to a man like Jerome who was too dense to simply climb on board so that his very capable wife could save them both. Instead, he seemed determined to drag his family down. She didn't know Brenda's husband that well, had only met him a few times but she was still angry at the pain he caused Brenda.

Yet, even as a trained psychologist, Renee didn't feel like she was in any position to judge her secretary's choice in life partners. Besides, who was she to judge? Her own marriage had been devoid of emotional energy and intimacy for years. This is what had led her to Deek in the first place. Though she found temporary solace in Deek's arms, adultery didn't feel right for her. It left a bad taste in her mouth and she felt consumed with guilt when the moment of ecstasy passed. If she couldn't conquer her own fear of loneliness and go it alone, how could she counsel Brenda to do the same? Brenda would do better seeing another marriage counselor, Renee decided.

"I know an excellent Christian therapist that I can refer you to," said Dr. Renee, patting Brenda's hand. "I hope he'll be able to save your marriage Brenda, if that's what you and Jerome truly want."

Brenda got up and hugged her, "Oh, yes, Dr. Renee. I want that more than anything. I want my family to stay together and I'm sure Jerome does too. He's sick with remorse," said Brenda, returning to her seat.

"Then that's what I want also," said Renee, nodding her head.

Renee was amazed at Brenda's capacity for forgiveness and unconditional love. She hoped she would one day get to that level in her spiritual growth. Brenda said the mere act of forgiveness felt liberating to her even if her relationship with Jerome didn't work out. Though she said she planned to do everything in her power to make her marriage work, and with God's guidance, hopefully it would work if that was His will.

Brenda gathered her belongings and rose to leave. She swung her purse across her shoulder and lifted the baby carrier, with Justin still asleep inside. "Oh, Dr. Renee, don't forget I'll be late on Monday because Justin has a follow-up doctor's appointment in the morning," said Brenda, "but I'll drop him off at the sitter's and come into the office right afterwards."

"I remember you said you weren't happy with Justin's old babysitter. Have you found someone else?" Renee asked.

"Not yet. But I'm interviewing a licensed day care provider on Monday. In the meantime, my mother agreed to watch Justin until I find a new sitter. Hopefully, she won't change her mind at the last minute like she usually does. I think you know after meeting my mother I have a real incentive to find someone else quick. And, for obvious reasons I can't trust Jerome right now."

"Oh, your mother has agreed to watch Justin?" said Renee, unable to hide her surprise and dislike of Brenda's mother.

"I know she's not the grandmotherly type but she does love Justin. And, like I said, I can't leave my baby home with my husband." Renee nodded. After what Brenda had just told her about what Jerome had done, no further explanation was needed.

"Take all the time you need. I'm sure it's not easy finding adequate daycare these days. Guess I'll find that out first hand soon enough," Renee smiled and touched her stomach.

"Thanks for being understanding. I really don't want to take any more time off if I can help it. With my mother watching Justin that makes it urgent for me to find a permanent babysitter right away." They both let out an understanding laugh and gave each other a hug goodbye.

On Sunday the next morning, Renee's telephone rang at 9:00 AM sharp, though because of her exhilaration about being pregnant she had been up for hours. It was Bill calling from Bangalore, India. "Hey, babe, I just wanted to let you know I got here okay. I'm staying at Maurya Hotel. If you need me here's the number at the hotel in case you can't get through to my cell phone," Bill rattled off a long series of digits while Renee wrote them down.

"What's it like in India and how was your flight? I miss you already,

Darling," said Renee, all in one breath. She burst with excitement to tell him the news about her pregnancy but resisted since she thought it would be better to tell him in person.

"It's amazing here, Renee. I can't begin to describe it all right now. I don't have much time, Hon, but look for something special from me in the next few days. It should be arriving by registered airmail. I know I messed up on your birthday so I'm sending you a present now and I'll surprise you with something else even more spectacular when I get home."

"That's sweet, Bill. When will you be coming home? I have a surprise for you too," she smiled.

"You do, huh? I can't wait to see it. Looks like I'll be getting in this Thursday afternoon if everything goes as planned. I've got a million things to do while I'm here. First, I have to make sure those employment screenings that the Embassy scheduled for tomorrow proceed without a hitch, and then I have to give the guys an Orientation about what to expect when they get to the States, among a hundred other things. I'll give you another call in a few days before I leave. I'd better get going, Babe. You know how to reach me if you have to."

"All right. Good-bye, Darling. Love you."

"Gotta go now. Bye," he said and blew a quick kiss into the phone, then hung up.

He ended the conversation a little too abruptly and forgot to say he loved her or ask how she was feeling. When the phone rang again a few seconds later, she thought it was Bill calling back to apologize. But it wasn't Bill. It was Deek.

"Good morning, Sweetheart. I thought it was probably safe to call since you said Bill would be gone for a few days. Forgive me for calling so early, but I just couldn't resist the urge to hear your voice after I woke up thinking about you this morning. Renee, I swear I can still smell your perfume from Friday night. I didn't wake you did I, baby?"

"No, I'm awake just not quite up yet. Are you in D.C. or did you go back to your Kent Island cottage?"

"I'm here in the trenches," he sighed. "I have to confess, Renee I was hoping I could see you again today," said Deek, "I know we just saw each other yesterday when I dropped you off, but can I take you to lunch at one of my favorite spots? There's this great Caribbean restaurant on 12th and U called The Islander. Their Calypso Shrimp melts in your mouth. Nothing fancy just good home cooking. You can come as you are. What do you say?"

"Hold on a moment Deek," said Renee, suddenly feeling nauseous.

She dropped the phone and held one hand over her mouth. Normally, she loved Caribbean cuisine but the thought of spicy food made her stomach feel queasy. She took a bite of a cracker that she had left on her nightstand and slowly swallowed it before coming back to the phone.

"Are you feeling all right, Sweetheart?" asked Deek, "You looked a little pale when I brought you home yesterday. I waited all day on Saturday, hoping you'd call me, but you didn't. Is there anything you need?"

"No thanks, I'm okay. Please don't worry about me. I'm sorry I can't go to lunch. I really need to rest today since I have a lot of commitments on my plate coming up this week. Deek, I have to go now, there's another call coming in. Goodbye." After Renee hung up, she realized she must have sounded just as rude and abrupt as Bill did when he had just called her. There was nothing she could do about that now.

Her priorities had suddenly shifted. She was going to have a baby and she knew it meant the end of her close friendship with Deek. She couldn't face the temptation. He would never want her anyway once he found out she was pregnant with Bill's child. Eventually, he would find out, but for now she didn't want to create any stress or complications. She didn't regret spending time with him on Friday. He always made her feel happy and alive. She still loved Deek and might always love him in a special way. Their time together had transcended her wildest imagination, but it would have to be only an unforgettable memory. Deek could no longer be a part of her life. Since she couldn't have both, she chose motherhood and her marriage. To her, they were one in the same because she could not risk imposing some future emotional scars on her child like the scars she had suffered growing up. Her unborn baby provided a new purpose and that meant letting go of her impetuous, fantasy life of a future with the handsome Detective Deek Hamilton.

Renee quickly got up and dressed and headed out to the bookstore. She spent hours combing through books about pregnancy, childbirth, and the first five years of baby's life. She bought over $200 worth of books for expectant mothers and a few fatherhood references for Bill. Hopefully, Bill's books wouldn't collect dust over the next seven and a half months and he'd actually get around to reading them. When Renee returned home, she curled up on the sofa with an afghan draped across her legs and poured through her new extensive library. The news of her pregnancy would be a blessing for everybody who loved her. She decided to not tell her father while he was still in prison. When he came home for Christmas he'd find out he was going to be a grandfather. By then she would certainly be showing. She felt so happy a permanent smile stayed on her face. When Angel suddenly leaped on top her lap and didn't get shooed away, Renee realized she had either entered a new state of bliss or complete insanity.

On Monday morning, Renee spoke to her OB/GYN at Sibley Memorial Hospital and made an appointment for an exam and a urine pregnancy test for the following Monday at 10:30 AM. Renee was disappointed that her doctor couldn't see her sooner. Next Monday was a full week away. Still, Renee preferred to deliver her baby at Sibley because of its advances and innovative techniques in obstetrics over the years. In addition to the pregnancy test, her doctor ordered a sonogram because of Renee's age and past medical history. Renee hoped she could convince Bill to come with her to her first prenatal visit since he'd be back from India by then. He'd be able to hear her prognosis straight from the doctor's mouth. Finally, after fourteen years of marriage they were going to actually have a baby. When he saw their baby growing inside her womb on the sonogram, this would certainly make him excited about becoming a father, she thought. Though nervous about her husband's reaction to becoming a father, she couldn't wait to tell him the news. His flight would be coming in at 3 o'clock on Thursday. How could she wait four whole days to tell him? Thursday seemed so far away.

Renee scanned the appointment book on her desk. To her dismay, patients were lined up back-to-back until five o'clock and her first appointment was due to arrive shortly at 9:30 AM. She'd be alone this morning. She recalled Brenda saying she had to come in late because of Justin's follow-up visit with the pediatrician. Luckily, Renee conducted new patient evaluations only on Fridays. All her appointments today would be longtime clients. After taking a gulp of coffee she suddenly worried if the caffeine and the Lexapro she had been taking might harm the baby. She jumped up and poured the coffee out in the bathroom sink. From now on, milk, juice, herbal tea or Evian water would have to suffice. She still had almost a whole bottle full of pills in her medicine cabinet, but she didn't need to take those pills now. It had been days since she was struck with an anxiety attack. In fact, she was feeling good about her life.

Renee pulled the patient files and placed the stack on her desk. She previewed the first patient's file. It occurred to her that she should cut back on her practice until after she had delivered a healthy baby. She couldn't take any chances with undue stress. Renee decided to refer some of her recently accepted patients to other colleagues. She didn't want anyone on her caseload that might turn aggressive and troublesome over the next nine months while she was undergoing a delicate pregnancy. She recognized her obligations as a therapist and felt bad about having to drop some new patients, however, she had to be concerned about her health and this pregnancy. That was her main priority now. At forty-five years old and with a history of at-risk pregnancies, she couldn't afford to take any chances.

Renee analyzed her current workload to see where she could cut back. She finally decided that the only one of her new patients she planned to continue to counsel was the pregnant teenager, Heather Hollingsworth that she had met last week. For many reasons Renee identified with this troubled teenager. She felt she had sparked a rapport with Heather on Friday and could eventually establish communication between the girl and her parents. Mrs. Hollingsworth was clearly one of those mothers who needed to be in control and who was always right—not unlike her Aunt Clara or Brenda's mother, she thought. There was no way Renee would abandon that young girl and send her somewhere else after establishing trust. That left Renee with only four active cases to deal with and one of the four was clearly asymptomatic, but she still met with Dr. Renee once a week out of habit.

Several hours later, after the morning patient rush had ended, Renee heard a computer boot up outside the office. She figured it was Brenda just getting settled at her desk. Renee opened the office door and walked out into the reception area to greet her and ask about her son. After finding out that Justin was doing fine, she returned to her office to prepare for the next patient. Throughout the day between clients, Renee floated about in ecstasy as if in a daze. She zoned in and out of what her patients were saying. After all, she had heard it before. Renee touched her stomach and could barely contain her joy or think about anything else. When she passed by a mirror and caught her reflection, she noticed a perpetual grin planted on her face. Some of her patients stared at her strangely but she didn't care.

CHAPTER 17 - JEROME

One of Jerome's favorite daytime game shows was playing on television, but instead of really listening to it, he sat slumped on the couch, momentarily lost in his thoughts. He hadn't been able to convince Brenda to leave Baby Buddha home with him this morning. From the way she acted you would think he had to pass Babysitting 101 to take care of his own kid. Instead of leaving the little guy home with his daddy, Brenda took their son to his mother-in-law's house. He knew his mother-in-law hated him and as far as he was concerned, he felt the same way about Mrs. Irene Adams. He already knew what Brenda's mama must be saying about him now that he had found himself once again broke, unemployed and living in his Grandmama's house. He recalled what Mrs. Adams had said to Brenda in earshot of him waiting in the next room just before they got married. *"That boy's a drugged out, lying, womanizing deadbeat and you can do better Baby Girl."* Irene's words had cut sharp and left no confusion about her feelings toward him. Jerome would never forget her hate spewing eyes that day as she tried to talk Brenda out of marrying him.

Jerome didn't want to think about Irene Adams. He let out a frustrated sigh and shook his head as he glanced about the cluttered house, wondering where to begin. Clothes and toys were scattered about, dirty dishes sat stacked in the sink, and the vacuum cleaner was parked in the middle of the living room floor, still untouched from Friday, the day Brenda discovered that he had been fired. Since he hadn't gotten up until close to noon, the day was already half gone and what did he have to show for it? The least he could do is cook dinner and clean the house before Brenda and Baby Buddha got home he decided. That might help start the week off right, he thought.

Jerome sprung from the couch and went into the kitchen. He swung open the freezer door and peered into it. Noise from the television game show echoed from the living room, but he decided to ignore it and focus on what to cook for dinner. "Wonder what my Baby'll want for dinner tonight?" Jerome asked himself out loud as he tried to decide what Brenda would like for dinner. "Hum, let's see ... pork chops, beef or chicken?" he wondered, while moving packages of frozen food around in the freezer. "Think I'll fix us a good ole country fried chicken dinner tonight with biscuits and gravy, just like Mama Etta used to make. I bet Shortie'll like that."

He had given to talking to himself out loud when nobody else was around. For some reason, the sound of his own voice helped to relax him. He'd give himself private little pep talks that seemed to boost his confidence and morale. Jerome took out a pack of fryer chicken parts and set the package on the counter. He grabbed a large bowl from under the cupboard and filled it with cool water. "Yeah, that's just what I'ma do," he nodded to himself, "Surprise my Boo with a clean house and dinner already cooked when she gets home from work this evening. I gotta do somethin' to make up for all the mess I got myself into again." Jerome picked up a silver serving spoon and admired his reflection on the back of the spoon. "But can a Brother help it if the good Lord made him fine as hell and irresistible to women?" said Jerome, rubbing his chin and smiling. "Seems like they either love me or hate me."

He removed the wrapping and plopped the frozen chicken in the bowl of water. Jerome looked around the kitchen as if trying to decide what to do next. "Let's see now. I might have to refresh my memory on how to cook this bird. I know I can put it down in the bedroom," he chuckled, "but I ain't no Emeril in the kitchen." Jerome shook his head when he thought about first, his ex-girlfriend, Leenae Lewis and now his former boss, Odessa Dillon who had unjustly fired him. Both women were crazy as hell as far as he was concerned. Neither one wanted to take 'No' for an answer, and now they hated him for rejecting them. Like it or not, they would have to accept it because more than anything he loved Brenda and his son. Nothing else mattered to him but doing right by his family.

He opened one of the cabinet doors and pulled down his grandmother's worn-out cookbook from the top shelf. He sat down at the kitchen table and thumbed through the recipes. When he found the recipe for country fried chicken, he smiled and pointed to it. "Yeah, that's it," he said and marked the page with a piece of torn newspaper. "I can read so I should be able to follow these here simple directions." He thought about how Brenda went out to work every morning and still managed to put things in order when she got home and whip up a decent meal in less than thirty minutes. He didn't see why he wouldn't be able to do that too when he had all day to accomplish the same tasks. "Let's see now," he said, rubbing his hands together, "I'ma need some Crisco, some flour, and some seasonings." He retrieved all the ingredients that the recipe called for and set everything out on the counter for easy access once the chicken had thawed enough for him to work with.

He returned to the living room and picked up the toys and shoved everything in the hall closet. Next, he sorted and folded the clean clothes that had been spread out on the sofa, separating the piles of clothes into his, Brenda's and the baby's things. As he was just about to start vacuuming he heard the doorbell ring. "Damn. I'm in no mood for company right now," he said, and headed towards the door to see who it was interrupting him from his housework. "That better not be no church people trying to get me saved."

He looked through the peephole and saw his buddy from work, Alonzo Woods, standing on the porch. Alonzo had on one of his more flamboyant outfits, matching red slacks, shirt, shoes, and socks. Jerome swung open the door and reared back laughing. "Man, you look like Superfly in that ridiculous getup," said Jerome, pointing and laughing as he waved Alonzo into the house. "Hurry up and get your ass in here, Fool before my neighbors see you."

"You just jealous 'cause you ain't got this hookup," grinned Alonzo, with his chest puffed out. "Man, even my drawers and T-shirt match. Check it out, Brother."

"No thanks," said Jerome, turning his head away just as Alonzo lowered his waistband to reveal a snitch of red underwear.

"Why ain't you at work, Buddy?" Jerome asked. "They bump you to the night shift or something?"

"Nah, Man. The Barracuda suspended me for three days for a methods violation so I'm out here just chillin'. You know what I'm sayin'?"

"Damn, Man. Now, she's starting in on you."

"Nah, she been on my black ass from day one, Slick," said Alonzo.

"Hey Man, you don't wanna piss-off Barracuda. You know she's horny as shit," laughed Jerome. "Why don't you just sleep with her? Ain't that what you told me to do, Partner?"

"She don't want none of my old meat, Jay," said Alonzo, shaking his head. Alonzo paused for a moment and Jerome detected a brief look of exasperation on his friend's face. "Why you think I'm here, Dawg? If I can get you to play nice with the lady, she'll fix that drug report and hire you back, Brother. Won't that be better than sittin' around here all damn day doin' nothin'?"

"Ugh! Alonzo, have you lost your damn mind? That woman's got more hair on her legs than I do. Naw, Man," said Jerome, waving his hand and shaking his head. "I have a beautiful wife and a baby boy. Why would I screw her fat-ass just to get my old job back?" Jerome gestured with open palms, questioningly.

"You should go on and tap that, Jay. She's got a decent-looking face. You can't deny that." Alonzo momentarily stared down at his red polished shoes.

"Maybe so, Alonzo. But she might hurt me with them big ass titties of hers."

They both laughed.

"Don't worry I'ma get my job back at UDS and with back pay too," said Jerome as he stretched out his arms confidently on top of the couch. "Once I prove she had no right firing me. In the meantime I got me a new job lined up as a night security guard. If everything checks out with my references, I could be starting as early as next Monday. So you see, Alonzo, I'm not desperate for Odessa's crumbs. Besides, I like being at home during the day, cookin', cleanin' and fixing things around the house."

"Okay, Martha Stewart," said Alonzo as he settled down on the couch beside Jerome, turning to face him. As Alonzo spoke, Jerome noticed that his buddy's eyes flickered about nervously. "But just so you know, she told me to tell you she'll give you a gravy run makin' 50 K if you drop the case."

"What kinda gravy run?" asked Jerome, folding his arms across his chest and giving Alonzo a skeptical look.

Alonzo played with a pack of unfiltered Marlboros and kept taking them out of his pocket and putting them back. "For starters, she said you can shift in the yard. All you gotta do is drive the truck from bay to bay. You don't even have to load, unload or sort anything. Somebody else'll do all that and you'll be makin' $50,000 a year," Alonzo explained. "You know Jay, I been at UDS ten years and I'm still on call and don't have my own route. Only the guys who been there 25 years get to shift in the yard for that kinda pay, Brother. So whaddya say, Man? Miss Dillon's offering you what the seniors get."

"Now she's Miss Dillon? Humph," said Jerome, wincing as he shook his head. "Beam me up Scotty—there's no intelligent life here."

Jerome plopped his feet up on the coffee table. "You not hearin' me Alonzo. Lemme put it to you this way … I ain't *never* gonna have sex with *that* woman."

"That's cool Jay," said Alonzo. "But don't say I didn't warn you. Hey, Man, you got a beer or somethin' in this palace? I know better than to light up in this air-fresh house, but at least a Brother can get a drink, can't he?"

"Nah, Man. I need to stay clear of alcohol. That's a trigger for me. My sponsor's coming by tonight at 8 to take me to my re-hab meeting. Want some lemonade or some orange juice?"

"You're kiddin' right?" said Alonzo, turning up his nose in disbelief. "Damn Jay, I see you really mean business this time."

"That's right. My wife took me back for the umpf-teenth time and I'm not gonna mess up again. I don't want nothin' to do with Odessa Dillon or UDS. Not until they receive my EEO suit papers that I plan to file against her and the company. Then I'll let my lawyer speak for me. I'ma ask my Uncle Ike to help me start the complaint next week as soon as he gets back from Las Vegas."

Alonzo gave Jerome a surprised look but quickly composed himself. "Oh, so that's where the old dude's been hiding out," said Alonzo. "On vacation, huh? So you goin' all the way with this suit, huh Jay?"

"Damn straight. Odessa's been getting' away with this shit for too long. I heard last year she was playing footsie with Hector Gonzales but he finally got Big C to put him on another route to get away from her. Everybody's scared of her, but I'm not."

"Does your uncle know about all the troubles you been havin' at work, Man?"

"Naw. I didn't wanna worry him about it. He stuck his neck out to get me that gig. He still don't know I been fired yet on that trumped up random drug test. Odessa's gone too far this time. Uncle Ike's been a supervisor at UDS for the last 8 years and he's worked there for twenty. I know he can help me file my complaint and get it to the right people."

"I dunno, Man," said Alonzo, shaking his head as he stuffed his hand in his pants pocket and began fidgeting with his cars keys. "I can't see how in the hell you gonna talk your way out of a positive random drug test. The evidence is pretty air tight against you, Man."

"Man, that test was bogus!" yelled Jerome. "I swear I didn't do no coke that day. I coulda ate a Poppy Seed muffin that morning for breakfast or maybe the test was off. I don't know what the hell happened, but I didn't do no damn drugs! At least not before I took that test."

"I doubt that poppy seed story is gonna hold up in court," laughed Alonzo.

"Go to hell, Man. I ain't got time for your bullshit. I gotta get back to my cleanin' before Brenda gets home." Jerome shot up from the couch, hoping Alonzo would catch the hint and split, but Alonzo still sat there. Jerome walked over to the picture window and drew back the drapes so he could see outside.

"Not that I'm justifying Odessa's behavior or anything," said Alonzo, "but her life ain't been easy. You know, her husband caught a bullet during a drive by shooting six years ago. She's been a lonely widow ever since."

"Good for him," Jerome turned and sniped back. "They put him out of his misery of having to live with her."

"You know you makin' it hard for everybody in the yard, Jay," said Alonzo with a frustrated sigh.

"That's not my problem, Man." Jerome stood in the middle of the living room. He rubbed his hand over his clean-shaven head.

"You a damn fool Jay," said Alonzo, staring down at his feet, but still not moving to leave. "If it was me, I'd go for the easy money and keep my damn mouth shut. Just sit back and reap the benefits. Nobody would be the wiser."

"Look Alonzo, when I wouldn't accept her advances, I kept

getting railroaded for methods, lateness, absenteeism, failure to follow directions. You name it, any little bullshit violation she could pin on me. But I kept on turning her down. Do you know one day she even ..." Jerome hesitated. He was almost trembling with rage. He couldn't bring himself to relate what had happened that day she actually followed him into the men's room. He was using the urinal and didn't see her come in. He felt someone's presence behind him, but he just naturally figured it was another dude. When he turned around and zipped up his pants, there she stood—grinning at him seductively. In complete shock, all he managed to say was, "What the fuck!" She tried to play it off and said she was just in there checking behind the new cleaning crew. He hadn't said another word. He just stormed past her, right out the door.

That incident was another thing he planned to put in his sexual harassment and unjustified firing complaint. But he couldn't tell Alonzo about that scene in the men's room. Besides, it was obvious this fool was going back and telling her everything. He'd tell Alonzo just what he wanted to get back to her. That way she'd know he wasn't one of those other chumps she'd been dealing with. He planned to get paid big. Just being relocated to some other supervisor was not enough. Her little gravy run offer to work exclusively in the yard for $50,000 a year was not enough either. Before it was over, he'd have enough to buy Brenda her own house.

Jerome turned to face Alonzo. "Naw, never mind. Anyway, next thing I know, I fail a random drug test and get fired. Doesn't that sound just a little bit suspicious to you?" asked Jerome, staring Alonzo in the face. "That's why I intend to put in a complaint to HR against her. Otherwise, this shit ain't never gonna end."

"Jay. Do you know how many fools have tried to go to HR before you got there?" said Alonzo. "Those assholes down in HR don't do shit. Man, nothin' ever comes out of those complaints." He waved his hand absently in the air.

"Yeah, I found that out too after talkin' to some of those guys. That's why I'ma school Uncle Ike on what's been happening to me as soon as he gets back from Vegas. And, I won't stop at United Delivery Services's HR department," Jerome explained, "I think I got a good shot at winning a sexual harassment case with EEO."

"Are you crazy, Man? You don't wanna bring the damn federal government into this. Nobody at UDS is gonna testify against the Barracuda. You'll be all alone."

Jerome slumped down in a nearby chair. "Well, I talked to Hector before he left to report to his new supervisor. He said he wished he had taken his situation further. But he's got eight mouths to feed and can't risk losing his job and being outta work while an EEO arbitrator looks into his complaint."

"And you *can* risk that?" asked Alonzo.

Jerome answered with passion in his voice, "That woman needs to be stopped and somebody has to have the guts to stand up to her. Odessa Dillon may be the boss and well, okay her face ain't half bad to look at, but I ain't nobody's stud."

Alonzo shifted in his seat and screwed up his face before he spoke, as if deciding what tactic he should try next. "You know Jay, word on the street is, you owe a couple of bad dudes some dough." That got Jerome's attention, so Alonzo proceeded on, "I'm sure Miss Dillon would give you the bread straight up if you started being nice to her. The way I see it, your narrow ass belongs to either those lowlifes you usta hang with or Big Mama. And, your homies don't like dudes."

"Listen Man," said Jerome, pointing a finger at Alonzo, "You need to get this through your big empty head. I don't need Odessa or her money. My Uncle Ike's gonna help me straighten everything out. I don't know who you been talkin' to out in the streets, but I'm cool with those dudes. Ain't nobody after me, understand?"

"Aw'ight, I gotcha Baby," said Alonzo with a half grin, "Don't be mad at me, Slick. I'm just one begger trying to help another Brother get a crust of bread."

"I ain't mad at you Alonzo. I'm just keeping it real."

"I may as well split then," said Alonzo as he got up and headed for the door, "I'm getting nowhere fast trying to talk some sense into you, Jay."

"Okay. Later, Man. Stay outta trouble," said Jerome and slapped the palm of Alonzo's outstretched hand.

"You the one, Baby. I'ma head on over to the Eclipse on Bladensburg Road so I can brush up on my Bop and hand-dance. Say Man, why don't you come on out to the club with me this Friday night? They gonna have Trouble Funk, EU, and Chuck Brown as a special guest."

"Chuck who? Nah, Alonzo. Think I'll pass, Brother," said Jerome, shaking his head and chuckling.

Alonzo shrugged. "Suit yourself. You youngsters today just don't know good music. Later, Slick." Alonzo waved, then, stretched out his hand. Jerome slapped him on his open palm one last time as a parting gesture of friendship.

After Alonzo left, Jerome slumped back down on the coach. He clicked the remote to a daytime talk show. Alonzo's visit had rubbed salt in his wounds. He had been trying hard not to think about his former boss and ruin his day. Now, he couldn't stop thinking about how she had railroaded him. "Uncle Ike'll help me clip that Barracuda's fangs." Jerome nodded. "Just wait 'til they slap my EEO compliant on that heifer's desk. This is one Brother, Odessa Dillon's gonna regret tryin' to set up." Jerome cringed at the image of the woman the guys in the yard had nicknamed 'The Barracuda.' Mid-fifties, big boned with an equal combination of fat and muscle, dark eyes that could turn on you in a second, and always horny as hell—this is how he would describe Odessa Dillon if anybody asked. He had to admit that some men might find her attractive—he just wasn't one of them. Jerome pushed the thought of her out of his mind. He forced himself to block out his former place of employment and everybody who worked there. He also couldn't quite erase the fact that Odessa Dillon wasn't his only problem.

He still owed the Jett Set Crew a lot of money and had no idea how he would get his hands on that kind of cash right now. Again, the only person in the world who could help him out of both fixes was Uncle Ike. With Uncle Ike's help, he'd pay back his debt as well as file a sexual harassment complaint against Odessa Dillon. That way he'd eventually get his old job back, Odessa would be the one they'd let go, and he'd have a nice pocket of change in the bank from the successful lawsuit. Of course, he planned to split the award money from his lawsuit with Uncle Ike. This was the way Jerome chose to see the outcome of his current problems.

Just then the doorbell rang again. "Now, who the hell can this be?" he said and raised himself from the couch in no particular hurry. Jerome took his time getting to the door. The doorbell rang at least four or five times in succession. Whoever it was at the door, sounded determined. This time he didn't bother to check through the peephole, but simply swung open the door. "What the hell! What the hell are you doing here, Leenae? asked Jerome, not bothering to invite her in. She held a shoe box under her arm and without invitation or uttering a single word, she elbowed past him and entered the house. Jerome didn't need an answer. He could tell by the scowl on her face that she was pissed and he knew why.

"Look Jerome," she finally spoke, jutting out her chest in defiance. "We both know you shoulda married me." Jerome didn't know what to say. Her eyes were charcoal-black slits of hatred as she glared at him. He found himself standing in the middle of the living room, facing her. Not knowing what to do and hoping Brenda didn't come home early and find her there, he stood defenseless against Leenae's rage.

"Why the hell did you walk out on me Saturday morning after all your promises Friday night. When I got up that morning, you were gone. All I found was this sorry-ass scribble you left on my kitchen table. Telling me you couldn't see me again. You know after all we been through together I don't deserve that bullshit. Friday night you said you was gonna move in with me, you remember that?" She still clutched onto the shoebox under one arm, and pointed her finger at him with her free hand.

Jerome finally found some words and coughed them up slowly. "I don't have no good reason for what I done this past Friday night," he said in a gentle tone, trying unsuccessfully to soften the stern look on her face. "I can see now it wasn't a good idea to try to stay friends with you after me and Brenda got married. When I got fired, I needed a friend. I couldn't tell Brenda what had happened at work. I thought you could be that friend but I took advantage of you and I'm sorry."

"Sorry don't cut it, buster."

Leenae placed the shoe box on the coffee table. He looked at it and hoped she didn't have a gun stashed in there. Then he reasoned she'd probably have her gun inside the leather pocketbook that hung from her shoulder, for easier access.

She placed both hands on her hips as she spoke. "Me and you go way back. We been knowin' each other since tenth grade. We had a good thing going 'til she went and stole you from me." He could tell her voice was rising and her face had started to look flushed. He had to be easy with Leenae because he knew this chick was not in her right mind. Jerome held out both arms to her as he tried to explain. "Look Leenae. I never lied to you. You always knew I loved Brenda. Now that we have a son together, I can't risk losing that. Not even to keep a friendship with you."

"I'm tired of your bullshit, Jerome," she said, "You came to me the other night, remember? You the one begged me to let you stay so she wouldn't find out your ass was fired. After smokin' up my stash and making love to me all night, all I get is some sorry-ass kiss off note!

Jerome's muscles tightened and he swallowed hard. She was right about that. He did go to her looking to get high and needing a place to crash. Now, that he was once again in his right mind, he didn't want to be bothered with her ever again. He took a deep breath and released it before speaking in a sincere tone. "Leenae, I'm truly sorry I hurt you. But please understand this fact. I am never going to leave my wife and son. And I am never going to be with you again. I don't think we should even try to be friends anymore. It'll be best for you and for me."

Leenae snatched up the shoebox from the table and pulled off the lid. She turned the box upside down and dumped its contents on his living room floor. The shoebox had contained a bunch of torn up photos of the two of them since high school as well as other things that he had left at her place over the years. "Go to hell, Jerome Asshole Johnson. You are one lying, no-good Negro that I regret ever trusting in the first place. I musta had brain damage to ever believe in you. Thanks for nothin' Loser." She hurled the empty shoe box at him, and stormed out of the living room, slamming his front door behind her. If any of his neighbors had been outside they would have seen her march out of there and probably would have heard her yelling at him even from inside the house since he had not bothered to close the front door when she barged in.

Leenae had only been there for five minutes, but it was long enough to make a bad day much worse. He bent down and began cleaning up the torn bits of photos and chucking everything in the shoebox to be tossed out into the garbage can outside. He did not want Brenda to come home and find any traces that Leenae had been there, even though she had torn up the pictures in tiny unrecognizable bits. He didn't think things could deteriorate much more, but they did. Not long after Leenae left, the telephone rang. When he picked it up he heard a loud, choppy, offbeat rhythm of percussion, guitar, and trombone playing in the background. Before Jerome could say anything, Bombillo from the Jett Set Crew spoke. "Where's our loot asshole?" Jerome sighed without answering. He stool there in silence and held the phone to his ear, trying to fake a relaxed demeanor. He could not let on to Bombillo that he didn't have things under control.

Jerome and Bombillo had been close friends in the old days. Back in middle school they called him Bruno Morales but now his former running partner was known as Bombillo to his drug-dealing Jett Set crewmembers. Bombillo had been promoted to the ranks of street runner for a known drug kingpin who had dominated the Northwest and Northeast corridor of the city for the past two years.

A Dominican who still spoke English with a Spanish, West Indian accent, he was born in Brooklyn but had lived in D. C. since grade school. Jerome listened while Bombillo talked. Because of their past ties, Bombillo was calling to give Jerome one last warning to show up with the dough he owed the crew for the five grams. Or, Bombillo explained, he wouldn't be able to hold off DL, the crew's official hitman, any longer.

Jerome finally spoke up with as much confidence as he could muster. "Yo, I need you to spot me a coupla more days, Man," said Jerome, "Talk to Delroy for me, Baby."

"Mira, if DL hears you callin' him Delroy, he'll smoke your ass just for that."

"Nah Man, like me and you … me and DL go way back, Dawg. We both knew that chump when he was Delroy McShore." Jerome knew better than to bring up Bombillo's former name.

"That old school shit ain't cuttin' it no more, homie. You gotta come up with the loot right now."

"I'm working on it, Bambillo, but ya'll gotta give me a few more days, Man."

"Aw'ight, I'll see what I can do, Bro. But your bama ass better come up with the cash in a couple days."

"'ppreciate it, Baby. Don't you worry 'bout a thing," said Jerome with an air of coolness.

"I ain't the one who gotta worry." Click. Jerome heard the dial tone after Bombillo hung up.

Jerome hung up the phone gently. He knew how to get the Jett Set Crew's money and he planned to take care of it as soon as he could talk to Uncle Ike. He tried not to think anymore about his money, his women, or his job problems.

Before he could get more than two steps away, the telephone rang again. At first he ignored it, figuring it was probably a tele-marketer this time. After the second ring he thought it might be Brenda calling and she'd worry if he didn't answer. Based on how he was feeling, if it turned out to be another person wanting him to pay off his debt, or even one of those damn telemarketers, he'd come through the phone and break his neck. "Yeah?" Jerome answered gruffly.

"Hey, handsome, how's it going, Baby?" said Brenda.

"It's going," sighed Jerome, not bothering to put on a pretense for Brenda.

"You don't sound so sure," she said. "I was calling to find out what you want for dinner tonight. I have to stop by the grocery store after I pick up Justin, just to get a few staples and stuff that I noticed we're out of."

Jerome perked up. "Don't worry 'bout dinner, Baby. I'm a cook dinner for us tonight. All you gotta do when you get home is put your feet up and relax. I'll even get Baby Buddha ready for bed and fix his bottle if I have time before my 8 o'clock rehab meeting."

"Hum, I could get used to this. But I'll be a little later than usual since I have to pick up Baby Buddha from my mother's. Mama and Daddy's house isn't as close as the old babysitter's place was. I'll be glad when I find someone qualified and permanent to look after him."

"You know, Baby, I can leave here in a few minutes and run by your Mom's to pick him up early. That way you don't have to go out of your way when you leave work."

"No, that's okay, Baby. He's fine with my mother. I just spoke to her and Justin's napping now. She told me that her stylist knows someone who runs a licensed home daycare center. I'm going to interview her after work tomorrow. If that works out, Justin'll have a new babysitter."

"I still don't see why he can't stay home with me until I find another job," sulked Jerome, "I'm here all day."

"It's too much responsibility for you right now, Jerome," Brenda sighed. Then she suddenly exclaimed, "Oh, I'm sorry, Baby, but my other line is ringing. I have to go, Honey."

"Okay, Baby, I'll see you when you get home," said Jerome, not able to hide his disappointment at not being trusted to take care of his son. "Love you like crazy."

"Love you too." Brenda blew him a kiss before hanging up to get to the other line.

Jerome felt bad that Brenda didn't trust him to watch their son until he found a job. If his flighty mother-in-law could baby-sit, he certainly could. But he knew he should just be grateful that Brenda had forgiven him. He wouldn't trade being a husband and father for the world. Nothing or no one could make him mess up again. His family meant everything to him. Hopefully, Leenae got the message and would get over it. Somehow he'd get Bambillo his money and file that EEO complaint against Odessa. That way he'd get his old job back and have a nice pocket of change in the bank from the lawsuit. In Jerome's mind it would all work out just fine.

CHAPTER 18

Several days had passed. Finally, it was Thursday morning and Bill was due home from India later that day. Renee sat at the kitchen counter and ate a light breakfast of croissant, orange juice, and fresh fruit. She folded back the newspaper and read the forecast: cool and cloudy all week. A blanket of fog concealed the view outside her picture window. There was no sign of life anywhere. Not even a squirrel darted through the yard or other small animals rusted in the bushes like they usually did. Outside it looked like a ghost town but inside her home a renewed life emerged. Now that she was pregnant, becoming a good mother became her main concern. If she wanted their child to be raised in a stable, two-parent household, she'd need to put more energy into saving her marriage. Renee hoped she could convince Bill to start marriage counseling with Helen before the baby's birth. She had not scheduled any appointments with her own patients today so she would be in a mellow frame of mind and would have enough time to get things ready for Bill's return home. After being gone a week, he called last night to say his flight would be delayed a few hours due to airline security. That meant he wouldn't arrive into Dulles until 5:30 and should be home by 7:00 PM.

So much had happened the week while Bill was away. No matter how hard she tried to control it, her infatuation for Deek had not faded. But she was so glad she had not slept with him that night at Kent Island. The more she tried not to think about him, the more he invaded her thoughts. He called everyday on the pretense of a general, friendly conversation, but the longing in his voice was evident. She wondered if he only wanted what he couldn't have. Was his persistence due to some kind of macho ego trip? No, she thought, to be fair, Deek was not that immature. Had she broken down and accepted any more of his daily lunch or dinner invitations while Bill was gone who knows where that seemingly innocent encounter would have led to next. Renee accepted the fact that people just couldn't have it all. She had found her soul mate in Deek and their moments together were always pure heaven, but they didn't last and it never would. She discovered she couldn't experience happiness amidst lies, secrecy, and guilt. The price to pay for happiness with Deek was too great. Finally, on Tuesday she had mustered the courage to ask him not to call her anymore and since then he hadn't. Renee convinced herself that after all those years of infertility and loss, she'd finally be able to find joy and fulfillment in motherhood. Perhaps she'd even be able to rekindle the desire that she and Bill once felt for each other at the beginning of their marriage.

Thursday was her housekeeper's regular day to come clean so when Renee heard the front door swing open she knew it was Chizuko entering with her key.

"Good morning, Miz H. I come early for you. Make things nice for Mr. H," said Chizuko in broken English, smiling broadly as she bowed often.

Chizuko Tanaka and her family had only been in the United States for less than a year. Although in her mid-fifties, she attended evening English classes at a high school near her home. Whenever she got the chance, she practiced her English on Americans and Renee always took time to engage her housekeeper in conversation.

"Good morning, Chizuko. How're you doing today?" asked Renee. The housekeeper carried several baskets of fresh flowers that Renee had ordered from the florist and began cutting and washing the stems in the sink as she chatted away.

"People not so nice, Miz H. This morning at bus stop I see young lady with dark eyes and skin a little more light," said Chizuko, pointing to her seashell-tinted arm.

"So I think young lady Japanese like me. I smile and bow to pretty girl and give greeting in Japanese. But girl speak English in mean voice. "What hell you want old woman? Why you no go back to China?"

"I say to mean little one, *Chizuko from Japan not China*! She say something again sound like mad words but I no understand," Chizuko frowned and shook her head while arranging the flowers in vases.

"Some people stay in terrible moods for no particular reason Chizuko, but we can't let them ruin our day, can we?" smiled Renee and sniffed a bloom full of pink lilies.

"No, Ma'am. Chizuko make things nice for when Mr. H get home today. I start downstairs first, okay Miz?"

"Yes, that's fine and thank you Chizuko. Everything always looks lovely on Thursdays after you've been here. As a matter of fact, I'm planning a special evening for my husband."

"Ohhh! Chizuko do good work for very special day," she smiled and bowed, "Big house but you and Mr. H not messy people. I stay late to help, yes?"

"That's great. Thank you, Chizuko. I'm planning an Indian-inspired evening, with candles, pleasant music, Indian cuisine and authentic dress. So if you can stay to help me I would really appreciate it. And you're right, Chizuko, this house is awfully large for just two people but that's about to change in the near future. There's some wonderful news I plan to surprise my husband with tonight at dinner," Renee smiled at her private thoughts as Chizuko glanced at her strangely.

Instead of asking her employer to explain and speak more slowly as she often did when Renee rattled on, the housekeeper took her supplies to the living room to start cleaning. She could tell her employer looked especially happy today and that's all that mattered to Chizuko.

Renee drained the last drop of orange juice and went downstairs to her office to complete a few hours of paperwork, check email and return some phone calls before getting things ready for Bill's arrival home. She was grateful for Chizuko's offer to help her prepare for her husband's homecoming. After her housekeeper finished her regular cleaning duties and decorated the rooms with flowers, she ironed the table linens and set the table using the best serving china and crystal. Renee guessed that Bill's palette may still be accustomed to Indian food so she ordered a traditional meal from Bombay Palace: an entrée of Tandoori chicken in a butter curry and marinated lamb with a side dish of saffron-seasoned basmati rice and an assortment of Indian breads. Chizuko volunteered to go downtown to the Indian restaurant to pickup the food for her. Renee called Remy, her regular driver and prepaid for the round trip since Chizuko could not drive or read the traffic signs. Just taking the bus to work and back home was still a feat for Chizuko. Renee also asked Remy to stop at a nearby French patisserie so Chizuko could bring back a jewel-like tray of pastries and chocolate-covered strawberries that Renee wanted for dessert.

Renee planned to serve small helpings at dinner and not overdo the food tonight. If Bill stuffed himself, he'd be too sluggish for lovemaking afterwards. And that's what their relationship needed to restart the fire and get him in a good mood before she announced her news. She drank lots of Evian water and nibbled on fruit and crackers so she wouldn't get too hungry in case his plane landed late. The food was a secondary treat. Renee fantasized about the evening ahead. She'd lock her eyes on his while slowly biting the juicy, chocolate-covered strawberries. Her eyes would send a clear signal that tonight was more about reconnecting as a couple and learning to fall in love again. It would be the perfect setting to announce that she was pregnant.

Chizuko returned from her errands about an hour later, carrying packages brimming with a complimentary mixture of culinary smells. She arranged the food in re-heatable, serving platters and wished her boss good luck before she left. Chizuko's help turned out to be a real timesaver because Renee had not anticipated all the time and effort it required to prepare for the evening. Her earlier attempt at creating a romantic evening had failed when Bill had unexpectedly left the country and threw out her invitation as junk mail. But tonight would be different, she smiled. The clock struck five—only a few hours remained she noted. Renee retrieved the matches from the kitchen drawer and sat them next to the dining room candles. She would light the candles just before he was due to arrive. She set out Bill's favorite Cognac and chilled a bottle of champagne. She dimmed the lights throughout the house then went upstairs to get dressed.

Renee showered in Boucheron's scented gel and massaged her skin with its lotion and cologne. Boucheron was one of her more enticing fragrances that she used only for very special occasions. She opened the gift box from Bill that had arrived at her doorstep yesterday, then pulled out the beautiful silk Sari from India. In addition to a sheet of decorative bindis, Bill's gift contained everything needed for an Indian woman's complete formal outfit: a hand-embroidered, purple silk Sari with gold, zari work on its border and end piece. There was a matching 'Choli' or blouse and a plain waist petticoat. Renee glanced at the picture of a lovely Indian woman wrapped sensually in her Sari pictured on the enclosed draping instructions. Normally not a flashy dresser, tonight Renee wanted to induce an adventurous side of her personality to come out by emulating the seductive effect of wearing this very feminine attire. Bill was in for a big surprise when he walked through the door this evening.

Renee recalled her husband's response last Thursday night when he saw her in that shimmering, low-cut, blue-black Neiman Marcus gown that she first planned to wear to the Boys and Girls Club fundraiser dinner. Her tummy-tucking, cellulite-shrinking, bosom-enhancing 'Flatter Me' corset transformed her into a sexy diva for about five minutes. She wondered now if her pregnancy had something to do with her short temper that night. But when she had to change into something sensible like a pantsuit in order to maintain the trivial function of breathing, Bill had not bothered to hide his disappointment. Renee knew what to do to get her husband's attention. She had tried the seduction plan the day before her birthday but an unlucky fluke of events kept Bill from reading her invitation to dinner where she intended to be the main course as well as the dessert. This time she hadn't bothered with mailing him a secret invitation but would have everything ready and waiting for him when he walked in at seven tonight.

After reading the Sari draping instructions several times, it didn't take Renee long to realize that she should have practiced wrapping her new Sari. She laid out the 242 by 45 inch rectangle of seemingly endless silk fabric on her white-carpeted floor and sighed. She decided to begin with the easy steps first and pressed a stick-on bindi over her forehead. Next she smoothed out her dark hair with the flat iron. Then parted it down the middle and twisted it in a neat bun at the nape of her neck the way the woman on the picture wore her hair. She put on the matching fuchsia-colored blouse and petticoat then nodded approvingly at her reflection in the full-length mirror. Not bad. She already felt beautiful and exotic but still had the most important part of the attire to drape, the Sari. Renee stood over the sea of purple fabric with both hands on her hips. Now she wished she had gotten dressed earlier while Chizuko was still there to help her figure this out. On second thought Renee shook her head at the idea of Chizuko wrapping her in the Sari. That would definitely end up being the blind leading the blind, thought Renee—a Japanese and an American woman trying to wrap an Indian Sari!

"Okay, you can do this Renee. Just take it step-by-step," she said aloud to herself. Renee bent down and lifted the top edge of the Sari and tucked it into the petticoat just as step 1 described. So far so good. But at step 2 she immediately ran into a snag. The directions said to tuck about a yard of the Sari to the left, back and front again in the top edge all around, keeping the lower edge in the same level. Renee switched from the left side to the right, then from right to left several times but couldn't make sense of the correct way to drape the cloth. Finally, she simply wrapped and tucked around her waist a few times.

The lower edge of her fabric dragged the floor instead of reaching just below the petticoat like the picture showed. To correct that problem, Renee started the circular tucking all over again and pushed in a few more inches until the border did not sweep the floor. The last thing she wanted was to trip over her own feet. When she got to step 3 and read the folding of the pleats part, Renee almost lost her nerve to continue. It looked like she'd need the multiple arms of an octopus to be able to fold those pleats. But she wasn't ready to give up yet. Her unborn baby counted on her to succeed in this mission to keep mommy and daddy together.

The directions for step 3 read, *Hold the edge of the sari in your right hand with your forefinger straight. With your left hand bring the edge of the sari over your forefinger of your right hand and back under the thumb of your right hand. This is your first pleat. Now use another 2.5 yards to fashion seven to eight more pleats just like the first.* Renee tied her fingers in knots trying to make the required number of pleats. To make matters worse her first pleats fell apart before she finished the remaining folds.

"You've got to be kidding," she said aloud and tossed the instruction sheet on the bed.

Frustrated, Renee took out her sewing kit and fastened together her own makeshift pleats with safety pins. After tucking the edges of the 'pinned together' pleats inside her petticoat she read where the directions said ... *The pleats should face towards the left and fall gracefully to level with the rest of your sari. The pleats can be pinned to the petticoat about 2 inches below the waist.*

"Now you tell me I can use pins! It figures," said Renee aloud, laughing at herself.

Since she had already fastened her pleats together with pins, she re-did the pins and this time attached them to her petticoat. When finally finished with this step, Renee checked her image in the mirror. Instead of the uniform, flowing pleats depicted in the picture, her bulky pleats made her look like a potbellied pig.

Renee spoke to her image in the mirror, "All right Mata Hari, let's move on to step 6 and see what's in store for us next. It can't get any worse." Step 6 instructed her to take the remaining 2.5 yards to the left and around the back. Pass it under the right arm and across the front. Then throw the 'Pallu' which it called the decorated end piece of the sari and drape the pallu over the left hand side shoulder and let it fall casually to just above the back of the knee. It said the wearer could pin her pallu to her blouse on the left hand side shoulder.

Renee took a deep breath before tackling this final step. Just as she suspected, the fabric did not drape flawlessly over her left shoulder and fall nicely down her back as the instructions indicated. After wrapping and re-wrapping umpteen times, she nearly strangled herself trying to get it to swing from the back and across her neck to the left.

"This is clearly a task that requires a level of expertise that I don't have," said Renee and threw up her arms. She collapsed on the bed and noticed that it was almost 7 o'clock. She still had to reheat the food and arrange it in the china platters as if she had prepared the meal herself and light the dinner candles. Chizuko threw out all the restaurant's bags but if Bill saw the food in microwave-able dishes he'd know something was up in the culinary department. So far everything had gone wrong. She looked nothing like the beautiful Indian model in the picture. In fact, she looked more like a desecrated mummy who had escaped from her tomb. How seductive was that?

The clock stuck seven. Renee was about to give up and unwrap herself from the yards of fabric when she got another idea. She studied the picture again and wished she had paid more attention to Aunt Clara's sewing lessons when she was nine. Renee threaded a needle with purple thread and began sewing the top of the fabric to her blouse to imitate the draped effect as closely as possible. This way it wouldn't come apart before she could wrap it correctly. For once she was glad Bill was late getting in. Thirty minutes later Renee grinned at the finished outcome as she stood before the mirror. "Now that's what having a logical, problem-solving, psychologist's mind gets you," she said to herself with satisfaction.

Renee carefully descended the stairs in her beautiful Sari and placed the bowls of food in the microwave. She lit the dining room candles and fantasized about how their evening together would end once upstairs in their bedroom. Perhaps she'd wait until that 'moment' to tell him her news. She lovingly dished out the meal and garnished the dishes with sprigs of parsley. Just as she had finished wiping up her mess in the kitchen and made sure the atmosphere looked inviting, an uncontrollable urge came over her to urinate. Damn, if only she hadn't been drinking so much water all day. Renee looked down at her neatly pinned and sewn together Sari and her eyes went wild when she realized there was no easy way to get out of it. This time she really had mummified herself.

"Now what Mata Hari?" said Renee frowning, "How are you supposed to pee in this getup? So much for your logical psychologist's mind." She practically tripped up the stairs trying to race to the bathroom. She couldn't risk untangling herself in the powder room downstairs. Bill was due to walk in any second. If she was careful maybe she could undo just the necessary parts and keep most of her Sari intact.

Bill walked through the door at 7:15 and dropped his bags at the foyer entrance. He noticed the subdued lights, fragrant smells, and mellow music that greeted him before he even saw Renee. He walked cautiously through the hallway and called her name. He poked his head in the dining room and his eyes gleamed in disbelief when he saw an Indian gourmet dinner on fine china plates spread out on a beautifully set table with flowers and lit candles.

As Renee came out of the bathroom she heard a rumbling noise outside. When she drew back the drapes and saw a minivan parked in the driveway, she wondered why Bill hadn't taken a taxi home instead of renting a minivan.

Bill looked mesmerized as Renee carefully descended the staircase dressed in her exquisite outfit. Before she even reached the bottom platform, he grabbed her and kissed her with an anxious longing that Renee regarded as strange behavior coming from him even if he had been away for seven days. He held her at arm's length and gazed admiringly.

"Wow, baby. You went through all this trouble for me," he said and kissed her forehead, "The dress, food, candlelight, the music? I guess you did miss me a little."

"I want to show you just how much after dinner, darling," she said and drew her body into his where he instinctively enclosed his arms around her waist.

Bill pulled a small, carved box from his jacket pocket and snapped it open to reveal a gold bracelet studded with crystal. "Here's part two of your birthday present, Hon."

"Oh, Bill, thank you. It's lovely and so is the Sari. Everything's perfect."

Just as she lifted her chin to kiss him again, someone knocked timidly on the door.

"Oh, sweetheart, there's something I should tell you. I wish I'd known you were planning all this because I'd have told you to put everything on hold for tonight."

"What do you mean?" She frowned and stepped back.

"Well, it's like this, Babe. With our flight being delayed I didn't have much time to make other arrangements, so I had to bring my twelve boot camp recruits home with me. They're a little grungy and tired and probably starving because the food on the plane was lousy. Bottom line—Shaw said I gotta have my recruits cleaned up and ready by eight o'clock tomorrow morning to present to him and a group of executives from several top IT firms."

Renee stood transfixed, too shocked to speak as Bill continued to explain.

"So Babe, the fellas need a place to shower and dress in the morning. We've got more than enough space to let them sleep here for one night. Tomorrow I'll get them settled in their own apartments in Alexandria. Anyway, that's probably one of the guys at the door now."

The knock sounded again, a little louder this time. Bill walked to the front door and swung it open. A slight, brown-skinned young man with jet-black straight hair, keen features, an unshaven chin and wearing a wrinkled white shirt, stood with hands clasped in front of him. He stepped timidly through the door when Bill invited him inside.

"Ah, Mahesh, I'd like to introduce you to my wife," said Bill as he motioned for his trainee to come closer.

"Renee, Mahesh here is being trained in Oracle RDBMS, relational database, performance tuning, security, and structure change control, among other things. He'll be groomed as one of our top Database Administrators."

Bill may as well have been speaking in the ancient language of Etruscan for as much as she understood. The young man pressed his palms together below his chin, with fingers pointing upwards and bowed slightly to greet Renee in a soft-spoken voice, "*Namaste, Shreemati.*"

Renee smiled politely and nodded her head. "Hello. Welcome to the United States."

"Tandoori chicken? It smells and feels just like home," Mahesh grinned.

"That it does, Son. Doesn't Mrs. Hayes look lovely in the Sari I bought her? Mahesh helped me pick out the most exquisite garment at the boutique."

Mahesh bowed and smiled to confirm his agreement.

"He's one of the brightest of our new recruits," said Bill, "You've gotta be pretty sharp to land a Database Administrator trainee position, right Mahesh?"

"If you say, respected Professor. You are most generous."

"Mahesh, will you please excuse my husband and me for a moment so that I can speak to him privately?"

"I apologize for the intrusion," said Mahesh, "May I be excused now Professor? I will wait with the others outside in the van until you summon us."

"Yes, that's probably a good idea. Ask the guys to wait a few more minutes until I speak to my wife. I'll be outside shortly. What was it that you needed?"

"Nothing that cannot wait, respected Professor," said Mahesh softly. He bowed his head to his professor and Mrs. Hayes before quickly exiting as he could clearly detect the tension on the face of his Professor's wife. The new technical recruit slipped quietly out the door, regretting his intrusion and offer to find out if one of his fellow trainees in the van would be able to use the restroom facilities as he had neglected to relieve himself at the airport when they landed. Mahesh would simply inform his fellow recruit that their Professor would be returning to the van momentarily and would provide further instructions, so he would just have to hold it.

"Bill, are you insane? All those men outside cannot stay here tonight. My whole evening for you is ruined. We agreed when we got back together that we'd try to make our marriage work. I don't see this as trying. Unless you're trying to upset me!"

"I understand how disappointed you are, Babe. I'll take them to a Motel Six or someplace for the night. Those discount motels always have rooms available for reasonable rates and the guys can double up. They won't mind. I'm sorry Renee. I had no idea you planned a romantic evening alone with me tonight." He tried to caress her once more but this time she was not receptive and pushed his hand away.

"You've been gone a whole week. Why wouldn't I want to be alone with my husband? Obviously, you don't feel the same way." She blew out the candles on the table and began removing the serving platters of food. She shoved everything in the refrigerator, ignoring Bill's attempt to explain as he followed after her.

"I do, Renee. But Shaw has been relentless over the past few days. I need you to be supportive right now. Once I get my foot firmly in the door of upper management, I can start calling the shots at Techands. Baby, I've got to make my company a success. I don't have anything else to fall back on if this doesn't work."

Renee put down the bowl of rice on the kitchen counter and turned to face him as she spoke. "I want to be supportive of you Bill, but I also need you to be supportive of my needs. This wasn't the way I planned to tell you my news but it looks like I have no choice because you just don't get what's really important."

"What are you talking about?" he held his hands out, imploring her to enlighten him.

"Come upstairs with me and I'll show you." He followed her upstairs to their bedroom. Renee slid open her vanity and retrieved the pregnancy test stick out of the top drawer. She held up a green tip stick in front of him. Bill looked at her even more confused.

"What the hell is that?"

"It's the results of a home pregnancy test I took last Saturday." Renee studied the confused look on Bill's face as he stared blankly at the stick.

"The what?"

"Bill, we're going to have a baby," she grinned, not able to hide her excitement despite her irritation with her husband.

Bill stood motionless and wore a blank look on his face. Renee still could not read his reaction at first. She held her breath. Then it became clear.

Bill's face contorted sharply as he asked, "When?"

"I don't know the exact date," she said, "I haven't been to the doctor yet. My appointment is 10:30 on Monday morning at Sibley Memorial Hospital. Can you come with me, Darling? They're going to do a sonogram. We'll actually be able to see our developing baby in utero, that means in the uterus."

"I know what it means Renee. I'm not stupid. Anyway, Monday morning is bad for me."

"What do you mean … bad for you?"

"Look, this shit isn't fair. You always knew how I felt about raising a kid and now that I'm over fifty, the idea is even more ridiculous."

"Ridiculous? How can you say those words to me?" she said as tears streamed down her cheeks. She turned away as she spoke. "This is what I've always wanted."

"Well, I don't want it. So it looks like we have a serious problem," he said grimly and folded his arms. "You've got a choice to make, Renee," said Bill sternly, "You can't be that far along in this pregnancy so I know it's not too late to take care of it."

"I hope you don't mean what I think you mean," she frowned. "Can't we at least go see my therapist, Dr. Stone, for joint marriage counseling and discuss it?"

"What for? I don't intend to change my mind about this. Not ever. So going to talk to your shrink would just be a big waste of time."

"The least you could do is try, Bill," she said, through her tears, "I've already thought of a name. If it's a boy we can call him Nathan, meaning the gift from God. That's truly what I feel this baby is for us … a gift from God."

Bill sneered sarcastically, "Isn't it a bit early to be picking out baby names? You're not even showing."

He paced the floor. "I guess you're forgetting what the doctor said five years ago. If you got pregnant again it would probably end up being another ectopic pregnancy and it could risk your life. Renee, if you're determined to go through with this nonsense at your age, I won't have anything to do with it and you'll be on her own."

"Then I'll be on my own." She glared as she faced him.

"Fine. I'll pack some clean shirts and stay at the motel with the guys tonight."

Bill hastily removed a stack of folded, boxed shirts from his dresser and threw them into his overnight bag without uttering another word. He slammed the dresser drawer shut. Renee grabbed his arm frantically to try to get him to stop but he pushed her arm away and proceeded towards the door.

"You can't just leave me tonight after what I've told you and go off with your trainees. Why can't we discuss this situation? I don't understand your feelings. Did something terrible happen to you as a child to make you feel this way? Please Bill, I beg you to trust me and open up about why you don't want your own child."

"Jesus, Renee, can you stop psychoanalyzing me all the time? I've just spent twenty hours traveling. I've got a bunch of foreigners outside in the van that have never been to the States. How can you expect me to deal with this now for chrissakes?"

"And I've just spent all day trying to make your homecoming special. Don't I mean anything to you? Is my happiness so trivial?" Renee threw up her arms in despair. She pulled off the draped garment from her shoulder and threw it at him, though it only fell to the floor at his feet.

Without answering any of her questions, Bill walked out of the bedroom, carrying his overnight bag with a shirt cuff still hanging out. He ran down the stairs and slammed the front door behind him. When she heard the van pull off, Renee sank to the floor and leaned her back against the mattress edge and cried. She had left the radio playing on a low volume while getting dressed earlier. Now she heard Luther VanDross crooning the lyrics from one of his old hits, 'A House is Not a Home.' Renee buried her face in her hands and sobbed. It seemed as though things had disintegrated over night, when in reality she knew their problems had been simmering on a slow boil for years. Just as Luther's song sorrowfully expressed a feeling of emptiness, she knew Bill would not be coming back home tonight and maybe not ever.

CHAPTER 19

Finally, the day of Renee's long anticipated doctor's appointment had arrived. On Monday morning Remy, her driver, let her out at the main entrance of Sibley Memorial Hospital on 5255 Loughboro Road, in Northwest. Renee had asked Bill to meet her in the hospital's Obstetrics wing at 10:30 and hoped he would be there and would stay long enough to drive her home after her doctor's appointment. She told Remy that she didn't think she would need him to pick her up after her appointment because her husband was meeting her there. Remy nodded and drove off.

Bill still hadn't moved back home since walking out Thursday evening, but she sensed his resistance was wavering each evening when they spoke briefly on the telephone. "You sure you're doing okay, Baby? Is there anything you need?" he'd ask her at the end of each of their 30 second long conversations. They didn't veer into any hot button topics and ended the phone calls before anything got too heated. It was a game of avoidance that they both played well. If Bill would just come to the ultrasound screening this morning, he might change his feelings about being a father, she thought. Once he accepted that her pregnancy was real he might be willing to make plans for their baby's arrival. She hoped this was not all wishful thinking.

On her way to Obstetrics, Renee purposely passed by the Nursery on the Maternity Ward. She stopped to peer longingly at the rows of multi-hued cherubic faces behind the large, glass window. In less than nine months her own infant would be snuggled inside one of those rectangular bassinets. She and Bill would finally attain the brass ring, a baby. Renee looked up and saw a familiar face smile at her from behind the partition. A petite, exotic-looking beauty with curly, black hair, laughing eyes, and a wide smile tucked the infant she had just finished feeding back inside his bassinet and waved at Renee. She came out of the nursery to greet Renee.

"Hello there. Dr. Renee Hayes, isn't it? I'm Sasha Rojas. Luke Hamilton's fiancé."

Renee still hadn't made the connection, but she did recognize her face as one she'd seen before.

"Luke is your friend Deek's brother. I met you about a week ago at that black tie fundraiser for the Boys and Girls Club. Remember me?" asked Sasha, giving Renee a warm hug as if they were old friends despite the fact that they had met only once.

"Yes, Deek introduced us. It's good to see you again, Sasha. I didn't realize you worked here."

"Oh yes, I love being a pediatric nurse at Sibley. Perhaps one day Luke and I will have our own babies," she said, displaying a wide grin.

"What brings you to Sibley Hospital's nursery ward, Renee?"

"I … um … well I have a doctor's appointment."

Renee quickly slid the *What to Expect When You're Expecting* book she had brought with her under her arm, but apparently not before the young nurse read the title. Sasha squealed and clapped in excitement.

"It appears congratulations are in order," she winked, "Hey, I have a fabulous idea. Deek is meeting me here at noon to discuss the wedding. My brother-in-law-to-be has been such a sweetheart filling in for Luke while he's been away at training. I already told Luke that his little brother should get the Best Man of the Year award for putting up with my fickleness," she chuckled. "Anyway, Luke and I are planning a Valentine's Day wedding next February and we still have lots to do. Why don't you join us if you're finished with your doctor's appointment in time? As long as you can stand cafeteria food, I know Deek would love the surprise of seeing you."

Renee wondered why Sasha hadn't asked one of her girlfriends to help her instead of enlisting Deek's help. Surely, a girl as friendly and outgoing as Sasha would have a few girlfriends, thought Renee. As if Sasha had read her mind, she piped up, "My maid of honor is helping me with most of the wedding particulars, but I still need to run everything by Luke, of course. And, since Deek is the only one who can get through to Luke while he's away, the poor guy's been drafted to listen to my ideas so he can take them back to Luke. I have to say though Deek's been a good sport about it. Otherwise, we'd have to delay our wedding plans until Luke gets back home." Renee thought about how effective Deek's connections had been in helping her father and she nodded in agreement that she understood.

"So Renee, can you join me and Deek for lunch today?"

"Thank you, Sasha, but I don't want to impose on your wedding plans."

"Nonsense. Any friend of Deek's is a friend of ours. Besides, it's obvious he cares a lot about you. Does he know yet?" she asked pointing to Renee's stomach.

"No, I … haven't officially announced it yet."

"Of course. Well, don't let me keep you from your appointment. Just stop by the nurse's station when you're done and ask for me, Sasha Rojas, okay?"

Just then a patient's call light flashed for room 9. "Oh dear, I'd better go, that's one of the patients who just delivered late last night. Bye Renee," said Sasha and started walking down the hallway to her patient's room, "Good luck and I hope to see you later."

Suddenly, Renee's stomach turned in knots. She had no intention of joining them for lunch. But what if Sasha said something to Deek about her pregnancy? Now, she wished she had told him herself when he called last Sunday and asked if everything was all right. She hated the idea of Deek finding out from someone else, especially after their last conversation when she told him not to call her anymore. But at least he would understand why she'd been acting cool towards him lately. He knew how much motherhood meant to her. Renee walked rapidly towards her doctor's office. She couldn't worry about Deek's reaction right now. The only thing that mattered was her baby.

Renee's heart sank when she reached the waiting room in Obstetrics and Bill wasn't waiting in the lounge. She signed the login sheet and sat down to wait for Dr. Louise Eckbert to call her into the examining room. Renee opened her book, *What to Expect When You're Expecting* but each time someone walked into the waiting room, she looked up to see if it was Bill. After waiting about twenty minutes the nurse called her name and led her to the examining room. Bill still had not shown up.

Renee stretched out on the examination table wearing nothing but a thin cotton gown and a sheet pulled over her stomach. Her eyes squinted up at the fluorescent light fixture. The antique white walls and stark, stainless steel medical supplies lined up along the counter made the frigid room temperature even colder. She rubbed the goose bumps on her arms to warm-up.

Dr. Eckbert tapped lightly on the door before entering. "Hello, Mrs. Hayes. I'm sorry for the delay," said Dr. Eckbert, "I was waiting for the results of your pregnancy test."

Renee greeted the physician warmly and hid her disappointment that Bill had not arrived in time. She studied the doctor's face. She prided herself on being able to read people. Dr. Eckbert looked at her askance without making eye contact.

"Is there something wrong with my pregnancy test?"

"The test turned out positive just as you suspected. But your HCG level of 13 is too low based on your last period. Perhaps, you're wrong about your dates and this level could be normal," said Dr. Eckert, forcing a weak smile of reassurance.

"Mrs. Hayes, I'd like to do an ultrasound and see what's going on. Your medical records indicate you suffered an ectopic pregnancy six years ago that had to be aborted. Is your husband outside? You may want him to come in."

"No, Doctor. He had an emergency at work and couldn't make it this morning."

"All right then, Mrs. Hayes, let's get started," she said, "I'm going to smear this sticky, cold gel on your belly so don't be alarmed."

Dr. Eckbert turned on the ultrasound machine and glided the cold instrument across Renee's stomach while studying the fuzzy, black and gray images on the monitor. Renee observed that the doctor's keen, blue eyes questioned the images before her. Dr. Eckbert pressed her lips together tightly. Her eyebrows and forehead burrowed together in a frown. Renee knew something wasn't right.

"What is it Dr. Eckbert?" asked Renee in a quivering voice.

The doctor turned off the machine. She gently wiped the gel from Renee's stomach without once lifting her eyes to meet Renee's puzzled face.

"I wish I had better news to tell you, Mrs. Hayes, but you have an embryonic pregnancy or what's called a blighted ovum. Sadly, no embryo formed in your uterus. The ultrasound shows there's only an empty yolk sac."

Renee felt like a brick had just landed on her heart. If she had not already been lying down on the examining table she would have collapsed.

"I don't understand, Dr. Eckbert. My pregnancy test shows I'm pregnant. Didn't you hear the baby's heartbeat? Perhaps, you're wrong."

"I wish I were wrong, Mrs. Hayes. I know how painful this must be for you. But there was no heartbeat, only the sound of the equipment churning. This type of pregnancy usually spontaneously aborts itself so there's no need to do a D & C today. I want to check you again in two weeks and if the pregnancy still hasn't miscarried itself, I'll perform a D & C. It's a routine procedure that should only take an hour."

Renee fought back a strong urge to break into a heart-wrenching scream, but she could not prevent the rush of tears. Dr. Eckbert grabbed a handful of tissues from the equipment counter and gave them to Renee.

"What's wrong with me, Doctor?" asked Renee through her sobbing, "Why does this keep happening to me?"

"It's no one's fault, Mrs. Hayes. Not yours or your husband's. There are a variety of factors. Sometimes, it's caused by the quality of the woman's egg but it could also be due to the fertilizing sperm. More than likely, it can be attributed to some chromosomal factor. Embryonic pregnancies tend to be genetically or morphologically abnormal. Since they end in early miscarriage, I believe this is nature's way of resolving its mistakes."

"My baby is not a mistake," Renee wailed.

"I'm sorry. That was a poor choice of words. Mrs. Hayes, I'm going to refer you to the Recurrent Pregnancy Loss program to help determine the cause for your history of losses," said Dr. Eckbert, "There's a two month waiting list so don't be upset if it takes awhile for you to get an appointment. I also have to advise you not to try to conceive again before six months. Your body, as well as your heart, need time to heal. I'd also like you to think about joining a support group."

After Dr. Eckbert left the examining room, Renee lay motionless on the table as tears streamed down her face and reality sunk in. Instinct, as well as, her undergraduate training in nursing prior to entering clinical psychology had revealed the bad news from the moment she saw the sonogram and heard no heartbeat. But Renee had denied her logical reasoning and medical training. She hoped Dr. Eckbert would assuage her fears. However, the doctor could not. She only confirmed the obvious. There was no developing baby inside her womb. Not now, not ever. Motherhood would remain for her an elusive dream.

Lying on the examining table, Renee couldn't see her impenetrable tomb, yet she felt buried alive. She felt buried in an endless existence of loneliness and a life without love. After about ten minutes, she willed her weighted down body to lift itself up. She dressed slowly. She slipped passed the nurse in the reception area and took a detour through Oncology in order to avoid the Maternity Ward. She didn't know what would be more painful, passing by those rows of beautiful, healthy babies in the nursery wing or running into Sasha and having to answer questions about her non-existent pregnancy. Renee didn't think she could ever face Deek again. Sasha looked like the bubbly type who probably couldn't wait five seconds to share what she perceived to be "good news."

Renee left the hospital and tossed her book on expectant motherhood in a trash container outside. An available taxi pulled up at curbside. She thought about the prescription of Lexapro that still remained in her medicine cabinet. She had stopped taking it, but something must have told her not to throw it away. Now she was glad for that inner voice. As soon as she got home, she would take a tablet, and she hoped it would take effect right away. Otherwise, how else was she supposed to deal with this? When the driver asked if she needed a ride, her stomach muscles trembled and words got stuck in her throat. Knowing she would probably cry in the cab the entire ride home, Renee shook her head at the cab driver and began walking until she could compose herself long enough to hail another taxi. She called Remy but he was in the middle of another pickup and could not get there for another hour. Worst case scenario—she would wait somewhere secluded on the hospital grounds until Remy could pick her up.

Even if she could get herself together long enough to take a short taxi ride to the Tenleytown or Van Ness Metro Station, this would be better than riding in a cab all the way home because the anonymity of a crowded train station would hide her grief from onlookers, she thought. She walked slowly and dabbed her cheeks with the balled up, overused tissue in her coat pocket. The streets of Washington at lunchtime swarmed with taxis, automobiles, and police cars. Pedestrians packed the sidewalks. They elbowed passed Renee, dashing everywhere with their cell phones pressed to their ears. The drone of everyone's conversations, horns honking, and sirens squealing buzzed around in her head. She felt like the entire world was oblivious to her pain.

At first she did not hear the familiar voice calling her name. Then she looked up and spotted his black Mercedes convertible. Deek was stopped at Dalecarla Parkway and Loughboro, obviously on his way to meet Sasha for lunch. Renee tried to pretend she didn't see him and stepped up her pace.

When their eyes met briefly, Deek knew immediately that something was wrong with Renee as he watched her hurring down the street. He knew there was a problem even though she quickly looked away from him. While still stopped on Loughboro, he manually dialed Sasha rather than use his cell phone's hands free voice command function. He had not yet updated Sasha's work number into his contacts phonebook so it was easier to simply pick up the phone and dial her. He could tell by the excitement in Sasha's voice, that she had some news she wanted to share with him, but that would have to wait. Before she could get out what she wanted to say, Deek explained to her that he had something come up and could not meet her for lunch this afternoon. Just as he thought, Sasha understood completely and was not upset by his last minute cancellation. He realized his brother Luke was lucky to have a caring and understanding lady in his life like Sasha. He drove only a short distance away and parked on the street, even though he parked illegally. That was the least of his concerns. He spotted Renee up ahead and ran to catch up with her.

Renee didn't respond when Deek casually walked up beside her and tried to sound nonchalant. "What a coincidence spotting you here,

Doc. Didn't you hear me calling you back there?" he said, taking easy strides with his long legs next to her fast trots to get away.

Renee lied and shook her head while keeping her eyes pinned to the ground and continued to walk away from him at a rapid pace. Deek grabbed her arm and stepped in front of her to force her to stop.

"What's the hurry Renee? Can we go somewhere private for a minute and talk about what's bothering you?"

"Don't you have a luncheon engagement with Sasha? I ran into her back there at the hospital. Besides, nothing's bothering me. Please go away, Deek. I want to be alone." He held her still. She looked up into his caring eyes only briefly before turning her face away again.

"You know you can't fool me, Doc. I've always been able to read you. Besides your eyes are red and I can see you've been crying. Come sit over here," he said and led her to a nearby, vacant bench.

"These people walking by don't give a damn about us so this is as private as any place else. You started acting evasive last Saturday when we came back from my cottage on Kent Island. Then you tell me not to call anymore. I want you to start at the beginning. Tell me now, Renee, what's wrong and what can I do to help you?"

Renee's jaw quivered. She opened her mouth partially, willed herself to speak with firmness and control but vocal cords disobeyed. She sat mutely with both hands clasped in her lap and felt the warmth of Deek's right hand resting over hers. A tear crept down her cheek but she left it there.

"Why were you at Sibley Hospital? Are you ill?" he asked. "Whatever it is, I'm here for you."

Suddenly, she blurted out that she thought she was pregnant and leaned into his shoulder, crying. Deek instinctively hugged her. When she finally broke away and composed herself she saw the bewildered look on his face.

"Isn't that good news?" he asked then added, cautiously, "Is the baby mine? Is that why you're upset?"

Now, it was her turn to give him a puzzled look. Why would he think that? Hadn't they always used protection? Then her mind flashed back to the one time they did not. In August late one evening after Renee's last patient had left, Deek had stopped by Dr. Helen Stone's old office where Renee had been temporarily seeing patients. He'd come by to escort her safely back to Shirley Ann's house, the foster mother she had been staying with in order to help care for a terminally-ill toddler. But things got too heated, as they always seemed to do whenever she found herself alone with him. Dr. Eckbert had estimated the time of conception to be about two months ago. The realization that Deek could have been the baby's father made the loss even more distressing to her. She had assumed the baby was Bill's but in fact it could have been Deek's. It didn't matter either way because there would be no baby at all.

Renee stammered through her tears, "There is no baby, Deek. My doctor just told me. In medical terminology, I have an embryonic pregnancy. The embryo did not develop in my uterus. I'll never be a mother and that's the only thing I really ever wanted. I feel so empty without it."

"I'm very sorry, sweetheart," he pulled her into him, hugging her gently. Then, he leaned back in order to look directly in her eyes, "You know, there could be other reasons you feel loneliness in your life," he hesitated, then continued, "Many women lead happy, fulfilled lives without giving birth to a child. But if that's really what you want, have you considered adoption?"

"Bill's vehemently against adoption. In fact, it's clear to me now he'll never want children at all, not his or anyone else's. He moved out a few days ago when I told him I was pregnant. That's why he didn't meet me at the hospital for my appointment this morning. I guess he'll be relieved when he finds out there's no baby after all."

"I don't understand why he didn't come with you today. It doesn't make sense for a man not to want his own child," said Deek, shaking his head.

"Bill never did want children. In the beginning of our marriage, I endured years of biopsies, medications, temperature record-keeping, and other invasive procedures to try to conceive. Each time a procedure failed, Bill seemed glad and kept telling me to give it up. He didn't even attempt to comfort me afterwards."

"Renee, I can't discuss your husband with you," said Deek, trying to hide his annoyance, "It's against my principles and besides I might say something I'd regret later like what an insensitive asshole he is. It's not fair that someone like him has a woman like you that he doesn't appreciate." He paused. "I've told you how much I love you, but for some reason you don't believe it or maybe you just don't feel that way about me," said Deek.

"I do love you as much as I can. But it's more complicated than that. Bill and I have a history together. I know what to expect. It's … it's complicated to just sever all those years."

"Renee, we could begin a history together too and it could start today. A baby isn't going to complete your life if you still don't feel valued by the man you're married to who's supposed to value you more than anyone or anything else. I don't understand why you stay with him when all I want to do is love and cherish you the way you deserve." Deek threw up his hands, "See, I'm overstepping my bounds again and saying too much. Just please believe me when I tell you I'll always be here for you."

"Right." Renee was suddenly angry. "Until someone younger and prettier like Sasha or your new FBI partner, what's her name. Until a woman comes along in your life who can give you children. Who are we kidding Deek? This was my last chance at motherhood. I'm too old for this and I can never give you the family you'll certainly want one day. I see how you are with children, even ones that are not your own. I just can't allow myself to fall deeply in love with you, then later get my heart broken. It's bad enough losing every baby I ever conceived but I know I couldn't survive losing you." Renee began to tear up again, then swiftly wiped her eyes. "What you think you feel for me now is not a lifetime commitment," she said harshly.

Deek shot up from the bench and raised his voice at her for the first time. He didn't seem to care about the strangers who turned around to look at him.

"Don't tell me how I feel or what I want. I'm a grown man and I've had enough relationships with women to know what I want and what I don't want. I'm not some kid playing games with you. My age has nothing to do with it, but you persist on penalizing me for being younger than you are."

He sat back down on the bench and took a moment to calm down. His face grew somber but without anger. Looking away from her, he stared reflectively at nothing. He then spoke some words in French that she did not understand. Though it sounded very beautiful when he spoke, there was unmistakable pain in his voice.

"C'est bien la pire peine,
De ne savoir pourquoi,
Sans amour et sans haine,
Mon coeur a tant de peine." ·

Renee turned to him, perplexed. "What?" she asked.

Deek lowered his head into his hand and spoke without looking at her. "It's nothing. Just part of a poem a 19th century French poet named Verlaine wrote. I remember it because my grandmother used to recite it all the time when I was a kid." He lifted his head and looked out, thoughtfully. "Let's just say I can relate to it. *Il est temps pour moi de laisser aller,*" Deek whispered to himself. From the anguished expression on Deek's face as he spoke the first language he learned as a child, Renee knew he was hurting inside. She didn't have to understand French to know that. She wanted to ask him what the words meant, but at this point it really didn't matter. After a moment of complete stillness, he rose from the bench and offered her his hand.

"Come, I'll hail a cab to take you home," he said, calmly. "If you change your mind and need someone to talk too, call me. I assume you still have my number."

She waited on the sidewalk while he practically ran into the middle of the street to stop the next taxi that whizzed towards him. The taxi came to a screeching halt. Deek opened the rear door and Renee walked slowly as he held the door for her. After she slid into the back seat, he slammed the door shut. Deek pulled out his wallet and handed the driver a twenty-dollar bill.

"Take her home, buddy," he said, "She'll give you the address."

Renee leaned out the window, "Deek, I'm sorry. I can't explain right now …"

"Forget it, Renee. Falling in love is just like living. Sometimes it requires risks and heartache. There's no playing it safe when it comes to love or life. Apparently, you just don't love me enough to take that risk." Deek tapped the hood of the cab and motioned for the driver to pull off. Then he turned and walked briskly back up Loughboro Road towards his car.

CHAPTER 20

Deek drove down Pennsylvania Avenue towards F. B. I. headquarters with one hand casually on the steering wheel and the other positioned on the clutch. He couldn't help thinking about Renee as he drove. Deek shook his head as he thought aloud, *I should have taken her home myself."* Oblivious to the traffic he felt more confused than furious. *"I don't get it. What kind of man wouldn't even show up at his wife's first sonogram appointment?"* Deek slowed down and came to a smooth stop at the red light. Renee—pregnant! He still couldn't wrap his mind around that declaration. And, to think the baby that Renee loss could have been his. He rested his forehead against his clenched fist while waiting for the light to change. Deek swallowed the lump in his throat that settled like a rock at the pit of his stomach. If he felt this bad about her lost pregnancy, he couldn't imagine how horrible she must be feeling right now. When the light turned green he took off—grateful for the heavy traffic that allowed him more time to think.

He didn't understand why Renee couldn't bring herself to believe that he really did love her, that their age difference made no difference to him. He came in contact with beautiful women his own age all the time, but had always felt that something was missing. Perhaps, it was simply a sense of vulnerability that he felt unexplainably drawn to. Renee made him feel important and more than that, she made him feel needed. She was beautiful and gentle-spirited and her vulnerability made him want to wrap his arms around her and keep her safe forever. But she didn't believe that feeling would be enough to sustain his love. It wasn't that he couldn't find that same need with a young woman his own age. It was just that so far he hadn't found it with anyone else but her.

Deek glanced at his 'hands free' mobile phone and thought about pressing the button to activate the voice command that would automatically dial her up. But Renee's parting words rang out in his ears and he hesitated to place the call. *"Deek, I'm too old for you. I won't ever be able to give you the children you'll certainly want one day. I just can't allow myself to fall deeply in love with you then later get my heart broken when you leave."* Suddenly, his anger at her overwhelmed him and he had to come to a screeching halt at the next red light. How could she allow her insecurities to come between them? He asked himself. She was dead wrong! He knew he would never leave her. Then a disturbing thought entered his head. If Renee hadn't already been married and unavailable, would he have still pursued her?

He pulled into the building's parking lot and found a spot to park. He turned off the ignition and sat there for a few moments thinking about this question that had drifted into his thoughts. *"Maybe you're just kidding yourself, Deek."* the voice inside his head replied. *"Maybe, the fact that she's married and won't let go is part of the attraction."* He closed his eyes and honestly considered the possibility that he was obsessed with having this woman only because she was already married to somebody else. Then, he shook his head. No. That wasn't it. He grabbed his jacket from the seat, got out, and pressed the automatic lock switch. Once he entered through the secure access and stepped on the second floor of the J. Edgar Hoover building, he could no longer indulge in his personal thoughts about Renee.

When Renee arrived home from the hospital, she slowly climbed the long, spiral staircase to her bedroom, clutching the banister for support. She stripped naked and searched through the blindness of her tears for her favorite cotton nightgown. She went into the bathroom and retrieved the Lexapro from her medicine cabinet and dropped one of the tablets into her hand, then gulped it down with a handful of tap water from the sink. She returned to her bedroom and slipped into bed in the middle of the day and closed her eyes, trying to induce her mind to erase Dr. Eckbert's news that there was no baby developing in her uterus. But she couldn't get the words out of her mind and for several minutes sleep's sweet escape eluded her. Renee spent the next half hour tossing in bed. After a fitful hour of sleep, she awoke groggy and glanced at the clock. She realized she had just enough time to dress and mentally prepare herself for her afternoon appointments that were still on the appointment book. She had no idea how she would get through those sessions, listening to other people's complaints that today seemed so miniscule in comparison to her own problems.

After her last patient left, she crawled back into bed with no desire for food even though she hadn't eaten all day. The only gratifying moment in her entire day had been seeing the progress she made with her newest patient, 15 year old Heather Hollingsworth. The pregnant teenager had been referred to her just a few weeks ago, feeling confused, unloved, and withdrawn. Today, Heather told Renee during therapy that she had decided to stay in school and keep her baby. The bonding activities that Renee had suggested to Heather's parents two weeks ago had begun to strengthen the family's communication. Remarkably, both parents agreed to be there to support their daughter in her decision to keep and raise her child. Heather accepted the fact that her carefree life would drastically change and she would be facing adult responsibilities once her baby was born. Renee was happy that Heather received the support she needed and did not have to experience the pain she herself went through when she got pregnant at 16 and Aunt Clara took care of the problem while she slept in a drugged-induced state, completely unaware of what was happening to her body. Renee wiped her eyes and forced herself not to think about her past or her bleak future. Even though she couldn't seem to save her own life, she was glad she could save someone else's.

Suddenly, Renee's cell phone on her night stand rang. She wanted to ignore it, but out of habit she picked it up and glanced at the name of the caller to see who was calling on her private number. It was her former patient, Veda Simms. Renee sat up in bed and answered it. "Hello Veda. How may I help you? Is everything going okay at your new job?" She tried to disguise her misery by sounding upbeat.

"Hi Dr. Renee. Yeah, I suppose things are okay. Other than my supervisor thinking she's running a slave camp," said Veda. "Dr. Renee, I wish you would come down here one day to this circus where I work at and see for yourself the type of lunatics they put in charge over here. But that's not why I called …" Veda's voice sounded anxious. She was never one to beat around the bush so she launched into the reason for her call. "Dr. Renee, there's something that's been bothering me for the past few weeks now. I finally realize unless I tell somebody, it's gonna eat me up, knowing what I know." Veda hesitated just long enough to catch her breath. "Dr. Renee, I think Brenda's husband might be in some kinda trouble and I'm not sure what I should do about it, if anything."

"What are you talking about?" Renee asked with concern. "Where are you now?"

"I'm still at work, but I had to come outside to call you from my cell phone because I think our desk phones are being recorded on the pretense that we're not suppose to be using business lines for personal calls. Whatever," said Veda glibly. Then, she continued explaining her purpose for calling. "I only have five minutes. I'm on my last break of the day, so let me get right to the point." Veda sucked in a deep breath and let it out before resuming. "A few weeks ago I was taking my normal cigarette break when I saw Brenda's husband, you know Jerome, right?"

"Actually, I've never had the pleasure of meeting the gentleman," said Renee. "I only know what Brenda has shared with me."

"Okay, I can tell from what you just said Dr. Renee that you don't know much about Jerome Johnson," said Veda, with an edge of sarcasm. "Anyway, like I said I saw Jerome outside talking to these three hood rats. I keep to myself around there, and I usually go to this isolated spot, pass the loading dock and across from an alley that sits between these two huge warehouse-looking buildings. It stays kinda dark in that alley no matter what time of day it is because those two big buildings block out the sun."

"Umhum," Renee responded, with the cell phone barely touching her ear.

"Anyway, to make a long story short that's where I saw them, standing not more than 25 feet away from me at the end of the alley. I also noticed a blue Jaguar XK8 parked off from the street and I assume that was their ride."

"Whah ... What ... did you do?" Renee said in a groggy voice, now starting to feel the effects of the Lexapro she had taken earlier in the afternoon.

"I didn't make a sound, Dr. Renee. I just stood back, watched and listened. One of 'em was short, dark and had a head full of crinkly dreads. He had a little pointed face like a rat and he was the one all up in Jerome's face. Rat-face was threatening him about something but I couldn't make out what they were arguing about because I wanted to keep back and make sure they didn't look up the alley and spot me eavesdropping on them. The other fella was this fine baby-faced Brother and he seemed to be the one in charge. And, the third dude could have been Puerto Rican or Mexican or something. But they all looked like they had criminal intent on their mind."

"You know ... that wasn't smart, Veda," Renee said just above a whisper, "You being there."

"I know. I know. I didn't stick around long because I wasn't sure if they were gonna drive back up the alley where I was standing. So I slipped away quietly. I haven't told anybody but you until just now."

"Are you absolutely sure no one saw you?"

"Umm … I'm pretty sure," said Veda, unconvincingly. "Later that day, I tried to find Jerome in the break room to talk to him about it, but someone said he had gone out on a last minute run to deliver some packages. Dr. Renee, I don't know if I should tell Brenda what I saw or just keep my nose out of it. That was a few weeks ago and rumor has it that Jerome got fired for drug use. Those dudes in the alley looked like drug dealers to me. Maybe everything blew over and Jerome's got it under control. Brenda's my girl and all. I don't wanna worry her for no good reason. But that husband of hers has a habit of getting himself into trouble. Besides, Brenda gets a little testy whenever me or Cha-Cha try to give her advice where Jerome is concerned. What do you think I should do, Dr. Renee? Should I just try to forget about it?"

After having listened as closely as she could to the entire story, Renee said, "What do you think you should do, Veda?"

"Damnit, Dr. Renee," Veda shouted, "Can you for once not act like my shrink? I need you to tell me what to do. Brenda's one of my best friends and she's your secretary for Chrissakes. I thought you cared about her. Was I wrong to assume that?" Renee could feel Veda's irritation with her. She knew Veda wanted a direct answer based on her professional opinion but Renee was in no position to give any more advice today. She began to feel tightness in her chest and shortness of breath. She placed her hand over her heart and recognized the familiar symptoms of anxiety. She took shallow breaths while staring at the bottle of Lexapro that rested on its side within her open nightstand drawer and debated whether or not she should take another pill. Right now she knew of nothing else that could so quickly and effectively knock out this enormous pain she was feeling. Tears welled up in her eyes and she blinked a few times to see more clearly. She grabbed a handful of tissues from the box on the nightstand and pressed the tissues to her face to try to mask the sound of her sobbing and sniffles. She hoped Veda would simply say good-bye and hang up. As long as she didn't have to utter any more words, perhaps she could keep it together for a few moments longer. Veda was already upset with her so what did it matter if she remained silent on the line?

"Dr. Renee? Are you there?" Renee could tell that Veda's voice had softened. "You're not crying are you? You are crying! Tell me what's wrong. I'm sorry I yelled at you. I had no right to do that. Dr. Renee? Dr. Renee! I know you didn't hang up. Speak it me." Veda talked into empty air because Renee was afraid that her voice would betray her if she tried to speak now. She took a deep breath and wiped her face with more tissue. The one balled up in her palm was completely drenched from her tears. Finally, she attempted to speak because Veda would apparently not hang up. "I … nothing. I'm … okay." She managed to stammer out between sniffles.

"The hell you are!" said Veda. "You don't sound okay to me. I'm coming right over there. It's almost time for me to punch out. I'm going back inside my building long enough to lock up my desk. I dare Odessa Dillon to give me some grief about leaving a few minutes early. And, screw Doctor-Patient whatever the hell ya'll call it. I'm not your patient anymore, Dr. Renee—I'm your friend. I'll be over there in ten minutes. You need a shoulder to cry on, Girl. And Veda's gonna be right on over there so go unlock the front door for me."

"No! … No, Veda. Please … Don't jeopardize your job by leaving early," begged Renee. "There's no need. Really, I'll be fine. I just had … I just …" Despite trying so hard to keep it together, Renee suddenly lost it. She dropped the phone on her bed and allowed her tears to flow freely. Despite her protests to the contrary, she was actually glad that Veda was on her way.

CHAPTER 21 - BRENDA

By 9:00 AM Brenda arrived at work thirty minutes late. Her arrival would have been even later had she dropped off Baby Buddha at Mrs. Walker's, his new babysitter. Fortunately, Jerome, who was still out of work, offered to take their son to the babysitter's for her this morning. That was only fair since arguing with him had caused her to be late in the first place. Brenda felt bad about hurting Jerome's feelings when he had asked if their son could stay home with his daddy today. Jerome had tried to convince her that the new babysitter she had hired was not reliable, but Brenda knew very well that it was her husband who was not reliable. As she waited for the computer to boot up, she sipped her coffee and thought about Jerome's recent accusation against the babysitter. "*You know Baby, I called over there yesterday to see how my son was doin' and I could hear him in the background cryin' his little heart out,*" Jerome had complained to her. Brenda easily recalled their conversation as she had hurriedly tried to get dressed for work.

"That's what baby's do, Jerome—they cry. Mrs. Walker is wonderful with kids. Whenever I pick Justin up in the evenings, he's always dry, fed, and happy," Brenda had said, dismissing his allegations.

The image of Jerome sulking while sitting up in bed with the covers draped over his knees came back to her, along with the sting of his words. "He's my son too, Brenda! I wanna spend time with him while I can. It wasn't my fault I got fired! I can take care of Baby Buddha better than some stranger."

"Well Jerome, if you think you're capable enough to handle a three month old baby by yourself then you're certainly capable of finding another job! Just focus on that, will you?" She had regretted what she said when she saw the look of betrayal on his face, but it was too late to take it back once she had said it.

Brenda had tried to soften the blow and reason with him. "Taking care of Justin is not as easy as you think. I have to think of his welfare first. Babysitting him for an entire day might be too much for you right now."

There was no mistaking the hurt and anger in Jerome's voice as he gave her a cutting glare. "That's bullshit! You just don't trust me with my own son. You believe what those fools at UDS said about me failing that drug test. But it's all a lie. I swear it."

Brenda had looked at the clock next to the bed and realized she was running late. When Jerome offered to pack Justin up in his car seat and drive him over to Mrs. Walker's this morning, she reluctantly said yes. She supposed it was a small compromise.

It was good that no patients were on the appointment book today. The office would be quiet since Dr. Renee had taken the day off, which was not like her, thought Brenda. With nothing to distract her, she could knock out one of her assignments for the MCSE class that she was taking online to earn her Microsoft Certified Systems Engineer (MCSE) certification. She spread the installation manual out on her desk and followed each network setup procedure carefully. The dialogue boxes on the menu screen displayed the exact outcome as her manual instructed. It took two hours to configure a successful network connection linking Dr. Renee's PC in the reception area to Mr. Hayes's computer in his office. Both PCs could now share data, the printer, and had access to each other's hard drive. Brenda felt confident that one day soon she would be qualified to apply for a high-paying technical position. Although, she still had to complete several more courses in her MCSE training program, she had just accomplished a successful network configuration without a hitch. She smiled at her accomplishment.

She began browsing around the newly networked system to see what capabilities her administrator security access allowed. That's when Brenda discovered that Mr. Hayes's PC also linked up to a central server for a corporate account. She checked the profile on the account, and its registered owner was listed as Clifton C. Shaw, Techands Inc., Arlington, Virginia. Brenda saw that access to the company's central server allowed Mr. Hayes, the operations manager, to see all the emails, electronic file attachments and PalmPilot™ files under Shaw's userid. That meant that anyone else connected to the server could also see this data. Brenda felt uncomfortable having complete access to corporate files. It had taken most of the morning to complete step one, the network connection. Now Brenda wanted to hurry up and tackle the last task on her class assignment sheet, which was to restore the hard drives to their previous state and thus, remove her access to corporate files. This step, she would be relieved to complete.

Having missed breakfast, Brenda took a bite of the ham and cheese sandwich that she had packed for her lunch then resumed working. Without removing her fingers from the keyboard, she briefly glanced at the clock. With any luck she'd be finished with her class assignment, the filing, and record keeping and be ready to leave work by four o'clock. The restoration process proceeded as expected, but she quickly realized it required total concentration. Brenda had to repeatedly switch between display screens to modify the settings. The sudden ringing of the telephone intruded on the silence and broke her focus. The light flashed on her private work line. She recognized the babysitter's name, Mrs. Walker, on the caller id panel and quickly picked up the telephone, causing her to lose track of her place in the restore process. That couldn't be helped now. She wanted to find out how Justin was doing. "Brenda Johnson," she answered.

"Uh, Ms. Johnson. This Ms. Walker ..."

"Is Justin all right?" asked Brenda, interrupting.

"Huh? Well, I dunno. I suppose so. Your husband called this morning to say he was keepin' the baby home today. I just wanna make sure you understand you still gotta pay me for a full week on Friday," the babysitter said. "I just now got a chance to call you. I been busy with these kids all day. I figure your husband already told you what I told him this mornin', but just in case he didn't I wanted us to be on the same page so to speak."

Brenda did not let on that she didn't already know about Jerome's decision to keep Justin home. She assured Mrs. Walker that she would indeed be paid for a full week and that Justin would be there tomorrow. She would deliver him there herself. After hanging up the phone, Brenda stared at the computer monitor but could not recall which machine was currently active. Her mind was distracted now that she knew Jerome had lied about dropping Baby Justin off at the sitter's. Why hadn't he called to tell her? Of course, he knew she'd be pissed. She immediately called home and got a busy signal. She wasn't sure what to do next. She couldn't leave the restoration process incomplete, could she? This was the last leg of the restoration phase, yet a terrible feeling that had suddenly come over her, would not go away. She frantically dialed home again expecting to get an answer this time. She let the phone ring and ring but the voicemail did not come on and Jerome did not pick up. Her uneasiness mounted. She took a deep breath to calm her nerves and tried the number again, much slower this time just in case her feelings of uncertainly and dread had caused her to miss-dial. Again, there was nothing but constant ringing. The insides of her stomach began to tighten. Brenda didn't take the time to shutdown the computer. She left the restoration step undone and retrieved her coat and bag from the closet, locked the front door, and rushed home.

Brenda tried to drive home cautiously but kept noticing the speedometer inch above the speed limit. She resisted the urge to run through every yellow light as well as the red ones. Red-light cameras were clearly visible at several major intersections and were the only thing stopping her from outright speeding. She tried to stay calm and think of a reasonable explanation for why Jerome had not answered the telephone. Maybe he had taken Justin out for a stroller ride in the park she told herself. But for some reason this possibility didn't assuage her growing fear.

At some point as Brenda drove past buildings, stores and neighborhoods, things that should have been familiar to her suddenly seemed strange, as if she had never driven that way home before. She stared out the window, her mind in a fog. The car seemed to propel itself forward. Heart drumming and teeth clinched in desperation, Brenda could not shake a crushing premonition that something dreadful had happened to her child. She should have just been late for work this morning and taken him to the babysitter's herself, she thought. She was a fool to trust Jerome to do it, knowing how badly he had wanted to keep their son home. What if Jerome had gone out looking for drugs and left the baby alone? What if Jerome had not locked the crib rail in place as she had shown him a hundred times and Baby Buddha had fallen out of his crib? What if Jerome had left the stove on and the house had caught fire? *"Oh God, Please Please,"* Brenda prayed aloud, *"Please don't take my baby! Please let him be safe and asleep in his crib. I won't ask you for another thing God. But Please don't make me live through this if something bad has happened to my child."*

Brenda couldn't shake the feeling of disaster that had swept over her and had lingered there. Then, as she crossed into her Southeast Capitol Hill neighborhood, she knew the reason why. Long before turning the corner onto her street, she heard the sirens and smelled smoke. Seconds later, she noticed grayish-black clouds rolling up into the sky up ahead and then saw the fierce flames shooting out the windows of her home. Brenda slammed on the breaks right in the middle of the street and jumped out the car, running and shouting frantically with her arms flailing about her. "My baby! My baby! No, God No!" she hollered again and again. She tried to run into the burning house but a neighbor grabbed her and prevented her from entering.

PART TWO

And thus I clothe my naked villainy
With old odd ends, stol'n forth of holy writ;
And seem a saint, when most I play the devil.
William Shakespeare *(1564 - 1616)*

CHAPTER 22

After torching the Johnson home, the killer cruised down 8th Street in Capitol Hill driving a rented black Chevy Blazer SUV. His darting eyes watched from behind an insulated hood. Too dangerous to leave a baby deserted here, he thought while searching for a safe place to dump the kid. The decision to park the rented get-away vehicle two blocks away from the Johnson house started out as a good one, he had thought. But now, it turned out to be chancy, running two blocks away from a roaring fire with a screaming infant hidden under an oversized jacket, and hoping not to be seen. Every step carrying that yelping bundle wrapped in a blue blanket, posed a threat to being noticed and caught. How the hell could such a perfect plan go so wrong? Letting that kid remain behind and burn to death wasn't in the plan. All that mattered was that the intended target, Jerome Johnson, was dead.

One hand rested on the steering wheel of the Blazer and the other nervously tapped on the dashboard to the rhythm of an old school hit, "War" by the Temptations that bellowed out from a CD changer. The killer didn't seem to care if the loud music bothered the crying baby that was lying lengthwise on the passenger seat without benefit of a car seat. He wanted to go faster but was concerned that the baby might roll off onto the floor. Glancing cautiously down the street from side to side, the killer weaved in and out of traffic to try to beat the lights. Being too close to the crime scene increased the arsonist's fear of getting stopped and questioned by the cops. Not to mention his fear of being pulled over for carrying an infant in a moving vehicle without a car seat! Perspiration stuck to his cotton underwear and went through the woolen sweat suit.

When the infant stopped crying, the killer glanced down and noticed the baby's puffy red, tear-stained face. His eyes were closed and his little chest rose and fell. The killer figured the baby had cried himself to sleep. "Good," he mumbled aloud. "Soon as I find me someplace safe to drop you off at without puttin' a noose around my own neck, you outta here, Partner. Don't blame me if your daddy was an asshole." The killer approached a crowded bus stop where a group of bums stood nearby. Street-corner drunks laughed out loud, cussed, and passed among themselves a whiskey bottle wrapped in a brown paper bag. Coming up on the intersection of 8th and Florida Avenue Northeast, the killer didn't notice the light turn red. Suddenly, a pregnant homeless woman walked out into the street. The killer slammed on the breaks. Distracted from looking around to see who was watching, he came just inches short of hitting the woman.

"Hey, watch it asshole," she swung her fist at the driver.

"Why don't you act like you wanna live then? Get your slow homeless ass outta the street," the killer yelled back at her.

The woman screamed back at the driver as she stood defiantly in the middle of the street with her belly poking out and both hands on her hips. "I'll kick your punk-ass right here, pregnant or not. Get on outta that truck and come say that shit to my face, Punk!" The homeless woman then picked up a broken bottle from the curb and threw it at the driver's vehicle. For just a few seconds she stared into the seething eyes of the driver behind the wheel and recognized the dilated pupils and agitation, signs of a fellow dope fiend. She had been there herself months ago before she got pregnant. Homeless, with no family, and approaching her nine month, all she had in the world was her unborn baby. Once she realized she was pregnant she had stopped drinking and doing drugs.

The killer's hand trembled on the wheel from an aching desire to leap out of the SUV and beat this woman half to death. Realizing the danger and certain capture that action presented, he remained calm and drove on. As he approached the intersection of 8th and Florida Avenue, the killer noticed a guard sitting inside a booth at the front gates of Gallaudet University. He peered out from under his knitted hoodie and saw the homeless woman's image in his side mirror as she chased after his vehicle, still shaking her fists and yelling something he couldn't hear. He realized the guard at Gallaudet's front entrance must have seen the dispute with this crazy homeless woman, but there was nothing he could do about that now. He needed to make a quick getaway and this was as good a place as any he'd seen so far to unload this kid. He brought the van to an abrupt stop and grabbed the blanketed armload from the front seat. "Come on, kid. It ain't gettin' no better than this," he said between clinched teeth. The killer jumped out the van, holding the baby in his arms as he ran towards the guard's station. He set the bundle down on the sidewalk in front of the guard's station and raced back to the van. Once back inside the van, … tires left skid marks as the killer raced off, running the red light.

CHAPTER 23

In this usually quiet Southeast Capitol Hill neighborhood, the approaching sirens and the smell of smoke had enticed everybody out of their homes. Onlookers swarmed around the burning rowhouse like flies on a week-old corpse.

Deek had just left F. B. I. Headquarters and was headed towards his car. His meeting with Special Agent Ana Santos and the other members of the SOS Task Force had wrapped up early and now he was on his way back to police headquarters on Indiana Avenue. He enjoyed working on the "Save Our Streets" (SOS) Task Force, a joint effort between the FBI and the Metropolitan Police Department that the Mayor had spearheaded over the summer. The police chief recommended him to serve on the task force and he had accepted, although it typically required him to work long days, juggling responsibilities for two law enforcement agencies.

Just as Deek pulled out of the parking lot, his pager went off signaling a message from one of the guys at the fire station where his older brother Luke was a Lieutenant. It was Firefighter Cooper Brown paging him. Cooper had been temporarily elevated to platoon commander in Luke's absence while Luke was away on special training. Since Luke had always kept Deek in the loop and alerted him whenever there was a major box alarm in progress, apparently Cooper was not going to break with tradition, thought Deek. After receiving Firefighter Brown's page, Deek detoured from his route, turned on the siren and police flashers installed on the dashboard of his sports car, then raced off to the duty station. Deek represented the Metropolitan Police Department's Homicide division so none of the guys in Luke's crew thought it odd that Luke would give Deek advanced notice when something major was happening. If the fire turned out to be intentionally started and fatalities occurred as a result, the investigation would quickly get handed off to MPD homicide. This way Deek would already be in place. Deek would stay clear of the burning building, but once the fire was out, he'd look for evidence along with the fire investigator, who would have also been dispatched, to determine what happened.

In less than two minutes Deek arrived at the firehouse. He noticed a full buffet style spread of barely-eaten food abandoned on a large wooden table that sat in the middle of the kitchen area where large aluminum pots hung from the ceiling. A well-used grill, black iron stove, oven, and chipped cabinets filled up the moderate cooking space. While inside the duty station he heard the dispatcher from CADS (Computer Aided Dispatch Systems) send out communications over the PA system repeatedly to announce the box fire on 6th Street, SE in Capitol Hill. The dispatcher announced house on fire, second level, heavy smoke, and gave the address. Dispatch had also alerted the arson investigator and building inspector as was customary for a box fire alarm of this magnitude. Like the fire fighters, Deek's ears were trained to listen to the commotion stirring around him and still quickly carry out his duties simultaneously without getting distracted by noise. Practically living in a police station for the past six years, the noise coming from the PA system and ongoing dispatcher announcements didn't bother Deek.

Firefighter Cooper Brown and his crewmembers stepped into their smoke stained, heavy padded suits and pulled them over their regular

District of Columbia Fire and Rescue uniforms of navy knit shirt, dark blue slacks, and black-laced shoes. Cooper handed Deek an armful of fire fighter gear, and he quickly slipped on a padded jacket and pulled a helmet over his head. Instead of taking his car, Deek accepted Cooper's invitation to ride in the engine with the crew. He took his position in the back seat, between two fire fighters. "Let's roll," said Firefighter Cooper Brown. The caravan of ladder trucks and fire engines pulled out of the station at full speed and blared down the streets at ear-piercing volumes like they owned the roads.

When the crew rounded the corner onto 6th Street, they saw billowy smoke and yellow-white snarls of fire erupting from the dwelling at full blaze. Unfortunately, they had not arrived at the fire's incipient stage. The police, fire trucks and engines from other units pulled up to the scene at the same time. The entire block was now full of commotion. A hysterical woman was trying to break into the burning house while two neighbors attempted to hold her back. The woman kept screaming, "Let me through! My baby and my husband are inside."

The truck's team lifted their arial ladder up to the roof. The crewmembers climbed to the rooftop and ventilated above the fire so the smoke would climb upwards. Even though the added oxygen from the knocked out windows in the attic fed the fire, smoke could be more deadly than fire.

Deek ran alongside the suppression team. While Cooper and his men headed straight for the burning house, Deek rushed to assist the distraught woman who obviously lived there. As he got closer he recognized the woman. He had met her recently at Renee's office when she was introduced to him as Renee's secretary. Deek dialed Renee from his cell phone and let her know what was happening out there.

The woman who lived in the house kept hollering that her baby and her husband were inside. The crew's adrenaline pumped up whenever the mission included rescue. Rescue, life—that was the first priority.

They'd deal with fire as they encountered it. But the first thing to do was to get inside and look for any survivors. As leader of the battalion, Firefighter Cooper Brown axed through the door and forced it open. Ash and thick, acrid, black smoke blinded them. Flames swallowed the oxygen. All they could see was smoke and flames coming from the second floor. The suppression team put on their air masks. Cooper instructed his lineman at the nozzle to follow closely behind him.

They proceeded up the burning staircase. Their routine consisted of a 'vent, attack and search' plan with Cooper searching for survivors upstairs, while the other firefighter attacked the fire. Cooper maintained radio contact with his unit. They relied on touch and smell to guide them. Another team searched the main floor where the fire had not reached yet. Just as Cooper and one of his crewmembers were about to step onto the second floor landing, they felt the rumble of wooden floorboards crumble and a burst of flames soar outwards. The second floor completely collapsed to the basement in a pit of ash, wood and nails. The firefighter nearly fell through the floor but Cooper grabbed him just in time.

Cooper's heart sank when he realized he could not complete the search without placing his entire crew in a dangerous situation. He felt frustrated, angry, and helpless, but he forced himself to deal with the incident and not the emotion surrounding it. He was the officer in charge and could not expose his own emotions. He calmly reported on the radio that the top steps and second floor collapsed and they could not continue to search for survivors. Cooper told his men to fall back. They would have to put out the fire from the outside and forgo any hope of a rescue. He radioed in that no further units must go into the building and his crew was coming out. How would he explain to the woman outside that he could not proceed forward without putting his men in danger?

Cooper and his crewmembers exited the smoke-filled maze and stepped through the hollowed out doorway into clear, brisk air. The police had already cordoned off the area with yellow tape to block neighbors, onlookers, and unauthorized entry to the crime scene. Cooper knew that once he could no longer address life and safety, their second priority was to put out the fire. He organized the suppression teams from several other units to fight the blaze from the outside. Eventually, the fire smoldered to ash and debris. The rowhouse stood gutted and soot covered. The fire had been contained in this one family's dwelling. All other residents from the adjoining houses were safely evacuated as soon as the fire started and their homes spared.

Out of the corner of his eye, Cooper noticed that Deek and another woman were consoling the bereaved woman. He hadn't seen this other woman arrive, but clearly she appeared to be close to the victim who had lost her loved ones. Cooper felt relieved they were there. Now that the fire was out, he would have to go back inside and search for the bodies. The Medic Unit, EMS, and the Fire Chief stood nearby. He was certain one of them explained to the woman why the rescue could not take place but that didn't make him feel any better. He had no idea what she would do if they found her child and husband's body and brought them out. It had taken three firefighters to hold her down to prevent her from going into the burning house. If not stopped, Cooper knew she would have gone inside.

Deek caught Cooper's eye and noticed that he signaled for him to come over. He left Renee and Brenda standing at the edge of the sidewalk and joined Cooper and another official who stood near by. Cooper introduced Deek to Marshall Fuentes, the fire investigator. The building inspector, as well as, a specialist from Hazardous Material (Haz Mat as they were called) also arrived on the scene and approached the burned-out dwelling. Haz Mat and the building inspector had been dispatched right after Cooper reported the collapse from his radio.

Deek knew that even if Cooper had not paged him as soon as they got the box alarm, as a homicide detective he would have still been at the scene to determine if a victim's death was caused by murder or accident. He had already begun questioning witnesses and neighbors about what they saw. Just like arson investigators, putting all the pieces together and finding evidence was also Deek's job. He loved solving crimes and bringing the guilty to justice. Despite the tragedy of this situation, he wouldn't want to be anywhere else and was glad that Cooper had paged him right away.

The police and fire department units worked together and everybody went through their own routine. The fire investigator could exercise police and arrest authority but he was primarily concerned with determining if this was a crime of arson or an unfortunate accident. Deek, along with the fire investigator and building inspector, all donned latex gloves and went inside the building to sift through the rubble to look for evidence. This dance between professionals proceeded simultaneously, each involved in their own unique mission. While Cooper searched for any victims' remains, Deek and the fire inspector collected evidence of how the fire started and looked for signs leading to a perpetrator, such as, fragments and forced entry.

With the fire now out, they hoped there would be enough of a preserved scene left to examine. Cooper shared with the investigators that his gut instinct told him that this was no accident and was deliberately set. Deek and the fire investigator agreed. Because of its strength and intensity, the investigative team suspected that a highly flammable material had been used to start the fire. While rummaging through the basement, Cooper spotted a gasoline can and pointed it out to Deek and the fire investigator. Just as he suspected, a rookie arsonist, not a professional, had probably set the fire and used a simple accelerator like gasoline. Once a match or lighter ignited the gasoline, the entire room became engulfed in flames in a matter of minutes.

After the fire investigator pinpointed the blast seat to be in the master bedroom, they removed loose debris and placed it in an evidence container. Deek found a charred matchbox near the door jam and sealed it inside a plastic bag, labeled it with an exhibit number, initialed, and dated it. Next he wandered through the smoke-damaged kitchen towards the back of the house. He found pieces of duct tape scattered on the concrete back porch. Deek bagged the duct tape as potential evidence.

"Let's hope the lab can lift some latent fingerprints from this tape," Deek told Marshall Fuentes. At that moment, Deek noticed a shred of dark fabric caught by a protruding nail in the window frame. "Looks like our arsonist entered through the kitchen window," said Deek with a satisfied smirk upon realizing that the arsonist ripped his sleeve either coming in or escaping through the window. He carefully removed the ripped fabric with tweezers and placed it in a labeled evidence bag.

"That's right, Lieutenant Hamilton," nodded the fire marshal in agreement, "It might be just enough threads for lab analysis to identify the type of material and possibly the manufacturer."

While Deek and Marshall Fuentes finished checking the exterior, the building inspector examined the extent of the structural collapse and damage. The inspector concerned himself with the building's safety for the homeowners as well as for adjoining residents.

Several minutes later, Cooper yelled out. He had found the remains of an adult, male victim, but still no baby. The burns on the victim were so severe that they showed bone destruction and covered large areas. If this was the woman's husband, he had been burned and blackened like charcoal beyond recognition. None of the fire fighters had found the infant's body anywhere. It could take several hours to locate the remains of a tiny, three-month old victim. But Cooper and his crew would work straight through their shift if they had to in order to bring closure to that poor mother. Deek and the fire investigator were the first to leave the house. The paramedics carried the victim's sheeted body out on a stretcher. They wouldn't ask the wife to look. The people at the morgue could deal with that.

When Brenda spotted them bringing out a body, she broke free from the Medic's grasp. Renee rushed after her but an officer blocked both their entrances through the yellow police tape.

"Officer, my name is Dr. Renee Hayes. I'm a psychologist but I used to be a nurse. Perhaps I can help here."

"Then help her stay out of the way," the officer said grim-faced, "This is a crime scene."

While Renee was talking to the police officer, Brenda tore through the yellow tape and dashed towards the covered stretcher, carrying her husband's body. She snatched the sheet away. Then, she crouched to the ground on her knees, screaming, and doubled over in pain. The burns had seared off his skin and hair to the point of being unrecognizable. Deek pulled her away and draped the covering back over the victim's body. Brenda looked up at him and shouted through her tears, "Oh God, No! This can't be happening." She buried her face in her hands, as Deek supported her in his arms. "Please God, please help me. Oh God, where is my baby? Where's my son?"

Renee hurried forward and bent down to help Brenda up as Deek inched back. Renee answered the fire investigator's questions for Brenda and gave him the names of both victims, even though the infant's remains had still not been found. Renee also gave the fire marshal her contact information where Brenda could be reached. Renee knew that right now this tragedy was too unfathomable for Brenda to deal with all alone. While Brenda wailed uncontrollably over Jerome's sheeted body, Renee gently grabbed her secretary to allow the paramedics to take over. The paramedics hoisted the stretcher into the waiting ambulance as Renee held onto Brenda.

"Where are you taking my husband?" Brenda shouted at the EMS crew.

The fire investigator spoke up. "To the morgue, Ma'am. We need the medical examiner to perform an autopsy. This will confirm the cause of death."

"What for? It's not like he had a heart attack," she yelled, "I don't want my husband cut up."

"I know how you must feel, Mrs. Johnson. We're all sorry for your loss but we have strong evidence that suggests arson. That makes this a homicide," said the fire marshal. "The ME will conduct a blood test to look for the presence of carbon monoxide. Then we'll know if your husband was alive when the fire started and succumbed to smoke inhalation."

"Who cares about that?" cried Brenda, "It won't bring Jerome back. My husband and my baby are gone. You can never understand how I feel."

The fire marshal explained to Brenda that the rescue team had not found her baby's body yet. "We're doing everything we can, Ma'am. But we need the ME's report as soon as possible," explained Marshall Fuentes, "It'll reveal valuable information so we can bring whoever did this to justice. It's possible your baby could have been abducted by whoever started this fire."

Long after they took her husband's body away, Brenda stood there looking disoriented as the tears steadily flowed down her face. She walked around the yard in front of her house in a daze—speechless. Brenda tried to scream but no sound came out of her mouth. She could hear the noise from the ambulance siren until it faded off into the distance. She detected a strong stench of smoke that lingered in the air. But to Brenda this was not the pleasant smell of a wood burning fire on a chilly night after the fire has gone out. It was the putrid smell of death. Brenda didn't notice the stares from curious onlookers that still collected along the sidewalk around her house. She felt Dr. Renee and Detective Hamilton's presence close by, but she was not able to make out the mumbled sounds of their voices as they spoke to her. Then, she heard a loud shriek as if it came from a wounded animal—at least that's what her brain had registered. A distorted image of someone's face appeared as a gray shadow in front of her eyes. This face was the last thing Brenda saw before everything went blank and she felt her legs give way.

CHAPTER 24

The guard in front of Gallaudet University had noticed a darkly clad driver getting out of an SUV, and looking around suspiciously as he left something on the curb in front of the gate. Then, the driver had dashed back to his SUV and sped off. The guard left his station and went outside the gate to investigate. To his shock, he saw that the driver had left a baby on the curb and the guard squatted down and gently lifted the infant. He went back inside the booth and called Central Administration to report that someone had just left a baby at the gates. "Call the authorities," said the guard, "I have an abandoned baby out here that some idiot just drove up and left on the sidewalk."

"Oh my God! Who left it?" asked the secretary in Central Administration.

"Don't know. The person was gone before I could open my door," said the guard, "But somebody better come out here ASAP and get this kid 'cause he needs immediate attention."

"All right, All right. I'll call the police to see if anybody's reported a missing infant and then I'll call child protective services. Even if someone has filed a report with the police, child protective services will still require proper identification. I'm sure the police will wanna talk to you when they get here."

"Fine, but I don't know what to tell 'em. Like I said I didn't see much. I couldn't even make out the license plate but I do know the car was a black SUV. Looked like a Chevy model to me."

"Well, that's something. I'll send Rebecca out to your booth right now to get the baby."

"Good," said the guard and hung up.

Rebecca drove down to the guard's booth, retrieved the baby and took him to the administration building where several University officials waited for the police and a social worker to arrive to pick up the infant.

When the call from Gallaudet University came into the police station, the authorities immediately notified Child and Family Services' Intake Division at 400 6th Street in Southwest. They had not yet received any report of a missing infant. Less than thirty minutes later, Miss Angela Shepherd, a social worker from Youth Division, accompanied by a uniformed officer, arrived at Gallaudet University. While the police officer drove down to the front gate to question the guard, Miss Shepherd went to the ladies room and attended to the infant's immediate needs with clean diaper and fresh clothing. She returned to the secretary's office and sat down to feed the infant a bottle of already prepared formula while she waited for the officer to come back. After the baby had finished the bottle, Miss Shepherd propped him up in the car seat that she had brought along and took out her Polaroid camera and snapped a few pictures of the abandoned baby.

"What happens to the kid now?" asked the secretary who had placed the call.

"Well, we don't know who he belongs to and no one's reported him missing. Right now he goes to foster care until a legitimate relative steps forward and can prove who they claim to be," answered the social worker as she removed the baby from the car seat and held him in her arms. "Since the little fellow can't make it easy for us and simply tell us his name and where he lives, I'm going to Court first thing in the morning to report a John Doe," said Miss Shepherd. "I'll ask the Court's permission to release the baby's picture to the media where it'll be seen on television and in newspapers. Hopefully, someone will recognize him. Don't worry. I'll do everything I can to find his folks." The secretary nodded, visibly relieved.

Miss Shepherd patted the baby gently on the back as she explained. "As soon as we get the Court's approval or until we receive new information, Officer Benson will do a TV broadcast for unidentified abandoned children and show his picture under a 'Do You Know This Child?' caption," said the social worker. "It'll list the contact information and I hope someone from his family sees it in time."

"He's a cute little guy," said the secretary, smiling at the baby from behind her desk, "What if no one contacts the agency in time?"

"That creates a big problem," Miss Shepherd said, frowning. "Child and Family Services will keep the case in a hold status for only five days. If a relative produces the proper identification within that five-day holding period, the child can be released to them without much hassle. But after our holding period, it could take as long as six weeks to get through the courts no matter what anybody says or does. I'd hate to see the little fellow separated from his family that long."

"That's awful," said the secretary, shaking her head, "Let's pray somebody sees that broadcast in time. I know his family must be going crazy right now not knowing where their baby is. I still don't understand why somebody would do such a thing. Maybe, his mama is just a scared teenager and didn't know what else to do."

"Maybe. I suppose that's the most likely explanation. A kidnapper would have asked for ransom rather than drop the baby off unattended like that," said Miss Shepherd, thoughtfully as she continued to rock the baby in her arms. "You'd be amazed at how many young mothers and even fathers drop their children at our agency or other designated safe places like churches because they can't take care of their children.

And since there's been no Amber Alert issued by the police yet, parental abandonment is still a real possibility."

"That's so sad, Miss Shepherd," said the secretary. "I pray somebody legitimate comes in and claims him soon."

"Me too," said the social worker with a faraway look in her eyes. "Like I said, once the Court has control of the child it's a whole different ballgame. I've seen these situations turn into a major drama for the family when they try to get their child back. I hope it doesn't have to come to that and we can get this little guy back home safely where he belongs."

When the officer returned, Miss Shepherd laid the baby on an unused desk and zipped him up in a green padded snowsuit that she had packed in a large purse. She flung her purse across her shoulder and scooped the baby up in her arms. The officer grabbed the car seat from the floor. They headed out, thanking the secretary for contacting them right away.

Once outside of the administration building, Miss Shepherd fastened the baby in the car seat in the rear of the police vehicle and she and the officer sat up front. They next headed towards Children's Hospital emergency room to have a doctor check the baby over. On route, Miss Shepherd speed dialed one of the Child and Family Services Agency's most valued foster mothers, Mrs. Shirley Ann Turner who lived on 20th Street in Northeast Washington. Mrs. Turner had come through for the Agency on many occasions such as this.

Miss Shepherd knew she could rely on Mrs. Turner in a pinch without having to go through a lot of red tape. Mrs. Turner's specialty was infants and young children. She hadn't accepted any new foster children since her last young charge, an eighteen-month old baby with AIDS, had died during the summer, only two months ago. Mrs. Turner always got very attached to her foster children and was devastated after the sick baby finally succumbed to her illness. Still, Mrs. Turner didn't hesitate to agree to take in the abandoned child left at the gates of Gallaudet University once the social worker had explained the circumstances. The social worker hung up her cell phone, relieved that Mrs. Turner had said to bring the baby directly over to her house after the doctor at Children's Hospital checked him over. At least this baby seemed to be healthy and well-cared for. Mrs. Turner wouldn't have to nurse another sick child, thought the social worker as she glanced back to check on the sleeping baby. Hopefully, the little one would be united with his real family soon, thought Mrs. Shepherd as she rode along in silence and tried to drown out the noise from the police radio dispatch.

CHAPTER 25

B renda had collapsed in front of Renee and Deek at the crime scene. Fortunately, Deek had grabbed her in his arms before she hit the pavement. He carried her to Renee's car, where stretched out in the back seat she soon regained consciousness, only to begin sobbing into her cupped hands that shielded her face. Renee knew that Brenda was in no mental or physical condition to answer any more questions. There would be time for questions and answers later. Right now, Renee needed to get Brenda back home with her where she could rest without disturbance. She would ask Helen to prescribe a mild sedative or some Ativan so Brenda could at least rest for a few hours and then she might be able to think more clearly. There would be phone calls and arrangements to make later. Renee would be there to help her secretary take each step one day at a time.

Renee nodded her good-byes to Deek and took off for home. In her rearview mirror, she watched him walk back to where the fire marshal and one of the head firefighters had been talking. As she drove towards home, Renee felt guilty about how badly she had treated Deek at Sibley hospital when she found out about her pregnancy loss. She had lashed out at him simply because he was a convenient target. Her therapist and mentor, Dr. Helen Stone, reminded her that anger, grief, and guilt were normal, healthy emotions after a pregnancy loss. When the time was right, she'd apologize and explain to him that her anger was not directed at him but at her own failure to carry a baby full-term. Despite how Deek felt about her now, she knew he would do everything in his power to find the killer who had committed this horrendous, cowardly act.

Brenda sat on the white sleigh bed in Renee's guestroom and stared out at nothing, her eyes transfixed and her mind a blank. She didn't notice the soothing periwinkle blue walls that surrounded her or the sweet aroma of white tulips sitting in a clear vase on the nightstand. The moss green stems of the tulips stood sturdy and upright while she herself felt bent and broken.

"Would you like me to call someone to come over?" asked Renee, "your Mom or perhaps one of your girlfriends to come be with you?" In silence Brenda shook her head no. Then, she turned and gave Renee a faraway look as she spoke. "Do you really think someone kidnapped my baby? But why? Who would do such a thing?"

"Here, this might help." Renee held out a sedative in the palm of one hand and a glass of water in the other. She didn't want Brenda to dwell on the unthinkable. What she needed was sleep, then she could face whatever was to come in the morning. Brenda gulped down the sedative then swallowed a sip of water.

"This room has a private bath," said Renee pointing to a closed door. "You'll find everything you need in there—clean towels and wash clothes on the shelf, extra packs of unopened toothbrushes and other toiletries. Since I sometimes stay in this room myself, you'll find clean nightgowns and a robe in the dresser drawer. Help yourself to anything of mine. I think we're pretty much the same size. I'll be in my bedroom down the hall. Just come get me if you need anything," said Renee.

"Thank you, Dr. Renee" whispered Brenda, and lay down on the bed with her eyes closed. "You're welcome, Dear," said Renee and gently closed the door as she left.

Like Job and Elijah from the Bible, Brenda prayed that God would be merciful and take her quietly while she slept once the sedative began to take effect. She didn't want to wake up and have to realize this was not a dream. Her husband was really gone. She didn't know what had become of her child. Had he been abducted by kidnappers? Would they want a ransom? Why was this happening to her? Not even Veda or Cha-Cha, her best friends, could help her through this. She knew seeing her mother right now would only exacerbate things. Her mother would only deluge her with a thousand questions that she had no answers for. Brenda's mind ran wild with agonizing thoughts as she ran down all the possibilities? Oh God, where was he? Was he somewhere frightened, cold and hungry thinking that his Mama had deserted him? Or worse, was her baby boy gone too, along with his daddy—his tiny remains somewhere lost in the rumble that the fire marshal had not yet unearthed? *"Lord, this is too much to bear!"* she moaned. She rolled over on her side and balled herself up in a fetal position. Her tears streaked the pillow case. Brenda forced her mind to drift back to the start of that day, a happier time when she awoke at five and began her morning routine as usual. She had found Baby Buddha asleep in his crib with milk stains on his chin. She recalled his fresh baby scent and the rosy-tint of his fat cheeks. She could even picture Jerome coming downstairs to breakfast that morning, wearing his wide boyish smile and kissing her gently on the lips. These were the pleasant memories that Brenda willed herself to think of as she finally floated into sleep.

Renee returned to her room at the other end of the hallway. It was past dinnertime but she wasn't hungry and knew Brenda could not eat a bite either after what she'd just been through. She placed a Nina Simone CD in the player. The husky voice of the blues singer from her father's heyday piped through the built-in speakers. She stretched out on the loveseat and let the music soothe her. Renee didn't think she could feel any worse than she felt after her prenatal appointment but she was wrong. Her doctor said fifty percent of first-trimester miscarriages were due to blighted ovum condition. Was that supposed to make her feel better knowing that many other women faced the same type of loss as she did? Her OB/GYN's words kept circling through her mind. *"Your embryo failed to develop from its fertilized egg. Nothing but an empty sac. No heartbeat detected. I'm sorry but you don't have a viable pregnancy."* It only takes a moment for things to change forever, thought Renee. At least that's how she felt upon hearing her doctor say those words. As soon as she got home from the hospital that morning, she had put in an emergency call to Helen. Her psychiatrist talked to her on the phone for over an hour but nothing had helped.

Angel purred at her feet, then suddenly jumped into her arms. She stroked the Persian cat's fur and looked into its slanted, green eyes. This was the first time Renee did not detect indifference or outright disdain from her former feline adversary. Angel had never climbed up on her lap to be petted before. Petting Angel actually helped Renee to feel better.

"Looks like we're in this together, huh kitty?" said Renee, rubbing Angel's coat. "He's deserted us both. I suppose the only reason you're being nice to me now is because I feed you Fancy Feast instead of those little dry pellets." Renee let a smile escape her lips.

She had grown fond of Angel and it appeared the feeling was mutual. They were no longer competing for Bill's attention. Angel felt more like her cat than Bill's now. She held Angel close and felt the warmth from her cat's thick, white fur and delicate bone structure. "It must be nice to have such a simple, uncomplicated life, Angel," said Renee, talking to the cat as if it understood. "All you need to be happy is a can of tuna delight and a clean litter box, huh?"

"As for me, I want to share my life with a loving soul mate and experience motherhood before I die. What I get instead is an empty yolk sac and a husband who can't express intimacy and doesn't want to ever be a father. So you see now how good you have it Angel?"

Angel purred again on cue as if she wanted to soothe her owner. It helped. Renee knew she had to stop feeling sorry for herself. After all, Brenda had to be feeling a thousand times worse. As she sat listening to the music playing in the background and enjoying Angel's company, she put aside her own disappointment at not being pregnant so she could be there mentally and emotionally for Brenda. This was no time to feel sorry for herself. Brenda was in a far worse situation and needed her support in the days and months ahead.

Renee knew that before this Brenda had always relied on scripture to comfort her and give her strength. Renee wondered if that would be enough to help her secretary now as the unthinkable had happened, something every parent dreads. Brenda's tragedy was magnified by the sudden loss of her husband on top of not knowing if her child was also lost. Brenda often quoted one popular verse that said if we only have the faith of a mustard seed, we can move mountains. Renee didn't know what verse from the Bible it was but she recalled Brenda saying it around the office from time to time. Renee got up and reached on the top shelf in the corner of her closet. She retrieved Aunt Clara's King James Holy Bible then blew and wiped off the dust. They both would need to depend on faith now more than ever to see them through whatever blows life had in store for them next. But as for Renee, she feared she had forgotten how to pray or how to trust in God.

CHAPTER 26

Later that evening on the same night as the tragic house fire at the Johnson's residence, Renee was sitting at her writing desk in the anteroom off from her bedroom with Angel curled up at her feet asleep under the desk. She had just finished the last entry in her diary. Brenda was in the guestroom resting. Renee hoped the sedative that she had given Brenda had taken effect. Renee took out a few sheets of stationery and started a letter to her father. After only a few lines into the letter, she heard her bedroom door open and shut. Angel awakened and stared expectantly at the door. Just as Renee started to get up and go see if Brenda wanted something, she looked up to find Bill standing at the French double doors of her anteroom.

The first thing Renee noticed was his new, expensive-looking leather shoes. Her eyes traveled upwards to the tailored, navy blue, wide pinstriped suit, burgundy silk tie, and monogrammed shirt. He looked like a gangster or even worse, a replica of his business partner, Clifton Corbin Shaw. In Shaw's case Renee believed that was one and the same thing. Not only had Bill consulted Shaw's tailor but he also wore the same arrogant smirk on his face. He held a legal-size folder in one hand and a cognac in the other. Angel skirted out the open door. The cat passed Bill without brushing his ankles with her backside like she used to do when he usually came home. Obviously, Angel was a good judge of character and Bill's disposition had drastically changed since associating with Shaw.

"Oh, it's you," said Renee with a distinct edge in her voice. "I needed you at the doctor's office this morning," she added, giving him a brief disinterested glance.

Bill walked up and tossed the folder on her writing desk. "Cliff suggested a divorce lawyer," he said and waited, looking pleased with himself she noticed.

Renee kept her gaze focused on the letter that she was writing, without looking up at him. She knew he expected her to react to his announcement, but she did not react.

Bill then continued. "I had my lawyer draw up a legal separation agreement. The papers are inside." He pointed to the portfolio. "You've left me no choice, Renee, if you insist on going forward with this risky pregnancy at our age. I made it clear this is not what I want. I have plans and fatherhood at 52 is not part of them." She didn't respond but kept writing the letter to her father, though she heard every word he said. "Renee, I've come too close now to getting everything I want to let this setback get in my way. For the first time I've got my own flourishing company. Techands already has dozens of clients lined up and a crop of new recruits on the waiting list to be trained."

"I, I, I. You seem to be using that pronoun a lot lately," said Renee without looking up at him.

"Listen, Babe, I'm not just thinking of myself. Have you forgotten what all those doctors told you six years ago? They didn't give you much chance of carrying to term anyway. Why put yourself through that agony again?" Sweat beads formed on his forehead as he spoke. Bill took a gulp of his drink then continued in a begging voice that Renee noticed had lost most of its initial haughtiness. "I've got my suitcase downstairs, Sweetheart and I wanna move back home. Just say that you'll consider giving up this foolish idea. At least think about terminating this pregnancy before it gets too far along."

Renee threw down her writing pen, snatched up the folder and pulled out the separation agreement. "Where do I sign?" Bill frowned and turned pale. "You mean you'd throw away fourteen years of marriage just like that for something that probably won't happen anyway? Don't be so unreasonable, Renee," said Bill with outstretched arms.

Ignoring Bill, she picked up her pen. Without even reading the separation papers, she scrawled her signature next to the pink 'Sign Here' tab. She stuffed the papers back into the legal folder then resumed writing her letter.

"Sweetheart, what are you doing?" he said, and grabbed her hand, forcing the pen to drop to the floor. "Let's talk and try to compromise."

Renee pulled her hand away. "What for? I agree with you, Darling," she said in a calm yet sarcastic tone. She scooted her chair back an inch and folded her arms, giving Bill a smug look. "I'm making it easy for you to continue with your important plans. You've obviously given this solution a great deal of thought. You want a divorce and I'm granting it to you, an uncontested, no fault divorce."

Bill sat his drink down on the edge of the desk, gently. He loosened his tie and knelt down in front of her. He took both her hands in his and held on tightly so she couldn't wiggle free. "Renee, I don't want this, Babe. I just want things back the way they were."

"And if I do what you want, then things will go back the way they were between us?" she asked, looking at him pointedly. Bill released his grasp of her hands and rose stiffly from his knelt position, holding onto the edge of the desk for support. He turned away from her direct gaze as he attempted an answer. "I'm not saying things were great before." He moved towards the middle of the room, staring at his polished leather shoes while she waited for him to look for the right words to say and for the confused look to leave his face. "It's just that ... Cliff thought it might be better this way ... for both of us."

"Cliff thought!" she yelled, "I don't give a damn what that weasel thinks. Why is he in our business? Besides, it doesn't matter anymore,

Bill," she said and turned away from him. "Things can't be the same between us because I'm not the same. Motherhood is something I will not compromise on any longer."

Renee picked up the pen that had fallen to the floor. Then, turned to face Bill as she spoke. "For once, I actually agree with you. It's over between us. If I can get through this morning at the doctor's office alone and everything else I've seen this afternoon, I can survive anything alone. That's what I've been doing anyway throughout most of this marriage, surviving alone."

"All right, all right. You win," he sighed and threw up his hands, "I'll try it your way. I'll come to your next prenatal appointment."

"That won't be necessary."

"No, Babe, I mean it. I really want to. Please let me at least try to change."

"I said it won't be necessary, Bill. My doctor told me this morning that I don't have a viable pregnancy."

"What ... what do you mean?" he asked as he approached her, stopping short upon seeing the palm of her upright hand. She summarized what the doctor had explained earlier that morning. She wanted him to feel as badly as she felt—if that were even possible.

"There is no baby growing in my uterus. I have what's called a blighted ovum. It's a condition that sometimes happens in pregnancies. And, this time it has happened to me." Renee saw that Bill looked stunned.

It took several moments for him to speak. Renee gave him a sidelong glance and watched as his expression switched from bewilderment to remorse. She noticed that a film of sweat had settled over his brow.

Bill picked up the folder with the signed separation papers from the desk and positioned the folder under his arm. He picked up his glass of cognac that he had placed on her desk. "I'll go make you a cup of green tea with a little honey," he finally said with a brief nod to himself. "You always used to like green tea. It seemed to make you feel better." As he headed for the door to leave, he turned back to her and with an inflection in his voice that sounded like hopefulness. "Maybe we can talk later."

Renee listened to the sound of his heavy footsteps as he slowly descended the spiral staircase to the first floor landing. She hoped he was not going to want to move back home. With her own emotions in shambles and Brenda's life turned upside down, now was not the time to try to listen to what Bill wanted. It didn't seem to her like he even knew what he wanted. She struggled to remember what it was that had attracted her to him in the first place. She recalled how funny he used to be in the beginning of their relationship and how he could always seem to make her laugh. Renee knew she had been the serious, more studious type, but dating Bill brought out a fun-loving nature that she didn't even know existed. And, he was kind and attentive in the beginning. She couldn't remember when or how it all changed. She was too exhausted to think about that now. She locked her diary and the unfinished letter to her father inside her writing desk and retired to the bedroom to lie down.

Downstairs in the kitchen Bill poured out his unfinished drink in the sink and dumped the signed separation papers in the hidden trash receptacle. He flung off his jacket and threw it across the back of one of the kitchen chairs. Then he snatched off his already loosened tie and laid it on top of his jacket. Scanning the kitchen's perimeter, he searched for something to make tea in. When he spotted the tea pot conveniently sitting on the back burner, he proceeded to fill up the pot with water. While waiting for the water to boil, he slumped down into a chair and let his head fall into the open palm of his hands. Bill couldn't help admonishing himself for what had just happened. "You really screwed that one up, Buddy," he said aloud to himself. "That's just what you get for listening to Shaw. Now what?" He tapped his fingers on the countertop. No ideas came to mind. He couldn't prevent Renee's words from playing back to him in his thoughts. "*It's over between us."* No, she couldn't mean that, he thought, shaking his head. He would give her more time and some space. He figured he'd better go back to his room at the hotel at least for a couple of nights. Let things simmer down, he thought.

"Damn, I shouldn't have listened to Cliff! I'm such a fool," he said, and slammed his hand down. Bill realized he didn't have the panache that his business partner possessed when it came to the art of persuasion. He had seen Shaw step into a room full of people and in less than ten minutes get anybody to agree with him. Bill knew he had really made a mess of things trying to be like someone he wasn't.

He had always resisted telling Renee the real reason he had never wanted to be a father. He had made that decision years ago. If he hadn't been so scared of the knife he would have gone and had a vasectomy done years ago, and that would have been the end of it. Though perhaps not he reasoned, since Renee still wanted to adopt a baby when she found out she was having problems carrying a child to term. She had begged him many times to open up to her and talk about what was causing his unnatural fear of fatherhood, but he had always skirted around her questions until he got angry when she veered a little too close to the truth. He knew how much she wanted to be a mother, but that wasn't enough to make him face his own demons and reveal what had happened to him as a child. One would think that an only child would be loved and cherished growing up, but that was not the case for him. Now, that all the parties involved were long since dead there was no use airing his family's dirty secrets. His parents had been deceased for ten years now, but he had lost touch with them years before they died in that plane crash.

The whistle of the tea pot startled him out of his thoughts. He jumped up and turned off the burner and slid the screaming teapot to a cold burner where the whistling receded to a soft hissing sound. He grabbed a cup and saucer from the cabinet and filled the cup with boiling water. He knew how Renee liked her green tea. She wanted the tea to steep in hot water for at least 5 minutes before adding honey and a squeeze of fresh lemon juice. He sat back down and stared at the cup as he waited for the tea to get good and strong and watched the steam circling the cup's rim, unable to block the memories that he usually managed to keep buried. Bill gazed at his distorted reflection through the tabletop for a few moments, then closed his eyes. Things that he had never shared with another living soul came back to him.

He had been a pre-menopausal baby, a complete and unwelcome surprise to his middle-aged parents. His mother wrongly assumed she was past her childbearing age and was in her late forties when she conceived. By the time they discovered she was pregnant, it was too late to do anything about it. They were stuck with the burden of an unwanted child, having decided early in their partnership that they would remain childless so they could devote their full attention to scholarship and research. Bill's parents were well educated and appeared to be normal from all outward signs. They were grant-funded, research doctors and spent all their time in the lab conducting studies at the University of Southern California. When they weren't writing grants to get more funding for their research they were in the lab working. Neither wanted to practice medicine and deal with patients, nor did they want children to hamper their lifestyle and commitment to science. Both parents were undeclared alcoholics throughout much of their adult lives that made their already short tempers even shorter. Cocktails before, during, and after meals were a staple in the Hayes household.

Bill had no memories of ever feeling loved or wanted in the three bedroom house where he grew up in Corona, California. In addition to razor-sharp, switch beatings and slaps that left hand prints for the smallest offense, such as getting a B on his report card instead of straight A's, he was regularly ordered to strip naked and stay locked in a dark, closet for hours without food or water. He could never figure out why it didn't occur to two seemingly intelligent people that they could have simply given him up for adoption. But for all he knew perhaps they had tried to go that route and no one wanted to adopt a black male infant. To any normal adult, let alone a child, that locked closet where they kept him isolated for hours would have seemed as awful as any thirty-day stretch in solitary confinement at San Quentin Prison.

He managed to hide from his teachers and classmates what went on behind the doors of 41 North Collins Lane. As a child, Bill never told anyone what his home life was like or invited friends over because he was too ashamed. He couldn't remember at what point he had made the conscious decision to never have children. He feared how he might raise them. God forbid if his parents' anger, impatience, and aversion to children turned out to be a hereditary trait. Bill knew he couldn't take that chance. He was petrified of being a father because he feared he might repeat the cycle of abuse that his parents had inflicted on him until he turned 18 and joined the Air Force, leaving home for good.

When the executor of his parents' will informed him that their plane had gone down on the way to a scientific conference in Munich, Bill didn't register shock or grief. All he remembered feeling was numbness. He quickly sold their house on North Collins Lane and closed that chapter of his life forever, vowing he would never discuss it with anyone. It was ironic when he met and fell in love with Renee, a psychoanalyst who could have helped him deal with those issues. So far he had successfully hidden that part of himself from her, just as he had successfully managed to deceive his teachers and friends throughout his childhood. He didn't want anyone to know how much he had been hated as a child.

Bill couldn't reconcile his belief that his genes might be contaminated with a strain of depravity that would only get released if he assumed the role of fatherhood. To save an innocent child from even the remotest possibility of that happening, he would not put an unsuspecting child in danger and have the cycle repeat itself. That was the only way he knew how to rationalize it, even though Renee would never understand and would always think he was being selfish and unreasonable. There was nothing he could do about that. She would never know how much they actually had in common by being raised in dysfunctional households. He knew about Renee's tyrannical aunt who had raised her, but she would never find out about his hateful parents who had raised him. He figured the best thing to do now was to give her some time to get over her disappointment of not being able to bear a child of her own. Once things got back to normal, he would show her that he could give her the kind of love and attention that she needed. Adopting a baby would not give her that, but he would.

Bill noticed there was no longer steam floating up from the tea. He felt the cup and realized it was lukewarm and the tea looked as black as coffee. Bill got up and poured the ruined tea down the drain. The hissing from the teapot was gone and the water had cooled down as well. He could either start the water boiling again or leave the house, which he figured was probably what Renee would prefer anyway more than she would want a cup of tea. He picked up his jacket and tie from the back of the chair. On his way towards the foyer he glanced up at the top of the staircase then on his way out he picked up his suitcase that stood by the door.

CHAPTER 27

Renee heard the front door slam shut. After Bill left she went to the guestroom to check on Brenda. She knocked on the door of the guestroom, but when she didn't get a response she cracked the door open just wide enough to peep in. Lying on the bed with an open Bible in her hand, and clinging to a string of white crystal beads, Brenda looked drained as if all life had been zapped out of her. Renee entered the room. "I knocked," she said, sitting on the edge of the bed, "you must not have heard me. What are you doing?" Renee asked, pointing to the string of beads in Brenda's hand. Brenda gave her a weak smile. "I was praying my rosary."

Renee nodded that she understood. "Oh, I almost forgot what I came in here to tell you," she said. "My housekeeper, Chizuko will be arriving shortly. I've asked her to stay with me for a few days to help out. My driver's dropping her off and he just called to say he should be here in about ten minutes. Chizuko's also bringing us a light dinner. When she gets here I hope you will try to eat something so you can keep your strength up, Dear."

"I'll try, Dr. Renee," said Brenda, unconvincingly.

"Brenda, would you like me to call a therapist that specializes in grief counseling? I know an excellent one who's good with helping people cope with unexpected loss."

Brenda laid her hand on the open pages of Psalm 91 in her pocket-sized bible that she always kept in her purse. "Thank you, but I already have my grief counselor right here. I am only strong because I have faith. I know my baby is alive and angels are watching over him."

"Of course, your baby is all right, Dear," Renee squeezed her hand gently. "I'm sure we'll hear something from the investigator soon."

"I know we will," said Brenda, straightening up in bed, her eyes wide with conviction. "I'm ashamed to admit Dr. Renee that I was feeling doubtful for a minute when I first got here. You know it's easy for Christians to praise God in good times, but in tribulations we sometimes forget and start blaming Him for bad things that happen to us. But, I'm alright now. I'll wait to hear what I already know."

Renee didn't know how to respond to that. "All right, Dear. Just tell me if there's anything I can do for you."

"You've done all you can do Dr. Renee and I appreciate you letting me stay here," said Brenda. "It's peaceful here and that's just what I need right now to allow me to pray and meditate."

Renee stared ahead blankly for several moments. She didn't understand how Brenda was able to be so strong. She wanted to ask her how she was managing this terrible tragedy, what was the secret? But she felt awkward and inept. As a psychotherapist, she was supposed to be the one trained at helping people get through their emotional and psychological difficulties. As if reading her mind, Brenda asked, "Would you like me to read you a few of my favorite verses from this psalm?" Renee turned to look at her secretary and nodded yes.

Hearing the calmness and assurance in Brenda's voice, sent a wave of peace through Renee as she listened. "I will say of the Lord, *He is* my refuge and my fortress, my God, in Him will I trust … Thou shalt not be afraid for the terror by night, nor for the arrow that flieth by day … Nor for the pestilence that walketh in darkness, nor for the destruction that wasteth at noonday …" Renee was enthralled with the words that Brenda read from her Kings James Bible.

Brenda ended with lines 9 through 12, her most comforting verses from Psalm 91. "Because thou hast made the Lord, which is my refuge, even the most High, my habitation; *There* shall no evil befall thee, neither shall any plague come nigh thy dwelling. For he shall give his angels charge over thee, to keep thee in all thy ways. They shall bear thee up in their hands, lest thou dash thy foot against a stone."

Renee hadn't realized that the soft muffled sobs were her own until Brenda had stopped reading. She wiped her eyes with the sleeve of her robe and took a few moments to collect herself. "Thank you, Brenda." The women hugged and Renee rose to leave, returning to her room where she could be alone to offer up her own prayers.

A few hours later ...

At around 8 o'clock that evening the doorbell rang. Chizuko went to open the door. A well-dressed middle-aged woman, wearing a black wool Greta Garbo hat with the brim cocked over her left eye, pushed pass Renee's housekeeper and stepped inside the foyer. "I'm Mrs. Irene Kenmore Adams, Brenda Johnson's mother," said the woman in a haughty voice. "I've come for my daughter."

"*Konbanwa*, Adams-san" said Chizuko with a slight bow. "I go get her now." Chizuko rushed to fetch Renee and to let Brenda know that her mother was downstairs.

Renee descended the staircase and met Brenda's mother at the foyer. "Good evening, Mrs. Adams ..."

Irene Adams cut her off. "I was out all day and just heard the terrible news about the fire and rushed right over here figuring my daughter might be with you. Is my baby girl here Dr. Hayes?"

"Yes, I brought her home with me earlier this afternoon when they took her husband away. It was horrible," said Renee, shaking her head, trying not to relieve the experience. "But I think she's doing fairly well under the circumstances. We still haven't heard anything from the fire investigator yet about her son but we're both hopeful. She's upstairs now preparing to retire. We've not long ago had supper together in my anteroom. At least she was able to eat a few bites."

Irene dismissed Renee with a wave of her hand. "Well, I've come to take my daughter home with me where she belongs," said Irene and swung her beaver fur coat over her left shoulder.

"She took a sedative after dinner so she'll probably go right to sleep. Shall I ask Chizuko to make us a cup of tea before you leave, Mrs. Adams?"

"Look, I didn't drive all the way over here for tea and chitchat. I'm going upstairs to get my daughter."

"That's probably not a good idea, Mrs. Adams."

"Brenda needs her mother at a time like this. Why didn't anyone call me? I had to hear about the accident from the six o'clock news."

Irene Adams pushed Renee and Chizuko aside then marched straight upstairs, yelling for Brenda. Neither one of them dared stop her. Dressed in a short, fitted, turquoise suit, matching suede shoes, and a coordinated, paisley silk scarf draped around her neck, Mrs. Adams looked too elegant for someone who had rushed over to comfort her daughter in a time of crisis. She had obviously put a good deal of thought into her appearance before 'rushing' over to see about her daughter, Renee thought. After about two minutes, she sailed back down the stairs.

"I can't get her to budge. At least that no-account husband of hers turned out to be good for something after all since she'll get his death benefit money now. Good thing she had the foresight to take out that $50,000 dollar life insurance policy on him."

"Brenda told you that?" asked Renee skeptically. She knew that Brenda rarely confided her personal business to her mother.

"Well, not intentionally. Saturday before last she called me. Frantic, she didn't know where that s.o.b. was. I didn't trust him and for good reason. Turns out he was up to no good instead of in some kind of accident like she thought at first."

Renee listened as Irene blathered on and on. Jerome's mother-in-law didn't have any qualms about talking ill of the dead.

"The day she called me over, she had just found out from his boss that he had gotten fired for using drugs at work. He told her he was out doing a midnight run when in fact he was holed up at his ex-girlfriend's place. Umhum, some midnight run," Irene said, rolling her eyes.

Renee managed to slip a few words in before getting cut off, "Well, I don't see how that ..."

Irene continued, not bothering to listen to whatever Renee was trying to say. "Anyway, the next day I told Brenda to get herself a life insurance policy on him before it was too late and nobody would insure him. She'd need some kind of safety net because people like Jerome don't live a long life I told her plain and simple. That's when she informed me that they both had policies on each other for 50 K since that's all the coverage they could afford. They wanted to be sure the baby would be okay in case something happened to either one of them. Turns out that was the best decision that girl ever made. Now that the fool's dead, she'll finally get some reparation for her years of heartache with him. She'll need that money to take care of her son and get back on her feet after losing all her possessions in the fire."

Irene Adams removed her black, felt hat and fluffed out blond tinted wisps of chemically dyed hair with a diamond-jeweled hand. Renee knew the insurance company would not issue any death benefits until they determined the cause of the fire. Mrs. Adams apparently did not know that her grandson was at the house during the fire since she appeared to be more concerned about the fifty thousand dollar insurance policy on Jerome. Apparently, the evening news did not reveal all the details or she failed to listen to it. The fire investigation team was still combing through the debris, looking for the baby's remains once Brenda informed them that the child had not been at the babysitter's at all that day like he was supposed to be. But Renee didn't know how to tell Irene this.

"Mrs. Adams, unfortunately, you didn't get the full details from the news report."

"What do you mean?"

"I'm sorry to tell you this but your grandson is missing. He was supposed to be at the sitter's but Jerome kept him home without Brenda's knowledge."

"Missing? Is my beautiful baby boy dead too?" she shrieked.

"That hasn't been confirmed yet. A crew of firefighters, police, and the insurance investigator are still at the scene, searching for evidence," said Renee, "It's late but I understand they've rigged up lighting. They said they won't give up until they find something. I'm just waiting for someone to call here with more information. I'm so very sorry about your grandson, Mrs. Adams."

"Oh my God, No," she cried and covered her mouth, "That child was supposed to be at his new babysitter's. Why was my grandchild in the house with that incompetent fool? Poor Brenda. She must be devastated. As a mother I know how she must feel," Irene wailed, "I'm sure she thinks it's all her fault. I told her repeatedly not to leave her baby with that worthless, drug addict husband of hers. I hope he didn't burn the damn house down doing crack. I have to be here for my baby girl when she wakes up."

"Oh God, I sure hope it was some kind of electrical overload that caused the fire, and not from that idiot doing crack," said Mrs. Adams, frowning. "Then the insurance company sure as hell won't pay Brenda a dime."

"Well, I doubt that Brenda's thinking about money right now," said Renee, in a curt tone.

"Lord, lord, lord, how did this happen?" Her eyes scanned the living room wildly until she found a comfortable chair and fell into it. Chizuko offered her a glass of water. Irene shook her head and waved it away.

"I need something stronger. A Vodka or scotch on the rocks if you have it."

Renee poured her a drink from the bar and handed her a half-filled glass of scotch. The woman would have to be sober enough to drive back home which Renee hoped would be soon. She didn't want Mrs. Adams to get too intoxicated to drive home. The last thing Renee wanted was to have to invite her to spend the night as a houseguest. Irene drank the scotch down in one gulp and held out her hand for another. "This is bad, this is real bad," Irene shook her head and wailed loudly without tears until Renee had re-filled her empty glass.

"Mrs. Adams, please don't mention anything about insurance benefits when you speak to Brenda." Somehow Renee didn't think finding her mother downstairs would be a source of reassurance to Brenda when she woke up. The telephone rang. Renee recognized Deek's cell phone number from the callerid view pad. She took a deep breath and exhaled before picking up. She hoped he wasn't calling with bad news. As soon as she heard him say hello, she could feel the frustration in his voice. Renee braced herself for another dreadful update. She hoped he wasn't calling with bad news about Brenda's baby.

"Renee, is Brenda able to come to the phone?" asked Deek.

"I don't think so. I sedated her after dinner so that she could get some sleep. What did you find out?"

"We examined the scene for five hours straight. No other body was found in the house. What it looks like we have now is a child abduction case in addition to the homicide and arson. They've already issued an Amber alert."

Deek told Renee he was at the police station and not planning on getting any sleep tonight. "When she's able to talk to us, we'd like to question her. Including, the FBI in case the kidnapper tries to extort a ransom. That fire was no accident," said Deek. "Someone broke in through the back window. We know for a fact foul play was involved. My partner and I will work closely with Marshall Fuentes. I can personally guarantee we're going to investigate this case until we catch the torch responsible and get her child back safe. Please tell Brenda that for me."

"By the way, I have a number for the Fire Victim Assistance program," he said, "Brenda's probably not thinking about that right now but they offer immediate assistance to victims of fire."

"I've got a pen. I'll take down the number," said Renee and wrote the telephone number that Deek recited.

"And, here … write down this other number for her. The Vanishing Children's Alliance," he said and gave her that contact as well. "VCA is a non-profit that should be able to offer help in case it takes longer than we hope for someone to come forward with information about her son. Let her know that I just entered the case into the National Center's Missing and Abducted system so VCA can get involved if it comes to that."

"Thank you Deek for all you've done," said Renee, "I hope her child will be found soon before all the paperwork even starts circulating."

"I hope so too, Renee. As I said, we've got alerts out and additional manpower working on finding her son along with investigating this crime. But we still have a long way to go," he said, the fatigue evident in his voice. "The first 48 to 72 hours are critical in solving a crime. Please assure Brenda we're doing everything we can to find her baby and catch her husband's killer."

"I know you are. Deek?" she hesitated, "I have a favor to ask."

"Sure Doc, what is it?"

"I'd like to be involved in the investigation. I'm not talking about heavy police work but I can offer a psychological criminal profile of the killer based on his actions, as well as, come up with some theories to help catch this person. If you want to check my credentials you'll see I do have expertise in criminal psychology."

"Renee, I really don't think that's a good idea and I'm sure …"

"Deek, please. I need something important to occupy my mind right now and I can't think of anything more important than this. I know I can help this investigation."

"I understand," he said, "but you haven't had time to deal with what your doctor told you this morning. And now, this."

As always, Deek honed right in on her feelings. He was so in tuned to her needs just like a soul mate would be for someone they loved. Yes, Renee desperately wanted to help Brenda find her baby and her husband's killer to make sure justice was done. She knew she certainly wasn't emotionally prepared to treat a full caseload of patients. But those weren't the only reasons she wanted to be involved in the case. Renee needed to be close to Deek as much as possible and working with him on solving this arson/homicide/abduction case would provide that opportunity.

"I can't promise you anything," he said, "Let me talk to my partner about it. But if we do decide to let you join the team, you have to promise to stay clear of going out on your own to follow-up on leads or doing anything that might jeopardize your safety. We'd welcome your insights about people and observations on the case, but that's the extent of it. Agreed?"

"Of course," she said, beaming like a schoolgirl, "Thank you Deek."

"Will you be okay?"

"Yes. I think so. I'm not thinking about myself."

"I know. Neither am I. Call me if anything comes up or if you just need to talk. I'll always be here for you. I'm sorry about the way I stormed off earlier this afternoon," he said.

"Don't apologize. You had every right. Listen, I can't talk about that right now. Goodbye Deek and thank you again."

Renee hung up the phone and started towards the stairs to check on Brenda. If she found her at least half-awake, she'd tell her what they found out so far. They knew her baby was not in the house during the fire because they didn't find any other victim's remains besides Jerome's. They still didn't know yet if the baby was safe or where he was. But at least there was still hope of finding him alive. That was something to be thankful for.

Irene Adams rushed towards Renee. "Was that news about my grandson?"

"Yes, they didn't find his body in the house. The police suspect he's been kidnapped. I have to try to wake Brenda right away and tell her. I pray the baby's safe somewhere and the person who took him will bring him home unharmed."

"Yes, me too," said Irene solemnly and dabbed at her dry eyes. "Did they find out how the fire got started? Could they tell if it was an accident or deliberately set?"

"No," said Renee and left it at that. She had no intentions of divulging anything else to this woman. There was no telling what she'd say to Brenda. Mrs. Adams would have to get her information like everyone else—from the 11 o'clock news.

"Why would somebody take a three month old baby? Maybe they plan on selling Baby Justin or torturing him for some sick, perverted pleasure," Irene moaned.

It was clear to Renee now why Brenda had not wanted her to call her mother to come over. This woman was incapable of consoling anyone's pain. As a therapist, Renee was able to grasp the depths of some people's criminality but she would never have revealed any of those terrible possibilities to Brenda or to her mother.

Renee couldn't stop Irene Adams from following her upstairs. Irene wore a concerned look when she saw her daughter lying on the bed in a drowsy lethargic state. Renee didn't want to tell Brenda everything that Deek had said on the phone with her mother there. She hoped after a brief visit she would see that Brenda needed rest and would finally leave. She would say no more in front of Brenda's mother than what she had already revealed to her downstairs. Irene shoved Renee aside and sat down on the edge of the bed next to her daughter. She gently rubbed Brenda's cold hand. To Renee's surprise, a real tear settled in one of Irene's eyes. "My poor, poor baby doll," said Irene, "Everything's going to be all right. Mama's here now."

Irene glanced up at Renee and noticed an icy look on the psychologist's face. Perhaps Brenda's boss wasn't as gullible as she first thought. Irene decided she'd have to keep a close eye on this nosey bitch and make sure she didn't meddle in her family's business and ruin her plans to get some of that insurance money now that Marvin had reduced her allowance to a mere pittance until she paid back that $20,000 in personal credit card debt. The sooner she got Brenda out of there and took her home, the better.

"Come on, get up, Baby Girl. Let's go home now," said Irene, lifting Brenda's arm and trying to hoist her up. "Let Mama help you, Baby." *Damn, I shouldn't have worn these high heel pumps,* thought Irene as she struggled to keep her balance and raise Brenda from the bed.

Renee made a quick study of Irene Kenmore Adams and summed her up in a few minutes. Renee saw before her a self-centered manipulator. And that was being nice. Brenda was the type who could be easily influenced and used. Renee could tell Mrs. Adams would have no moral issue with taking advantage of her daughter's trusting nature. And, she seemed a little too interested in that insurance money.

"Excuse me, Mrs. Adams but I think it might be best for Brenda to rest here tonight if she'd like to," said Renee, "Then she can decide what she wants to do in the morning. She's more than welcome to stay here as long as she wishes. Brenda's become like part of my family."

"But she isn't, is she, Dr. Hayes? My daughter belongs at home with her own family during a tragic time like this."

"Mama, do you mind if I speak to Dr. Renee alone for a minute?" asked Brenda.

Irene cast a wicked glare at Renee, then smiled at her daughter and said, "Of course not." She sailed out the room, leaving the door slightly ajar as she waited just outside the room in the hallway. Renee closed the door tight and went to sit on the bed next to Brenda. She saw the open bible on the nightstand where Brenda's favorite Psalm 91, was highlighted.

"I guess you know I've read this psalm over so many times I've practically memorized most of it," said Brenda, and with her eyes close, she recited the first verse. "He that dwelleth in the secret place of the Most High shall abide under the shadow of the Almighty."

"What does that mean?" asked Renee, holding onto Brenda's hand.

"It means that if you believe in God, you become fortified through your belief," Brenda explained. Renee nodded. She knew Brenda's faith in God was strong and she'd need that faith to see her through these next few days. She told her everything that Deek had said on the telephone. Brenda cried with relief at the news that her son had not been consumed in the fire with Jerome. She dried her eyes. Renee watched as Brenda silently mouthed a prayer of Thanks to God for saving her son from the flames. Even though she still didn't know where he was she still gave thanks to the Lord.

"Dr. Renee, I don't know why this terrible thing happened but I know everything will be okay in time," said Brenda, "and I know my baby is safe wherever he is and he'll come back to me."

"I only wish I had your level of faith," said Renee and turned away so Brenda would not see the tears welling in her eyes.

"What's wrong, Dr. Renee? I can tell you're hurting too. Everything happened so fast with me that I haven't taken a moment to see your pain. Forgive me for not noticing before."

"It doesn't matter, Brenda. Don't worry about me," Renee started to rise, but Brenda drew her back.

"Yes, it does matter. I've noticed enough outside of my own misery to see that your husband hasn't been here for you. And something's weighing heavy on your heart, isn't it?"

"You're right, Bill hasn't been here. My husband and I split up and this time I think it's for good. I know it's time I stop fooling myself about my marriage," said Renee, "But that's not the worst of it. The thing is Brenda, I found out at the doctor's office this morning that I have a rare medical condition. Even though my pregnancy test turned out positive, no embryo developed inside my uterus."

Brenda stared at Renee with a blank, horrified look.

"Bottom line, I'll never be a mother like you. It's not in the cards for me."

"You don't know that, Dr. Renee," said Brenda. "Nobody knows that but God."

Both women hugged and clung to each other for several seconds. Somehow, they understood and it felt better to know they weren't alone.

"I didn't want to go home with my mother anyway, Dr. Renee. Now I know I belong here with you. We've both suffered a terrible loss. We need to see each other through this."

Renee nodded and wiped her face with tissues from the box on the dresser.

"We'll be okay," said Brenda, patting Renee's hand, "Sometimes it seems like there's no hope, no way out. You're lost. But I believe whatever the problem or the tribulation, He will deliver us if we have faith."

"I'll try to believe that Brenda. I really will. I'll try to learn from your strength."

"I'm not always strong," said Brenda. "Like everybody else I have my bouts with spiritual failure from time to time, but do you know what Dr. Renee? Talking to you earlier today and reading those scriptures to you, helped me reaffirm my faith. They'll find who's responsible for Jerome's murder. My baby is safe some where and he's coming home to me. I can see the whole thing in my mind."

Suddenly, they heard a forceful knock, followed by the door swinging open and Irene Adams's irate presence waltzing through the room.

"How long is this girl talk crap going to last?" snapped Irene, "It's getting late and your father expects me home soon. Are you ready to leave now?"

"I've decided to spend the night here, Mama. Why don't you go on home and I'll call you tomorrow. I promise."

"Well! This is really just too much, Brenda Jewel Adams," said Irene, posed at the end of the bed, with both hands on her hips.

"I'm still Mrs. Brenda Johnson, Mama. I'm not dropping my late husband's name," sighed Brenda, wearily and leaned her head back on the pillow.

"Humph. I'd never expect this kind of disrespect from you."

"I'm sorry, Mama. I'm not trying to disrespect you. I think I can calm my nerves better here. I just want to spend a quiet night alone so I can pray and meditate. Please try to understand."

"Well, I don't understand! I don't understand any of it. Sometimes I wonder whose child you really are because you sure as hell don't take after me," she said and snatched a linen handkerchief from the crevice of her breast. She cried dramatically into the handkerchief. "I've devoted my entire life to being there for you and all I get is ridiculed." Irene whined, "Your father's not much better. He completely ignores me now. I can't get two words out of him these days except 'How much did that cost?' What am I suppose to do if I'm no longer needed as a wife and a mother."

Brenda massaged her aching forehead. Irene, suddenly, grabbed her daughter by the torso and attempted to lift her from the bed. "Come on, Baby Girl. Enough is enough. You're coming home with me," she said, forcefully.

Brenda pushed her mother's hands away, "No, Mama. I said I'd like to rest here tonight."

Renee stepped closer to Irene until she was inches from her face. She didn't know what had come over her but suddenly she felt as though she was transferring her suppressed anger for her long deceased Aunt Clara onto Irene Adams who actually reminded her of her overbearing aunt. Renee never had the nerve to stand up to Aunt Clara, but if she had been able to tell her off, she knew what she would have said. Renee gave Irene a hard-eyed stare. "Look Mrs. Adams, I know you're Brenda's mother but let's get this straight. This is not about you or your need to control everything."

In a shift move, Irene unfastened the single button that tugged at her midriff and flipped her jacket open. She crossed her arms and stood in front of Renee. Her squinted up face wore the distorted look of someone who was not only capable of violence but who was quite comfortable with it. "I know you don't want me to take off my earrings," said Irene, defiantly. "I can tell you're an uptown girl and might not know what that means. But let me make it clear, you don't wanna rumble with me tonight."

"Mama, please! You're making me feel worse. You really should go home now and stop worrying about me. God wouldn't bring me this far to let me down now."

"Goodness gracious, Brenda, I wish you would be more realistic about people. You trust strangers too easily. You've always been that way. That's why you got stuck with that Jerome Johnson in the first place."

Brenda tried to reason with her mother. "All I want to do right now is be alone so I can get down on my knees and pray for my dear husband's soul," Brenda said, wearily. "I know Jerome's at peace. It's not going to be easy the next few days putting him to rest but I'm not alone. None of us are. I only wish you had enough faith to believe that."

"Humph, you'll find out soon enough, Baby Doll, just who you can really count on. It's not your so-called friends," Irene said, her eyes like bullets that shot at Renee, "and not some mythical spirit in the sky. The only thing you can count on is blood kin, Baby. Everybody else will end up betraying you sooner or later."

"Mama, if I didn't know better I'd think you just got initiated into the Mafioso. You sound like something straight out of The Godfather."

"That's all right, Brenda. Go ahead and make fun of me but you'll see what I'm talking about one day." Irene stormed out the room and went downstairs to get her coat and hat. Renee and Brenda didn't know what to say after that. A few seconds later, they heard the front door slam shut.

CHAPTER 28

The next morning Renee woke up like clockwork at seven and accepted two stark realities: Her marriage was over, and there was no baby growing inside her. The half-million dollar house in Foxhall Crescent Estates that she shared with Bill for the past fourteen years now felt more like a place of entombment for the dead. The clock struck its last chime. Yesterday, Bill had presented her with separation papers and to his surprise she signed them. His ploy to force her to go back to their sterile existence backfired. Seeing the beginning of the end in writing, made her realize their marriage was suffocating them both. The last time their problems escalated to the point of discussing divorce, her attorney explained that either spouse could be granted a no-fault divorce after being separated for one year. There was no way she could stay in that house alone for one year. She'd put the house on the market and look for a small place of her own. Her thoughts turned to Deek.

Renee recalled how Deek had told her how he had narrowed down the hunt for his getaway cottage on Kent Island by simply keying in the location, price range, and other desired amenities into a real estate website that even gave the buyer a three dimensional view of every room in the property. She decided she would try out the world of virtual reality on the Internet later that evening. Searching the Net sounded a lot less time-consuming than driving around the city house hunting with an agent. Renee already knew she wanted a metro-accessible condo or brick rowhouse, something near a secure building downtown where she could rent office space to see patients. If anyone had told her that in less than a month's time her life would tumble into a myriad of major changes, she would not have believed them.

Over this short time span, Renee had discovered she was two months pregnant but without a growing fetus, was on the verge of legally separating from her husband, and suddenly entangled in an arson/murder/kidnapping investigation. Nothing made sense anymore. She was glad today didn't fall on one of her bi-weekly Tuesday mornings where she served breakfast to the homeless at Charlie's Place inside a church on Connecticut Avenue NW. Brenda needed her more today. Renee got up, took a leisurely shower, and got dressed. By the time she finished dressing it was close to nine o'clock.

She slipped quietly down the hallway to check on her secretary, not wanting to wake her in case she was still asleep. She found the door ajar. Brenda was up but still in her nightgown and she was talking on the telephone to someone. Renee caught the tale end of the conversation. After Brenda hung up the phone she greeted Renee with a weak smile that revealed fatigue and lack of sleep. "That was Mrs. Johnson, my mother-in-law on the phone just now. She's already contacted the funeral home that took care of everything when her husband's mother passed away last year," said Brenda, hugging herself as she stood by the nightstand, completely still. "Mrs. Johnson wanted to make sure I wouldn't have a problem with her making the arrangements for her son. I know as Jerome's wife that's my responsibility but I'm so relieved she's handling it." Brenda sank down on the edge of the bed. "Making arrangements for my husband's funeral would just about send me over the edge if I had to deal with that on top of everything else."

Renee nodded. "Yes, that's good Jerome's mother is handing things under the circumstances."

"She also told me that they'd be releasing Jerome's body for burial in time for the funeral service that she's already arranged for Friday. Naturally, it'll have to be closed casket," said Brenda, seemingly without emotion. But Renee understood this reaction was just her defense mechanism kicking in so she wouldn't break down. Still, Renee wasn't sure what to say to Brenda after that. It was obvious looking at her that she hadn't slept well last night. After what seemed like a long pause, Renee asked, "Would you like to have your breakfast brought up or do you feel like coming downstairs?"

Before Brenda could answer the telephone rang again. Renee picked it up. Brenda stared at the phone in Renee's hand and hung on every word. "Yes, this is the Hayes residence. Yes, I do know a Veda Simms. She did? Oh, how wonderful! Thank you very much. Yes, Mrs. Brenda Johnson is here in fact. Just a moment please." Renee's voice lifted in excitement as she held the telephone out to Brenda, "Veda recognized Little Justin's photo on a television news broadcast last night and she called the number on the screen. It's a Miss Shepherd on the phone, a social worker from Child and Family Services. She wants to speak to you."

Brenda held the phone to her chest for a few seconds, closed her eyes and whispered 'Thank You Lord', before she answered. Renee watched as Brenda's grin widened and her face turned exuberant. Although Renee could only hear one side of the conversation, she could tell from the expression on Brenda's face that everything would be all right. "Thank God, my prayers have been answered," said Brenda to the woman on the phone. "Where's my baby now? Can I come get him?"

Brenda nodded, "Yes, Ma'am, I understand. I'll be there this morning with my documentation. Thank you Miss Shepherd for calling me as soon as you found out."

Brenda hung up. Out of breath from her excitement, she explained to Renee what the social worker from Intake Division had told her she needed to do in order to get custody of her son back. Miss Shepherd said Baby Justin had been examined by a pediatrician at Children's Hospital and had suffered no outward or internal injuries from his ordeal. He was currently being cared for by a very competent foster mother. Brenda grabbed a pair of Renee's jeans and a pullover sweater that had been neatly folded in the bottom drawer and went into the bathroom to get dressed, leaving the door partly open so they could still talk. "See Dr. Renee, didn't I tell you? God is so good," said Brenda as she threw off the borrowed nightgown and stepped into a nearly new pair of jeans. "I knew my baby would be all right."

"What did Miss Shepherd say we have to do in order to get Justin returned to you?" Renee asked, while Brenda glided the sweater over her head and splashed water on her face.

"First, I have to go down to Child and Family Services' Intake office and show them proof that I'm who I say I am. My driver's license should be enough proof. I sure hope so because all I have left to my name is what's in my purse and what I carried with me to work that morning. But that's all right as long as my little boy's fine."

Brenda came out the bathroom fully dressed and ready to go. She picked up her purse from the nightstand and checked its contents to make sure she had everything she needed. "I hope my driver's license will be enough for them because I don't have my birth certificate, social security card or Justin's birth certificate either. I'll have to request duplicates of everything from Vital Statistics." She took out her cell phone and dropped it on the nightstand, "This won't do me any good now because the battery's dead and I don't have the charger."

"I'm sure you have pictures of Justin in your wallet," said Renee, "I should think that would be sufficient proof."

"Just in case it's not, I hope Miss Shepherd isn't one of those types who go strictly by the book and forces me through a bunch of red tape."

"Don't worry, Dear. As a CASA volunteer I've worked with Child and Family Services plenty of times and I've dealt with the Courts. If necessary I can call in a few favors."

"That's a relief," said Brenda as she picked up her purse. "What's a CASA volunteer?"

"CASA stands for Court Appointed Special Advocate. At the CASA program I work with at-risk children on a regular basis where children are placed in temporary foster care. I'm certain Justin is with a nurturing caregiver. Just waiting for his mama to get there and bring him home," Renee smiled.

"I'm sure too, Dr. Renee, but not for the same reasons you are," Brenda said, reflectively.

"Okay, let's go then. Would you like to drive my car? I think it'll be better to take it rather than calling Remy, my driver, since who knows how many stops we'll have to make along the way," said Renee, turning out the light switch. "I just need to stop in my bedroom to get my bag and the keys."

"Certainly, I can drive if you want," said Brenda, following her.

On the way downstairs they smelled a buttery aroma mixed with sweet spices from the cinnamon Streusel coffee cake that Chizuko had just removed from the oven and placed on the counter to cool. The scent from homemade cake baking in the morning, combined with the rich fragrance of French roast coffee, was a good start for Renee. Chizuko had also cut up two small bowls of fresh melon and had set the table in the breakfast room for her employer and house guest. Renee thanked Chizuko for her efforts and let her know that after breakfast they would be going out for awhile and she would not need her help for the rest of the day. She would get her driver, Remy to pick her up, and Renee would cover the cost as usual. Chizuko bowed and thanked Renee, then quietly exited to her small room on the first floor to pack up her things. Renee dialed Remy. He was used to getting her last minute requests so he assured her that he could be there in about an hour to take Chizuko home.

That solved, Renee hoped Brenda would not mind sitting down to a quick breakfast before they left for the agency so as not to offend

Chizuko. Brenda assured her she did not mind and in fact admitted that she was indeed starving, having not eaten barely anything for the past 24 hours. Now that her spirits had been uplifted at hearing the good news about her child, her appetite had returned. The coffee cake was delicious and Brenda marveled at how well Chizuko who was Japanese could cook American food, especially considering that according to Renee she hadn't been in this country that long. Relishing each bite, they both surmised that Chizuko must be a natural-born chef.

Not to be left out Renee's cat, Angel nibbled at a dish of chicken in gravy that sat on the floor off to the corner. The cat had been trained not to jump up on the kitchen counter so Renee didn't worry about having their breakfast arranged buffet-style on the counter. When Angel had consumed her fill of gourmet cat food and sipped from the water bowl, she curled on the floor and licked herself clean. Then, she padded over to the table where Renee and Brenda sat and hovered under it, purring around Renee's feet. Renee didn't bother to shoo the cat away as she ate. They'd become friends since Bill moved out, or at least, they tolerated each other better.

Actually, Renee realized as she smiled across the table at Brenda that it felt good to have a friend to share things with, both the good and the bad things. She didn't know if Brenda regarded her as one of her girlfriends like Cha-Cha and Veda, but she hoped that one day she would be able to fit in and have a group of close female companions the way Brenda, Cha-Cha, and Veda were with each other. They looked out for each other. That was something Renee had never experienced before. She couldn't really count her mentor Dr. Helen Stone as meeting those qualifications because she was her psychiatrist not her girlfriend. Renee was glad that she was able to be there for Brenda. It felt good to be able to help someone else. She would see Brenda through all of it, the funeral, getting her son back, and helping to find out who was responsible for Jerome's murder. Suddenly, she realized she needed to call Deek and update him but she'd wait until they were underway and call him from her cell phone since she wouldn't be the one driving to the agency.

After breakfast, Renee quickly stacked the dishes in the sink, knowing that Chizuko would finish cleaning the kitchen before she left. She and Brenda were both anxious to get downtown to the intake office. Renee called out to her housekeeper to tell her she was leaving. She then dropped the keys in Brenda's open palm. They left through the garage.

While Brenda drove Renee retrieved her cell phone from her purse and called Deek. She noticed that Brenda took Canal Road to Whitehurst Freeway, but didn't pay much attention to the route Brenda took after Deek answered on the first ring. "Good Morning, Doc. Good of you to call. I was just about to call you as a matter of fact."

Hearing Deek's voice put a smile on her face. A warm sensation came over her as she listened to him speak. She recalled the last time they had been alone together at his cottage on Kent Island. Now was probably not the time, but she couldn't deny the ache in the pit of her stomach and admitted to herself that she missed him. Oblivious to her thoughts about him, Deek updated Renee on the investigation in a matter-of-fact tone. Renee was careful not to respond in any way that might upset Brenda, so for the most part she listened to Deek without comment. He told Renee that the police were still tracking down the victim's coworkers, family members, and friends for questioning. Officers had been canvassing the neighborhood to find out if Jerome had any enemies, anyone who wanted to see him dead. They would backtrack again today to catch anything they might have missed. So far no eyewitnesses had come forward.

He told her that the primary physical evidence that investigators had collected from the debris and exterior premises consisted of, a shoe print picture taken near the exit area, pieces of a burnt-out gas can, bits of duct tape found strewn under the rear kitchen window, and a miniscule piece of fabric caught on the window frame. No ideal, preserved crime scene existed because the entire top structure of the house had collapsed in the fire. Investigators hoped DNA and laboratory analysis would be able to provide some answers from the evidence Deek sent them. Right now they had nothing conclusive to tie anyone to the crime. When Deek finished giving her his update Renee realized she had almost forgotten to tell Deek the reason for her call.

She then told him that she and Brenda were on their way to Child and Family Services office. She explained how Veda Simms had recognized Brenda's son's photograph and had contacted the agency right away. Veda had guessed correctly that Brenda might be staying with Renee and she gave them her home number. As a backup she also gave them Mrs. Adams' full name so they could locate Brenda's mother in case Brenda had not been at Renee's place. Veda did not know Mrs. Adams' phone number or address, but she figured that the agency could locate her if they had her full name. Deek was relieved to hear that Brenda's son had been found safe. He offered to help if things didn't run smoothly at the agency when they got there.

"Renee, do you think Brenda would mind if Lieutenant Bradford and I dropped by later this evening for a few minutes to question her a little more about her husband's associates? There're a few loose ends we'd like to get clarity on."

"Hold on, let me check with her." Renee turned to Brenda and told her Deek's request. Brenda looked conflicted. Renee could see the tension in her face from the clamped lips and rigidness of her jaw. She could almost tell what Brenda must be thinking, knowing how she herself would just want to spend time with her baby after more than an entire day of not knowing if he were alive or dead. Renee returned the phone to her ear and let Brenda's silence give her an answer. "Deek, I'm not sure how long all this will take or where we'll be. How about I call you later with something more definite?" Brenda nodded her agreement as her mouth formed a silent 'Thank You' to Renee.

"Good. I'd appreciate it if you'd let me know. My partner's itching to put this case to bed. You don't have to tell Brenda this, but we're on our way to her husband's autopsy now. There's no doubt about his identity. Dental records came in last night and confirmed that the victim is Jerome Antonio Johnson."

Renee didn't know what to say. She held the phone to her ear in silence as Deek continued. "We've got Forensics and the D. C. police crime scenes lab checking for any trace evidence and latent prints collected yesterday. I'm hoping for a clear set of prints or anything that'll tie the person responsible to the crime."

"When will you know something?"

"I stayed at the precinct late last night to finish the transmittal letter and put a rush on it. All the significant evidence went out this morning so hopefully the lab results should come back in a few days."

"You are moving fast. Are you getting any sleep?" she asked.

"Sleep? What's that?" he laughed.

"I wish you and Detective Bradford would let me help Deek. Did you get a chance to speak to your partner about me working with you on the investigation?"

"Yep, sure did. He wasn't too keen on the idea. But after some convincing and serious blackmailing," said Deek, lightheartedly, "He agreed that having a psychologist on board could be beneficial. But one slipup Doc and you're out."

"Don't worry, I'll abide by all your rules."

"All my rules? Hum, I like the sound of that."

"You know what I mean Detective Hamilton," said Renee, with a flirty tone in her voice.

"Okay, Doc, we'll give it a try. Good to have you on the team, partner."

Renee hung up, relieved that their conversation ended on a lighter note. She didn't go into the details of her conversation with Deek. She was relieved that Brenda could not hear what he had told her about the police's progress on the murder investigation. When she looked out the window she saw that they had turned onto Independence Avenue in Southwest DC and weren't that far away. Like Brenda, Renee had taken to silent prayer and she said one for Brenda, praying that the agency would not give them any resistance. They arrived at the Child and Family Services office on 400 6th Street, SW just before 10:30 AM.

When Brenda and Renee entered Miss Shepherd's small cramped office, they found the social worker perched behind a cluttered desk. She was in the middle of a telephone conversation but smiled at them as they walked in. Still talking, she pointed to a set of chairs in front of her desk. Miss Shepherd snatched off her eyeglasses and rubbed the space between her dark eyes and frowned as she listened to the person on the other end. She held her hand over the telephone mouthpiece and whispered apologetically to Brenda and Renee. "I'll be with you in a moment. I can see it's going to be one of those days." The social worker nodded and grunted "um hum" to the person she was talking to on the phone. "All right. Call me back as soon as you speak to Judge Riker's calendar clerk," said Miss Shepherd in an authoritative voice. "I need to be there when the judge hears that juvenile case for disposition. Fine. Okay, Bye."

As soon as Miss Shepherd hung up, she extended her hand in a greeting and everyone introduced themselves.

"I'm sorry about that," said Miss Shepherd, "This place stays hopping as you can see." She walked over to the file cabinet to retrieve Baby Justin's case file. She took out the Polaroid of the abandoned baby and showed it to Brenda. "Is this your son, Mrs. Johnson?"

"Yes, that's my Justin," Brenda beamed, "I have another picture of him when he was first born that I keep in my wallet." She pulled out the photo and handed it to her. "All my more recent photos were destroyed in the fire at our home yesterday. I'd been meaning to add a more recent picture of him in my wallet, but just hadn't gotten around to it. But you can clearly see it's the same child."

"Well, it looks like it could be him," said Miss Shepherd, wrinkling her nose.

"Can I go pick him up at foster care now?" asked Brenda, "I know my baby must be frightened and confused without his mama."

"I'm sorry Mrs. Johnson but before I can let you take possession of this child you'll need to show me some identifying information to prove you're his mother. Do you have Justin's birth certificate and your driver's license or a social security card?"

Brenda dug through her wallet and took out her driver's license. She explained that she would have to get duplicates of her social security card and her son's birth certificate. However, she was sure her mother had kept her original birth certificate if the social worker needed that. She could easily retrieve it from her mother if necessary.

"Do you mean this birth certificate for Brenda Jewel Adams?" asked Miss Shepherd and held up a copy of Brenda's birth certificate.

"Yes, that's mine. Adams is my maiden name. Did my mother come here?" Brenda asked, in surprise. "Is she still around?"

"Unfortunately, yes your mother did come here this morning and fortunately, now she's gone. She showed up ranting and raving about her grandson and demanding to know where he had been placed. The woman carried pictures of your baby and your birth certificate as you see here," said Miss Shepherd. "Obviously, because of custody issues we couldn't be responsible for placing the child in this woman's care without speaking to you first, Mrs. Johnson and validating your ID. When I tried to explain that to your mother, she became so hostile that we had to call security to throw her out I'm sorry to say."

Brenda covered her face with her hand for a few seconds then looked up. "I'm sorry about that Miss Shepherd. I hope you won't hold that outburst this morning against me. I'm a good mother. My employer, Dr. Renee here can vouch for me."

Renee nodded her head vigorously. "Of course I can. I can assure you Miss Shepherd that Brenda is a responsible, level-headed young woman. As you can see from her driver's license she is who she claims to be. You would be doing the right thing for all concerned by returning her baby to her immediately."

Miss Shepherd leaned back in her swivel chair and clasped her hands together. "Mrs. Johnson, I honestly don't feel comfortable releasing the child into your family's care until you bring me the baby's birth certificate as final proof," said Miss Shepherd. "The Child and Family Welfare agency is quite rigid about requirements. I can only keep the case in hold status up to four more days."

Brenda's face grew tense. "What do you mean by hold status?"

Renee had wanted to stay out of it as much as possible. The last thing she wanted to do was to appear to take over like Brenda's mother had tried to do this morning, but she now felt it was time to speak up. "Miss Shepherd, I understand the procedure but couldn't you simply accept the picture in Brenda's wallet and her driver's license as valid proof? You already have a copy of her legitimate birth certificate that her mother provided, what more do you need?"

Miss Shepherd's thoughtful expression encouraged Renee to continue in a pleading tone. "We're here because of tragic and unfortunate circumstances that you're well aware of. We both know that if this case gets out of holding status and the court takes control of her son, there's simply no telling when this mother will be reunited with her son."

Brenda's face grew distressed. She demanded to know what being out of holding status meant. Miss Shepherd explained to her that when an abandoned child is brought to Child and Family Services, the case goes into a five-day holding period. If Brenda had brought in her baby's birth certificate while the case was still in holding status and could successfully prove that she was his mother, the child could be released to her without going through any more red tape. One day had already passed. After the holding status, it would be out of the social worker's hands in which case it could take six weeks to get through the Court system no matter what. That's when an attorney called Guardian Ad

Litem would be appointed by the Court to represent the baby while Child and Family Services would have its own legal representation.

"There's no need to get all these lawyers involved!" said Brenda, leaping from her chair. "Why is all this necessary? I've shown you everything?"

Renee could see that Brenda fought back her tears. She touched her arm and nudged her back down in the chair.

"Because Mrs. Johnson, my superiors could challenge my authority if I give the go-ahead to release the child to you without proper evidence that the Court itself would recognize. And if the case were to be turned over to the Courts, they still wouldn't release the child into your custody until the minor's appointed attorney and I visited the home where he would be residing. Will you be staying at your mother's house temporarily or permanently?"

Brenda cupped her forehead in her hand and spoke in a soft tone. "You mean you'd actually make a home visit before returning my baby back to me?"

"That's right, ma'am. So to avoid all that hassle and red tape you must bring the child's birth certificate within the next four days while the case is still in holding status," said Mrs. Shepherd with finality in her voice.

"Try to understand, Mrs. Johnson. Our main concern is the protection and safety of the children. We have to be very careful. You can say you live somewhere in a decent neighborhood, but for all we know you could be living in an alley or a crack house somewhere. The Court requires us to check out everything before an abandoned child is released to you."

"Just for the record, my son and I will be staying with my parents on Primrose Street in NW Washington until I can look for my own place. I'm sure you and the Courts would find my parents' home more than adequate."

"I'm sure you're right, but like I said that won't be necessary if you bring me what I need to close this case," said Miss Shepherd, leaning forward and planting her elbows on the desk. "I'm not trying to be difficult, Mrs. Johnson. I know you've been through hell, but we have to ensure that the baby turned into us is really yours. Please try to see it from our point of view."

Just then they heard a soft knock on the door followed by the door opening. Another social services representative popped her head through the door.

"Sorry, Donna but one of our foster mothers is outside and she says it's urgent."

"Oh, good grief, what is it now!" Mrs. Shepherd rose from her chair and headed towards the door. Before she could get to the door a woman walked in carrying a sleeping, bundled baby in her arms. Renee looked surprised when she saw Shirley Ann Turner, the foster mother that she had grown close to this past summer when they shared in the responsibility of caring for Susannah, a child born with AIDS. Though Renee gave total credit to Shirley Ann who had assumed the bulk of taking care of Susannah on a daily bases. Renee had just been the relief pitcher when Shirley Ann needed a well-deserved break. The women rushed to hug each other. Ever since retiring from the federal government and raising her own kids, Shirley Ann Turner had devoted herself to taking care of foster children. Renee had worked with her ever since joining CASA and loved this lady's dedication and kind spirit.

"Shirley Ann! How have you been?" said Renee, "I had no idea you'd resumed doing foster care so soon."

"You know me. I can't stay away. It's good to see you, Dr. Renee," said Shirley Ann, shifting the sleeping baby to her other shoulder. "I got a call from Miss Shepherd last night to say this little angel's mama would be coming in this morning to identify his photo," said Shirley Ann, gently patting the baby's back as she spoke. "I know if it was me, I'd want to see my baby and not some photo of him. I know that's what I'd want," said Shirley Ann, nodding her head. "So I decided to bring this little dumpling in person to see if he's the one. I'm praying for a happy family reunion."

"You two know each other?" asked Miss Shepherd.

Brenda got up cautiously and approached the baby in Shirley Ann Turner's arms. She had been staring at the blanketed bundle ever since the foster mother walked in but because of how Shirley Ann carried him and because the blanket was partially draped over his head, Brenda couldn't see his face. As Shirley Ann began rocking the baby, he woke up from his nap and started to cry. Upon hearing him cry, relief swept over Brenda's face. She held out her arms.

Brenda recognized that cry. The sound of his cry brought back her memory of him being born. It took what seemed to her like an eternity for the doctor to siphon out the mucus from his passageway. For every deafening second of silence between his first breathe, Brenda and Jerome had clinched each other's hand and waited for sounds of life from their newborn. Baby Justin's first strong cry confirmed to everyone in the delivery room that he would be okay. This was the same way he was crying now as if he were taking his first breathe of life.

Shirley Ann released the baby to Brenda's outstretched arms. Brenda scooped him up and held him to her breast as she rocked him back and forth. Baby Buddha looked into his mother's tearful eyes and immediately stopped crying. He cooed and smiled at the familiar loving face looking down at him. Brenda silently thanked God for placing her baby safely back in her arms. She realized then that this moment had happened just as she had seen it happening in her mind's eye when she had prayed and meditated in bed last night. She silently asked for forgiveness for momentarily doubting the outcome when it appeared that Miss Shepherd was not going to make any exceptions to the agency's rules. Brenda didn't perceive this outcome as a miracle. She attributed it all to faith. A feeling of warmth and protection washed over her as she held onto her baby. She knew God would be there with her through the next ordeal ahead—her husband's funeral.

After signing all the necessary paperwork, Miss Shepherd released sole custody of the minor child, Justin Johnson back to his mother and closed the John Doe abandoned baby case. Brenda thanked Mrs. Turner for taking such good care of her child. She thanked Dr. Renee for always supporting her, as well as, Miss Shepherd for waiving the requirement of the baby's original birth certificate. Under the circumstances, the social worker agreed to let Brenda mail her a copy of Justin's birth certificate after she received it from Vital Records in the next six weeks or so. The three joyful women assembled in Miss Shepherd' office and gave each other departing hugs before they left. Brenda asked Dr. Renee if she wouldn't mind dropping her at her mother's house. She explained to Renee that she knew her mother had meant well this morning, she just went about it the wrong way. Renee knew that Brenda was right. While she didn't want Brenda to leave her alone in that big house, she realized that Brenda needed to be with her own family, especially with the funeral looming ahead. Brenda strapped Justin in the car seat and sat in the back, cooing and playing with her son while Renee drove in silence to Irene Adams house on Primrose Street.

CHAPTER 29

On Friday morning at 10 o'clock a long, black hearse stood stationed near the carved double doors of Nativity Catholic Church on Georgia Avenue. Inside the church Brenda Johnson with her family and the family members of the deceased took up the first two rows. Dr. Renee Hayes sat on the same side as Brenda, but in the last pew. Renee and Brenda's eyes met briefly when Brenda turned around and glanced towards the main entrance. Both women smiled and nodded at each other. Brenda wore a stylish black, military-collared suit, tasteful black pumps, a black felt hat with a short mesh veil that did nothing to conceal her red, puffy eyes. Pearl posts were clamped to her ears and served as the only adornment to her outfit. Brenda sat between her father, Marvin Adams and her mother, Irene Adams. After having met Brenda's mother, Renee was not surprised by Mrs. Adams's brash wardrobe selection for the funeral. Unlike everyone else, Mrs. Adams stood out in a red Chanel suit, red hat, leather clutch purse, and red stiletto pumps. The rest of Brenda's family sat directly behind her on the second row, a few cousins and an aunt who Renee had never met. She noticed Brenda's two best girlfriends, Cha-Cha Taylor and Veda Simms, also seated nearby on the second row to console her. Jerome's family claimed the first two pews on the opposite side of the sanctuary, his parents, grandmother, siblings, and more relatives.

Baby Justin slept peacefully as Brenda gently rocked him in her arms. Media attention had heightened around the arson/murder case. Watching Brenda from afar with her baby son cradled close to her breast, Renee knew that the recent stories being reported about her had to be lies. Renee was committed to doing everything in her power to prove them wrong. Just yesterday on yet another news headline, a station reported that Brenda Johnson had tried to file an insurance claim the day after her husband died in the fire. Renee hadn't had a chance to talk to Brenda since she moved back home with her parents several days ago, but she didn't believe a word of the negative press. To Renee the only explanation she could come up with was that someone must be out to destroy her trusted secretary. Fortunately, Deek still seemed to have an open mind about the case and she hoped that wouldn't change. He confided to Renee the other day that his partner, Detective Melvin Bradford, the lead investigator, was being pressured by their superiors, the DA, and the public to make an arrest. Renee wished someone would come forward soon with new information leading to other suspects since time seemed to be running out for Brenda.

Renee spotted Deek sitting inconspicuously towards the rear of the church, but still several pews ahead of where she sat. He looked back and noticed her too, and gestured for her to come sit with him. Renee walked down the aisle, faced the altar and genuflected before easing in the spot next to him. She took in the spicy scent of his familiar cologne. Whenever they ran into each other the tension escalated. Being in church at a funeral didn't seem to make a difference. To avoid being distracted by him, she read the program. The program couldn't hold her interest because Deek looked as good as he smelled. Even at a funeral, he appeared 'James Bond' savvy in spit-shine, black loafers and trim, lightweight gray, woolen trousers that curved against his muscled legs. He wore a matching single-breasted jacket over a soft-striped shirt and woven silk, black-on-royal blue tie. Renee felt guilty getting turned on in a church but that was difficult not to do sitting so close to Deek.

Renee composed herself when she saw Father Emanuel, Brenda's priest, lead the processional of pallbearers, carrying the closed casket up to the altar. The organist played a passionate and forceful Rachmaninoff concerto. If the mood wasn't already somber, the music cast an even deeper gloom over the funeral service. Renee didn't even know Brenda's husband that well, but her eyes glazed and she dabbed at them frequently with her handkerchief. In accompaniment to the music, the robed priest chanted a sorrowful praise to the Lord. After the hymn, he knelt before a statue of the Virgin Mary and bowed his head in prayer. He held a string of rosary beads within his clasped hands. The priest stood up and turned around to face the mourners and those who had come to pay their last respects to the deceased. Father Emanuel had a full, round face, glittering, brown eyes and stock of dark curls laced with copper tints that fell over his ears and down his neck. When he spoke, his message sounded like a symphony of rhythmic intonations that Renee found soothing.

"We are not here today to mourn, but to celebrate life. Jerome Antonio Johnson was a devoted husband, father, son, and brother," said Father Emanuel, his melodic voice echoing through the church. "Although he faced temptations from the snares of the secular world and made many mistakes, Brother Johnson repented. He was on the road to overcoming his obstacles with the support of his loving wife and her unwavering faith in our Lord."

The priest looked down at Brenda momentarily before continuing. "Tragically cut off at only 28 years old in the prime of his season, some of you may be asking why does God allow such terrible things to happen? People ask these questions all the time. Why did God take this one? He or she was so dedicated to God. Children, it's not God's fault when people kill each other or hurt each other," said the priest with emphasis and scanned the congregation with his dark, liquid eyes, "God gave Man free choice to decide to commit good deeds or the free choice to commit sin. These terrible things happen because of sin and evil in this materialistically driven, sinister world we live in today."

He placed both hands on the podium while his gentle eyes swept over the mourners before him. "I see the sorrow in your faces and sense the heaviness in your hearts. Some of you seated before me may be asking yourselves something even more personal, like, 'Does God really care about me? Why did God put me in this situation? Why did he let this happen to me?' Yes, life's blows will hurt for a while but God says 'I am with you'. Don't give up children. Don't feel hopeless. You are never alone."

Father Emanuel took a sip of water and continued. "God is about goodness and about bestowing blessings to his faithful servants. We may not understand his intentions but we must maintain faith because we never know the day or the hour when we'll be called home," he said. "My Sisters and my Brothers, don't be afraid of death. It is as quick as closing your eyes and opening them back up again. When you open your eyes you are on the other side where there's eternal peace. Have faith in Our Savior, Jesus Christ and you will be ready to pass over to the other side whenever your time comes." Father Emanuel flipped open his bible and read the marked passage. "In Ecclesiastes 3:1, the Lord says, 'For everything there is a season, and a time for every purpose under heaven. A time to be born and a time to die'."

"Life on Earth is short and we suffer many trials and tribulations along the way but there are also moments to be cherished. Think on all the precious moments you shared with Brother Johnson and keep the memory of your loved one alive." He closed the Bible and performed other rituals at the altar that Renee did not pay much attention to. Instead, she reflected on what the priest had said.

The priest's words had comforted her deeply. When he spoke she couldn't help thinking about her own recent loss upon finding out her uterus bore no growing baby inside of her. Last week Dr. Eckbert had told her that the pregnancy would spontaneously abort itself within days since no fetus existed to sustain hormone levels. At sunrise that morning Renee woke up with cramping and light bleeding and knew it was all over. Another failure at motherhood. Just as Dr. Eckbert expected, nature took care of its own non-survivable mistake. But somehow she got through it. Not long ago she would have needed strong medication and denial to numb herself against feeling anything, but over the past several days she discovered she could take whatever life had to throw at her.

Renee knew she was growing emotionally stronger. Watching how Brenda maneuvered through her crisis and how she relied on faith to get her through hardships had opened up a door of understanding for Renee. Renee realized she still had much to learn about experiencing life and love, things that she had never learned before in her medical and psychiatric manuals. But at least she realized there was hope now that the door had been slightly cracked open. This cracked open door is what had allowed her to get up that morning, wash away her own sorrow and attend this funeral despite her own loss. She felt Deek squeeze her hand. When she turned teary-eyed to face him, he took the balled up handkerchief from her fist and gently dabbed each corner of her eyes. Renee hoped he would assume her tears were brought on by Father Emanuel's touching words. She didn't want him to think that she wasn't emotionally stable enough to focus on the investigative work as a criminal profile consultant. In fact, helping Deek with the homicide case was exactly what she needed right now.

Renee looked out at the mourners to see if they too felt moved by the service. At that moment, she felt a strong awareness that she was being watched. Every so often a man seated a few rows in front of them and wearing a brown suit and a colorful orange and royal blue kinte cloth around his neck, surveyed the back pew and peered in her direction. Renee finally recognized him as the obnoxious customer from Good Looks beauty parlor but she couldn't recall his name.

"I have to get out of here," she whispered to Deek, "I passed a private office in the basement coming in this morning. Can we talk for a few minutes? I have something I want to show you." Deek nodded and followed her out to the vestibule. There was intermittent sobbing coming from the deceased side of the church as they quietly exited the sanctuary.

Once outside in the vestibule, Renee and Deek descended a narrow stairway that led to the church basement, and they entered one of the unlocked counseling chambers. They sat down on a striped Chippendale sofa. Before he had a chance to ask what she wanted to talk about, Renee removed a folded clipping from that morning's Washington Post Metro Section from her clutch purse and handed it to Deek. "Have you had a chance to read this morning's paper yet?" she asked. "It's nothing but lies about my secretary."

He took the clipping and unfolded it. Then read the caption aloud. *Young Washington area mother suspected of arson and murder. Police suspect co-conspirator could also be involved.* Deek's face didn't register any surprise as he read the rest of the clipping in silence. Renee already knew exactly what it said, having read it several times earlier that morning in disbelief.

In the aftermath of Monday's arson at a Southeast Capitol Hill rowhouse that left 28 year-old Jerome A. Johnson dead, the lead investigator on the case, Detective Melvin Bradford, says attention is now being focused on the victim's wife, Brenda Adams Johnson. Mrs. Johnson is the sole beneficiary of a fifty thousand dollar life insurance policy on her husband's death. After receiving an anonymous tip and questioning witnesses, police uncovered a hidden web of lies, infidelity, and drug abuse that could have sparked the domestic turmoil within the Johnson household that led to the crime on Monday afternoon. As yet, no formal charges have been filed. Investigators are awaiting lab results of physical evidence before making their move to arrest Mrs. Johnson on suspicion of murder, conspiracy to commit murder, arson and insurance fraud. The Johnson family maintains their daughter's innocence and retained the nationally renowned criminal attorney, Mr. K. C. Bloodstone as their daughter's legal counsel.

In a recent chilling discovery based on an unidentified caller's tip, this was not the first time Mrs. Johnson has come under suspicion for murder and insurance fraud. Police later confirmed the informant's claim by searching police records. Records reveal that nine years ago an unwed, 19 year-old Brenda Adams, now known as Johnson was charged with involuntary manslaughter in the death of her six-week old infant daughter. At that time Miss Adams collected a $15,000 death benefit on her infant's life insurance policy that had been taken out on the very day of the child's birth. However, due to lack of physical evidence to prosecute, the DA dropped the charges against Miss Adams (aka Mrs. Johnson) and marked the infant's death accidental. Uncovering this new skeleton in Mrs. Johnson's closet has shed further suspicion on her credibility.

"It doesn't look good for Brenda," said Deek, refolding the news clipping. He then handed it back to her. Renee gave him a pained expression without knowing what to say. Deek leaned back against the couch with his arms folded, apparently reflecting on his own private thoughts. She had hoped he could shed some light on where all these lies were coming from. But were they all lies, she asked herself. Could Brenda really be guilty, she thought. People were not always who they seemed to be. As a trained psychologist, she recognized the many faces of deceit. Brenda presented herself as a loving mother, devoted wife, and she called herself a Christian woman. But could she in fact be a cold-blooded killer motivated by money and greed? Renee decided that Brenda's mother certainly came across as conniving, selfish, and greedy. But, what about her daughter? She wondered if the apple fell close to the tree in the case of mother and daughter. For a second she felt puzzled, but then her head cleared. No, there had to be another explanation.

Renee refused to believe she could be that wrong about a person's character. Instead of believing rumors she'd help investigate the facts and find out what happened to Brenda's first baby nine years ago. Renee didn't like the way this investigation was heading. She turned to face Deek. "Before we jump to conclusions we should find out the identity of this unnamed source and what their motive is," she said, her voice trembling with anger.

Deek leaned forward and clasped both hands in front of him. "I agree, Doc. Bradford's theory is pretty much based on rumors and circumstantial evidence. Until lab results come in and give us some physical proof that points elsewhere, he won't back off Brenda. In fact, that's the reason I'm here. I'm supposed to take her in for re-questioning after the service," he said matter-of-factly.

"You can't be serious. Brenda's already been through so much. Don't tell me you believe these awful lies they've been printing?"

"No, I'm not 100% convinced of her guilt so I want to give her a chance to respond to the accusations. But it was either me or Bradford so I volunteered to come today."

"I want to be there when you question her," she said firmly.

"Your role is to advise, remember?" he turned to give her a stern look, "You're not trained for law enforcement, Renee."

"I know that Detective. It's not necessary to keep reminding me what my limited role is on this investigation. But Deek, there are too many other possibilities to pin everything on her. For instance, suppose the torch is simply a pyromaniac who gets gratification from setting fires?"

"Don't worry, Doc, I won't let Bradford railroad your secretary. But I do have to consider all the evidence even if it points to Brenda," he said, "In my book we can't afford to exclude anybody as a suspect who knew the victim, had opportunity, and good reason to want him dead."

Renee rose from the sofa, "We'd better get back upstairs." Deek agreed and followed her to the door. Just as they had exited the room and were about to return to the sanctuary, a man appeared in front of them, standing at the bottom of the stairway. His attention was focused solely on Renee. "Hey, ain't you that fine sistuh I'm always running into at Good Looks on Thursdays?" the man said, grinning and stuck out his hand for Renee to shake. "I'm Alonzo Woods, you remember me, don't ya?"

The scent of cigarette breath preceded him as he edged too close to her, invading her space and accidentally stepping on one of her black, patent leather pumps. Renee stepped back a few inches away from him and briefly shook his outstretched hand out of politeness. His hand felt hot and sweaty, and when he wasn't looking she wiped her hand on the handkerchief from her purse. She hoped if she didn't talk or introduce him to Deek, he would get the hint and go away. That never worked at the beauty parlor and didn't work any better at the church either.

"Ya'll don't mind if we talk for bit?" asked Alonzo, and without waiting for a reply he led them back into the counseling chamber. Deek and Renee sat down on the couch while Alonzo sat across from them in a wing-back chair.

"I'm Lt. Detective Degas Hamilton, MPD, Homicide. And you obviously already know Dr. Hayes. What can we do for you, Mr. Woods?" said Deek.

Alonzo stared down at his shoes as he spoke. "It sure is a damn shame how my man went down," he said, shaking his head, "Jerome was my ace boon coon at Union Delivery Service. I was just at his crib a coupla days ago right after he got suspended from work for failing one of them piss tests. I mean a random drug test. Man, I can't believe it. Just the other day, we was layin' back, chillin'. Now this. Ain't life a bitch?"

It didn't seem to matter to Alonzo that he was in church since he didn't bother to modify his language, Renee thought.

"Mr. Woods, I'm one of the detectives investigating the Johnson murder case," said Deek and pushed back his jacket to reveal the badge attached to his belt. "Since you and the deceased were good friends do you mind if I ask you a few questions about him?" Deek retrieved his Blackberry™ from the inside pocket of his jacket, which Renee knew would have every feature activated. She also noticed that Alonzo got fidgety when Deek asked him questions.

"Uh, from what I been reading in the news lately, looks like ya'll already got your mind made up as to who done it," said Alonzo.

"You can't believe everything you read, Mr. Woods," said Renee, tersely. "I'm helping Detective Hamilton with the case as a criminal profile consultant. I assure you there are still more suspects left to uncover."

"Me and Jay was best buddies ever since he started at UDS as a driver. I wanna do whatever I can to help ya'll catch that mutha ... the asshole that killed him. I don't care what the papers say, I can't see sweet, little Brenda doin' something like that to anybody much less to Jerome."

"Do you know Mrs. Johnson well?" asked Deek.

"No, not really. Only what Jay used to say about her. His locker's full of her pictures and the baby. Some he claimed he couldn't show me," said Alonzo with a wicked grin. He and Brenda still acted like newlyweds hear him tell it."

"Would you be willing to testify in court if it should come to that confirming their close relationship?" asked Deek.

"Sure Detective Hamilton. Believe me, Jay loved his family and he tried real hard to beat his drug addiction. Jay said his wife forgave him a lot of times in the past and he didn't want to disappoint her again. That's why at first he was scared to tell her he got fired for failing that random drug test at work."

"Did Mr. Johnson have any enemies that you were aware of?"

"Enemies? I don't know if I'd call 'em enemies but lemme put it to you this way. My man Jay had a whole lotta drama queens in his life. From his ex-girlfriend, on down to his nosey mother-in-law. Me and him was just talkin' 'bout all his female troubles a coupla days before ... you know, before he died."

"Exactly how did these ladies cause Mr. Johnson problems?"

"Well, for one thing that damn mother-in-law of his was always in the mix. I think ole Jay woulda rather got both his eyes dug out with a rusty nail than get into a rumble with the Ice Queen. That's what he called her behind her back. Not to her face of course. I think he was scared of her and who wouldn't be? Have you met Brenda's mother yet, Detective?" Deek shook his head and encouraged Alonzo to continue, which didn't take much encouragement. Alonzo talked incessantly with a nervous edge in his voice. He kept licking his dry, chapped lips.

As Alonzo did what Alonzo did best—gossip nonstop, Deek took down his statement, typing rapidly into the word processing program installed on his hand-held Blackberry™ device. Renee marveled at how adeptly Deek handled the palm-sized device. He always kept up with the latest trends in technology. She recalled how his house overflowed with high-tech gadgetry and computer equipment. When they had first met at the beginning of the summer, Deek had told her that he always loved electronics and technology. After graduating with a BS in Information Systems at 21, he landed a contractor position at IBM Corporation as a systems engineer. He stayed there for a few years until the corporate routine bored him. Eventually, he joined the Metropolitan Police Department and moved up the ranks to Detective Lieutenant in Homicide Division at just 28 years old. Going from a world of developing and installing software to catching criminals responsible for murder was a huge leap. But apparently, Deek still considered himself a techie at heart.

"All that's interesting Mr. Woods, but other than these two ladies from his personal life, did Mr. Johnson have any problems with anyone at work?" asked Deek.

"No way, man. Everybody at UDS loved Jay. He was a funny cat. Always kept us goin'. More'n half those folks takin' up seats upstairs work at UDS. Even our boss is here and nobody in the yard likes her."

"Hum, I see. So as far as you know nothing out of the ordinary happened at work before Mr. Johnson got fired for using drugs?"

"Now that you mention it, I do recall one incident. A coupla weeks ago, my load was running late so I waited out my time in the breakroom 'til I could punch out. Anyways, I overheard Jerome talkin' to this dude on the phone about payin' back some loot. When he got off the telephone, he broke down and told me he was in trouble." Alonzo paused and looked down at his feet, shaking his head.

"Yeah, go on." Deek prompted.

"Jay told me he used to be down with this DC Mafia crew called Jett Set. He ran up a tab for about two grand and couldn't pay it back. But growing up he was tight with some of the dudes so they gave him a few extensions. He told the crew he was gonna ask his uncle to take out a home equity loan and spot him the dough. Anyway Jay told me he was worried 'cause Unk had bad credit. I dunno what happened after that. I doubt it worked out good for him the way the economy's been going down."

"Got any names for me, Mr. Woods? Did Mr. Johnson tell you who he spoke to from the Jett Set crew that day?"

"Naw. Jay got tight-lipped after he calmed down. Besides, those guys only go by nicknames. Nobody knows what name they Mama gave 'em." Alonzo's face suddenly turned agitated as he spoke. "Maybe Jay couldn't pay up in time and one of those Jett Setters whacked him."

Deek glanced at his watch. "Thank you for the information, Mr. Woods. I'll discuss your statement with my partner this afternoon. In case we have further questions, is it okay if we stop by your house sometime tomorrow morning?"

"Let's see, tomorrow's Saturday, ain't it?" said Alonzo, rubbing his forehead, "My only day off is Sunday but they got me on night shift so I'm usually home in the daytime. Sure thing, Detective, I guess tomorrow morning's okay if ya'll wanna stop by around nine or so."

"I appreciate your cooperation, Mr. Woods," said Deek, writing down Alonzo's telephone number and address of 19th Street, SE in the Lincoln Park neighborhood.

"Wait a minute Detective, if ya'll do drop by tomorrow, it's best if we trek on up to the corner store so I can talk in peace," said Alonzo, "Otherwise Izza, that's my wife, Isabelle—she'll hang on every damn word. Sometimes I talk too loud 'cause I can't hear so good no more.

Now, Izza can hear a fly walk. I can't keep none of my damn business to myself. We been married 30 years and that woman's 'bout to get on my last nerve."

"Whatever you prefer, Mr. Woods. I'll go over your statement with Detective Bradford, my partner and I'll call if we need further information. Thanks again for your cooperation."

"No problem, Detective. I'm glad to do my civic duty to help ya'll fight crime. I hope you find the dude that done it," said Alonzo.

"Don't worry. We'll get the person responsible, sooner or later."

Just then Deek's cell phone rang and he stepped out of the room to answer it. Alonzo got up from his chair and moved closer to Renee on the sofa. "You know Dr. Renee the repast is gonna be at Brenda's mama's house right after service. Ya'll comin'?"

"I would like to be there for Brenda," said Renee and hoped Alonzo Woods wouldn't be attending, "I haven't had a chance to talk to her privately for several days. I'm sure all the publicity around this case has been stressful for her." She was relieved when Deek returned.

"Looks like I have to head on back to headquarters now. That was my partner on the phone. Something's come up."

"Roger that, Detective," Alonzo winked, "I'll look after the Doc for you." Alonzo let out a yawn and stretched his arms. "Lord, this funeral is deader than poor Jay layin' up there in that damn coffin. I hope I can hold on 'til the repast. I dunno what the hell that priest's been talkin' about all this time. That priest don't know my buddy from Adam. This is probably the first time Jay's even been in a church. And now, looks like it's his last."

Deek and Renee glanced at each other briefly. Renee forced herself not to comment while Deek simply shrugged and shook his head. Their silence didn't keep Alonzo from continuing the conversation on his own. "Me, I was raised Southern Baptist. I expect folks to be wailin' and fallin' out on the floor at a funeral. You know, something to keep you awake. This funeral's too tame for me."

"Mr. Woods, do you mind?" said Deek as he walked to the door and held it open, "I need to speak to Dr. Hayes before I leave."

"'course not, Detective. I get the hint." Alonzo rose from the couch. "I'ma go on back up there and comfort the widow. I guess this thing's almost over." Alonzo left and Deek closed the door behind him. Renee exhaled a sigh of relief. She picked up her purse from the couch and approached where Deek stood by the door.

"I dread running into that man whenever I'm at the hairdresser's and now I find him here."

"I don't care who he is. If he's got information pertinent to this case, I need to talk to him," said Deek, "Right now, we don't have any eyewitnesses or strong physical evidence that would take the heat off Brenda. Bradford just called to tell me he has more incriminating information against your secretary."

"What did he say?"

"I can't discuss it right now until I have all the facts. But let's just say we need as many personal statements as we can get and hope it points somewhere else. Unless a confession drops in my lap, I have to depend on information sources like Mr. Woods to provide other leads."

"You're right Deek," said Renee, "but from the tall tales I hear Alonzo Woods dishing out to the girls at the beauty shop, I wouldn't put much stock in anything that man has to say."

Deek smiled, "Well, Doc does that mean you're not interested in coming out with Bradford and me tomorrow morning to further question Mr. Woods?"

Renee wrinkled up her face, "Surely you jest. I consider your partner to be several notches below Alonzo Woods on the obnoxious scale."

"If I recall, Doc, you did say you wanted to work with us on this case."

"I guess you do have a valid point, Detective," she said while looking up into his dark, brown eyes.

"Good. I like having you around," he said and pulled her waist close to his body as he kissed her gently with a few brief pecks.

She felt the soft, moistness of his lips, defined by a neatly trimmed mustache. Deek didn't have those tickly, annoying facial hairs like some lazy men who wrongly believed regular grooming was only for women. And, he smelled so good. She closed her eyes and interlocked her arms around the small of his back as if to urge him not to leave just yet. She was surprised to realize that she had abandoned her fear of getting hurt because he might grow weary of her. Neither did she care that they stood only inches apart in the basement of a church. Renee only wanted to relish in how wonderful she felt at that moment. Deek teased her lips with his in a slow, circular motion then playfully met her tongue. They lingered in a tight embrace and tasted each other's lips. Renee felt the hard metal glock fastened to a shoulder holster under his jacket. The gun didn't bother her because she only focused on listening to his breath, and smelling the alluring, spicy fragrance of his cologne, while keenly aware of his body's increasing hardness.

"I'd better get out of here," he said in a whispered voice, "I shouldn't be thinking what I'm thinking right now in church."

They ended their kiss as innocently as it began with a playful peck on the lips then reluctantly let go their grip on each other. After Deek left the church, Renee calmed down and returned upstairs to the funeral service.

Luckily, she found an opening in the pew directly behind Brenda, near Veda and Cha-Cha—familiar faces that smiled at her and made room on their pew.

At the end of the mass, Jerome's oldest brother came up and eulogized him in a touching tribute and relayed anecdotes from their childhood. In the midst of Father Emanuel's songbird vocalization of Psalm 116, a woman seated in the middle pews sobbed uncontrollably. Renee turned around but did not recognize the woman who appeared to be close to Brenda's age. However, she did notice how Mrs. Adams looked back and cut her eyes at the sobbing woman whose makeup had started to run through her crying. She also overheard Mrs. Adams when she leaned over to Brenda and whispered in a voice that was not particularly quiet to anyone sitting near her. "What's that tramp doing here," said Mrs. Adams, "Has she lost her mind showing up at Jerome's funeral? That's just the epitome of bad taste." Brenda rocked Baby Justin and ignored the woman's outbursts as well as her mother's outrage.

Now the whole church had begun to stare as the woman bent over screaming and clutching her midriff. Renee silently mouthed the question, 'Who is that?' and Veda, who sat right next to her, answered that it was Leenae Lewis, Jerome's girlfriend from when they were all in high school. If Brenda heard Veda identify the woman as Jerome's high school ex-girlfriend, she didn't react. Instead, Brenda sat as rigid as a mummy with her lips clamped shut. By this time the noise had awakened the baby and Brenda's father reached over to take him from Brenda and carried him quickly out into the vestibule. Suddenly, the woman leaped from the pew and sprinted down the aisle yelling, "Open it. Open the casket now. I wanna see him." Brenda stood up, transfixed and speechless. Everyone stared in shock as Leenae ran towards the casket. Father Emanuel stumbled down the short steps from the altar in his haste to restrain the woman.

"Please, madam, stop," begged Father Emanuel waving his pudgy arms, "This is a closed casket ceremony."

People sat motionless with mouths gaped open, too stunned at this sudden outburst to move. In a flash, Leenae got past the priest and flung open the casket while people gasped in horror and disbelief. The severely burned body lay in the coffin, encased in white, silken padding. A white sheet covered most of Jerome's burned remains. Leenae screamed, covered her hands over her face, and then turned away. Father Emanuel rushed to close the casket, at which point Jerome's mother doubled over into her husband's arms and began weeping.

"What in God's name are you doing, Leenae?" Jerome's brother shouted, "Are you insane?"

Two men grabbed Leenae by each arm and tried to guide her back to the pew, but she snatched away from them. She stood in the aisle yelling something unintelligible at the dead body in the casket. When she spotted the two men coming towards her, she ran out the side exit.

Alonzo grinned from his seat. "Now that's what I'm talking about. Some drama up in here."

"This is a shameless spectacle in the House of God!" said Brenda. "Lord, forgive us." Brenda crumpled onto the seat and cried softly. Veda and Cha-Cha quickly moved up to the front row and put their arm around her and squeezed her shoulder. Renee followed and came forward to try to comfort Brenda.

Mrs. Adams, Brenda's mother, readjusted her red brimmed hat with a manicured red polished hand, and then crossed her leg to the other side. "Ya'll should have known better than to set up a dignified funeral for Jerome Johnson. You know the type of riffraff he hung around with. Would have been easier and quicker to have him cremated like I said."

Once things had settled down after Leenae's tirade, Father Emanuel ended the service and signaled for the pallbearers to carry the casket out to the hearse. The family had paid the additional cost for police escort through the city, so the funeral procession proceeded straight to the cemetery, unencumbered by rude motorists breaking into their convoy or honking their horns.

CHAPTER 30

T he investigative homicide team, Detectives Melvin "Mel" Bradford and Degas "Deek" Hamilton pulled up at the front gates of Galludet University at 8th and Florida Avenue, N.E. to question the guard. Bradford, the seasoned veteran on the team, short and stocky with thinning hair, and Hamilton, his younger partner, were following up on a tip they had received on Monday October 6, the day of the Capitol Hill fire. When the detectives approached, the six-foot five, muscled-bound guard stepped out of his booth to speak to them.

"Mr. Todd, is it?" said Det. Bradford, reading the nametag on the guard's uniform, "We're Detectives Bradford and Hamilton. We'd like to ask you a few questions." The detectives flashed their badges and Ids simultaneously.

"Like I said, I didn't see much behind that booth. I couldn't even make out the license plate but the car was a black SUV. Looked like a Chevy model."

"Your description matches what we got from some of the neighbors who thought they saw someone fleeing the scene that afternoon in a dark-colored sports utility vehicle," said Bradford, "But unfortunately, it's not enough."

The guard furrowed his bushy eyebrows together in deep thought. "Wait, there was a pregnant, homeless woman that wanders the streets around here sometimes. She had a run-in with the driver that afternoon when the driver almost hit her. She probably got a better look at the vehicle and maybe even saw the suspect."

"Well, that's something to go on," said Deek, "Where can we find this witness?"

"There's a group of homeless people that squat in those abandoned rowhouses in Trinidad, N.E.," said the guard, "It's cold today and when it's cold outside or the weather's bad, some of them go there to keep warm, or dry if it's raining. You might track her down over there."

"I know where you're talking about," said Bradford, "The doors on these abandoned houses are always broken open. We get complaints all the time from owners who can't keep the homes boarded up. It's easy for squatters to break in. Thanks, Mr. Todd, if you remember anything else, give us a call."

Detectives Bradford and Hamilton jumped back into Bradford's police-issued midnight blue Crown Victoria and sped off. They traveled down H Street towards the Trinidad neighborhood in Northeast Washington, D. C. The car slowed down in front of an L-shaped track of nondescript, brick red, graffiti-covered walls as the detectives peered out both sides of the window. Bradford told Deek how ten years ago when the housing complex was first built, a well-kept lawn of lush green surrounded the entire residential area. He said at one time there had been a park with functional playground equipment. Now, the swings were broken and the only thing standing on the basketball court was the backboard, and a dangling, net-less hoop that had been partially ripped off.

They continued slowly down the street, hoping to catch sight of the homeless, pregnant woman the guard had said might be a potential witness. Flanked by a twelve-foot high-wired fence and a forest of densely populated evergreens in the distance, the projects looked more like a maximum-security prison. A construction crew had left stacks of metal slabs, a bulldozer and a front loader on a nearby abandoned lot. A group of young men huddled on the lot but when they spotted Bradford's car inching towards them, they ran.

The subsidized housing and abandoned dwellings that the detectives passed had been overrun by homeless people, thieves, drug users, and their dealers. Wasted young souls slouched in doorways, their youth and bodies used up by drugs. The homeless squatted in clusters with their bundled possessions close by. As he stared out the window, Deek felt a lump in his throat. He realized that at one time many of these people could have had jobs, homes, and dreams. Too many working people today were only two paychecks away from being in the streets.

Suddenly, something shadowy with a speck of red flashed from behind a dense thicket of poplar and catalpa bushes. Bradford slammed on the breaks and both detectives jumped out the car. The shadow fled but didn't get far before Bradford and Deek caught up with her. She was pregnant. Her large, glassy eyes glared out at them with mistrust. She removed her red knit cap and twisted it in her hands.

"I didn't do nothin'," she stammered before the detectives could speak.

After Bradford and Deek introduced themselves and explained what they wanted, she grew even more reticent.

"What's your name?" Deek asked.

"Belinda, but folks around here call me Billi."

"Listen, Billi we just spoke to the guard at Galludet University. He told us you had an argument on Monday with someone fitting the description of our suspect. Could you tell us what happened?"

Billi folded her arms around her shivering body and stared at her scruffy shoes without answering.

"Do you have family anywhere?"

Billi shook her head.

"I can try to get you some help Billi if you let me. You should be going to a clinic for regular prenatal care," said Deek. "Take my card. It's got my number at the precinct and at FBI headquarters."

He stuffed his business card and some bills in her hands. "Go get yourself a decent meal. When I get back to the station, I'll make some calls to find out about permanent shelter and other services for you and your baby once it's born. You haven't been drinking or doing drugs, have you?"

Billi assured Deek she wasn't. She said when she discovered she was pregnant she stopped drinking and smoking crack. No family, homeless, and approaching her ninth month in the pregnancy, all she had in the world was her unborn baby.

"Let's get back to the reason we're here," Bradford piped in, "Don't keep us in suspense, lady, tell us about the driver in the black SUV. We think this is the person responsible for that fire Monday afternoon on 6th Street in SE that resulted in the death of a 28 year old man."

"No, I don't know nothing, man. I'm not getting mixed up in this." Billi shook her head vehemently. She refused to get involved in a murder investigation.

"Maybe we'll just take you down to police headquarters and charge you with trespassing on private property," Bradford threatened, "Unless you're ready to make a formal statement."

"I ain't goin' nowhere and I ain't talkin' to no cops," said Billi.

Deek took his partner aside and spoke in a whispered tone so the witness could not hear. "Mel, can't you see this woman is afraid and needs help?" said Deek, "Your scare tactics are a misuse of authority here."

Bradford sighed and shrugged his shoulders, "You can play Santa Clause on your own time Young Blood. But I'm getting the hell outta here. This is a waste of my goddamn time."

Detective Bradford turned and walked away. He plopped his heavy frame behind the wheel and slammed the door. Deek talked to Billi for a few more minutes before leaving. He asked her to call if she changed her mind about cooperating or if she needed anything.

"All right, let's head back to the precinct," said Deek, wearily then climbed in the passenger's side, "Maybe something's come in from the lab."

CHAPTER 31

After the interment at the cemetery, Renee made a brief appearance at Mrs. Adams's house, but still didn't get a chance to speak to Brenda privately. Renee wasn't thrilled with the idea of Brenda moving back home with her manipulating mother. But having Brenda safe at her own home did free up her time to work on the case with Deek as the investigative team's criminal profile expert. In just four days, the media's portrayal of Brenda had degraded from innocent widow to vilified murderess. The press painted a conniving, greedy woman who launched a scheme to collect on her husband's $50,000-dollar life insurance policy by burning down an elderly lady's house and all her memories. They projected a heartless criminal capable of killing her husband who she knew was home at the time of the arson, kidnapping her baby and leaving it to be found by authorities. In an attempt to show a rising trend in killer mothers, the press dug up past cases where mothers had willfully harmed or murdered their children.

Renee did not know this woman they depicted in the newspapers and on television. As far as she was concerned, that woman did not exist. There had to be other suspects to consider. Hopefully she could convince Lt. Melvin Bradford, the lead investigator for Jerome's case, to explore different possibilities. When she volunteered her services as a civilian, Chief Frye and Detective Bradford agreed to accept her help.

She headed for D.C. Police headquarters at 300 Indiana Avenue, NW and hoped Deek would be there instead of at the FBI building. Deek had been working double time, dividing his responsibilities between the Save Our Streets (SOS) FBI joint task force, designed to reduce drug-related crime in the city and his regular MPD homicide caseload.

When Renee arrived at headquarters, the desk sergeant told her that Detectives Bradford and Hamilton were on their way back to the station after questioning witnesses. Renee rode the elevator to the homicide division on the third floor to wait for them. She sat down on a bench amid the processing room's somber decor of drab pea green walls, black metal desks, hard chairs, and metallic gray filing cabinets. A tower of boxed paperwork sat in a corner waiting to be filed. Now she understood why Deek kept his notes and paperwork electronically organized on a PDA and his laptop computer. In seconds he could access law enforcement databases and computerized systems to manage his cases and analyze evidence. All around the room, she heard the constant noise of phones ringing, conversations, and witnesses being questioned. Investigators huddled in their spaces, poured over stacks of case files, and charted their evidence on a large white board.

"Here come Beauty and the Beast," said a female detective when Deek and Lt. Mel Bradford walked into the homicide area.

"I must be Beauty, huh?" smiled Mel, carrying a brown lunch bag with grease spots from something obviously fried and fattening. Deek and Mel took off their overcoats and hung them on the rack.

"Guess again, Asshole," she said and rolled her eyes at Mel, "Here's a hint—one of you is fine, wears sharp threads, and drives a two-seater Mercedes. The other one is full of shit, wears cheap ass suits, and drives a Ford Taurus that's older than my mama."

"Easy on the compliments, Galloway," said Mel, "If you're trying to ask me out on a date, I'm busy tonight."

"Ugh! Don't make me vomit. And do us all a favor, will ya Bradford? Stop feeding the rats. Your mama don't work here."

Lt. Bradford plopped his 5'9" thickset frame in the chair behind his cluttered desk and with a pudgy hand swept old take-out food wrappers and empty coke cans into the wastebasket. Renee saw that nothing had changed with Lt. Melvin Bradford since her last unpleasant encounter with him over the summer when he wrongly accused Veda Simms, one of her former patients, of murdering her boyfriend. He had the same sarcastic attitude. He was still balding on top, wearing the same rumpled, brown sports jacket over a dingy blue shirt that clinched his sagging belly.

"You better make your move soon, Galloway, 'cause I'm outta here after December 21st. That's your last chance. I'll be retiring and heading out to my favorite fishing spot in Virginia. Got my gear all set," said Bradford in between chews of French fries and double cheeseburger.

"Humph. Good Riddance."

"Hey, Mel, you should come out to my new spot on Kent Island," said Deek, carrying a case file and pulling up a chair, "we can do some fishing out there. They've got a huge fishing pier. It's right after you make that first exit off the Bay Bridge."

"What's bitin'?"

"A little Rockfish and Perch so the locals tell me."

Detective Galloway looked up from her paperwork. "Deek, you still working on that federal task force?" she asked.

"Yeah, I'm still working with the feds on the SOS Task Force. But the chief asked me to also work the Johnson case with Mel since our department's short on manpower."

"Oh, I almost forgot. Some woman called a little while ago. Said she remembered something about the Johnson arson/murder case but she only wanted to talk to you."

"Thanks, Galloway. Did she leave her name and number?"

"Nah, said she was calling from a phone booth and she'd call you back."

Ever since he had arrived, Renee had tried to make eye contact with

Deek so she could talk to him alone, but he didn't see her standing by the window. Finally, she braced herself for a reunion with Bradford and walked over to his desk where he and Deek had begun looking at the Johnson case file. Renee cleared her throat.

"Excuse me, Deek … uh Detective Hamilton, may I please speak to you privately for a moment in the coffee lounge."

Deek stood up, but before they could walk away, Bradford stopped her. "Dr. Hayes, I hear you're helping out with the suspect profile," he slid his chair back and swept his hungry eyes over her body, stopping at the crevice of her V-necked Navy-blue, fitted jacket with its tiny, pearl buttons. "Whatcha got for us?"

It was warm in the processing room but Renee would not remove her jacket. She wore a filmy, sheer white blouse over a white lace camisole and did not want Bradford leering at her breasts.

When Renee didn't answer him, Bradford pressed on. "If what you wanna say to my partner is about the Johnson case, you can speak freely right here," said Bradford and pulled up another chair close to his desk. He patted the chair and motioned for her to sit down.

Renee continued to stand. "Brenda didn't telephone the insurance company the way it was reported in the News," she said. "Her mother, Mrs. Irene Adams, admitted to me after the funeral this morning that she placed the call and had pretended to be her daughter. Plus, Mrs. Adams hated her son-in-law. My secretary is not the only person with motive."

"Is that right, Inspector Clouseau?" Bradford said with an amused look. "I still say the wife had a more compelling motive—50 K in cash from her husband's life insurance policy. That's a lotta dough for somebody like her. Besides, Mrs. Adams could be lying to take the heat off her daughter. She's probably just being a protective mother," said Bradford, fixing his sleepy eyes on Renee.

"Then you haven't met Mrs. Adams. Protective is not a word I'd use to describe her unless it's towards her own self-interest."

"Ouch! Remind me not to get on your shit list, Doc." Lt. Bradford ran his finger down the case file, then pushed the open page in front of her. "Take a look at this, Dr. Hayes," said Bradford.

Renee silently read the entry that he pointed out.

At 8:35 AM on Tuesday October 7, the morning after her husband's death, Mrs. Brenda Johnson called MegaLife.com Insurance Company to notify the claims rep that her husband had been killed in a tragic house fire. The victim's wife requested that they start processing her husband's claim as soon as possible. The claims rep immediately called the police to alert them that insurance fraud could be involved and put a hold on the claim.

"Not only that, but Mrs. Johnson found out a week before the murder that her husband had been cheating on her with a Miss Leenae Lewis," said Bradford, "So let's add another motive on top of greed—revenge."

"When Deek and I questioned Mrs. Johnson about her whereabouts on Monday, the 6th from 11:00 AM to 1:00 PM, she claimed she was at your office, working. Unfortunately, no one was there to corroborate her story, so she doesn't have an alibi. That gives her opportunity, especially if she used an accomplice. Greed and betrayal caused Brenda Johnson to kill her husband," said Bradford, wearing a satisfied smile.

Renee slid the extra chair next to Deek and sat down. Fatigue and anxiety swept across her face.

"Can I grab you a cup of coffee while I'm in the lounge?" Bradford asked her. "I'm about due for a re-fill."

"Yes, thank you, Lt. Bradford, coffee would be nice. Cream and sugar, please," she said, realizing that at least she'd have five minutes without him around.

Bradford got up and headed for the coffee lounge. "Can I get you something too, Partner?" he hollered back at Deek.

"No thanks. I'm good."

Before Renee and Deek could get into a conversation, an attractive young woman burst through the door. "There you are, Hamilton," she said. Renee and Deek looked up at the same time when the petite, honey-toned woman with striking black eyes strutted in and honed in on Deek, ignoring Renee completely.

"Hey, Santos, what's up, Partner?" said Deek.

"*Todo esta bien, Pápi*," said the woman, smiling seductively.

Her long, dark hair was pulled back in a ponytail and flounced as she walked. She wore a tailored, burgundy suit, high-heeled shoes, and carried a portfolio under her arm. Renee recognized Agent Ana Santos, Deek's partner, from the FBI SOS Task Force that she had met weeks ago at the Boys and Girls Club fundraiser dinner. The Johnson case belonged in MPD homicide territory however the FBI helped the local police force when resources were low and they requested help. Because of all the unsolved murders, Chief Frye authorized new strategies to centralize the homicide unit, utilize FBI resources more, and increase police presence on the streets. When Agent Santos offered to share information with the MPD homicide investigators working the Johnson case, the chief welcomed her input. Lieutenant Bradford, on the other hand, wasn't so grateful. At this point, neither was Renee, but for personal reasons.

"Ana, what do you have?" said Deek, pulling up another chair for her to sit down, "By the way, you remember, Dr. Renee Hayes. Dr. Hayes is working with us on the Johnson case as a criminal profile consultant."

Agent Ana Santos nodded at Renee then pulled out a cassette player and tape, along with a thick manila file from her portfolio.

"What happened to you last night, Partner?" Agent Santos asked Deek with a flirty smile.

"Working on this case," said Deek, "I haven't had a good night's rest or eaten a decent meal in over 48 hours."

"Well, you missed a feast at my Tia Rosa's, man. We had *arroz y habichuelas con pollo* and her *sancocho* melted in the mouth. And, her *ceviche*! Unbelievable! Mi Tia makes her *ceviche* with huge shrimp instead of the chunks of fish. I'll get the recipe from her and make it for you. Would you believe I ate three bowls of it?"

"You don't look like it," Deek smiled, "Not everybody can eat whatever they want and still look fantastic."

He didn't notice the color draining out of Renee's face and her eyes narrowing into fiery slits.

"After a few bottles of Corona and the music got pumped up, I worked off those calories dancing the *Merengue* and *Bachata*. You should have been there, man."

At that moment, Bradford waddled in carrying two mugs of coffee and a Hostess Twinkie cupcake from the vending machine. "Too bad I missed the *fiesta*, Santos," he grinned, after catching the last part of her conversation.

"*Disculpe!*" Agent Santos glared at Lt. Bradford. "Who says you were invited, man?"

At least she and Agent Santos shared a common contempt for Melvin Bradford, thought Renee. And, it seemed obvious to Renee that they shared a common affection for Deek.

"Look, I don't plan on being here all night again," said Bradford, "So let's cut to the chase. Right now, we're looking at a bunch of rumors, gossip, and speculative information so we better start sifting through this crap. We already got too many damn cooks in the kitchen as it is." He looked at Renee.

"You're right Mel, let's look at the facts to see what we got so far," said Deek, "I don't know why it's taking forensics and the crime scene lab so long to get back to us with their results from the physical evidence I sent them."

"Like I said, so far my money's on the wife as the prime suspect unless somebody can show me different," said Bradford, "I could arrest her now on suspicion of murder but then I'd have to charge her within 48 hours. I gotta bring the DA hard evidence before I do that."

"You got anything substantial on the Torch yet?" asked Santos, replacing her playful smile with a serious demeanor.

"Not exactly. Mel and I tried to talk to a witness who was seen arguing with the suspect in front of Galludet University. But she refused to cooperate with us," said Deek, "the woman was homeless and looked like she could give birth any minute. Under the circumstances, I think she had other priorities. Plus, Mel pissed her off."

"I need another Twinkie," said Bradford, looking bored as he got up to return to the vending machine.

Deek told Renee and Agent Santos everything the guard at Galludet University had said and what the homeless woman had said, which wasn't much of anything. "They did both confirm that they saw someone in a black SUV near the time of the arson/murder and not far from the crime scene. Mel and I finally tracked the witness down at one of those abandoned houses."

"Will she testify?" Agent Santos asked.

"I doubt it. Says she won't get involved in our murder investigation now that she has her baby to think of. I gave her my business card in case she changes her mind. But I don't expect to hear from her. Bradford's lousy attitude throughout the questioning didn't help," said Deek, "She could have been a possible eyewitness. The only chance we had so far of finding one."

"That's too bad Deek," said Agent Santos, handing Deek her cassette tape. "Here, I don't know if this'll shed any light or just add to the confusion. I've been clocking this Jett Set crew and their leader going on six months."

Deek went to get Bradford from the coffee room to come listen to the tape Agent Santos brought in. Santos explained that the FBI did a tape and tap on the phone lines at Lucia Delgado's apartment. Lucia was the Dominican girlfriend of a Jett Set crewmember named Bombillo. Coincidentally, this was the same crew that Jerome Johnson owed $2,000 to and that the FBI had under surveillance. Based on the FBI's voice print analysis, Agent Santos said the tape contained a phone conversation between two men who agents identified as Delroy McShore—alias DL, right-hand man of suspected drug lord, James

Ian Mathias, and another crewmember named Bruno Morales—aka Bombillo. Santos believed Ian Mathias ordered DL to kill Jerome Johnson for not paying his drug debt. Deek re-winded the tape and pressed the button to play back the conversation as they all listened.

"Sounds like the honeymoon's over," said Bradford, after listening to the two alleged drug runners on the tape argue about how to deal with Jerome's reluctance to payback his debt.

"I got a plan to bait and catch this *maricon* DL then maybe he'll give up the main Man to save his own skin," said Agent Santos.

"Sounds like you're only worried about solving your own case against Mathias, Santos," Detective Bradford said. "Besides, your case sounds speculative. What else you got on these Jett Setters? All I see is a tape implicating DL in a murder and conspiracy to commit murder. DL's hotshot lawyer will have him out before you finish all your goddamn paperwork."

"Maybe not, Mel. Not if we can scare DL and get his cooperation to rat out his don," said Deek, agreeing with Agent Santos. "This chump DL might think he could beat the drug dealing rap but not if murder and arson are tacked on."

"I'm not trading my girl for your boy," said Bradford, "If that's your game plan, Santos, you can forget it."

"Look Bradford, your Johnson murder case and my Mathias drug dealer case might be linked," said Agent Santos, with excitement in her voice.

"They actually pay you a salary for these brilliant deductions?" said Bradford, sarcastically. "Damn, just what I need—another rookie Fed getting in the way of my homicide investigation. I practically got everything wrapped up on this Johnson case. All I gotta do is tie a bow on it."

"Listen Lieutenant, we can help each other," said Santos, almost begging.

Santos explained that their FBI special task force already outlined the details of using an undercover cop to trap DL. By threatening DL with a capital murder charge, they could work out a deal. With DL's testimony, the feds could bag Ian Mathias for multiple gang-related slayings, tax evasion, and drug conspiracy. Agent Santos read from police reports and her own case files while Bradford stared off into space not even wanting to consider another suspect, other than Brenda Johnson. Renee had always suspected Bradford of being unprofessional and now she was convinced of it.

Agent Santos vehemently argued her theory. "Lt. Bradford, there is enough motive for me to wonder if the Jett Set hitman, DL could be responsible for Jerome Johnson's murder on October 6."

"If you charge Mrs. Johnson for her husband's murder, I won't have any bargaining chips to make a deal with DL," said Santos.

"Sounds like a personal problem," said Bradford, yawning.

"Look, Detective, we know from a close acquaintance and our wire taps that Jerome Johnson, the victim, owed Mathias $2,000 that clearly he could not pay."

"That's right, Mel. What we need is enough leverage to convince DL to go for a plea bargain and turn government snitch against Mathias," said Deek, backing up Agent Santos.

Agent Santos stood up and leaned across Bradford's desk until she was right in his face. "What else do you need, Bradford? I've got a vested interest in both these cases because I truly believe they are related and that Ian Mathias is behind a string of multiple killings throughout the city." Ana Santos continued. "So I'm gonna stick around to make sure that poor widow doesn't get blamed for a crime she didn't commit just because you wanna close out all your case files before you retire. Any problems with that Detective Bradford?"

"I hate to blow out your candles, Santos, but ... you better light 'em up again and make another wish," he said, wearing a sneer on his face and a toothpick stuck between his teeth. "You guys are gonna have to dig that hole a little deeper to nab your boy, Mathias. Anyway, why would this guy Mathias order a hit for a lousy two grand?" asked Bradford, "That's chump change to a big time drug lord like Mathias."

"It's not about the amount of money, Detective, it's about respect," said Santos, "You should know that! Mathias can't just ignore it or other crackheads might try to get away with it. Or worse, his crew might lose respect for him and take him out one day."

Bradford shrugged and stretched out his arms behind his head. "I don't believe the Johnson woman's statement. I think this broad's guilty as sin," he said, scratching his rotund belly.

Agents Santos threw up her arms and sighed in exasperation.

"I gotta go to the john," said Bradford, as he rose and headed towards the bathroom, "What I really need is to get myself a case of beer, get loaded, then crash for about five days."

Agent Santos called after him. "Mel, all I'm asking is that you consider the possibility," she said and ejected her cassette tape from the machine. "Until I see a set of fingerprints or an eyewitness tying Mrs. Johnson to her husband's murder, I'll stick to my claim against Mathias."

Agent Ana Santos gathered up her documents and gave Renee a polite nod, good-bye. Then, she looked directly at Deek and smiled. "*Llamame esta noche*," she said only to him and strutted out the door. Renee did not know what she said to him, but it was clear Agent Santos had a thing for Deek, and what woman wouldn't, she thought.

When Deek and Renee were alone at the desk, or as alone as they could be amidst a half dozen detectives working on their own cases, Renee turned to Deek with a concerned look on her face. "Come to think of it, I believe my beautician, Cha-Cha Taylor, has been seeing that drug lord, Ian Mathias, the one Agent Santos talked about. It sounds like the same man. I hope he's not using her. Cha-Cha puts on a tough exterior but she can be very naïve and trusting at times. I think I should warn Cha-Cha to stay away from Mathias without telling her anything specific, of course."

"I don't think that's a good idea Renee. Though I understand your concern for her. You might be putting your own safety at risk if Mathias finds out you're working with us and thinks you know too much," said Deek.

"I know Cha-Cha can be overly dramatic at times, but if it turns out that this Ian Mathias really is responsible for Jerome's murder I'm sure Cha-Cha had nothing to do with it. But I can't help worry that if she continues to see this man she might become an unknowing accomplice to his crimes or worse, another one of his victims."

"I see your point. Mathias is dangerous. But let me talk to her, okay? That way she won't need to know you're behind it. If for some reason she doesn't believe me and goes back and tells Mathias, at least you won't be implicated. And if she refuses to sever ties with him, she'll have to face the consequences when he gets busted."

"All right Deek, but please speak to her soon. This is Friday so she'll be at the shop late. Make her understand how dangerous it is being involved with this man."

"Don't worry, I'll talk to her as soon as I can," said Deek and squeezed Renee's hand.

CHAPTER 32

A uniformed officer approached Deek and called him away. While he was gone, Renee went to get a drink of water from the cooler and caught sight of her image on a wall mirror. She flinched at the tired, lusterless eyes, pallid skin, and turned-down corners of her mouth that reflected back at her in the mirror. The past ten days had taken a heavy toll. It seemed like every time she came within reach of what she wanted, it got snatched away. She thought of losing her mother at the young age of 7. Renee no longer trusted that happiness would ever come her way unless she really worked hard for it. When Deek returned he immediately read the troubled look on her face. As usual, he intuitively sensed her moods and feelings. He stood behind her chair and gently massaged her neck and shoulders until the tension lifted.

"Thanks, I needed that," she said, with a relaxed smile.

"I think I'll call the crime scene lab to see if the technicians have anything yet," said Deek, "Hopefully, they were able to lift fingerprints off the duct tape we found behind the Johnson house."

"Can they do that?"

"Sometimes. Nowadays, we have cutting-edge science and technology to bring killers to justice. I'll put the call through on speaker phone so you can listen in," said Deek as he dialed one of the specialists at the police CSI lab.

"Hey, Roberts, Detective Hamilton here. How are you, buddy?"

"Backed up but I started your analysis, Lieutenant."

"Good. What's it look like so far?"

"Nothing from the duct tape or fabric threads yet. But I'm applying gas chromatography analysis on the gasoline can and debris residue you sent in."

"I've heard of that procedure but educate me a little, will you Roberts?"

"Gas chromatography is a technique that's become so accurate it can differentiate between different makes and grades of gasoline," the specialist explained, "each grade of gasoline has its own fingerprint so to speak, depending on the chemicals present."

"That's fascinating, but what'll it buy me?"

"I should be able to trace the residuals from the gas can used in the crime to an individual gas station or even to the fuel tank of a particular vehicle."

"That should narrow the search a bit for us," said Deek, "how soon do you think you'll have something conclusive?"

"Because it's you, Lieutenant, I'll work on it this weekend. Should have something by Monday."

"Appreciate it, buddy. I owe you one."

"I'll hold you to that, Detective."

Just as Deek hung up the phone, Bradford returned. He filled his partner in on what the crime lab specialist explained but Bradford didn't seem impressed. The lead investigator stuck to his belief that starting a gasoline fire was too amateurish for a notorious drug crew like the Jett Setters. Why wouldn't they just shoot the guy? Deek admitted that Bradford had a valid point. Then his partner opened the front drawer of his desk and took out a piece of paper.

"I have a warrant of arrest upon probable cause, signed by the magistrate, said Detective Bradford, waving the paper in the air. "I just got a call from the DA. She wants me to proceed."

"Why didn't you discuss this with me first, Mel?" asked Deek.

"'Cause I'm the lead investigator, not you, Young Blood. Those media sharks, Chief Frye, and Mayor Latchette are on my back every day to make an arrest. The public is fed up with all these so-called good mothers committing crimes for their own selfish gain."

Bradford's voice rose to an emotional pitch. "Brenda Johnson thought she'd be sitting pretty with that insurance money. And, at the same time gettin' rid of her cheatin' husband. This isn't the first time she's tried to pull a fraudulent insurance scam. Check the police files for yourself." He paused, looking straight at Renee. "Well, I've got news for her, by Monday morning, she'll find her ass in C-10 in D. C. Superior Courthouse for arraignment," said Bradford, "If her hotshot attorney can't get her ass out on PR, she'll stay locked up until the trial."

"Detective Bradford, this is a double tragedy. A man is brutally murdered and his wife falsely accused," Renee said.

"That's not how me and the rest of the world see it. Brenda Johnson had motive and opportunity. Look at the facts. The wife finds out her husband got fired for using drugs, is having an affair with his old girlfriend, and she inherits fifty grand if he croaks. As for opportunity, I don't think Mrs. Johnson would have any trouble getting somebody else to do her dirty work for a nice share in the profits. She's a pretty little thing at that. How hard would it be for her to convince some idiot to knock off her husband for say a couple of grand once her insurance money comes in?"

"Your theory is bogus, Detective," said Renee, "I know my secretary and she is as good and honest as they come. She's a Christian and a believer."

"The worse kind if you ask me," said Bradford. "Anyway, this is what you say, Doc, but I happen to know things aren't always as they seem."

"Don't be so quick to put this case to bed, Mel," said Deek, "There're still too many unanswered questions and nothing but circumstantial evidence to pin it on Mrs. Johnson. I want to close the case while it's still hot too but only if we catch the real killer."

"This Johnson case has gotten too much media attention. I'm the lead investigator and everybody's breathing down my neck to solve it."

Bradford folded the arrest warrant and placed it in his inside jacket pocket. "You two continue the party without me. I'm going home for some shut-eye. I'll be back in a coupla hours. Deek, can you follow-up with the victim's ex-girlfriend, Leenae Lewis? Make sure her alibi checks out too"

"Looks like I'll have to. Catch you later, Partner," said Deek.

"If it makes you feel any better, Dr. Hayes, I don't think Brenda Johnson acted alone. I believe she had a flunky boyfriend in on it," Bradford winked. "Like I said, greed, betrayal, and revenge. It's all there, folks." Bradford got his coat and headed for the door. Before leaving, he turned around. "Ya'll remember that old school tune by the Pretenders?" Without waiting for their reply, he began singing the lyrics off-key, "It's a thin line, between love and hate ... a thin line, between love and hate ..." His voice trailed off, but he kept singing until they could no longer hear him.

Lt. Bradford left Renee seething mad but as usual she was able to successfully mask her anger with him.

"Deek, I have to see Brenda right away and find out what happened nine years ago with her first child and the insurance money she collected from that child's death. Bradford is obviously using that case to establish a precedent against her."

"You're right, Doc. Call me when you have something. I need to hang around and finish some paperwork on another case. Bradford's not even waiting for the physical evidence from the lab that could implicate someone else. This isn't like him, Renee. Something must be causing him to have tunnel vision against Brenda Johnson."

Just as Renee was about to leave to go see her secretary, a pregnant woman who appeared to be homeless ambled into Homicide's processing room. Renee stood frozen in place as she stared into the homeless woman's sorrowful dark eyes. The woman's bony shoulders drooped and she was dressed in layers of oversized, threadbare, dirty clothes and a dingy-looking, red knit cap. The woman nearly collapsed in front of Detective Galloway's desk. Tall and thin, except for her bulging stomach and swollen feet, she braced one hand on the detective's desk and clutched a business card in the other hand.

"Can I help you?" Detective Galloway asked.

She glanced at the card in her hand. "I need to see Detective Degas Hamilton," she said between puffs to catch her breath.

Deek and Renee rushed towards the woman and grabbed her on each side by the waist and elbow. They led her to a more comfortable couch in the coffee lounge where she immediately collapsed. She wiped the perspiration from her face with her coat sleeve. Then snatched off her red knit cap and smoothed down dark strands of straggly, unwashed wavy hair. Renee noticed that if this woman's hair had been groomed and cared for, its texture would have resembled the beautiful mane of what the old timers used to call 'good hair' like Renee's mother had possessed when she was alive.

"Billi, can I get you anything?" asked Deek, helping her to remove her ratty wool coat.

"Water," she said in a weak voice, still out of breath.

"I'll get it," said Renee and hurried out front to the water fountain. Renee returned a few moments later and offered her two water-filled Dixie cups. The woman gulped down one then placed the other cup on the table.

"Bless you sistuh," the homeless woman grinned, revealing a few missing and chipped front teeth.

Despite the lack of dental work and gaunt expression, Billi had an attractive face with large, chestnut eyes, a small, button nose, and naturally rose-tinted lips. She was just a shade lighter than Renee's own tender brown complexion. Grimy, dirty, multiple layers of clothing covered her back. This was all she owned to shield her from the cold.

Living on the streets branded Billi's once-pretty face with healed scars, a weather-beaten skin tone, and blemishes.

Renee sat down next to Deek, facing his potential witness. At that moment, they noticed her face cringe as she hugged her belly.

"Are you all right Billi?" Deek asked.

"Yeah, just let me sit here and catch my breath a minute. Took me over an hour to walk here."

Renee thought that Billi appeared to be in the late stages of her pregnancy.

"When is your baby due?" asked Renee, "I'm Dr. Renee Hayes, a psychologist but I also have previous nursing experience. You look like you are near delivery and should be seeing an obstetrician at least weekly."

Billi shrugged, "Don't know when I'm due exactly. I ain't seen no doctor yet."

Renee shook her head and sighed. This woman should have been receiving prenatal care and treatment, not living on the streets. That poor woman was about to bring a life into the world with no way to take care of it.

"You shouldn't have walked so far in your condition," said Deek, "why didn't you call me? I could have gotten someone to pick you up."

"I used my last fifty cents in change tryin' to call. Didn't that lady cop out there tell you I called?"

"Yes, I got the message but I didn't know it was you calling, Billi. I'm glad you changed your mind about cooperating with us. We need more support from the community and witnesses willing to come forward in order to solve these escalating murders and crimes."

"I'm only talkin' to you Detective Hamilton. Not your partner."

"All right, Billi. Do you remember anything about that Monday afternoon when you argued with the driver of the van?"

Billi's face contorted as if she were experiencing pain. She took a deep breath, relaxed and then nodded her head as an answer.

"What can you tell me about the vehicle?"

Before she could speak, Renee interrupted and suggested that they take Billi to the nearest clinic to be checked out first. They could question her later. Deek agreed and got up to offer his hand to help Billi up.

"No clinics and no hospital," said Billi, waving his hand away, "They ask too many damn questions. When my time comes, I'll know it and I'll call the ambulance to take me to the hospital."

"All right," sighed Deek, "but before you leave here I'm going to give you a pre-paid cell phone with enough minutes on it to last you a few weeks. I want you to contact me any time. Or if you need anything, you understand?" Billi nodded her head.

Renee didn't like the sound of the pregnant woman's garbled speech. She didn't think the woman would last a few weeks, and felt conflicted about interfering in Deek's questioning of her.

After catching her breath, Billi confirmed that the kidnapper who almost ran her down Monday afternoon around 12:30 drove a black, Chevy Blazer sports utility vehicle. After they argued, she threw a broken bottle at the right side of the vehicle. She said it could have left a dent or scratch. When the driver passed her, she had to jump out the way to avoid being hit.

"The Galludent University guard said he couldn't make out a license plate number. Did you see it, Billi?" Deek asked.

"I don't remember the license number but I saw a sticker on the back of the car that had an E on it."

"That sounds like the stickers Enterprise uses on some of their rental cars. Wait one minute. I wanna get somebody from the squad to check that out," said Deek and poked his head out the door, shouting, "Kane, can I see you please?"

Moments later, a young rookie detective appeared.

"Yes, Lieutenant?"

"Kane, I need you to contact all the Enterprise car rental places in the city. See which one rented out a black, Chevy Blazer SUV on

Monday as well as the day before," said Deek while Kane wrote down his instructions on a tiny notepad.

"When you find the rental location, get a name and address of who rented the vehicle and when it was returned. Find out if there was a dent or scratch on the right side when it came back. Then check the trip-sheet to see where the vehicle went. Let me know what you find out."

"I'm on it," said Kane and rushed out the door.

"Billi, was the person you argued with a man or a woman?"

"I dunno for sure what they was. They had on a dark hooded parka. The voice sounded kinda deep and scratchy for a female but I guess it coulda been a shortie. Some chicks have a deep voice," said Billi, "Whoever it was looked high off a little Whoula too."

"What's that?" Renee asked.

"Whoula? That's a blunt mixed with cooked coke or crack sprinkled on it," Deek answered.

"About how tall was the person and could you tell if they had a thin, average, or heavyset build?"

"Couldn't really tell since they was sittin' down in the car."

After taking her statement, Deek wanted to be sure Billi could be a credible witness. He asked if she had a record. "Tell me Billi, if I pull up your rap sheet will I find anything?"

"Yeah, man, I did some time a few years ago. I was a mule and my partner ratted me out."

"When we first spoke you told me you hadn't taken any drugs since your pregnancy? Are you telling me the truth about that? And, what about your HIV status? Do you know what it is?"

"Yeah, I'm clean. When I found out I was gonna have a baby, I stopped copping dope and drinking liquor. I quit cold turkey. That's no lie, man. I had my HIV status checked by one of those mobile health vans just a coupla months ago. They did the oral test right there and everything was cool. I'll swear on a stack of bibles."

"I believe you, Billi," said Deek.

Billi looked down at her protruding stomach. "Before I knew about the baby though," she said, rubbing her belly, "all I could think about was my next hit. But not now."

Renee kept her thoughts and concerns to herself. She couldn't be absolutely sure if this woman's garbled speech resulted from alcohol, drugs, or just plain fatigue and despair. She could only hope that the woman was telling the truth about her negative HIV status for the sake of the unborn child. But what if she were lying or in some type of denial? What if she had contracted a venereal disease before she got pregnant that could infect her newborn? Renee had already witnessed tragic results that summer while volunteering for CASA when 18-month old Sweet Baby Susannah had died of AIDS that she contracted at birth from her HIV-positive, drug-addicted mother. Renee pushed those horrible thoughts away. She wanted to believe what this poor mother-to-be had said—that she had stopped using drugs when she discovered she was pregnant and that she was clean.

"That's good to hear, Billi," Renee added with a smile. "There's a new healthcare program you might qualify for." Renee glanced at Deek as she continued, "Detective Hamilton and I are going to get you enrolled at Mary's Center so you can start receiving prenatal care and get linked up to other community services that can help you after your baby is born."

Deek nodded. "That's right, Billi. You'll need job skills and permanent housing. Unfortunately, the situation with permanent housing for the homeless is getting worse since everything's more expensive," he said, "but between Dr. Hayes and myself, we'll use our connections to do whatever we can to get you on your feet. I might be able to pull some strings to get you in public housing."

"Yeah, right. Dream on man. I've heard those promises before. But at the end of the day when it's friggin' below forty degrees outside I'm still sleeping under some freeway or sneaking into boarded up row houses if I'm lucky."

"Why don't you go to the House of Ruth for shelter?" asked Renee. "They take in single women. And the city has churches that'll open their doors when it's cold."

"Dr. Hayes is right, Billi," said Deek. "LaCasa in Northwest also provides shelter. In fact, there're about a half dozen homeless shelters in D. C. And if you don't want to go to a shelter, I'm sure you know the city provides sleeping bags and blankets. You can also spend the night in these vans that come by when the temperature gets really low."

"Naw. No thanks. No privacy," said Billi, "and not enough cots in the shelters most of the time. Those vans and shelters ain't for me, man."

"Regardless, when the weather gets below freezing, you can't stay outside, Billi," said Deek, firmly, "That's not healthy for you or your baby. You could die from hypothermia. I want you to call me whenever you need help."

Billi nodded and mumbled okay. Deek placed a few twenties from his wallet into her grimy hand. "In the meantime, take this for your baby."

Renee saw how the woman's eyes lit up when Deek gave her the money. While it was a nice gesture, she knew it was not enough to fix the problem. There were too many more Billi's out there in the streets with nowhere to go. "Do you know who the baby's father is?" asked Renee.

"You mean do I know which one is the daddy out of the three juvenile delinquents that beat me up and gang raped me nine months ago?"

"Did you report this assault to the police?" said Deek.

Billi laughed a gut wrenching belly laugh.

"Yeah, man. Like the cops are really gonna break their neck to look into my case. Besides, I couldn't see too well after those little thugs knocked me over my head. I musta blacked out. I didn't know I was pregnant until a month or two after the attack."

Renee felt sorry for this woman and embarrassed by her own earlier lapse into self-pity. No matter how bad one's situation appeared to him or her, there was always someone in far worse shape. Life wasn't fair.

"Billi, would you be willing to testify what you saw on Monday when you encountered the alleged arsonist?" said Deek. "My gut instinct tells me this is the same person responsible for the arson, abduction, and murder at a private residence."

"Yeah, man, why not?" she said and wiped her runny nose on her sleeve, "You seem like a cool dude for a cop. And you Doc, you're not so bad for a shrink," she said, turning to Renee and giving her a gap-toothed smile.

Suddenly, Billi frowned and a look of panic swept across her face. "Hey, man, something ain't right here."

"What is it, Billi?"

With face contorted, she pointed to her lower belly and screamed. "This baby wants to come out now!"

CHAPTER 33

Renee leaped from her chair. "Billi, don't push yet. Deek, call the ambulance."

Deek's face flushed. He ran out to ask Sergeant Kane to put an emergency call through to dispatch and then he returned in seconds.

Billi wailed. "Look Doc, I ain't kidding, I really gotta push."

"Resist the urge to push, Billi. If you push too soon it could harm your baby. The cord could be wrapped around the neck and your baby might get strangled. I don't have time to explain all the consequences, just trust me. Don't push yet, wait until the ambulance gets here."

"I don't know if I can wait that long, Doc."

"They'll be here soon. Try to relax. You'll be fine, said Renee. "Billi, may I examine you to see what's going on? Like I said before, I used to be an emergency room nurse."

Billi groaned in pain but nodded her approval. Renee asked Deek to go get something to cover up the window so they could have some privacy. "But don't take too long" she said as she helped Billi to recline on the couch, "I'm going to need your help." Deek nodded and rushed off. When Renee next glanced out the window a few moments later, she saw that he had salvaged a large pad of flipchart paper and a roll of masking tape. He managed to induce several of the uniformed officers to help him cover the window. While the window was being plastered with large sheets of flipchart paper, Renee examined Billi. Renee's eyes narrowed in concern when she saw that Billi had dilated to about 8 centimeters and her contractions increased rapidly. She was already in transition stage, which Renee knew meant that Billi was in the final part of active labor. Billi shivered as her contractions intensified. They kicked-in every two minutes. Once Billi reached 10 centimeters her baby would be born no matter what any of them wanted, thought Renee.

Deek returned to the coffee lounge, carrying a washcloth moistened with cool water. He placed the damp folded hand towel on Billi's forehead. When he saw the look on Renee's face he frowned. "What's the matter?"

"Oh my God, I see the baby's head! Deek, we don't have time to wait for the ambulance."

"Wh-what do you mean Renee? We have to wait."

"This baby is coming now and we have to deliver it."

She told Deek they would have to help Billi onto the table because the couch was too narrow for her to get into position for the baby to safely pass through the birth canal. By that time, several people outside the lounge area knew about the delivery in progress. Even though their view was now blocked by the paper taped to the window, Renee could still hear the commotion and knew that an audience had congregated outside the lounge. Deek went to the door and motioned for young Sergeant Kane to come inside and help them. Kane's jaw dropped and he remained transfixed behind the covered glass window. He fiercely shook his head no.

Renee and Deek grabbed Billi and she slumped into Deek's arms. He helped her climb on top the table. Deek removed his shirt as Renee instructed, and stood with nothing covering his brown sugar toned muscular torso except a white-ribbed undershirt. Renee folded his shirt and placed it nearby on the couch so it would be handy when it came time to quickly catch the baby. The baby would come out slippery and wet and she didn't want it to slide out of her hands and fall to the floor.

Billi could no longer talk but she could still scream. She held such a tight grip on Deek's T-shirt that it ripped from his body, revealing his bare chest. Sweat dripped from Billi's brow as she panted, breathed, and yelled until her mouth went dry. She hollered each time a contraction came. And continued screaming in anticipation of the next one. No one else in the station would come in and help them. They simply gathered behind the wall of the makeshift birthing room and waited for the outcome. Renee could swear she detected the sounds of someone starting a bet as to whether the baby would be a boy or a girl. When Renee gave the okay to push, Billi pushed and her water broke. She stammered a weak apology for making a mess but said the gush of liquid felt like a warm bath. Billi's eyes protruded out of their sockets as she shrieked in pain. "You're doing good, Billi," said Renee, "We're almost there." Renee tried to get her to breathe and relax but it was useless. She appeared to get weaker and Renee feared the baby might be in distress. It seemed like hours but only a few minutes had passed. She prayed the ambulance would get there soon.

"Deek, do you have something sterile to cut the umbilical cord with?"

"No, but there may be roller gauze in our first aid kit to tie it off with. I'll go get it," he said.

"That'll work until the ambulance gets here and they can clamp and cut the cord with something sterile."

Deek rushed out to get the first aid kit. Billi grimaced from the pain. There was nothing sterile to use to make an episiotomy incision so her delivery could go smoother, no drugs or IV to reduce the pain. Billi tightened her muscles and gave another strong push. Seconds later, a full-term baby girl with a stock of coal-black, curly hair, plunged into the world. Renee caught the baby with Deek's shirt and wrapped it around her. Renee checked her watch and saw that it was 4:57 PM.

At that moment, Deek ran back into the lounge with the first aid kit. He stood by looking helpless with the kit in his hand while Renee quickly used her fingers as a suction to scoop out the mucus from the baby's mouth and clear her passageway. The baby let out a hearty cry. The audience behind the covered glass panel clapped and cheered. The infant's dark brown vibrant eyes looked at Renee with a startled expression. Her forehead and one eye were bruised from the difficult birth but at least the baby could breathe on her own.

Deek cut a strip of roller gauze and tied off the umbilical cord. Renee laid the bundled baby on her mother's chest. Billi forced a weak smile but something didn't look right in her color. A stricken expression came over Renee as she examined Billi. The new mother breathed heavily and her pulse felt faint.

"Billi has a placenta abruption and if the ambulance doesn't get here immediately, it will be too late," Renee whispered to Deek.

"I don't understand," he said, looking worried, "I thought the hard part was over."

"Once Billi's labor began and her water broke so fiercely, the large gush of fluid leaving the uterus caused an increased risk of placental abruption. That means the placenta detached too early."

"Is there anything we can do in the meantime?"

"I'm afraid not. She's at a higher risk for postpartum hemorrhaging because her uterus is not contracting the way it needs to after labor," Renee explained.

Suddenly, they heard the ambulance outside. "Good, they're here," said Deek, "I was just about to put her in a squad car and drive her to GW myself."

When the EMS personnel reached the homicide unit, Billi was unconscious. The EMS staff cut the umbilical cord with sterile instruments and discarded the afterbirth. Renee requested to ride with Billi in the ambulance but they told her she had to follow in her own car because only family members were allowed in the ambulance. Deek headed to his locker to put on a clean shirt. On the way he showed Renee where she could wash up in the Ladies Room. A few minutes later, they met up in the squad room of the homicide unit. He told Renee he would drive her to George Washington University Hospital where the ambulance was headed since it was the closest hospital. On the way out, he grabbed his jacket off the back of the chair and helped Renee with her coat.

They arrived at the hospital only minutes behind the ambulance. Deek and Renee rushed through the emergency room door and asked several desk attendants and medical personnel about Billi. No one wanted to take the time to give them information about a homeless woman who had just given birth with life-threatening complications. Deek stopped a nurse on her way down the hall and showed her his badge. He asked what happened to the maternity patient just brought in.

"Are you family?"

"No, she has no family. Ma'am, I just introduced myself as a homicide detective working on a case so it should occur to you this is police business," said Deek with annoyance in his voice.

"Please wait here Detective. I'll go check on her."

Renee sat down while Deek stood nearby. A short time later, they saw the nurse coming down the hall towards them. Renee got up and they both approached her hoping to hear everything was fine. They couldn't tell anything from the flat expression on the nurse's face.

"How is she?" Renee blurted out.

"The patient you asked about died from hemorrhaging in the ambulance on the way to the hospital. The body's been taken to the morgue. Do you know who she was?"

"Her name was Belinda," said Deek. "I don't have a last name." Renee covered her mouth and looked away. She said a silent prayer for Billi's soul.

"What happened to her baby?" asked Deek.

"The baby's healthy. She weighed 7 lbs. 8 oz. and measured 20 inches long. Her Apgar score was 10, which is good," said the nurse and went on to explain. "Apgar's a test we use on newborns to check their activity or muscle tone, their pulse rate, reflexes, skin color, and respiration. Everything looked good on all counts."

"What's going to happen to this baby?" Renee asked.

"We notified Child Family Services because we don't have facilities to keep border babies here at the hospital. Due to the quick delivery though, the baby still has some amniotic fluid in her lungs that she has to expel before we release her to Child Services. She'll be in the nursery overnight for observation then she can go home."

"Home?" said Renee, "that little baby has no home and no mother."

"That's all the information I can give you, Ma'am. If you'd like to go to the nursery to see the infant, she's on the 3rd floor," the nurse said and walked away.

Deek looked at Renee and knew the answer to his question before he even asked it.

"So what do you want to do?" he asked anyway. Deek waited but Renee didn't answer right away.

"I've been having this same dream lately," she said in a subdued voice, "where I see the fuzzy outline of a baby suspended in the clouds with its umbilical cord still attached and dangling. I feel a desperate need to hold the baby in my arms. So I reach out to grasp it but just as I touch its fingertips, it suddenly vanishes. The hurt is so real I can actually feel the pain in my body when I wake up."

Deek glanced down at her with sincere, dark eyes. He smiled and grabbed her hand. Without uttering another word, they walked hand-in-hand to the elevator and got on. He pressed the button for the third floor.

CHAPTER 34

At the GW hospital lobby, Deek offered to take Renee home but she could clearly see he was too exhausted to drive all the way across town. She called her driver, but Remy wasn't available, so she ended up calling a cab instead. By seven PM that evening, daylight had turned to dusk when the taxi dropped Renee off in front of her door. She walked passed the For Sale sign that her realtor had placed on the front lawn. Thanks to the recovering D. C. housing market, her house had only been listed three days but already attracted several interested buyers.

Renee unlocked her front door and lumbered up the long staircase. She still wanted to call Brenda and ask her secretary to explain that damaging story in this morning's paper. She knew Bradford and Deek would follow-up as part of the investigation, but she needed to hear it from Brenda herself. For right now though, she only wanted to go straight to her haven—the bathroom with its large, step-down tub bordered with scented candles and colorful soaps along its ledge. After quickly undressing and leaving her clothes in a heap on the bedroom floor, she soaked in a tub of foamy suds until she closed her eyes and drifted off to sleep. When the telephone rang, Renee's eyes sprung open and it took a moment to recognize her familiar surroundings. She'd been swept away in a fantasy dream about her and Deek making love.

"Now who is this?" she said out loud and reached for her cell phone on the bathtub ledge and answered it.

It was one of her colleagues, Dr. Hershel Goldbaum. After a brief perfunctory greeting, she found out Dr. Goldbaum was calling about a former patient that she had transferred to him three months ago. The last thing she wanted to do was discuss this former patient that she had only talked to once at an initial screening session. Renee promised her friend Hershel she would FAX him the information he needed about his patient as soon as possible. She hung up the phone and climbed out the tub, cursing Hershel and the patient under her breath. After patting herself dry she slipped on a black silk robe hanging from the door hook and went downstairs to her office.

Dr. Hershel Goldbaum was a clinical psychologist like herself who in addition to family and relationship counseling also specialized in chemical dependency, personality disorders, depression and attempted suicides, compulsive-obsessive behaviors, identity confusions, and bereavement counseling. Hershel said he needed her notes from the patient's initial session so he could conduct an evaluation to submit to the courts in the morning. Renee always screened new patients and tended not to get involved with people who were referred by the courts if she could help it. Not only was this patient a court referral, he had been convicted of pedophilia. Renee refused to accept any patient who abused or harmed children. This time she'd delete the patient's records so she would not have to recall his session again.

Renee turned on the computer in the outside reception area where Brenda worked. Since hiring Brenda she had little need to use the PC because her secretary maintained patient records electronically and retrieved whatever she needed in a flash. Brenda had once instructed her on what to do to locate a patient record but that was months ago. Renee fumbled through the document storage application that Brenda had installed, but the program was not intuitive for an average, non-technical user like herself. Since she had a working knowledge of Windows Explorer, as a last resort, she opened Explorer to try searching for the patient's file. All she found was a list of meaningless filenames sorted by 'date modified' and that didn't tell her anything. The first file that appeared at the top of the list had a filename of TSS1001.xls. Since it still wasn't sufficient to identify its contents, Renee opened the document and noticed Microsoft Excel displayed on the screen. Upon glancing at the file, she realized it was some type of company budget spreadsheet from the President and CEO of Techands Inc, Clifton Corbin Shaw.

Renee wondered how this file showed up on her computer. Of course, Deek could explain it but she didn't want to disturb him. He was either home resting or back at the police station. Then she remembered that Brenda had set up a network linking her PC to Bill's as a practice exercise for her computer class. With the recent trauma in Brenda's life, it was no wonder she forgot to disconnect the link.

At first Renee dragged the mouse up to the 'x' to close the file but her curiosity got the better of her and she slowly read the file contents. Renee did not trust Shaw and wished her husband had listened to her numerous warnings about him. If there was something important that affected Bill's future, she wanted to know about it. Just because they were separated and getting a divorce didn't stop her from caring about him. In the biblical sense, they were unevenly yoked as husband and wife but hopefully they could still be friends. She used this reasoning to justify her snooping as she read the company's budget sheet and private memo to executives that she was also able to retrieve from her PC's hard drive.

The report showed that a benefactor named James Ian Mathias funneled large sums of cash to Techands Inc through company president, Clifton C. Shaw. Earlier that day Renee had learned from Deek and FBI Agent Santos that Mathias was the alleged drug kingpin and leader of the Jett Set Crew. Upon studying the spreadsheet, Renee saw where thousands of dollars were being laundered through Shaw's corporate account on a weekly basis. If Mathias was really a drug lord then Techands Inc. appeared to be a front to receive his illegal earnings. That was the only way she could explain the regular influx of cash from Mr. Mathias. Mathias was named as investor and William Hayes, her husband, was listed as a general partner. Techands Inc's legitimate business of providing software support was purely coincidental. The company's main mission seemed to be a laundering service for drug money. She refused to believe that Bill had knowingly gotten involved in a money laundering scheme. She felt certain that Mathias and Shaw were using him without his knowledge. She had to warn him.

Renee immediately dialed Bill. As usual, the line was busy on his cell phone and his voicemail came on. She left him an urgent message to come to the house as soon as possible so they could talk. She printed out the Techands company documents and turned off the computer. She didn't have time to spend all evening searching for those damn patient records for Hershel. Hershel would have to wait. She hurriedly called him back and said she couldn't locate the patient's file on her computer and her secretary was not available. Once her secretary came back to work in a few days, she would have the notes sent. Renee hung up the telephone and returned upstairs to her bedroom to wait for Bill to arrive. Moving day into her new place would be next Saturday so in the meantime she could start packing.

Less than an hour later, Bill walked into her bedroom. Renee had not heard him pull up outside or enter the front door. As she closed her suitcase, she glanced at him briefly with an expressionless face then went to her closet to retrieve another empty suitcase. She didn't trust herself to speak at that moment. Either he was a crook or he was naive. For his sake she hoped it was the latter. Renee threw the suitcase on top the bed and returned to the closet to pull down an armful of garments.

Bill approached her with both arms outstretched. "I knew you'd come to your senses My Love," he said with a sardonic grin and distinct smell of alcohol on his breath, "I got your message that you're ready to talk now so I rushed right over."

Renee continued to busy herself packing while trying to remain calm.

"What's all this packing about?" he said, pointing to the suitcase. "I also noticed that 'For Sale' sign outside. Should I assume you're moving in with me tonight, Sweetness?"

She didn't answer him so he kept talking.

"That's fine Babe but I could've used a little more notice," Bill said with a cocky grin," If you don't mind waiting until tomorrow, I'll get my housekeeper to come by in the morning to straighten things up a bit. I guess you heard about my new two-bedroom apartment uptown at Park Connecticut. The rent is over three grand but I can easily afford it now. The business is going great."

Renee couldn't restrain herself any longer. "That's what I called you about," she said, "The Business."

"You don't wanna discuss us getting back together?" he asked with a confused look.

"No, I didn't call to get back together. Anyway, you appear to be doing just fine," she said. "Last week I saw you at McCormick and Schmick's sitting with a bunch of pasty-faced suits and a twenty-something blond hanging on your arm."

"Oh, that was nobody. She's just an associate of Shaw's. You should've stopped over to the table to say hello."

"Whatever. Your private life is your own business now," said Renee, "My attorney filed the legal separation agreement you gave me." Renee saw his eyes flinch but she continued. "I fished the papers out of the kitchen trash bin later that afternoon when I went downstairs to make a cup of tea. My attorney says after a year, the court will grant us a no-fault divorce. But I'm sure your attorney already told you that by now. I intend to file after the waiting period if you don't."

"Is that why you put the 'For Sale' sign on our front lawn?"

"Yes. I hired a real estate agent a few days ago and put the house on the market. We already have several qualified buyers so we can just split the proceeds on the sale."

"I haven't agreed to any of this, Renee," he said, standing rigidly in the middle of the floor. "You're moving too damn fast." Then, he stuffed both hands in his pockets. With drooped shoulders, a crestfallen look spread across his face. "I guess there's someone else in the picture. That explains the rush."

"No, Bill. This is about me." She stopped packing and turned to face him. "I need to bring meaning to my life. I'm the only one who can rescue me. And in case you've forgotten, we used *my* Aunt Clara's money as the down payment on this house. I didn't need your approval to list it since only my name appears on the title. Although, I did try to contact you many times over the past several days but you never bothered to return my calls."

"I'm sorry Renee. I've been a little distracted lately. Do you mind letting me in on your plans now? After 14 years of marriage is that too much to ask? Where are you moving?" He advanced towards her and sat down on the bed.

Renee resumed packing as she spoke. "I found a three-story, brick Victorian rowhouse near 24th and I Street in NW. Plus, it's fully decorated because the owners had to leave the country. It's near George Washington University and Metro-accessible. I'll be able to lease office space in a secure building nearby when I'm ready to go back to seeing clients full-time."

"Renee, please don't do this, Babe. Give me another chance. Just because someone doesn't love you the way you want them to doesn't mean they don't love you with all they have to give. I'm not the type to be overly expressive with my feelings," he said with a wounded look in his eyes. "You've known me long enough to understand that."

"I know that Bill, and I don't blame you. But it's taken me a long time to gain the courage to start becoming the person I want to be. I'm sorry but I can't go back to the way it was."

Bill's facial muscles tensed as he waved his arm about, gesturing at their possessions. "What are you gonna do with all this stuff throughout the entire house?"

"Estate sale. If there's anything you want, take it. There's no need for us to argue about material things. The auction's not scheduled to take place for another two weeks," said Renee, with decisiveness. "You'll get half the proceeds from the estate sale as well. I plan to donate the bulk of my half to charity, especially to those groups helping the homeless."

As if Bill finally realized it was hopeless to argue, his demeanor turned bitter. He got up from the bed. "Since when did you turn into Mother Theresa? Guess I missed your coronation to sainthood. But then you always did think you were better than everybody else," he sniffed.

"I'm not in the mood for your sarcasm today. You couldn't begin to understand what I've been through these past few days." Renee inched closer to him, not afraid. "We have other serious issues to discuss and that's why I called you. I actually want to help you Bill, because I truly don't believe you have a clue about what you've gotten yourself into with Shaw."

"Again, you seem to enjoy insulting me. So, what the hell is all this about Renee? I had to drop everything to rush over here."

Renee explained to Bill how she knew that his business partner, Clifton Corbin Shaw, was connected with a known drug lord named Ian Mathias, who the FBI had been investigating for six months. She said that the company Shaw started with seed money is really a front for money laundering. To prove it Renee retrieved the documents she had printed off her computer and handed them to Bill. As he read the company documents, the color drained from his face. "I can't believe it!" Bill shook his head and clenched the sheath of papers in his fist. "There must be some explanation." He looked up at Renee. "Huh ... How did you get this?"

"Before you left for India you gave my secretary permission to practice setting up a network by connecting both our computers. Do you remember?" When Bill nodded 'yes', Renee continued. "My secretary, Brenda has been going through a rough time in her life this past week and in her distraction she forgot to remove the connection or simply didn't have time."

"When I had to search through my patient data, I stumbled upon these Techands company documents, which as you can see clearly show that Ian Mathias is the only investor and major stockholder," said Renee, "and this man is under suspicion by the FBI."

Bill sat back down on the bed slowly, looking lost and stricken. A film of perspiration settled on top of his mustache. He crushed the papers into a tight mass and hurled it at the wall. He buried his face in his hands and curled himself into a ball. If this was a ploy to get her to feel sorry for him, it was working. She could tell by his reaction that he had no idea what his business partner was involved in. Renee felt relieved that her instincts about her husband had been right. She sat down next to him on the bed and touched his shoulder. She sensed his body tense up under her touch. He straightened his posture to regain control. Renee waited for him to speak.

Bill closed his eyes and spoke just above a whisper. "I'll write my letter of resignation today. I've been so busy training the guys I didn't pay attention to where the investments were coming from. Once I trained Mahesh to maintain our corporate server, I didn't bother to go through the records that Shaw stored on the server," said Bill, thoughtfully. "I'll think of some excuse without tipping Shaw off that I know he's just been using me." Bill's voice cracked. "He's been giving off the appearance of running a legitimate company. But really if what you say about our investor is true and I have no reason to believe you're lying to me, Shaw's just been stockpiling illegal drug money. No doubt using this money to fund his future political aspirations. Seems you were right about him all along."

Renee squeezed his hand. With eyes still closed, Bill couldn't see her nodding in agreement. Suddenly, his eyes snapped open and he grabbed her arm. "Listen to me, Renee. Don't tell anybody that you know about this connection to illegal activities at Techands. Let the cops or the FBI or the IRS do their jobs and figure it out for themselves. I don't want you to get dragged into this mess. It might be dangerous if Shaw and this guy Mathias suspect you know what they're up to. Do you promise me you'll stay out of it?" Bill looked at her with a wild-eyed expression.

Renee saw the desperation and fear in his face. He wouldn't let go of her arm until she agreed not to get involved. "Yes Bill, but even if I don't go to the authorities, the FBI are close to building their case against Ian Mathias. It won't take them long to find out about all of Mathias's associations, including Shaw, you, and Techands. Just quitting Techands won't be enough," said Renee, "You have to turn in state's evidence to show that you weren't involved and you have to do it without tipping Shaw off. If you suddenly resign, he'll know something is not right and he'll get suspicious. What are you going to say to him?" she asked.

Bill stood up and clasped his hands together under his chin. He looked past her in deep reflection for several moments. Then, he spoke. "I don't want you to worry about that. I'll say I have to resign for medical reasons. I'm going back to my office in Virginia now to see if I can gather more evidence to turn into the authorities. I think you're right," he nodded, "I can't just sit back and let them figure it out because they will figure it out. And my name will still be associated with Shaw on all the company documents. I need to make sure my recruits aren't implicated in all this. Maybe I can work out a deal so they can return home to India. Just let me take care of it, Renee. I'm not going to come around here any more because if something goes wrong … well, it's just better that you stay completely out of it. You know how to get in touch with me if you need me."

Renee watched as Bill walked out the bedroom and slowly closed the door behind him.

CHAPTER 35

The tension boiled inside her from the strain she'd been under. Days of unreleased stress had mounted up, beginning with trying to stay strong for Brenda to delivering Billi's baby into an uncertain, motherless world. On top of those things, losing the homeless woman to childbirth complications. Had Billi not been homeless and afraid to seek prenatal care throughout her pregnancy perhaps she would have survived. Renee thought about the infant she delivered yesterday afternoon and wondered if it would be fair to try to adopt the baby now when her life was so unstable and uncertain.

Next week, she planned to move into her new house near George Washington University, alone. While she and Bill both still cared for each other in their own way, this passionless existence between them was no longer enough for her. In the beginning, Bill had been funny and attentive, but over the years he had become closed off emotionally and she did not know why. She would always hold feelings for Bill, but she now knew that he was not her true love. For these reasons she planned to go through with the divorce proceedings even though he said he didn't want her to. She had sacrificed for too long who she was to please others. The dispassionate and guarded persona that Aunt Clara had clothed her in during her childhood did not fit any longer. Life was too short to live without happiness.

Renee had failed to create the perfect 'white picket-fenced' family that she had always wanted—a loving couple and happy children. She might not ever be able to offer the baby girl that she had delivered yesterday a traditional home with both a mother and father present, but she could offer all of her love. Renee had always yearned for what she perceived as the ideal family although she had never experienced it herself as a child. Perhaps that's why she came to regard it as the ideal. Should she deny this to another child? All she could guarantee the child was her own love, nurturing, and security. If only she could be sure that would be enough. What *she* needed right now was to be with Deek and feel his arms around her. All these other decisions and uncertainties could wait. Ever since their kiss yesterday in the church's private sanctuary in the basement, Renee couldn't get Deek out of her mind.

Renee now understood what kind of man she wanted to spend the rest of her life with. She wanted a man who was secure with his manhood, one who knew what he wanted and was not afraid to unleash passion with his whole heart and soul to the woman he loved. Fear of rejection would not frighten such a man because he would be confident and sure of his desires. There was only one man she knew of who fit that description, Deek.

Thinking of him made her feel playful and sexy. She reached into the top drawer of her dresser and pulled out a sheer, Swiss-dot, black chemise. When she put it on just for fun, the lingerie showed off her sexy, hourglass shape and accentuated her large breasts. The lettuce edged hem just barely skimmed her derriere. She slipped her legs through its matching thong and immediately felt wicked. A pale-jade pendant encircled with green peridot semi-precious stones and matching drop earrings, that had been her mother's, glowed against her brown skin. A pair of black, ankle-strapped high heels completed the look, and she felt transformed into a beautiful adventurous woman, full of passion.

Dreaming and fantasizing about Deek wouldn't satisfy her any longer. Renee picked up the phone and punched the first five digits of his telephone number then slammed the phone down. Her heart beat excitedly. It wasn't like her to openly display her emotions and sexual needs. But if she didn't take a proactive approach to show Deek how much she wanted him perhaps some other sweet, young thing would—someone like Ana Santos who had been working closely with him for several months. Ana Santos did not bother to hide her attraction to him. Renee picked up the phone again and this time dialed her driver, Remy. While she waited for Remy to arrive she quickly tossed a few essentials in an overnight bag. She hoped Deek wouldn't be angry with her for showing up at his place so late without warning. But if she called first she knew she would not have the nerve to go through with this plan once she heard his voice. She hoped it wasn't too late to finally reveal her true desire for him.

Twenty minutes later, she heard the doorbell ring. Renee removed her mother's full-length, dark chestnut mink coat from its plastic, dry cleaning bag, and wrapped the fur coat around her scantily clad body. The fur felt warm and luxurious next to her bare skin. She took one last look in the foyer mirror for encouragement before opening the front door. Remy's moon-shaped, dark cocoa tinted face displayed his usual white, toothy grin. Her Nigerian driver wore his typical, chauffeur's uniform—a bargain-priced, dark suit with an obvious sheen to its texture, crisp white shirt and tie. Remy offered his elbow and escorted her to the car. Both being 5 feet 4 inches tall, she usually met him eye-to-eye but in three-inch heels Renee towered over him. Remy opened the door of his black sedan then she carefully climbed in the backseat. Since meeting Remy Adu two years ago from a colleague, Renee could always count on her driver to talk nonstop. But this time she didn't mind. His banter distracted her from thinking about visiting Deek's home unannounced wearing nothing but a see-through chemise and thong under her coat. She had never initiated anything this bold with him before. Deek had always been the one pursuing her and usually receiving mixed messages for his trouble.

Listening to Remy talk about his childhood in Lagos Calebar and the odd jobs he had in college before starting his limo service helped her relax. For a few minutes, she forgot her nervousness about Deek's reaction to her visit. She had heard most of Remy's stories before but he never remembered what he told people and seemed to enjoy the storytelling. All she had to do was respond with an occasional "Uh huh" or "Really?" to encourage him to keep talking. Remy bobbed to the cheerful music bursting from his CD player that he described as African Sukous and Makossa tunes from Cameroon.

When Remy announced that 23rd and Alabama Avenue was just a few blocks ahead, Renee started to get anxious once more. She clasped her hands together in her lap and realized they felt like sandpaper. In her nervousness and rush to leave the house, she forgot to put on Saphir, her favorite French perfumed lotion. Remy stopped in front of Deek's house and she could see that his lights upstairs were on. Out of desperation, she asked Remy if he had any lotion because her hands were dry and she had forgotten to pack lotion in her purse. Remy fumbled in the glove compartment in a near pitch dark car until he found a small bottle and handed it to her. She couldn't see the bottle but it felt like oil so she rubbed it liberally on her hands, the crevice of her breasts, neck and behind her ears. Then took a depth breath to calm down. Suddenly, after applying what she assumed to be oil, a strong, pungent smell of cheap, men's cologne permeated her senses and filled the car.

"Remy, what is this?" she shrieked and placed the open bottle to her nose.

"Is it not lotion, Doctor Hayes?" he asked innocently.

"No, Remy. It smells like men's cologne, even worse it reeks of Brute! What am I going to do now? I smell like a man."

And not even one wearing something pleasant like a KL or Davidorf scent that she could possibly pull off if Deek had been drinking heavily that evening. No scent was better than Brute. At that moment she panicked and thought this was a bad sign of things to come. She should just ask Remy to turn right around and drive her back home. He apologized for accidentally giving her his cologne instead of lotion. She couldn't really blame him. It was her fault for not smelling the damn stuff before dosing it all over herself. There was no time to discuss the mistake because Remy was getting out to open her door. She mentally re-grouped and decided that as soon as she got inside the house she'd ask Deek where the powder room was so she could scrub the cologne off. Remy held out his hand for her to exit and she climbed out the car.

"Would you need me to come back later to pick you up, Dr. Hayes?"

"No, Remy but can you please wait here in the car for about ten minutes. If I don't come back then it's okay to leave."

"Yes, Ma'am," he said.

Renee opened her purse and paid him for the ride and the extra time to sit parked out front of Deek's house until she could determine if this was a good idea or a serious mistake in judgment. Renee stood on the steps for several seconds and contemplated leaving before pressing the buzzer. Just as she was about to turn around and head back to the sedan, Deek appeared at the door wearing an army-green Polo Ralph Lauren ribbed T-shirt and stretch-cotton boxer-styled underwear that barely reached mid-thigh. She fought the urge to stare down at the peekaboo crotch opening that couldn't hide much on Deek, but instead studied his sleepy eyes. Though somewhat drowsy, he looked surprised yet happy to see her. For a moment she felt her legs weakening from the arousing scent of his cologne, a light combination of spices that immediately drew her in.

"I ... I shouldn't be here," she finally blurted out, "You were already in bed. Forgive me, Deek ..."

He grabbed her arm and pulled her inside then re-bolted the door shut. As he reached for her coat, Renee pulled back.

"May I use your bathroom, please?" she asked hurriedly. Hopefully, he hadn't yet noticed that she smelled like cheap men's cologne from CVS drugstore, on sale at two for $5.00. If he thought she was crazy, he didn't show it.

"Of course," he said and pointed to the powder room down the hall.

Renee almost ran inside the bathroom and locked the door. Stupid, stupid, stupid. She admonished herself repeatedly as the hot water filled the basin. She wanted the water to reach boiling point if she could stand it. How else was she going to get that horrible smell out of her skin? Renee took off her coat and drenched a hand towel in the water. Fortunately, there was a bar of pleasantly, scented soap on the sink and she rubbed it on the dripping, wet towel until the suds reached the top of the basin. To avoid getting her skimpy chemise wet, she slipped it from her shoulders and washed her arms, chest, neck and every inch of skin that Remy's Brute cologne had sullied. She re-applied the soapy towel again and again until she could no longer smell the men's cologne.

When she stopped splashing and running water, she could hear a faint sound of jazz music outside the bathroom door. Renee dried off quickly with another hand towel, fixed her lingerie, and put her fur coat back on then clamped it shut from top to bottom. She wasn't ready to reveal her intentions just yet. She realized that by now Remy must have left so there was no turning back.

When she stepped from the bathroom, she saw that Deek had covered up with a green and maroon, plaid silk robe tied at the waist. He lay stretched out on an off-white leather recliner with his head leaning back, eyes closed and feet propped up on the ottoman. The brightest light came from the fire in the living room and it cast a soothing glow across the darkened room. A full glass of champagne waited for her on a large coffee table that also held a chess board with a game in progress. Next to the chess board sat two books, *Dreams From My Father* by Barack Obama and *A Long Walk to Freedom: The Autobiography of Nelson Mandela*. When she approached he slowly opened his eyes and smiled. He rose and leaned close to her. She thought he was about to kiss her. Instead, he placed his warm lips tenderly on her cheek and held out his hand for her coat. "Here, let me take your coat. Sit down and stay awhile," he said in a soft-spoken, sexy voice.

Renee stepped back and pulled her coat together. "In a minute, Deek. I'm still a bit chilly." She sat down in an armchair near the couch and suddenly felt foolish showing up unannounced and virtually naked under her coat. She would need a little more time to relax, though the music was beginning to ease her tension. "What are you listening to?" she asked and picked up the champagne flute from the coffee table and took a large gulp, hoping the alcohol would relieve her uneasiness at showing up uninvited.

Deek sat down across from her, rested his elbow on the arm of the coach and smiled. "A little mellowing out Miles," he said as he nodded to the rhythm of the music.

Renee closed her eyes in deep concentration as she listened. "That sounds like something my Dad might have listened to when I was growing up but I don't remember the name of it," she said and swayed her head to the melody.

"That's 'Flamenco Sketches' playing now. Out of Miles Davis's *Kind of Blue* CD."

"Oh yeah, I do remember that tune now. I was very young but my Dad used to listen to it over and over again."

"There's not a bad track on that album. It's a classic," said Deek. "And, Bill Evans' sensitive piano is such an intricate part to me." He repositioned himself on the coach and leaned back with one leg stretched across the length of the sofa.

"Yes, it's nice and mellow. I like it. I can see you're quite the jazz aficionado," said Renee, noticing that he wore only his underwear beneath the loosely belted robe.

"Well, I don't know how much of a jazz fanatic I am. I just know what I like," he said and gave her a smile of approval.

Renee took a deep breathe and drank another generous swallow of her champagne. Just as she unclamped the first hook at the neck of her fur coat, the doorbell rang. Deek glanced at the clock above the fireplace ledge and got up to answer it. Renee hoped it wasn't her driver ringing to ask if she wanted to leave. It was now after ten o'clock. Who else besides herself would be visiting Deek at this hour? Suddenly, an unpleasant thought gripped at her stomach. Suppose it was Ana Santos, showing up unexpectedly with the same idea she had?

CHAPTER 36

Whar Renee heard Detective Mel Bradford's loud voice and heavy feet coming down the hallway, she felt both relief and dread all at the same time. At least it wasn't Ana Santos. She quickly re-clasped the top hook to her coat and looked around for a means of escape but there was none. Bradford grinned when he saw Renee sitting in the living room. She clutched the coat collar tightly about her neck as a feeling of alarm came over her. Suppose Bradford wouldn't leave? Now she remembered why she never acted spontaneously.

"Looks like I interrupted something, kid," he winked at Deek. "And, I see you got Miles playin' in the background. Smart move. You can't go wrong with Miles."

Ignoring the obvious, Bradford proceeded to plop his large frame down on the leather recliner next to Renee. "You got any Scotch or Vodka, my man? I wanna run a coupla things by you about the Johnson case. And you're not gonna believe what went down after you left. But I see you're busy so I won't stay long."

"I've got Drambuie and Vodka, which do you want?"

"Surprise me, Young Blood."

"Okay, but let me hang up Renee's coat first. She just got here too. It's a little chilly outside but I'm sure she's warmed up by now," said Deek, while reaching out to slip the coat from her shoulders. But before he could grab it, Renee leaned away and shook her head. "No, that's okay. I'll just keep it on a little longer." Panic! This would be the last time she did anything on impulse. There was no escape.

To make matters worse, Deek pitched a few more logs in the fire. Fortunately, he didn't see her wipe the sweat from her forehead.

"If you'd prefer something hot to drink like an Irish coffee or something I can make it while I'm in the kitchen," he said, reaching for her glass, "I thought you might like the chilled champagne but …"

Renee quickly scooped up the glass to prevent him from taking it. "No, nothing hot," she said a bit too fast, "the champagne's fine, thank you."

When Deek disappeared into the kitchen, Bradford stared at her suspiciously. Renee got up from the armchair and sat down on the far edge of the sofa and wrapped her arms tightly around herself as if still cold. Gratefully, Deek returned quickly and offered Bradford a glass of Vodka. Deek stood by the fireplace with his arms folded.

"So what's so urgent Mel that it couldn't wait until tomorrow?" said Deek, "I'm really wiped out tonight."

"Don't be so damn impatient, Partner. I got an idea how we might nail the Johnson woman for that insurance scam she pulled nine years ago," said Bradford, gulping down his drink.

Renee rolled her eyes upward to the ceiling as Bradford explained his plan. "Why don't we pull the good cop/bad cop drill on her tomorrow during interrogation? Make her think we got something substantial so she'll spill her guts and confess to get a plea bargain on both crimes. And, I'm not ruling out her odd-ball Mom who I finally met the other day as an accomplice. She's a piece of work that one."

"What makes you think she'd fall for that routine, Mel? Everybody's hip to it by now."

"You're right, most career criminals are wise to the game but I think Brenda Johnson's naïve enough to fall for it," said Bradford. "I'm having her picked up tomorrow morning. And since you say I don't tell you what the hell I'm doing, I'm letting you know now. So I figured we'd go over our parts tonight."

"Look Mel, if it's all the same to you, I'd like to wait another day before we take Mrs. Johnson in for interrogation. There's something I want to check out first. Besides, I already told you I'm tired as hell. The last thing I feel like doing right now is rehearsing a good cop/bad cop scenario with you."

"I get the hint, kid. I know a young 'jitterbug' like yourself needs his rest," said Bradford, sarcastically then winked at Renee.

"Mel, I really wish you'd stop referring to me as young or a kid all the goddamn time. I'm a grown man just like you are. I'd appreciate some respect and I'd like you to call me by my given name."

"Well, what the hell else are you then? You weren't even born when Malcom, Martin, and the Kennedy brothers were shot? I bet you still can't get a 'Thirty & Over Club Card' from Majic 102.3 radio station. Am I right?" Bradford grinned and tipped his glass in the air.

"I'll be 29 in January. That's only a few months away."

"I rest my case, *Degas*. Is that respect enough for you?"

Deek sighed in frustration and threw up his hands. "There's no reasoning with you, Mel. How 'bout you just avoid calling me at all."

"Don't blame me. I didn't name you," he said then diverted his attention back to Renee. She cringed. Bradford was like a school yard bully.

"I betcha me and you got more in common age-wise," said Bradford with a crooked grin, "Not to say you look bad 'cause you look damn good for any age. But you must be almost ready for your AARP card. Me, I've been a member for nine years so I can get discounts on things. Anyway, exactly how old are you, Doc?"

"Detective Bradford, let me educate you about something. There're three questions a gentleman should never ask a lady. How much do you weigh? How old are you? Or when is your baby due, if he's not absolutely certain she's pregnant. Got it?"

"I got it, Miss Manners, but those rules don't apply to me 'cause I ain't no gentleman. So what's all the mystery for? Just tell me how old you are."

"None of your damn business," she said and clutched her coat tighter. She imagined her fingers gripped around his thick, pudgy neck.

Bradford just wouldn't let up, thought Renee as he launched his next observation. "You look like you're roasting in that hot ass fur coat," said Mel, "Why don't you take it off?"

Deek walked over to the couch and felt her forehead and cheeks. "You are perspiring and your face looks flushed. Let me hang it up for you and I'll turn up the heat if you're still cold. I don't want you to catch pneumonia."

"No, Deek. I'm fine. I should just call my driver back and leave," said Renee, getting up from the couch, "You said you were tired and I'm sure you don't need all this uninvited company." Renee gave Bradford a piercing glare.

Deek grabbed her by the hand and pleaded with her not to leave while Bradford pulled back the recliner to get more comfortable.

"Your driver, eh? You use a driver?" asked Mel, "I'm going blind over here looking at those rocks on your ears. Must be nice. Hey, if you need a lift home I don't mind dropping you off," said Bradford, swallowing the last of his Vodka.

"No thanks. That's kind of you to offer, Detective Bradford, but I can manage."

Bradford handed Deek his empty glass. "Can you fill her up for me Partner? That first round was a bit short."

"I'll go with you," said Renee and followed Deek out to the kitchen.

When she was certain Bradford could not hear or see them, she confessed to Deek that she felt embarrassed and ridiculous being there. She opened her coat slightly so he could see some of what she was wearing or not wearing under the coat. She told him that she had planned to be alone with him but now the mood was gone. Deek told her to wait in the kitchen while he got rid of Bradford. A few seconds later when Renee heard the front door open and close, she came out of the kitchen and met Deek in the hallway.

"How did you convince him to leave?" she asked.

"Mel doesn't get subtle hints. Trust me, you don't want to know the exact words I used, but it's what he understands."

"Do you have anything for a headache Deek?"

"Sure sweetie, there's some aspirin in the powder room cabinet. I'll get it for you."

"That's okay, I can find it. Will you get me a glass of water though?"

Renee disappeared into the powder room and closed the door. When she heard him return to the living room, she cracked open the bathroom door slightly.

"Deek, can you come in here please?" She called to him after a few minutes.

"Are you okay, baby?" he asked and rushed into the bathroom.

When Deek ran in, he found her standing in the middle of the floor—the fur coat dropped to her feet and heels kicked off in the corner. She wore only her see-through, black chemise and thongs. Her eyes expressed a seductive, come-hither look. Deek stood still in the doorway for a few seconds. He looked mesmerized by her outward display of sexuality. He unbelted his robe and let it fall to the floor. Then he slowly stepped closer. They embraced and began slow dancing in place to the mellow sounds of Miles Davis coming from the living room. When their bodies touched she felt his hardness press against her navel. Deek held the back of her head with one hand while the other caressed her back. He bent down to meet her waiting lips with a sweet kiss. She felt the tip of his warm tongue trace her mouth slowly as both their tongues and lips joined.

"How's your headache?" he whispered and nibbled her ear.

"What headache?"

They kissed while in a close embrace as their feet dragged slowly to music.

"You make me feel like another woman, not myself"

"Is that good?"

"Oh yes. When I'm with you my body feels like it's been electrified back to life. I'm not my usual repressed self."

"Really? You're just trying to flatter me, aren't you?"

"No, it's true."

"Well, let's see if I can do even better. Would you like to go upstairs?"

Stopping to get the bottle of champagne, he led her to his contemporary-styled bedroom, aglow from a luminescent blue light. It felt like walking into the space age. On one wall, incandescent lighting displayed a gallery of modern art. An ergonomically designed chair leaned against the wall under steel shelves that held a huge collection of CDs. Next to that stood a smoked glass and black metal armoire.

Deek placed the Moët champagne bottle and glasses on the nightstand by the bed and they both removed their underwear. He folded back the terra-cotta brown, plush velvet spread to reveal champagne-colored, cotton-silk sheets. She lay down on the bed first and he braced himself on both arms above her as they stared into each other's eyes. Whatever cologne he was wearing, smelled tantalizing. It was something she had never smelled on him before. She would have to ask him what it was later because at that moment she couldn't talk. Relaxing music played in the background from a continuous selection of CDs but the only sound they listened to was each other's gentle breathing. He instinctively closed his eyes when she started caressing his face. She began at the well-arched brows, then moved down to the feathered lashes of his dark eyes—lashes that were long, yet still masculine and quite alluring. Next, Renee slid her index finger down the perfectly-shaped, curved nose and played with the fine hairs of his mustache, then followed the neatly trimmed growth around his chin and jaw line.

Deek leaned forward and kissed her neck, and behind her ears while she moaned from the sensation of his lips on her skin. Not wanting to rest his full 180-lb. weight on her body, he supported himself with one arm and linked her hand in his. His kisses felt lingering as they softly brushed against her knuckles and the open palm of her hand. He closed her hand and sealed it with another kiss. He kissed all the way up her arm, then slowly sliding downward, kissed around her hips, inner thighs, legs, and behind each knee. He gently grasped her foot, massaged and sucked her toes. Renee was so glad she had included the pedicure with her French manicure the other day and tried a more vibrant crimson polish. The stripe of red across each toe made her toes look like candy drops. He sucked each toe as if it was a sweet, sugarcoated treat. He kissed and caressed every inch of her, purposely avoiding her genital area until she felt herself throbbing from the tension and wanted to grab his fully erect penis and insert it herself. But Deek was a patient lover, and enjoyed caressing her body. He touched her so delicately as if he were stroking a luxurious fabric of silk, velvet, or satin. Prolonging the ecstasy and having a man take his time was not what she was used to, but she knew she could easily get used to it. She was in ecstasy!

In one swift motion, she slid from under him and changed positions so that she lay on top. Renee touched and kissed Deek's bronzed-toned body with a light, feathery touch then applied more pressure to experiment and discover what he liked. He was already aroused so she simply focused on enjoying how good the hardness of his muscles felt and the warm, moist perspiration of his skin. She glided her fingertips down his tapered torso and rubbed the tiny, erect nipples on his chest and felt his steady breathing intensify. With a light touch she stroked his tight abdomen, and circled his navel with her pinkie finger. When she glanced down below his waist, she saw that his body announced how badly he wanted her. But she wanted to enjoy touching him a little longer as much as he had relished kissing and fondling her.

"Do you have any lubricating gel, baby?" she whispered in his ear.

Deek reached over and retrieved a tube of lubricant from the top drawer of the nightstand and gave it to her. She squeezed a tiny amount in the palm of her hands then rubbed her hands together to warm them. She caressed his penis in long, slow delicate strokes at first then varied the pressure with faster, firmer motions. Suddenly, he pressed the base of his penis and allowed himself to relax.

"Did I hurt you, honey?" she said with concern.

"No, baby, I wanna be inside you when I come," he said and pushed back the strands of sweat-soaked hair from her forehead so he could see her eyes. "Just wanted to slow things down a bit."

"Does it work? I mean, does that actually stop you from coming."

"Um hum. But don't stop touching me, baby. It feels good."

"Which do you like better, my hand or my tongue?"

"Both. Either. Hell, do whatever you want to me. I'm yours." He lay on the champagne-tinted sheets that shimmered next to his medium-brown complexion with his eyes closed and a contented smile on his face.

For how long will you be mine, Deek, she thought? Just for tonight? Why would you want to spend your life with me when you could have just about any woman you wanted, women much younger, prettier, and that you have more in common with? Maybe Bradford was right, she was too close to AARP's eligibility age. She was crossing over into the dangerous zone of a broken heart without heeding her internal warnings. And why the hell should she? Nothing was guaranteed to last forever; not love, not health or happiness. Tomorrow wasn't promised to anyone.

Renee went to the bathroom and heated a small, terry clothed towel with warm water. She gently dabbed the warm, moist towel around his entire pelvic area. Then she bent down and tasted him, feeling his erection harden on her lips, tongue, and deep within her mouth. When his eyes looked down and pleaded with her, she slithered her body upwards and guided him inside. They made love with such intensity, she didn't know which sensation to savor—the feel of his body blending with hers, his hardness against her softness, their racing hearts, or the sounds of their pleasure. The light spicy scent of his skin and firm, tightness of his body gave her all the pleasure she needed at that moment. She released her fears about finding everlasting love and happiness, and soared in the present joy she felt.

CHAPTER 37

On Saturday, the next morning, a ringing telephone next to Deek's bedside woke Renee up. The ringing stopped after the first shrill-pitched noise. Still groggy from a restful night of sleep at his place, she turned over to snuggle next to him but found his side of the bed empty. A quiet stillness filled the room except for the constant strumming of sleet against the window. Slits of grey horizontal daylight radiated through the mini-blinds. Renee sprung from the bed and wrapped a thick, terry robe around her body that Deek had left across the bed. She bent down the blinds and looked out the window to see if his car was still parked outside. Powdery white snow mixed with sleet descended in a diagonal path and covered everything for as far as she could see.

She was glad she had paid attention to the weather forecast yesterday and packed her cowl neck black knit jersey dress and ankle boots. Renee liked how the dress swathed her curvy figure from breasts to mid-calf, and was fuss-free enough to ball-up and take anywhere. Finally, she pinpointed his black Mercedes convertible parked near the end of the block. She was relieved to find he hadn't left.

"Did the phone wake you sweetheart?" said Deek, walking in with a tray laden with rich smelling coffee, lobster omelets, and a red rose set in a crystal bud vase.

He was already dressed and looked handsome in a blue-gray shirt, slate blue silk tie, and charcoal wool slacks.

"Yes, honey but it's okay," she smiled, "How long have you been up? I didn't hear you make a sound this morning." Renee curled back on top the bed.

"At least a couple of hours, I guess. I went to the gym, came back, showered, got dressed, and still had time to fix breakfast," he said and set the tray down on the nightstand beside her.

"You should have wakened me," she said, stretching, "I had no idea it was this late."

"You were sleeping so soundly, I didn't want to disturb you."

Deek leaned over and kissed her as she wrapped her arms around his neck and returned the kiss.

"Where's your breakfast darling?" she asked, eyeing the single serving of food and two cups of coffee.

"I already had my usual Pineapple-Carrot shake but I'll have a little coffee with you."

"This looks delicious. I had no idea you were a gourmet chef."

"I'm not. Foodnetwork deserves all the credit, not me."

"I doubt that sweetheart," said Renee as she admired the tray's presentation—a two-egg omelet with generous bits of lobster, sprinkled with pepper and chopped chives and thinly sliced fresh cantaloupe, garnished with mint leaf. He had placed a tiny gold box of Godiva chocolate truffles next to the bud vase. Renee took a bite of the omelet and felt like royalty. The lobster's meaty texture blended with the herb and butter-flavored omelet sent immediate pleasure sensations to her taste buds. "Umm, this omelet tastes wonderful," she said, pointing to the plate with her fork. "How did you make this?"

"Nothing to it," he said and took a swallow of his coffee before explaining. "First, I baked the lobster in the oven for a few minutes. When that was done I cooked the eggs in cooking spray and allowed them to set in the frying pan. After the eggs set a bit, I sprinkled lobster on top. Now here's the important part," he gave her a between-you-and-me smile. "Once your eggs start to cook, you must roll the omelet instead of trying to flip it. Flipping is no good. The secret is to roll it."

"Got it, Master Chef." Renee nodded with an amused smile. "And, how many other hidden talents do you have besides your culinary talents in the kitchen, handsome?"

"Stay with me again tonight, beautiful, and I'll show you a few more," he winked and then leaned across the bed to kiss her.

"As tempting as that sounds, I can't. I'm moving into my new house next Saturday, remember? I still have a lot of packing left to do at home."

"Let me help with that. I have to go downtown to the precinct first but I should be able to break away for a couple of hours later this afternoon."

The scenario flashed through her mind of what would happen if Bill dropped in while Deek was over there helping her pack. Bill had said he was going to stay away from the house to avoid implicating her in any of his business's dealings until he had a chance to sever all ties with Shaw's criminal element, but who could depend on anything Bill said? She agonized over whether or not to tell Deek about Clifton Shaw's money laundering scheme with James Ian Mathias, the man FBI agents suspected of drug trafficking. She wasn't sure if she would be able to convince Deek that Bill had not known anything about the company's hidden agenda when he partnered with Shaw. Bill wanted her to stay out of it and let him handle it. Hopefully, he would do this soon because she knew it wouldn't take Agent Santos very long to uncover Mathias's business associations with Shaw, which would eventually point to Bill's involvement.

"No, thank you, honey," she said, "I hired professional movers to do all the heavy work."

"So, that's all I'm good for, eh? Brawn and muscle," he said, teasingly.

"Not hardly, Detective," she smiled and kissed his lips, "You've proven yourself to be quite multi-talented."

"By the way who was that calling so early this morning?" asked Renee, changing the subject.

"My partner. I mean Detective Bradford, not Agent Santos."

"I should have guessed. What's he up to now? Do you really suppose he's serious about arresting Brenda and her mother on nothing but circumstantial evidence, rumors, and innuendo?"

"Serious as a heartache. He just now told me the US Attorney's Office is going for a conviction in federal court instead of the D. C. Courts. That way they can seek the death penalty."

Those last few words stung Renee's ears. She couldn't believe how quickly the case had evolved into a lynch mob against Brenda.

"Aren't there any other suspects?"

"I checked out Leenae Lewis's alibi. She was the victim's old girlfriend if you recall. Well, Miss Lewis claims she was visiting her brother in Philly on the day of the fire and he backed up her story," said Deek. "On the other hand, Brenda Johnson has no alibi and her motive appears stronger, at least to Bradford. I investigated the tip about her first baby's death nine years ago and the subsequent $15,000 death benefit she collected. Unfortunately, it's all true." Deek opened the armoire, removed his packed gun holster and shield and fastened them to his waist. He placed one foot upon a chair and strapped another concealed pistol around his ankle under his pants leg.

"Where are you going?" she asked.

"To work, baby. As much as I'd love to stay here and make love to you all day," he said and walked over to the bed to kiss her goodbye, "I've got too many unresolved cases on my plate. Besides, I need to be at the precinct when Bradford interrogates your secretary and her mother. My partner's been known to misuse his authority to get a suspect to say what he wants," said Deek. "You're welcomed to stay here as long as you like, sweetie."

"The hell I will just lie here and do nothing. Detective Hamilton, I hope you don't think I'm going to stay in bed waiting for you to get home and not do anything to help solve this crime that your partner is trying to pin on Brenda. I'm not so sure her mother is innocent but I'm certain Brenda is."

"Renee, how many times do I have to explain it to you? I have the training, shield and the gun," he said, patting his weapon, "You don't."

Renee jumped out the bed, pushed passed him, and ran towards the bathroom to shower and get dressed. "Give me ten minutes. Don't leave," she demanded and slammed the bathroom door.

By mid-morning, the white snowflakes had lost their firmness and turned into wet mush. On the drive over to headquarters, Deek suddenly turned quiet. The only sound for several minutes came from the swish of the windshield wiper.

"What are you thinking, honey?" she asked.

"I was just thinking about Billi and her baby. I feel responsible, Renee. I should have insisted that she go to the clinic instead of continuing to question her when we first found her."

"No, Deek. By then it still would have been too late to undo the damage of no prenatal care for nine months. It would have happened anyway. When she went into labor at the police station even if we were in route we would have lost the baby too because I wouldn't have been able to safely deliver her."

"I hope you're not just trying to make me feel better."

"No, I'm being honest. Billi should have been receiving prenatal care. She had a serious medical condition that needed to be constantly monitored by an obstetrician. The city needs more local shelter space and services for the homeless, especially for women in Billi's situation. You didn't let her down, Deek, we all did."

Renee placed her hand on his and leaned in to give him a kiss on the cheek. "You smell so good, Darling. I meant to tell you that last night but I was a little distracted," she smiled. "Is that something new you're wearing?"

Deek took his eyes off the road long enough to turn to her and smile. "It's a cologne called Lalique from France. Glad you like it, Sweetheart." "I do. It's light yet spicy. The scent is so addictive. I can't stay away from you," she said and inched closer, placing her hand on his thigh.

"Hum. Well, in that case I'll make sure to keep a steady supply on hand," he glanced over and smiled. Deek was quiet for awhile. She studied the serious look on his face as he appeared deep in thought.

For the next few minutes, they both maintained their silence, each locked in private thoughts. Renee wondered if now was the right time to tell Deek that after she got home from the hospital yesterday, she called an adoption lawyer to look into the possibility of her adopting Billi's baby or at least seek guardianship until adoption could be granted. Renee had fallen in love with the baby girl as soon as she'd laid eyes on her. She couldn't stand the thought of her being a border baby or placed in a cycle of temporary foster homes.

A telephone call on Deek's phone interrupted the silence and Renee's private thoughts. He accepted the call using voice command on his hands free cell phone. It was Tyrone Wallace, the sixteen year-old kid that Renee had met through Deek during the summer and who Deek had befriended six months ago when he spoke at Tyrone's high school on Career Day. Ever since Career day, Deek had slowly assumed the self-appointed role of father-figure to Tyrone who Deek had learned did not have a father in the household.

Deek's tone of voice changed to denote male bonding. "Sure thing buddy, you know I'll be there when you get signed in at Aberdeen. I'm your mentor, where else would I be?" he chuckled. Renee noticed that his face lit up whenever he spoke to Tyrone. "Hey man, you need me to get you any gear to take up there with you when you go?"

From the speakerphone, Renee heard the excitement in Tyrone's voice. He rattled off things he would need like underwear, socks, sweat suits, and pajamas. Deek nodded as Tyrone went through his list of supplies that he'd have to bring with him to Aberdeen. Deek must have committed the list to memory since he didn't write anything down. "No problem. I got it covered, My Man," said Deek.

It was clear from the gist of the conversation that Tyrone would be going away to school soon, but when Deek hung up the phone Renee still asked him what all that was about. Just as she suspected, Deek had used his connections with someone at a quasi-military alternative school in Aberdeen, Maryland to find out if Tyrone would qualify for their highly successful program to train and mentor at-risk youth. Tyrone had just called to tell Deek that he received his letter of acceptance to Freestate Challenge Academy, where he would be living on-campus for the next 22 weeks as a cadet. Renee could see the relief on Deek's face after his phone call from Tyrone.

She was already aware of Deek's involvement with Tyrone over the summer to help keep the teenager occupied. He invited Tyrone to stay at his place from time to time. For the last few weeks of summer, he had enrolled him in a Youth Flight School sponsored by The East Coast Chapter of Tuskegee Airmen with his mother's permission. But once the flight program came to a close, Tyrone's mother reported that her son had resumed hanging out with the wrong crowd. A single-mom who worked two jobs and had two other younger children at home, she had her hands full. She welcomed Deek's help and advice. The Freestate Challenge Academy sounded like a good opportunity for Tyrone and it would help take some of the pressure off his mom from worrying where her son was at night.

Not long after talking to Tyrone on the phone, Deek and Renee arrived at D.C. Police headquarters. When they walked through Homicide's processing area, a uniformed officer informed Deek that Brenda Johnson and her mother had been brought in for questioning earlier that morning. Lt. Bradford was in the process of questioning Brenda in interrogation room one. Deek entered the interrogation room and politely asked his partner to step outside. Detective Bradford leaned across the table in front of Brenda and shoved a notepad and pen in front of her.

"In case your memory comes back while I'm gone," he snarled at Brenda and left the room to speak to Deek.

The two detectives returned to the open bullpen area of desks positioned in rows against the walls. Lt. Bradford sat down at his own desk while Deek loomed over him and tried to hide his annoyance.

"Mel, I told you I was on my way when you called. How long has Mrs. Johnson been in there?"

"Since about nine-thirty. I sent a uniform detail out to the Adams residence this morning and she agreed to come in for questioning. I explained her rights when she got here. She said she understood and waived her right to legal counsel."

"Yeah, I bet you did everything by the book."

"Of course, Kid, you know me. Playback the goddamn tape if you don't believe me," said Bradford, "Besides, lately your ass is always MIA—between the FBI and your extracurricular activities. I can't afford the luxury of dragging my ass on this case waitin' for you to show up."

"Have you found out anything important?"

"Hell no. She claims she wants to help us figure out who really murdered her husband. But all I've heard so far is bullshit. And she's real closed mouth about the insurance money she collected when her first child died nine years ago."

"Where's Mrs. Adams, her mother?" asked Deek.

"I've got her cooling her jets in box three. Talk about nutcases, that dame's a class act."

"One guess who ratted out her own daughter so she could collect 25 grand in reward money for information about the case," he said, leaning back and resting his clamped hands behind his balding head. Renee looked shocked to hear that but Detective Bradford's nod and sly grin confirmed that he was referring to Brenda's mother.

"Are you saying that Mrs. Adams actually called to tell police about her daughter's unfounded charge of insurance fraud nine years ago?" said Renee, "That's unbelievable even for her."

"It didn't exactly happen that way," Bradford said, then took a bite of powdered donut that he retrieved from a bag on his desk.

"Mrs. Adams got her flunky lover to call the tip line. Some idiot who goes by the name of Hercules. I guess she figured she'd collect that reward money her husband put up a lot sooner than she could wrangle a few coins away from her daughter outta the fifty thousand dollar death benefit." White flecks of powdered sugar dotted his mustache and avocado green shirt as he spoke between chews.

"I guess it finally dawned on her that insurance companies don't pay out when fraud is suspected. Anyway, last night she sent her 6' 5" 300 pound dimwit over here to claim the reward. It took less than two seconds to bust his game. Hercules confessed that Mrs. Adams put him up to it then broke down and cried."

"So her plan backfired," said Renee.

"Exactly. It just made me suspect her motives even more. I must say you were right about that one, Doc," said Bradford, between bites before continuing. "When I threatened to arrest Hercules if he didn't talk, he started blabbering faster than a parakeet on Ritalin. Said Irene Adams owed $20,000 in credit card debt and her husband cut off her allowance."

"Did you arrest this Hercules?"

"Naw, I shoulda booked him but I figured he had enough problems dealing with that crazy Adams broad," said Bradford, "But she knows I'm onto her slick ass now. She's in room number three sweatin' bullets by now."

"I don't understand how she could do that to her own daughter?" said Renee, shaking her head.

"Actually, she was trying to hang the crime on her son-in-law's ex-girlfriend when she told Hercules to report the information to us," said Bradford, "But I dug deeper and got the whole story."

"That still doesn't let her off the hook," said Renee. "She's got about as much maternal instincts as my shoe."

"Mrs. Adams thought her tip would lead us to suspect Leenae Lewis. What she didn't expect was that the media would find the case of a wife allegedly killing her husband to collect fifty grand a more interesting scoop," said Bradford, "Her meddling ended up hurting her daughter instead of Jerome's ex-girlfriend."

"Are you planning to tell us what happened Mel or do we have to guess?" said Deek.

"That's what I stopped by to tell you last night, Young Blood, but you told me to get the fuck out, remember?" he said, grabbing another donut.

"Basically, the short and sweet of it is this. Leenae Lewis and Jerome Johnson were charged in a mail fraud bust out scheme nine years ago."

"What's a bust out scheme?" Renee asked.

"Leenae's brother, Davon Lewis owned a retail bargain store in Northeast where he ran a "wholesale jobbing business" in the store's back office. Davon convinced his sister and Jerome to use phony credit cards to help him buy merchandise wholesale and then resell it to other "mom and pop" retail stores. They bought everything on credit with no intention of paying their wholesalers. Essentially, they sold the goods, kept the money, and Davon declared his business bankrupt after he made a nice profit."

"Davon Lewis, the mastermind behind the bust out, claims to be his sister's alibi," said Deek, "Just how reliable do you suppose that corroboration is?"

"Not very in my opinion," Renee said, "Were they convicted for this scheme, Lt. Bradford?"

"Police records show the charges against Miss Lewis and Mr. Johnson were ultimately dropped but Davon Lewis had a previous record of insurance scams against him and the jury convicted him of mail fraud."

"But how did the tip from Mrs. Adams' boyfriend lead you to find out about Brenda?" Renee asked.

"Coincidentally, that was around the same time the first Johnson baby died of SIDS and Brenda Adams collected $15,000 on the baby's insurance death benefit. When I checked out Hercules's tip, that stuff about Brenda rose to the surface like fat in cold soup."

"In addition to reporting the Lewis-Johnson case, the newspapers headlined the story about the then unwed mother, Brenda Adams collecting a death benefit after the sudden death of her and Jerome Johnson's infant daughter."

"So the whole thing smelled rotten to the press," said Deek, "that's why they dug deeper."

"Leenae Lewis and her brother may be inventing a fairy-tale about their whereabouts, but my instincts tell me either Brenda Johnson or her mother planned this latest insurance fraud or they hatched the scheme together," said Bradford. "It's no surprise that Mrs. Adams hopes to get a nice chunk of change if we can't convict her daughter."

"I wouldn't put anything past Irene Adams, but Brenda is innocent," Renee insisted.

"One thing seems certain, the victim had a lot of enemies," said Deek, "Now we got Davon Lewis doing time for mail fraud nine years ago while his partner, Jerome Johnson walked."

"Tell me, Dr. Hayes, how did this dude, Jerome Johnson, a drug addict who didn't have a pot to piss in, get two fine honeys to lose their mind over him?" asked Bradford, "One at home and one on stand by when I can't even get an ugly woman to give me directions."

"I wouldn't want to comment on your personal failure to attract women, Lieutenant," said Renee, "But Jerome probably appealed to women because he projected a 'bad boy' image. From dealing with love-obsessed female patients, I've discovered that their attraction to 'bad boys' is one reason these women are in therapy in the first place. They always seem to go for the 'bad boy' over a nice, clean-cut, stable guy. Not that you're 'the nice, clean-cut' type either Detective Bradford."

"Sorry, I asked," he said looking dejected.

"If you don't mind, I'd like to speak to Brenda for a moment. May I?" Renee asked Bradford.

"Be my guest, Doc. She sure as hell ain't opened up to me yet," he said. "Me and Deek can watch from the observation room. She won't know we're behind the two-way mirror and might tell you something she wouldn't say to me. So that's probably not a bad idea."

Renee opened the door of the interrogation room and walked in. Brenda didn't look up. The room felt like an isolation chamber: bleached-out gray walls, no windows or telephone—nothing but a table and three uncomfortable chairs. A tape recorder, some paper for her statement, and a cup of water sat on top the black, metal tabletop. Brenda sat shivering at the far end of the room. She looked uncomfortable and frightened slumped forward in a straight-back wooden chair with elbows on the table and her hand barely holding up her drooping head. Renee didn't see a thermostat to turn up the heat and noticed that the four, bare walls didn't even have a light switch.

"Brenda?"

When she recognized Renee's voice, Brenda jerked her head up.

"Dr. Renee? I'm so glad you're here. Have you seen my mother? The son of Satan lied and said she went home but I don't believe him. She wouldn't leave me alone in this place."

Renee couldn't argue with Brenda's new nickname for Detective Mel Bradford. It somehow did seem to fit. She was glad she didn't have to outright lie and just shook her head 'no' to Brenda's question because she really had not seen Irene Adams yet. Renee took Brenda's hands in both of hers to warm them and tried to console her.

"Brenda, I realize it's hard but can you tell me what happened to your first child nine years ago?"

Brenda hesitated for a moment before speaking in a whispered voice. "Dr. Renee, little Janica's death still haunts me to this day. That's why I've never talked about it to anyone, but since it's plastered all over the news I suppose it doesn't matter now."

She looked down and closed her eyes briefly. "It was really hard on Jerome too. That's when he first started experimenting with crack. Before that he only smoked weed but he needed something stronger to wipe out our baby's death. I had my Lord and Savior to see me through it, but Jerome had never been strong in faith. After it happened, we never talked about it. But things were never the same between us." Renee nodded for Brenda to continue.

"I know you'd say that wasn't healthy to keep it locked inside, but we wanted to forget. Even though the doctors said Janica died from Sudden Infant Death syndrome and there was nothing we could have done to prevent it, I think we blamed each other. It's something I never wanted to talk or think about ever again. Even when Baby Buddha was missing for almost 24 hours, I wouldn't allow myself to think, what if it's happening all over again. I had to believe I would get Justin back. Or that would have been the end for me. There would have been no point in me going on. After the loss of my first child, any time the memory came back, I blocked it out again as if it never happened. I guess Jerome tried to forget too and drugs became his crutch. I know he was still hurting. I guess that's why I kept taking him back."

"I understand, Brenda," said Renee, and looked softly into her eyes. "I really do, more than you realize." Renee thought about her own teenage pregnancy that was stolen from her while she slept in an anesthetic state. From that time on, she had never been able to successfully carry a pregnancy to term. Renee thoroughly understood the need to erase bad memories through disassociation.

"We broke up soon after Janica died but got back together five years later. Then I got pregnant with Justin. He was our second chance. I wasn't going to let anything happen to him."

"What did you do with the $15,000 insurance money you received after Janica's death?"

"That was nine years ago. Before we lost our daughter to SIDS, I was an unwed, 19 year-old mother, Dr. Renee. When I got pregnant I dropped out of community college to move in with Jerome. I had only finished one semester. My parents disapproved and refused to help if I didn't go back to school and give the baby up for adoption. But I just couldn't give her up once they put her in my arms," said Brenda, "Besides, Jerome and I were in love. Or at least I thought we were."

Brenda hesitated. Renee prompted her to continue. "Go on, Brenda."

"Well, right after Janica was born of course I couldn't work. Then Jerome lost his job and I ended up selling my car so I could apply for welfare. A few weeks later our baby daughter died in her sleep. Jerome talked me into filing the insurance claim to get Janica's death benefits. But the money didn't help."

Brenda stared at her folded hands as she spoke. "Jerome slid further into depression and drugs. It didn't take long for him to smoke up all that insurance money on crack. Especially when Leenae and his homies became his full-time "getting high" crew and kept him dependent. That's when I got fed up and left him … then one day out of the blue, Jerome and I ran into each other at a nightclub. It was obvious our feelings for each other were still strong. This time he promised to cleanup and to kick his addiction for good. So eventually we got married and the rest is history as they say. So here we are."

"Brenda, I need to go outside and talk to the Detectives handling your case. Will you be okay for a while?"

"Sure, Dr. Renee. Thanks for listening. Do you think you could ask that Lieutenant Bradford if I could use the rest room?

"Of course, Brenda. Can I get you anything?"

"Maybe a cup of tea if they have it."

"I'll see what I can do, dear," she said and patted her hand, before exiting out the door of the interrogation room. She knew Deek and Lt. Bradford had heard every word.

CHAPTER 38

After Renee left the interrogation room, she asked Detective Bradford if he had followed through on Brenda's request for tea. She knew he had heard them behind the mirror. Bradford assured her that he already instructed someone to bring Brenda a cup of tea. He asked one of the guards to escort Brenda to the ladies room as she had also requested. Renee followed Bradford and Deek back to the squad room to discuss what Brenda had revealed to Renee.

"So I'm the son of Satan, huh?" snarled Bradford, "Why the hell didn't she give me some straight answers when I asked her about the infant's death and the insurance money she collected back then?"

"I believe Brenda has been suffering from a disassociated personality disorder since the tragedy nine years ago," said Dr. Renee. "When you tried to bring up those memories, her natural mental defenses threw her into disassociation."

"Doc, I'm shy a few cups of coffee to comprehend the drift of your lingo," said Bradford, "Can you explain what the hell you're talking about in plain English?"

"Disassociation occurs when someone takes himself or herself out of a situation. They're not present on an emotional level and they don't have control over it," Renee explained in laymen's terms. "That way they don't feel the horror and pain. They can actually block it out. So they disassociate and remove themselves mentally."

"I still don't get what you're talking about, Doc," said Bradford, waving his hand away. "It doesn't matter anyway 'cause I don't buy it. Brenda Johnson's pity party is over."

"Perhaps, you could establish trust with her if you'd turn up the heat in that icebox you call an interrogation room," said Renee, "It's like the Antarctica in there."

"Yeah, I could do that but I'm not. Look, this ain't the Hyatt, Doc. I don't want Brenda Johnson or her mother getting too comfortable in our interrogation rooms. When they've had enough, they'll talk and tell me what I wanna know."

Bradford and Deek entered the interrogation room where Brenda waited, while this time Renee watched from behind the two-way mirror. Bradford turned the tape recorder to record and continued his questioning. He assumed his usual domineering position for interrogations and loomed over Brenda with his arms folded across his overhanging stomach as Deek stood nearby.

"Neighbors heard an argument at your place between your husband and Leenae Lewis about a week ago," said Detective Bradford, "Do you know anything about that?"

Brenda remained mute and refused to answer any of his questions. When her secretary shutdown from Lt. Bradford's 'tough guy' approach, Renee couldn't resist the urge to peep in through the two-way mirror at Irene Adams, still waiting in interrogation room 3. Irene Adams, dressed in a fitted, aqua-blue, jacquard suit, paced the small, enclosed space like a caged tigress. Her silver fox collared, gray mink coat lay draped over a chair.

Renee could never let Brenda know what her mother did to incriminate her own daughter. Most children assumed their mothers loved them unconditionally and they're devastated to find out otherwise. But somebody needed to straighten out Mrs. Irene Adams and Renee decided to volunteer for the job. Brenda's mother was a greedy egocentric bitch but could she also be a murderer? Renee didn't think Irene was the type to get her hands dirty by doing the deed herself, but she could have easily hired or tricked someone gullible like Hercules to carry out the crime for her. Irene Adams' intense hatred of her son-in-law was common knowledge and now police had uncovered another possible motive—financial gain. She desperately needed to pay off her personal debts so she could resume her frivolous, self-serving lifestyle.

Renee slipped out the observation room. The officer guarding the door to interrogation room 3 knew she was working on a case with the detectives so he allowed her to enter. Renee was glad the room was soundproof so she could tell that woman exactly what was on her mind.

"Oh, it's only you," sighed Irene, turning around when she heard the door open. "What do you want? Where's that fat-ass, Cro-Magnon piece of shit whose been keeping me cooped up in this hellhole all morning for no good reason?" Hours waiting in an interrogation room had removed all semblance of Irene Adams' phony, high-class manners. Though she was never effective at keeping up that charade for long. "Where the hell is he?" Irene spewed, glancing at her watch. "I have an appointment at the spa this afternoon."

Renee approached Brenda's mother with a determined look.

"May I speak to you for a minute, Mrs. Adams?" she asked firmly.

"What the hell do you want?" Irene sneered in a tone even more biting than usual.

"I just thought I'd warn you, watch that you don't implicate yourself in this crime by letting your greed get the best of you."

"And what is that supposed to mean?" she said, cocking her head to one side and folding her arms under her breast.

"I know it was you who called Brenda's insurance company right after Jerome's murder," said Renee. "If you had thought about someone else besides yourself for half a second, you would have realized that pretending to be Brenda and initiating the claim right after her husband's death would cause police to think your daughter was a suspect. But maybe you really didn't care about that."

"I have never intentionally hurt my little girl," Irene raged. "I love her and she knows it. I don't need to prove a damn thing to you."

"Mrs. Adams, you don't even know the meaning of the word love. And if that wasn't bad enough," Renee continued, "when Brenda did not automatically receive her payout on the claim you initiated, you had to think of another way to get your hands on some fast cash, didn't you? It's a shame about that pesky, little insurance stipulation that a person suspected of intentionally causing a policy holder's death is prohibited from collecting his insurance," said Renee, shaking her head sarcastically while glaring at Mrs. Adams.

"So you instructed your lover to reveal past evidence on someone else that also happened to lead police to damaging information about Brenda. All that scheming just so you could collect the reward money your husband put up to find legitimate leads."

"That was not my fault," Irene yelled, "If Marvin had just given me the goddamn money in the first place I wouldn't have to resort to these tactics. And who knew Hercules was such a fucking idiot? I realize now he's only good for one thing."

"You are beyond pathetic, Mrs. Adams. I don't understand how a mother can betray her own daughter and still look at herself in the mirror as much as you do without reproach."

"Who the hell are you to judge me, you tight-ass bitch?" Irene shrieked. "I'm not too much of a lady to whip your ass right here so you'd better leave while you still have a chance."

"I will leave Mrs. Adams because it's obvious you don't see how you've hurt Brenda. Talking to you is a waste of time. And just so we understand each other," said Renee, "the only reason I'm keeping quiet about what you've done is to avoid hurting her more, as well as, your husband who I don't know at all, but feel immensely sorry for." Renee tore off a page from the notepad sitting on the table and scribbled the name and telephone number for her colleague, Dr. Helen Stone. She slid the paper across the desk in front of Mrs. Adams.

"That's the number for a good psychiatrist," Renee said calmly, "I suggest you use it. Perhaps Dr. Stone can help a fifty-plus year old woman stop behaving like a selfish, oversexed teenager."

"Fifty-plus!" Irene shouted, "How dare you imply …"

Renee left the room and closed the door without listening to the rest of Mrs. Adams outburst. Did Brenda's mother realize how lucky she was to have such a lovely and kind-hearted daughter like Brenda? How could anyone be that wrapped up in themselves and so ungrateful about the precious gifts God had given them? She'd give anything to have a child of her own—just one. Renee didn't want to waste another thought on Irene Adams.

She returned to the two-way mirror behind room number one where Lt. Bradford still carried on his interrogation of Brenda. Detective Bradford conducted the questioning while Deek stood at the opposite end of the room and listened, wearing an unreadable expression on his face.

"If you didn't do it, Mrs. Johnson, who do you think did?" snapped Lt. Bradford. Brenda stared down at her hands without answering.

After several moments of silence, Brenda told him she remembered a telephone call Jerome received a little more than a week before he was killed. She said her husband acted nervous and frightened after the phone call and then soon left the house.

"Who called? You got a name?"

Brenda shrugged and shook her head.

"Who did you conspire with to concoct this scheme? Was it your mother and her boy toy, Hercules?" said Bradford. Brenda didn't respond as Bradford continued badgering her. "Looks like things worked out pretty good with you getting your child back safely in less than 24 hours. Sure seems nice of the killer to conveniently drop off your baby in front of a guard's station," he added sarcastically.

"Yes, thank God for that," Brenda responded wistfully.

"Maybe you should be thanking whoever you conspired with to concoct this arson/kidnapping/murder offense. You expected to rack up another insurance payoff didn't you Mrs. Johnson?" said Bradford, leaning forward across the table. "A real windfall this time, 50 thousand bucks of free money. Not to mention the added benefit of getting your revenge for finding your husband cheating on you again with Miss Lewis." That got a reaction from her. Brenda's face flushed and she gave him a scorching look. Still, her mouth remained clamped shut.

"The crime lab lifted your fingerprints off pieces of duct tape that the arsonist ripped from the window to break in."

Brenda looked up. "That's not surprising Detective Bradford since I'm the one who sealed up the window in the first place. Mama Etta's house was over fifty years old with poor insulation. I used the duct tape to try and block out the cold air that was getting in."

"Hum, convenient," he said, undeterred. "We also collected a sample from the arsonist's clothing that got caught on a nail as he or she escaped through the window. Do you have a black knit Coogi sweat jacket in your possession?"

"No, I do not."

"It's amazing what lab analysis can determine from just a few strands of fabric."

"Good. I hope it leads you to who really killed my husband," said Brenda.

"You slipped through the cracks nine years ago 'cause they didn't have enough evidence to charge you. If you think I buy that disassociation crap Dr. Hayes is selling, think again, Mrs. Johnson," he said, "If you cooperate now, it'll go better for you in the long run."

"I'm cooperating as much as I can, Detective," said Brenda near tears, "I want to go home to my baby."

"Too bad. At this rate you'll never see him grow up."

"What do you want from me, Detective Bradford?"

"A confession."

"I'm not guilty."

"Would you be willing to take a lie detector test?

"Of course, I have nothing to hide," she said, "I'll do anything to convince you I'm innocent so you can start looking for the person responsible."

"Fine, I'll schedule the test for one day next week."

Deek gave Bradford a signal that meant let's talk outside. The two detectives left Brenda again and they met out in the squad room.

"I think we should let up off Mrs. Johnson for awhile," said Deek, "I'm still waiting on the gas chromatography analysis. Roberts says he'll have it by Monday. Then we'll be able to pinpoint where the arsonist bought the gasoline and maybe directly to the perp's fuel tank."

Bradford stuffed both hands inside his pants pocket and shook his head.

"Can't you wait until Monday before scheduling a polygraph, Mel?" said Deek, "It's only a matter of time before we fill in the missing pieces."

"Whaddya have against putting her through the test, Kid?"

"It's obvious this suspect is under a great deal of emotional stress. Strapping her to a chair with sensors will only make her anxiety worse," said Deek. "Testing someone this emotional could produce a false positive result even if she's telling us the truth. Since we don't have an eyewitness, why not wait for more lab results."

"Right, there's no eyewitness but there's a helluva lot of compelling evidence against her. And, since I don't think she pulled this off alone, I'm willing to bet it was a Mother and Daughter operation. I'm trying to get her to confess now to make it easier on her and you're not helping. You know the DA's going for the death penalty and the city's top prosecutor is taking the case."

"With the flimsy evidence we're giving them, just how do you think the prosecution can build a case of guilt beyond a reasonable doubt?

The only finger prints at the crime scene are explainable and no witness can place her there."

"That's their job description, Hotshot, not ours," snapped Mel. "I've got my orders to charge her. So let's put this thing in overdrive and call it a day."

"If that's the game they want to play it's a big risk," said Deek, "They still want to go ahead and try the case on conjecture with very little hard evidence? If Brenda Johnson is truly guilty and gets off, it'll be for good. They can't ever try her again for this crime."

Bradford shrugged, "That's their fuckin' problem. I did my job."

Deek gave his partner a disgusted look.

"Look Kid, despite our lack of physical evidence, a strong motive and opportunity still exists. In other words, no alibi and there's a past precedent for insurance fraud. I'll bet my badge that Brenda and a possible accomplice were in on this crime together. And since the apple doesn't fall too far from the tree, my money's on the mother. Lemme go find out what Mommy Dearest has to say, "said Detective Bradford, "I bet she's ready to talk by now. It'll be a helluva lot easier to offer her a deal to give up the dirt on Brenda. I bet she'll jump at the bait to plea bargain for a lesser sentence."

Just then the Captain walked up.

"How's the Johnson case going, Mel?" she asked, "About ready to put this case to bed, I hope."

"Sure thing, Captain. I was just going in to break down a deal to the alleged accomplice in this Thelma and Louise outfit. Louise is tight-lipped but I think I can make Thelma crack. Stick around and watch me operate," he bragged to his boss.

Detective Bradford dubbed Mrs. Adams as the feisty Thelma in what he believed to be a mother-daughter crime plot. He entered room 3 to interrogate Irene Adams alone. Captain Frye, Deek, and Renee positioned themselves behind the mirror so they could observe Bradford questioning the suspected accomplice. Bradford asked Irene

Adams to sit down. Then pulled out a chair and sat down across the table from her.

"You've known the victim, Jerome Johnson since your daughter was in high school. How did you feel about your son-in-law, Mrs. Adams?"

"He wasn't on my list of top favorites but I had nothing to do with his murder and neither did my daughter. She's practically a saint."

"Listen, I'm on your side, Mrs. Adams. I think the cheating, crackhead bastard got what he deserved," he said.

"Despite what you think, Detective, I didn't hate my son-in-law," said Irene. "It's true, I didn't like some of the people he associated with, especially that slut, Leenae Lewis. But since Jerome was the man my daughter chose, I accepted it and tried to make him feel like part of the family."

Mel gave Irene Adams an expressionless look. "You must think I'm as dumb as a box of rocks to believe that crap. We got witnesses who'll attest to your intense hatred of your son-in-law from day one. Where were you on October 6th between eleven in the morning and one PM?"

"Detective Bradford, we aren't getting anywhere this way," she said, sweetly.

Irene rose slowly from her chair and walked around the table then sat on top the table facing him. She let her skirt rise several inches and crossed her legs to the opposite side where he had a clear view of her exposed thigh. She removed her jacket and unbuttoned the first three buttons of her sheer, black blouse to reveal a generous cleavage under a turquoise satin bustier.

"Did you know I used to be stripper in my younger days?" she said, "Men told me I had Tina Turner legs. You like Tina Turner, don't you Detective?"

"What do you think? I'm not dead," said Bradford and wiped the sweat from his brow.

Irene leaned forward, stared into his widening eyes while he tried unsuccessfully not to look directly at her breasts. Irene pointed to her satin bra. "I'm wearing matching thongs," she said and licked her bottom lip, "would you like to see them?"

Bradford turned and glanced briefly at the blacked out mirror behind him. Sweat beads settled on his forehead. His breathing increased but he sat speechless and watched as Irene re-crossed her legs to the other side.

"You're a man of the law so let's negotiate a quid pro quo," she smiled seductively, "In other words, you do something for me and I do something for you."

Bradford stood up, removed a handkerchief from his jacket and quickly brushed it across his face. "Yeah Mrs. Adams, you can do something for me. You can tell me the truth in exchange for not getting cuffed and fingerprinted. That'll be your quid pro quo. Your daughter's been jerking my chain all morning and I'm not about to waste all goddamn day on you too."

"I don't like your tone or your language, Detective Bradford," said Irene and leaped off the table. She straightened her skirt and re-buttoned her blouse. Then snatched up her jacket and mink coat from the back of the chair. "I want to call my lawyer and my husband now. If you aren't going to charge me, release me immediately. I know my rights."

Bradford stormed out of the interrogation room enraged. He ordered an officer standing nearby to direct Mrs. Adams to a telephone. When Deek and Renee walked up to his desk, his attention remained fixed on the affidavit in support of arrest warrant. He didn't look up although he knew they were standing there.

"Mel, you can't take your frustration out on Brenda just because her mother's a piece of work," said Deek. He tried to convince his partner to wait until Monday to make an arrest but his argument fell on deaf ears.

"Sorry, Young Blood. I'm filing formal charges against her right now. In my book, the spouse is always a prime suspect unless somebody can show me otherwise and so far, that hasn't happened."

Lt. Bradford ordered an officer to escort Brenda downstairs to the receiving area to be booked. Her motives: an insurance payout of 50 thousand dollars, and secondly, a woman scorned when she discovered her husband cheating on her with his old girlfriend. Bradford told Deek and Renee he had enough circumstantial evidence to detain Brenda Johnson based on probable cause. And, since he also thought her mother was involved—in fact Mrs. Adams might have even been the mastermind, he'd keep looking for evidence so he could eventually book her too. Bradford handed them his warrant and supporting documentation to review.

On the affidavit in support of arrest, Brenda faced federal fraud and first-degree murder charges that accused her of improperly trying to collect on Jerome Johnson's life insurance policy after allegedly setting or conspiring with an accomplice to start a fire with the intent to cause her husband's death. An additional charge listed was intent to destroy property. The charges included information from witnesses and several neighbors.

After reading the affidavit, Deek threw up his hands and walked away. Renee followed him to his desk and sank in the chair in front of him. Brenda's lawyer, Mr. K. C. Bloodstone, would have to perform a miracle to get her out of jail tonight, thought Renee.

"So what happens to Brenda now?" she asked Deek with a worried look on her face.

"Now that she's been arrested, she'll appear for arraignment in D. C. Superior Courthouse on Monday. The judge will weigh her lawyer's argument and determine initial pre-trail detention status at the arraignment hearing. That means whether she stays in jail or gets out on bail."

"What are her chances of getting out on bail?"

He shrugged his shoulders, "Don't know. If we go by past precedent, not very good."

"But it really comes down to how good her lawyer is," said Deek, "and I hear K. C. Bloodstone is one of the best criminal attorneys in D. C. Then it could also depend on who the judge is."

"So basically, you have no idea," said Renee, folding her arms with a frustrated sigh.

"Generally speaking when somebody is accused of a violent crime like murder, her attorney will have to convince the judge that she's no danger to the community, there's no risk of flight and that she won't get involved in the kind of conduct that she's accused of while out on bail. The District's pre-trial contention laws are so severe I doubt that she'll be able to get out before trial."

"My God, this is terrible. She could be locked up for months with no one but Irene Adams to care for little Justin," said Renee. "Though it sounds like if Bradford gets his way Irene Adams will be occupying her own cell. I doubt that any of her relatives can take the baby to his sitter's every day. And, who would pay the sitter? That is, if Bradford doesn't try to arrest Mrs. Adams too as an accomplice."

"I don't think Mel wants to tangle with Mrs. Adams based on nothing but his intuition after what we just saw in the interrogation room," said Deek, with a subtle grin. "He is going to have to dig for some credible evidence."

"Deek, this isn't funny. Those charges against Brenda are serious. We need to do something. The real killer is still out there somewhere."

"Sweetheart, I realize it's serious and I didn't mean to sound glib. But I don't know what else I can do. Mel is lead investigator on this case and he can pretty much do as he damn well pleases. In his mind, he already has the real killer in custody and he's working on getting her accomplice put away too."

"It's absurd to think Brenda had anything to do with this. We can't just sit here and let this happen to her."

At that moment Marvin Adams, Brenda's father and her attorney, K. C. Bloodstone, a squat, no-neck man, walked in. Renee leaped from her chair and re-introduced herself to Mr. Adams, whom she

had met at Jerome's funeral a few days ago. She identified herself to
Mr. Bloodstone as Brenda's close friend and employer. Renee asked the
attorney what could he do to get Brenda released on bond with charges
as serious as suspicion of murder, arson, insurance fraud, and filing a
false report.

"Dr. Hayes, it's obvious your concern for my client and her little
boy's welfare is genuine," said Mr. Bloodstone. The attorney explained
his strategy for getting Brenda out on bond, while Mr. Adams nodded
in approval.

"I reviewed the arrest warrant and intend to use the fact that the
police don't have any physical evidence against her," said Bloodstone.
"I'll suggest that she be on an electronic monitor inside her parents'
house until trial. In her favor, Mrs. Johnson has no prior convictions."

"I should be able to convince the Court that she's not a danger to
the community because she won't be out of the house and won't flee
because of the ankle bracelet," said the attorney using animated hand
gestures. "I've just come from speaking to my client in lockup and we'll
be entering a plea of not guilty to all charges. If the judge grants bail,
the longest it should take to get her out is one week."

"So she'll be spending the weekend in jail for something she
didn't do," said Renee. "I know Brenda's innocent and shouldn't be
locked up at all. She's so fragile after losing her husband and having
her baby missing for an entire day. I really don't know how much
more she can take."

"Mr. Bloodstone, I'll put up whatever bond money is necessary
to get my daughter released," said Mr. Adams. "Now, where is that
Detective who had her arrested? Lt. Bradford, I believe my wife said
his name is."

Renee pointed Bradford out to Marvin Adams. Detective Bradford
had his back to them and was talking to a police officer.

"I'll contact you later this evening, Mr. Adams," said Bloodstone,
"I'm on my way to file a motion to have your daughter's bond status

reviewed and request that it be expedited. Don't worry, Mr. Adams, we'll have Brenda out of here and back home with you and Mrs. Adams as quickly as possible."

"Thank you, Mr. Bloodstone," said Brenda's father, grasping the lawyer's outstretched hand, "I have every confidence in you, sir."

Marvin Adams approached Lt. Bradford from behind and demanded to see his wife.

"Sure thing Mr. Adams, your wife's waiting for you in the coffee room. By the way, you have my deepest condolences, Mr. Adams," said Bradford, "and I'm not talking about your late son-in-law." Bradford walked away. He didn't see the confused look on Marvin Adams face.

Deek clasped his fingers together and rested folded hands against his chin as he reflected on the case. "There's still one thing that doesn't add up, Renee."

"What's that, Deek?"

"Brenda said she was certain her husband had stopped using drugs and there was no indication of problems at work. Alonzo Woods, Jerome's coworker basically said the same thing when I questioned him at the funeral, remember?"

"Yes, that's right. What's your point?"

"If Jerome was clean, why did he fail a random drug test that resulted in his termination?" Deek asked. "If everything had been going so great prior to him getting fired, what suddenly happened to change all that?"

"Perhaps Brenda missed the signs," said Renee, "Quitting is not as difficult as staying quit. Addicts often incur so many physical and mental changes that they need to get their fix merely to sustain homeostasis."

"Homeo-what?"

"In layman's terms, withdrawal can be very rough. It's easy for a recovered crack addict to slip back, especially when pressures escalate."

"What pressures though? He had a decent job, a loving wife, nice kid."

"And an ex-girlfriend he couldn't stay away from. That's pressure right there," said Renee.

"Exactly. I think we should backtrack and talk to Leenae Lewis again," he said, "but first I want to stop by Union Delivery Service where Jerome worked and get a copy of those drug test results from Jerome's boss. Deek searched his PDA for the telephone number. "Ah, here it is, Odessa Dillon. Let's see, it's after two now. She might still be there on a Saturday."

"Mrs. Dillon is also Veda's supervisor. From the tidbits of information that Veda has told me about working for her, I think you may be right," said Renee. "I hear this woman is a classic workaholic."

Deek called Odessa Dillon at UDS and caught her at her desk just before she was about to leave for the day. She agreed to wait for him since he said he could be there in twenty minutes and it wouldn't take long. As for Miss Lewis, they decided to pay her a surprise visit afterwards. Deek helped Renee with her coat and they left without telling his partner anything. Bradford had moved on to his next case and they knew he would not pursue any other leads to help Brenda. It was up to Deek and Renee to find new leads and find them fast so that Brenda wouldn't have to be away from her child any longer than necessary for a crime they truly believed she did not commit.

CHAPTER 39

Twenty minutes later, Deek turned into Union Delivery Service's rear parking lot. He maneuvered his low-to-the-ground, tire screecher around drivers handling 'tractor trailer' sized cabs. It was a busy late Saturday afternoon. The lot was full of UDS's regular blue trucks pulling in, as well as others on their way out to deliver packages. Deek parked in one of the few visitor spots. Renee did not expect to find Veda in her office since she was normally off on Saturdays.

Deek and Renee walked carefully through the loading dock area. They passed drivers that steered their trucks from one bay door to another, receiving incoming and outgoing packages to be unloaded, sorted, and reloaded. Deek went over to speak to a security guard, while Renee stood in the walkway and looked around. Suddenly, she spotted Alonzo Woods standing in front of Bay 25 smoking a cigarette. Alonzo loafed around and watched as a petite-framed woman struggled to unload packages from his truck. At that moment he noticed Renee staring at him. He stamped out his cigarette then strolled up to her in a cool, bopping gait.

"Yeah, Miss Dillon just gave me a raise to 50 K this morning," he bragged. "I been shifting in the yard for the past few days. That means all I gotta do is sit on my sweet ass all day long and move my cab from bay to bay," he grinned, "I ain't gotta make no deliveries or pick up no packages. Those other losers gotta do all the heavy loadin' and unloadin'."

Renee realized he was trying to emphasize his importance since that was his typical behavior at Good Looks Salon where he was always trying to impress the girls at the beauty parlor. "Good for you, Mr. Woods. Congratulations on your promotion."

"You like barbecue, Dr. Renee?" he asked, "'cause I know this little rib joint around the corner. Man, the meat just melts off the bones. They got cornbread, biscuits, baked beans, 'tata salad, you name it."

"I, uh, don't ..."

"Maybe you might lemme take you one day," he winked.

"Didn't you tell us yesterday at Jerome's funeral that you'd be home this morning in case Detective Hamilton and his partner, Detective Bradford wanted to question you further? So what are you doing here at work today? It's a good thing they didn't waste their time going over to your house to see you."

"Well uh, yeah, guess I did tell ya'll that. But I decided this morning to get the hell outta Dodge. My wife, Izza's on the rampage with her damn 'honey do' list. I had to come to work so I could take it easy and get me some peace and quiet. Izza was spittin' bullets when I left. I know I'ma catch hell when I get home. So may as well keep my ass out all night since I'ma catch it anyway," he grinned. His relaxed body stance straightened up abruptly and the suggestive leer on his face turned serious when he saw Deek walking towards them.

"Mr. Woods, how are you?" said Deek, shaking Alonzo's hand. "If you're not too busy right now, can you direct us to your supervisor's office. She's expecting us."

"Sure Detective, Miss Dillon said you was comin' by to pick up Jerome's things outta his locker. I boxed everything up for you. I didn't know Dr. Renee was coming too. Anyway, follow me, I'll take ya'll to Miss Dillon's office."

Alonzo pointed out an office with the name Odessa Dillon, Supervisor, printed in gold lettering on the closed door. Alonzo pimped away, trying to be cool and nonchalant on his way back to the yard. Deek knocked and waited for Mrs. Dillon to invite them in.

"Who is it?" said a firm voice behind the door.

"Detective Hamilton, Mrs. Dillon. And Dr. Renee Hayes." They heard lumbering sounds and heavy footsteps approach and the click of a door latch as Mrs. Dillon unlocked and opened the door. A fairly attractive, mid-fiftyish woman with a round, overly made-up face stood before them. Creamy eye shadow in shimmering bronze made her honey-colored, oval eyes glint like jewels.

"Won't ya'll come in," said the robust woman, wearing a tailored beige pantsuit and a forced smile on her caramel complexioned face. She motioned them forward into her office and returned to her desk. When she walked, her extra-wide, one-inch pumps suffered under her weight. The coppery toned medium-length hair flipped up at the edges in a relaxed bob softened her square jaw and gave Mrs. Dillon a polished, well-kept look of professionalism.

"Thank you for agreeing to see me on such short notice, Mrs. Dillon," said Deek in his deep, mellow voice, "We won't take up much of your time." Deek and Renee still stood near the doorway and did not remove their coats. The stark, white walls and shades of khaki and pale army green gave the office a chilly, distressed aura.

"I hope not, Sugar. Actually, I was on my way home when you called. I'm not sure what else I can tell you Detective Hamilton. I already told everything I know to your partner on Tuesday." Mrs. Dillon spoke in a mid-western accent and volunteered that she hailed from Houston, Texas but had lived in Washington, D. C. for the past twenty years yet still couldn't completely shake her roots. She unbuttoned the double-breasted jacket over her thick middle and sat down behind her desk.

"There's Jerome's locker contents, already boxed up and ready to go," she said, pointing to a box sitting on a round conference table. "I doubt there's anything in there that you'd consider evidence, Detective. I already went through it, of course."

"Of course," nodded Deek, and walked over to the box to check its contents. He pulled out pictures of Brenda and Baby Justin. A bottle of shampoo, lotion, a tube of deodorant, a change of clothes, and a picture of Leenae Lewis in a heart-shaped frame with an inscription 'Always yours' written in the bottom corner.

"Looks like you were right, Mrs. Dillon," he said and packed everything back in the box, "I'll make sure Jerome Johnson's family gets his possessions."

"That's good, Darlin'," she curved her full lips, painted and glossed, into a half-smile.

"'Course, I meant to mail that stuff to his parents' address but hadn't gotten around to it yet. Jerome left in such a huff two weeks ago on Friday when he failed that drug test. He didn't even bother to clear out his locker," Odessa explained.

"I've been pulling double-shifts myself right along with my guys so it just slipped my little 'ole mind to take care of it. You know, we at Union Delivery Service aim to please and serve our customers 24 hours a day."

Renee thought to herself, this is UDS and they don't have time to ship a terminated employee's possessions? Odessa Dillon stood up as if to see them out when Deek helped Renee out of her coat. He sat down on one of the contemporary chairs in front of Mrs. Dillon's desk and draped his overcoat across the arm of the chair. Renee sat down nearby on the muted sage sofa. Mrs. Dillon pursed her lips but followed suit and sat back down as well. Renee noticed a stack of fashion magazines spread out on the chrome-rimmed, glass end table. She stared curiously at a glossy folder labeled National Park Seminary Historic District that rested on top of an end table.

When Odessa saw Renee staring at the folder, she piped up, "I'm interested in old buildings and the Seminary's full of interesting structures with their own history."

"I understand you're a busy woman, Mrs. Dillon and I appreciate your time. This will only take a few minutes. If you don't mind I'd just like to clarify a few things you told my partner on Tuesday. I'd also like to take a look at Jerome's employee record."

"Good Lord, Detective, don't ya'll talk to one another? No wonder crime is out of control in this dang city. I already showed his records to the other fella, the short, chubby guy. And answered every last one of his questions."

"Please, Mrs. Dillon, this will go faster if you cooperate. I have things to do just like you do," said Deek, "The employment records, please Ma'am."

Odessa unlocked the bottom drawer of her desk and pulled out Jerome's file then handed it to Deek.

Deek saw that during Jerome's first two months of employment, he showed exemplary work habits working under his uncle, Issac Temple. However, when his route shifted to Odessa Dillon's unit, he received a total of seven days worth of suspensions in four months based on deficiencies and violations with: methods, lateness, absenteeism, personal differences with supervisor, stubbornness, and failure to follow instructions.

"I gave Jerome Johnson many a verbal warning first before resorting to suspending him and notating his permanent record," she said, as Deek read the file, "but I guess he was just a square peg that refused to fit into a round hole, if you know what I mean."

After reading through the file, Deek passed it to Renee to study. On Jerome's skills inventory sheet under qualifications Renee saw where it indicated that he had obtained his CDL license prior to joining Union Delivery Service. He trained and prepared for the feeder driver position beforehand she was sure in the hopes of one day getting a promotion. Renee didn't think this demonstrated the typical behavior of a drug addict. She believed this supported Brenda's claim that Jerome hadn't touched drugs in the past 18 months. But what other reason would Odessa Dillon have to fire him other than drug use? The deficiencies noted on Jerome's record were reported solely by Mrs. Dillon and couldn't be substantiated by anyone else at UDS.

"Jerome appeared to be doing well reporting to his uncle who supervised another division. So why was he assigned to a different route after just two months?" asked Deek.

"Nepotism. Ike had already used his influence to get his nephew hired. I guess somebody complained to the head office about favoritism."

"I suppose you have no idea who complained to the head office, do you Mrs. Dillon?"

"Not a clue."

"When we spoke to Mr. Temple, Jerome's uncle, he said Jerome left him an urgent message while he was away on vacation last weekend. Jerome said he needed to speak to him about a problem at work as soon as he got back. Unfortunately, by the time Mr. Temple returned, Jerome was dead. Any ideas what that problem at work could have been Mrs. Dillon?

She clasped her hands together on top of her desk and looked directly at Deek with a sphinx-like expression. Then repeated her pat answer. "Sorry. Not a clue, Detective."

"We questioned several of your employees but one in particular gave us the most useful information. A close friend of the victim's, Alonzo Woods said that Mr. Johnson was terminated about two weeks ago right after failing a random drug test. Jerome's wife also said she spoke to you when she tried to track down her husband and you told her he had been fired for failing a random drug test earlier that same day. If that's correct, I'd like to get a copy of the test results for all those employees who were randomly selected to undergo drug testing that day," said Deek, firmly.

Renee noticed that Mrs. Dillon's unwavering look of calmness began to crack.

"Uh, Alonzo was mistaken as usual. And Mrs. Johnson, poor thing, was so hysterical that night I doubt she could recall anything we talked about. Fact is, the test wasn't quite random, Detective. I requested that Jerome be tested on the basis of reasonable suspicion."

"What suspicion, Mrs. Dillon?"

"Well, like it says on his record he'd been coming into work late, his eyes looked red, and 'course I was suspicious since I knew about his prior drug problem. I just wanted to be sure he wasn't slipping back into old habits."

"I see. Since you specifically requested this test for Mr. Johnson based on your own belief of his using drugs," said Deek, "I'll need you to explain your company's drug testing procedure in detail."

Odessa Dillon removed her jacket and leaned back with her arms folded under her chest. She attempted to hide her annoyance but wasn't able to disguise the chill in her stare. She explained that UDS used a private company but they still followed federal government regulations mandating that drivers and personnel operating heavy equipment be randomly tested. However, a supervisor could request that an employee be tested if they suspected drug use. That was her justification for requesting that a drug test be performed—reasonable suspicion.

"How does the technician identify the person being tested? In other words, how do they ensure that the sample matches the person being tested and this person is who they claim to be?" he asked.

"Ah, I see why you're an investigator, Detective Hamilton. You do have a suspicious mind, just like me," she smiled. "Well you see, the contractor comes to our work site and brings their own testing supplies, cups, and whatnot. I sign what's called a chain of custody form to authorize the drug testing. On the form there's a pre-printed form number, say, 456 as an example. The form also has a peel off label with the same identifying number of 456."

Deek took notes on his Blackberry™ as Mrs. Dillon explained the company procedure.

"This form has the employee's name, phone number, social security number, and other information to identify him. The technician peels off the label and affixes it to the urine sample cup. Next the employee shows his or her picture ID like a driver's license to the technician and the technician matches this to what it says on the form."

"Umhum, I see," Deek nodded, "Go on, Mrs. Dillon."

"The employee then provides his urine sample in the labeled cup. Afterwards, the technician sends the sample to the laboratory for analysis and the results are recorded in an automated system called HEIDI. Is that detailed enough for you, sugar?"

"Yes, Ma'am. Please continue," said Deek, crossing one ankle over his knee. "Who has access to the results?"

"As the supervisor I can access HEIDI to obtain the results of my employee's test results by typing in his social security number. The results will show either positive (presents of drugs) or negative (no presence of drugs)."

"Is there a printed record of the results?"

"Yes, I can print out these results and show them to the employee, which is exactly what I did with Jerome. Positive results can be justification for dismissal. That's why Jerome was terminated two weeks ago. His test results turned up positive."

"Thank you for explaining the process so thoroughly, Mrs. Dillon. It sounds full proof enough. Would you mind pulling up Jerome's test results now and printing out a copy for me to take with me?"

"Of course, Detective. Is that about all you think you'll need 'cause I'm running late for an appointment."

"Yes, Ma'am. That should be sufficient and we'll get out of your way."

"No problem, Darlin'," she said and turned to her computer to key-in Jerome's social security number that she obtained from his employment record.

In seconds the drug test results printed out on the printer next to her workstation. Deek read the report that Odessa handed him and verified Jerome's identifying information in the top half of the document. He read the test results that indicated Positive for traces of cocaine and marijuana in Jerome's system. He folded up the report and placed it in his coat pocket.

"Everything appears to be in order. Thanks again for your cooperation, Mrs. Dillon." Deek held Renee's coat while she slipped her arms through. As they walked out, he placed his arms around her waist. "Well, that didn't turn up much," he said, "Let's hope we have more luck talking to this ex-girlfriend, Leenae Lewis. Even if she's innocent, she may know of someone Jerome dealt with who wanted him dead."

Renee sensed the frustration in Deek's voice and the hopelessness on his face. It didn't give her much hope that they could help get Brenda out of trouble any time soon. She knew she had to get home today to check on her cat, Angel and finish packing. Although, her housekeeper, Chizuko had been coming daily to feed the cat, Renee had grown very fond of her former nemesis and wanted to make sure she wasn't too lonely in that big house all day. Angel would love the small, cozy rowhouse they were moving into next Saturday. It marked a new beginning for both of them. Ever since Bill left, Renee was surprised that Angel didn't seem to miss him any longer. She had to admit, neither did she.

Deek held the car door open while Renee climbed in. She was glad she didn't see Alonzo in the yard with the other workers when they left. A single dose of his flirtatious behavior was enough for one day. Just as they were about to drive away, Deek's pager went off with an urgent message. He put the car in park and returned the page from his cell phone. After the call, he flipped the phone shut and turned to Renee.

"That was the Assistant US Attorney's office calling about another case," he said, "I'm also assigned to an ongoing investigation involving a series of unsolved murders. They have a witness and all detectives working on the case must be present to question this witness. If I'm not in the room, they'll postpone it and that won't be good. I gotta go Sweetheart. They're starting in twenty minutes and it'll probably take a couple of hours."

"I understand, Deek," she said, disappointed, "You go ahead. I'll catch a cab home."

Deek dialed a taxi from his cell phone and gave the taxi service the location at UDS's main office. The taxi service said they had a cab in the area and one would be there in five minutes.

"Wait right out front, Baby and promise me you won't go traipsing off to see Miss Lewis without me. As soon as I get out of the meeting, I'll stop by your place and pick you up, okay?"

Renee nodded but didn't seem thrilled to just sit, wait, and do nothing. He got out of the car to open her door and they leaned against the car and kissed good-bye.

"What about Jerome's possessions, Deek? Do you want me to take them to the Adams residence?"

"No, that can wait. Brenda's in no position to receive these things now anyway. I'll take care of it later."

"Don't forget to take out Leenae's picture before you return Jerome's things to Brenda's family." she said.

"Most definitely. It's settled then. You go home and I'll meet you there in about two hours," he said. "We'll pay Leenae a visit later this evening. Then I'll take you someplace quiet for dinner and we can go over the facts again and try to come up with a new strategy. I'm not giving up on Brenda, so don't look so defeated, Renee."

"All right Deek. I trust you, Honey."

"Oh, I almost forgot. I have something for you," he said, leaning into the car to retrieve a package from the glove compartment. "Perhaps, this'll cheer you up. I was saving it to give you tonight but you may as well have it now." Deek held out a beautifully wrapped small gift box and a letter.

"It's a belated birthday present, Darling. Promise me you'll wait until you get home to open it. Make sure you're somewhere comfortable and romantic with no distractions," he smiled, then kissed her again.

"I promise. Thank you, Sweetheart," she whispered and buried the gift and letter deep inside her purse.

Deek hopped back into the car and dashed off. A late afternoon spate of sunshine had melted the early morning snowfall. The wet pavement glistened from a slick coating of slush. Renee walked carefully to UDS's front entrance and stood at curbside to wait for her taxi. The same guard that Deek spoke to earlier when they first arrived ran towards her just as a taxicab turned the corner into UDS.

"Good thing I caught you, Doctor," the guard said, out of breath.

"I believe that's my taxi pulling up. I was on my way home. Can I help you with something, Mr. Fletcher?" said Renee, reading the name on the ID tag pinned to his shirt.

"The Detective said you folks came to pickup Jerome's belongings from his locker. I forgot to mention to him that we also got employee mail slots. I checked Jerome's mailbox and found this."

The guard gave her a sealed white envelope with Jerome Johnson written on front.

"Will you make sure his wife gets this?" said the guard, "and tell his family I'm really sorry. Jerome was a good man. I'll miss him."

"I'll be glad to, Mr. Fletcher," said Renee and put the envelope in her purse, "Thank you.

"I guess this is your cab," said the guard and opened the rear passenger door.

"Looks like it."

"Are you here to pickup Dr. Renee Hayes?" she asked the taxi driver.

The cabdriver nodded and turned down his music when Renee climbed in the back seat.

CHAPTER 40

O dessa Dillon burrowed her eyebrows together in a frown, and the muscles in her face grew tense. She tried to remain calm and not read anything into that Detective's questions about the drug test. But she couldn't shake the feeling that he and Dr. Hayes suspected something. What if they realized that Jerome's drug test had been falsified to give her a legitimate reason to fire him? He had been good at his job and customers loved him. No matter how often she probed the regulars on his route for negative feedback they always gave glowing survey responses about him. So she also had to fabricate some trumped up charges on his employment records since the only complaints Jerome ever received came from her.

Odessa tapped her pen rapidly on the desk and went back over her plan to make sure she hadn't made any slipups that could lead the cops back to her. Unfortunately she had needed to rely on that ignoramus Alonzo Woods to carry out her dirty work. She knew Alonzo was used to being controlled by a woman at home because she had met his bossy wife, Izza at a company picnic last summer. And when Odessa found out that he indulged in recreational drug use with cocaine and marijuana, she knew she had him by the balls. He was just four years away from early retirement and he would lose his pension if she fired him. Odessa started Alonzo out on small tasks like sending messages, and being her eyes and ears in the yard to find out who the troublemakers were. Even though he tried to play macho around the young ladies at work who didn't know any better, Alonzo Woods didn't stray too far from his wife's apron's strings. Like his wife at home, Odessa manipulated him at work like a puppeteer working the strings.

Just before planning the arson-murder, Odessa had sent Alonzo over to Jerome's house to tempt him with an easy run and a raise if he'd come back to work and be her boy toy. But Alonzo came back and reported that not only had Jerome rejected her offer, he planned on filing a sexual harassment lawsuit and hostile workplace complaint against her. If Jerome talked, other complaints about her might start to surface, especially from Hector Gonzales who might get the idea to join Jerome's lawsuit. She had no choice after learning what he planned to do once his uncle got back from Vegas. Jerome Johnson had outlived his usefulness on earth, if he ever had any.

Odessa recalled the moment she realized that Jerome was not going to play footsie with her like Hector had reluctantly done in order to save his job. She had ordered her flunky, Alonzo to come to her office and let her know the minute Jerome had returned from his afternoon run. She had waited all day for him to get back from his Thursday afternoon deliveries. Odessa watched him at the break room entrance for several minutes like a lioness stalking her prey. She saw that Jerome relaxed and joked around with the other guys in the break room. Not one to hide her robust figure under a tent-sized, muumuu or loose clothing, she sashayed up to him wearing a tight, too-short skirt and matching polyester-blend jacket in shouting tomato red. She had planned to make a move on Jerome that day so she purposely wore red since red always made her feel hot. Underneath the suit, she wore a white shell in stretchy fabric that revealed her large, dark nipples. Odessa knew she had failed the managerial professional dress code miserably that day and didn't give a damn. She easily recalled their conversation in the break room.

"I need to talk to you for a minute, Jerome," said Odessa, standing over him and trying to sound professional in front of the other workers.

"My load ran late and I'm waiting out my time, Miss Dillon, since I didn't get to take lunch," Jerome explained.

"I understand Jerome. I just wanna speak to you for a minute in private before you punch out," she said.

Jerome followed his boss to her office and she locked the door once they were inside.

"Sit down, Darlin'," said Odessa in a sweet voice and pointed to the couch.

When he did, she sat in a chair across from him and crossed her legs. Her skirt rode up her thighs when she sat down. She knew it would. She could see that Jerome had tried not to stare at her big legs but couldn't help looking. She knew her legs were her best feature. She rubbed her hand down one bare leg, pleased that he hadn't been able to look away. That's when she told him that she never wore stockings even in winter because stockings chaffed her thighs when she walked. She gave him a red lip-glossed smile and puckered up her lips in an air kiss.

"Like what you see, Sugar? I know I do. Lawd, I declare, Brother, you are so fine." At first she mistook Jerome's gawking at her as one of desire but he soon made his true feelings known when he abruptly rose from the sofa. "If that's all Miss Dillon, I wanna get back to my break time."

That's when Odessa's smile abruptly faded. She was humiliated by his rejection and even worse, she feared he might make fun of her to his buddies. Her flirtations had worked with Hector Gonzales, but it hadn't worked with Jerome Johnson. She could tell Jerome wasn't afraid of her the way Hector had been. She walked over to her desk and opened the bottom desk drawer and pulled out his employment record. She showed him a list of customer complaints that said he was too slow making runs and where it said that customers didn't like his attitude.

"Who said that about me, Miss Dillon? 'Cause I get along with everybody as far as I know."

"You know I can't divulge that information, Sugar. They responded to the satisfaction survey anonymously. Looka here, Honey, this whole misunderstanding with those silly customers can be forgotten. I got an opening for a feeder driver and I see here in your file where it says you got your CDL license before coming here. If I was to recommend you to Mr. Clarke upstairs you know the job's as good as yours, Darlin'."

"No thanks, Miss Dillon. I like my route and I don't mind working extra shifts if I have to."

Then his face turned serious. "I hope you dig where I'm coming from and we can act like this never happened. If you think I'm just gonna play along with the game you worked on Hector, you messin' with the wrong dude. I'm here to do my job and that's it."

Jerome unlocked the door to her office and left, leaving Odessa standing with her arms folded and a scowl on her face. Odessa recalled that's when she decided to come in late one night when no one was there and install a hidden camera in the break room so she could watch and listen to see if he made any slipups. But after several days of monitoring the hidden camera and not seeing anything incriminating, she hatched her plan to have Jerome tested for drugs so she could have grounds for firing him. Realizing that he would more than likely pass the drug test, she made Alonzo switch his urine sample for Jerome's and trick the technician into believing it was Jerome's sample. That way Jerome was certain to fail since she knew Alonzo had a serious substance abuse problem.

Odessa knew the technicians checked driver's license as a form of valid ID before collecting the sample. So the first step was to get her hands on a fake D. C. Driver's license with Alonzo's picture on it and Jerome's name, address and other identifying information printed on it. Odessa was able to easily find everything she needed from the Internet.

She ordered the fake driver's license online made to specification with Jerome's information that she wrote on the order form and a photo of Alonzo that she provided. The license arrived in no time, shipped right to her door, next day air. When she received the so-called novelty driver's license in the mail, she was amazed at how authentic it looked. The hologram was flawless, and even the bar code and magnetic stripe worked. Jerome took the drug test that day as scheduled and so did Alonzo. As she suspected, Jerome's results came out negative but Odessa destroyed them and printed out Alonzo's positive test result that matched with Jerome's ID.

The ID card was the only loose thread that could tie her and Alonzo to Jerome. She had to follow-up just to make sure that idiot Alonzo destroyed the fake driver's license like she had told him to do. Odessa paged Alonzo and ordered him to report to her office immediately. She paced the floor nervously until he knocked lightly on the door before entering. Before he had a chance to get through the door, she pounced on him.

"What did you blab to that homicide cop with your big mouth?"

"Nut'n. I threw him a bone about the girlfriend and his mother-in-law always givin' Jay the blues, that's all, Boss. Oh yeah, and I may have mentioned a phone call he got a few weeks ago while we was in the break room. Some bad ass dudes who wanted the loot he owed 'em," Alonzo explained, "But I swear I ain't say *nada* 'bout you, Boss."

He wiped the sweat from his brow. "Miss Dillon, you know how hard I tried to get Jay to go along with the program like Hector did but Jerome wasn't buying."

"Yeah, well, I tried to convince him too but the Brother just didn't want no parts of this. And he would have liked it too. Unless he was gay. Yeah, I bet that was it, Jerome Johnson had to be gay. Why else would he turn down all this good lovin'?" said Odessa, reflectively.

"Yeah, I'm sure that was it, Boss. You never know nowadays when a Brother is on the down low. Just 'cause he got a wife and kids at home or a girlfriend, that don't mean shit."

"That's right, and I don't have any problems with that. But when he told you he was planning to file a sexual harassment claim against me as soon as his uncle got back from vacation, that was going too damn far. You know I had no choice after that," she said with a wild-eyed expression. "No way could I let that weasel destroy my empire I spent over 20 years building."

"Alonzo, you did get rid of the fake driver's license right away, didn't you? That ID had your picture on it so you could take the drug test using Jerome's name and information. That means it ties you and me to the crime."

Odessa dazed out the window to reflect again on her brilliant plan and how everything had worked like clockwork. She didn't notice Alonzo's face had turned red and he was still stammering some explanation that she wasn't listening to until she heard him say "I lost it."

Odessa lunged at him. "You did what?"

"I think I lost it in the parking lot outside. I'm sorry, Boss," he stammered.

Alonzo described what happened the day he took the drug test while he was leaving work. He put the license in his coat pocket but at some point while he was walking across the lot, maybe after he reached in his pocket to get a cigarette, the ID fell out without him realizing it. As soon as he got home he felt inside his pocket for the ID so he could cut it up and throw it away, but it wasn't there. So he drove back to work and searched the entire lot but didn't find it. He figured somebody turned it into lost and found. Then the mail clerk must have dropped it into Jerome's mailbox since his name and address was on it. If the person who found it didn't know Jerome personally, they wouldn't know the picture wasn't him. Alonzo admitted he was too scared to tell Odessa about his blunder.

"You are such a fuck up, Alonzo Woods!"

She picked up the telephone and called the security guard. "Fletcher, I need you to go by Lost and Found in the mailroom and see if Jerome Johnson has anything sitting in his mail slot. Bring me whatever's there, you hear?"

"Yes, Ma'am, I already done that just now and I found an envelope with Jerome's name on it."

"Good, then bring it to me immediately. It's probably his driver's license that I need to turn into DMV," she said, silently giving thanks to the Lord that Fletcher found it in time.

"You know Miss Dillon, come to think of it, that envelope did feel sorta like it had a plastic card in it—somethin' like a driver's license," said the guard.

"Just bring the goddamn envelope to my office right now, Fletcher! I don't have all damn day to sit here and listen to your simple mumblings."

"I can't do that right now, Ma'am."

"Fletcher, I'm giving you a direct order. You don't want me to write you up for insubordination do you?"

"No, Ma'am. What I mean is I already gave that envelope to Dr. Hayes. She and the Detective said they came in to get Jerome's things to return to his family. I didn't know what was in the envelope but since it had Jerome's name on it, I gave it to the lady doctor. The Detective had already gone and I just caught her in the neck of time before she got in the taxi to go home. You didn't say nothin' about giving you Jerome's things. You told me they came to get his stuff so I gave it to 'em."

"Never mind," she snapped and hung up. "I'm surrounded by incompetents."

Odessa grabbed a D. C. directory and frantically looked up Dr. Renee Hayes's residence.

"There it is. Foxhall Crescent Estates in Northwest Washington. I know exactly where that is," she grinned.

"If she hasn't looked inside the envelope yet, I'll sweet talk it out of her and tell her that it's a company ID badge and we don't release those to terminated employees and she will have to return it so that the badge can be deactivated. Yeah, that sounds good," she said to herself.

"But what if she's already opened the envelope and looked inside, Miss Odessa, Ma'am?" said Alonzo. Odessa jerked her head around to glare at Alonzo. She had forgotten he was still standing there. "Then she's one dead pigeon," said Odessa and slammed the phone directory down on her desk.

"I'm not gon' hurt Dr. Renee for you or anybody, Boss."

"Fine, I'll do it myself. You'd probably screw it up anyway."

"I don't like this," he said, shaking his head, "Dr. Renee's a nice lady. I don't know how I lit Jay up with that gasoline. Musta been so fucked up on that shit I didn't know what I was doin'."

"That sorry excuse won't even buy you a pack of Kools, Idiot," said Odessa. "No jury's gonna feel sorry for you just because you happened to be doped up at the time."

"I can't let you kill Dr. Renee, Boss."

"Look, Dimwit, let me spell it out for you. We don't have a choice because you screwed up. If Dr. Hayes finds out what's in that envelope, she'll show it to those Detectives and they'll be on our asses like flies on shit," said Odessa. "I'm going to get that envelope back. With any luck I won't have to off anybody else to do it. But I will if I have to."

"Now go home and stay put. If anybody asks you anything keep your stupid mouth shut for a change," she snarled, "Wait for my call. I'll let you know when we're in the clear."

Odessa snatched her coat off the hanger and ran out the door.

CHAPTER 41

When Renee walked in the door, she heard her telephone ringing and ran through the hall to pick it up. It was the adoption attorney who told her that he was able to get the court to grant her legal guardianship of the border baby at George Washington University Hospital. As soon as her attorney uttered those words Renee nearly dropped the phone. She covered her grinning mouth with one hand and held onto the phone with the other as her eyes grew moist from happiness. She felt lightheaded listening to the attorney run down all the details so she sank down into the closest chair. He told her that he had had no problems convincing the Court since Renee had a past history working with CASA and Child and Family Services. The attorney said he had been working with a licensed child-placing agency to ensure that they satisfied all the Court's requirements. It also helped that she had already gone through background checks, attended counseling, and parent classes over the summer when she had re-initiated adoption procedures to try and adopt a child with her husband. Not only that, her colleagues had given her glowing recommendations for guardianship. Renee nearly laughed out loud at being on the receiving end of so much good news all at once, after just a few days ago hearing nothing but distressing news. This time she had finally completed the adoption process—alone.

However, Renee was disappointed, but not surprised to learn that the closed adoption records contained very little information on baby Jane Doe. Belinda, the baby's biological mother, had no last name that anyone knew of, and the records noted that she was deceased. Under father, the adoption records indicated unknown. The last piece of information her attorney needed for the birth certificate was to record the child's name.

"Have you thought of a name for your baby, Dr. Hayes?" her attorney asked, "We've been referring to her as baby Jane Doe but now that the paperwork is practically complete, I'd like to request that a name be put on her birth certificate."

This was all too wonderful to be true! Just like that, it was the moment she had been waiting for practically all her life—the moment other parents looked forward to—the honor and responsibility of naming their baby. Now it was her turn! Renee closed her eyes and pictured the baby in her mind. A medium brown complexion similar in shade to her own skin tone. Soft black curls, dark brown oval eyes, a tiny upturned nose, and bow-shaped, pink lips—all inherited from her biological mother's best features. Suddenly it came to her that she'd name her baby after Deek's grandmother Katia who he often said he admired so much for her strength, wisdom, and gentleness.

"Her name's Katia Belinda Hayes. That's the name you should have them record on her birth certificate," said Renee, with finality in her voice.

When she hung up she still couldn't stop grinning at the idea of becoming a mommy, which was now no longer an idea, but a reality. Everything had happened so fast! She had a million things to do to prepare a nursery in their new house and buy baby necessities. She knew she could count on her friend, the foster mother, Shirley Ann to help her shop and give her advice. If Brenda were not going through her own troubles right now, she would have been there for her too. Renee couldn't be too sure about Veda or Cha-Cha, but strangely enough she was beginning to understand what it felt like to have actual girlfriends to share good times as well as the bad times. Of course, the first person she planned to tell was Deek when he stopped by later that evening to pick her up. He had told her that she had a good chance of being approved when she confided to him that she had contacted an adoption attorney, but Renee didn't want to get her hopes up so she didn't want to believe it could really happen. Deek wouldn't be at all surprised. He knew she had fallen in love with the baby the moment she burst into the world and landed in her arms and he was right.

Renee went into the kitchen to check on Angel's food dish and found Chizuko had already been by earlier and left food for her cat. She poured Evian water into a crystal glass and went upstairs to her bedroom to open the gift and letter from Deek. This was truly a day for excitement, she thought as she reclined on her loveseat. Angel immediately leaped up and curled in her lap. Renee removed the sealed envelope addressed to Jerome and placed it on the end table beside her. Then she dug deeper in her purse until she found the gift box and Deek's letter. Renee stroked the cat with one hand and neatly unwrapped the small box with the other. She gasped in awe as she lifted out an 18 karat gold necklace with a single row of three descending diamonds, each diamond larger than the next. She dropped the necklace back in the box and ripped open his letter. As she read, a perpetual smile remained on her face.

My love,

Hopefully you are reading this letter while soaking in a warm bath or lounging in your favorite chair and enjoying a glass of chilled Chardonnay. I bought this gift for your birthday over two weeks ago but didn't think it was appropriate to give to you until now. If you are opening the gift box, you see it has an 18 karat gold 'three stone' necklace. The smallest diamond represents our past, the middle one symbolizes the present, and the last and largest diamond is for our future together. I wanted to do something special for your birthday even then, but as you were still living with Bill I didn't feel comfortable interjecting myself in your life. Now that things are different, I want to shower you with all the gifts, love, and attention a woman like you needs and deserves, if you let me. As my Martinican grandmother used to say, in French, of course, "Quand une porte se ferme, un meilleur s'ouvre" ... which simply means "When one door closes, a better one opens." I want to be the man standing behind the next door you open. I promise it will be a better one.

Renee, I understand how the events in your life could lead to insecure feelings. Why you sometimes doubt that others truly love you and happiness is elusive. But from the first moment we met, I felt drawn to your beauty and warm demeanor. There was an unexplainable desire to get to know you and it didn't go away. I knew there was something special, something that comes only once in a lifetime. However, as with any true love, you have to let it go for a while. This feeling has to be put to the test of time. Although we've only known each other four months I feel closer to you than I have to any other woman I've been involved with.

Sweetheart, I know you need time to heal from the terrible loss of your baby and resolving any lingering ties you still have with Bill now that you are legally separated. I know you've suffered hurts and disappointments and I can't make them go away but I want to be there in your life for the pleasure and the sorrows. Renee, you are a beautiful and passionate woman. Your age, my age—does not matter to me. I only bring it up now because I know that is another doubt you have about our compatibility. I know you're not perfect and neither am I. It takes two people to make a relationship go bad and two people together to make it strong. I have confidence that you and I can build a life together. I hope one day you'll feel strong enough to completely let go of all superficial routines just because they're familiar to you and take the risk to truly love. When you're ready, Darling, I'll be waiting.

Je t'aime ma chérie.

Deek

Renee wiped a tear from her eye and refolded the letter then stored it in her box of treasured mementos. She checked the clock on the end table to see how much longer it would be before he'd get there and realized it would be at least another hour. She missed him already. The envelope addressed to Jerome Johnson leaned against the lamp base. She thought about how awful Brenda would feel if she had picked up Jerome's belongings and discovered the heart-shaped picture of Leenae among his things. She wanted to be sure the envelope didn't contain anything that would cause Brenda more pain. Renee picked up the envelope and tore it open. A driver's license fell onto the carpeted floor face up.

"This doesn't belong to Jerome," she said out loud to herself, "That's Alonzo's photo."

She picked up the license and examined the information printed on it. It listed Jerome Johnson's name and address, a birth date that she knew was too late to be Alonzo's date of birth, as well as a height and weight of 5' 10," 165 pounds. These vital statistics belonged to Jerome not Alonzo Woods. That's when she realized the driver's license had to be a fake.

Odessa Dillon, Jerome's supervisor had explained that an ID was required to identify the person taking the drug test. Now, Renee understood how Odessa and Alonzo falsified Jerome's drug test results so that he would fail but she didn't know why Odessa wanted to terminate him. Jerome didn't start having problems at work until they reassigned him to her unit and he began reporting to her.

Renee picked up the phone to call Deek but placed the receiver back. She didn't want to leave a message about something this important. She figured he would not be able to get away from the interrogation in order to take her phone call. She'd have to wait for him to get there since he told her he couldn't be reached during the meeting in the Assistant US Attorney's office. Briefly, she considered contacting Detective Bradford but dismissed the idea as a waste of time. She didn't trust him to follow-up on a new lead. Bradford wouldn't prolong the Johnson investigation a minute longer even if it meant getting to the truth. He'd probably think the novelty license with Alonzo's picture and Jerome's information was just a practical joke. Perhaps, it was, but she wanted to find out why. She called UDS and requested that the receptionist on the evening shift page Alonzo. Perhaps, he was still there. When the receptionist finally came back to the phone, she told Renee that Alonzo Woods had left work for the day.

Renee knew she was taking her role as consultant on the case too far. If either Deek or Bradford knew what she was thinking of doing, they'd remove her from the case for breaking one of their cardinal rules. But she had to do something. Brenda was being charged with a capital murder offense that Bradford believed had been executed with the aid of a co-conspirator. Renee had to pursue her hunch that Odessa Dillon was the one behind Jerome's murder so Brenda could be vindicated. She shouldn't have to spend the weekend in jail for a crime she didn't commit.

Renee thought back to Jerome's funeral when Deek had questioned Alonzo. At that time Alonzo told them where he lived on 16th Street, SE in Capitol East. Renee figured she could get Alonzo to talk easier if they were alone. He would feel threatened if Deek were there. That's the one thing Alonzo loved to do, talk to the ladies. She'd go see Alonzo and accept his offer to take her to that rib joint. There had to at least be a salad on the menu she could eat. Once on his own turf and relaxed, she'd break down Alonzo's defenses and get a confession out of him. She ran down the stairs, picked up her camel-colored wool coat, and stuffed the fake driver's license inside one of the pockets. With her coat draped over her arm, she opened her front door only to find Odessa Dillon standing on her porch about to ring the bell.

"Mrs. Dillon? How did you get through the neighborhood security gates without the pass code?"

"Hah, some security ya'll got in this fancy place," said Odessa and elbowed her way pass Renee to step inside. "All I did was wait for a resident to enter and piggy-backed behind him. Sugar, I coulda gone down the block and back before those dang gates would close."

A look of distress crossed Renee's face when she recalled Deek telling her a few weeks ago to contact their security management firm and let them know the gate was defective. But with everything that had happened in the past several days, she had forgotten to call. Now here was this demented woman who she knew was at least partially responsible for Jerome's murder, standing less than a foot away from her and blocking the exit.

"What do you want, Mrs. Dillon? As you can see I'm on my way out," Renee said in a curt tone.

"You know very well what I want? You opened that envelope didn't you? I can tell by the scared look on your face that you know. That's too bad, Dr. Hayes. Just like Jerome, now you've given me no choice."

"Why did you kill him, or did Alonzo do it for you?" Renee asked, trying to appear calm while her heart pounded.

"I tried to give Jerome another chance to come back to work but he wanted to sue me for sexual harassment instead. He was gonna betray me so I had to eliminate him. My only mistake was getting that idiot Alonzo Woods to be my hitman. Damn, how could I have been so stupid!" she cursed herself aloud, "I shoulda taken care of Jerome Johnson myself instead of relying on a moron to be able to follow simple orders. If you want something done right, do it yourself. Now, hand over that fake driver's license," Odessa demanded and held out her hand.

"I can't. It's evidence."

Renee clutched her overcoat and ran up the stairs as Odessa followed. If she could just get to her bedroom and lock the door, she might have time to call 911. Just as Renee made it to the door and was about to slam it shut, Odessa's large hand grabbed her wrist and held it tightly. Odessa held her from behind and twisted her arm. The coat fell to the floor. She sensed Odessa's hot, panting breath at the back of her neck.

"Now, I'll ask you again—nicely. Where's that ID, Sugar?"

"In my coat pocket," said Renee, gasping out of breath from the sprint up the stairs.

Odessa released Renee and reached into her handbag then pulled out a stun gun. She pointed its neon blue bolts of electrical probes menacingly at Renee while stooping down to pick up the coat. She searched each pocket and yanked the fake ID out then tossed the coat across the floor.

"Good. Now, all I gotta do is take care of you. Let's go," she said and shoved Renee forward.

"Go where?" She was trying to stall for time in the hopes that Deek would soon get there.

"For a ride. You don't think I'm stupid enough to whack you in here, do you? I know just the deserted place to dump your body where nobody'll find you for a long, long time, if ever," said Odessa with a lurid smile. "After a few days, the flies and maggots'll get a buffet feast off your rottin' corpse. Now walk, Sistah. My car's conveniently right out front."

Odessa held Renee around the waist from behind and clutched the stun gun in her free hand as she nudged her victim from the bedroom into the hallway. Suddenly, Renee whipped around and pinched Odessa in her plump upper thigh as hard as she could.

"Ouch! Damnit, bitch!" she hollered and released her hold on Renee long enough to rub her bruised inner thigh.

Renee dashed downstairs and bumped into a marble pedestal, knocking over a baroque statuette that crashed to pieces on the foyer floor. She ran out the door with Odessa chasing behind her. Renee was in better physical shape than Odessa and she seemed to be making ground as Odessa struggled to catch up. She headed for her neighbor's estate and prayed someone would be home to let her in. She yelled for help but the street was deserted and no one responded. Suddenly, she tripped over a loose tree branch and bruised her leg. Odessa was now right up on her. Renee didn't get much farther before Odessa's strong arm wrapped itself around her neck and pulled her backward. Then Odessa shot her with the stun gun. Renee stumbled forward from the electrical zap and immediately felt disoriented. Her vision turned blurry. She tried to scream, but nothing came out. Still she tried to will herself to remain conscious. Renee fought to resist the numbing effects of the stun gun but now she didn't have the strength to release herself from Odessa's grip after being stunned. Her feet dragged behind as Odessa hauled Renee's temporarily incapacitated body towards the car. Odessa looked around briefly before shoving Renee into the passenger's seat.

As if coming out of a trance, Renee began to stir from her listless, incoherent stupor. She didn't know how much time had elapsed. It was dusk and a slate-gray fog had drifted low to the ground. She glanced out the car window for a street name or some familiar landmark as Odessa drove along a narrow winding road. Moments later, her abductor turned into an empty graveled lot and climbed out the car then pulled Renee to her feet.

The temperature had dropped to a biting cold wind. Without a coat, Renee folded her arms around her body to keep warm. She stumbled over her feet when Odessa propelled her forward and stared out to study her surroundings through blurry eyes. An enclave of decaying buildings dwelled amidst a vast, open track of sloping landscape interspersed with densely populated evergreens and wild undergrowth.

Trees had begun to shed their needles from the onset of winter. Renee jumped when a gray squirrel dashed in front of her and scampered across the tall brown grass.

"Where are we?" asked Renee.

"I guess it won't hurt none to tell you now, Sugar," answered Odessa with a crooked half-smile, "since we're completely isolated here and it's about to become your burial grounds."

"We're at the National Park Seminary. As you can see it's got a heap of land and a whole mess of condemned buildings plopped up on it and not a soul in sight," said Odessa, waving her arm as a pointer. "Since it's been designated a historic site these old buildings won't be demolished any time soon. That means by the time somebody comes digging through here, the only thing left of you will be your bones."

Renee saw a highway in the distance but there was no way to get to it. "Are we still in the city?" she asked, trying to get her bearings in the hope of escape.

"No, Darlin' we're in Forest Glen, Maryland, in the suburbs, just outside Washington, D. C. I came upon this place last year when I had to go out to UDS's Maryland branch office. Since I'm a bit of a history buff, I did some research on it."

Renee recalled seeing the folder about the Seminary in Odessa's office. She figured if she could keep the woman talking, it might buy her more time. "So what did you find out?" asked Renee, feigning interest.

"Some of these buildings have been here since the late 1800's. The Seminary used to be a finishing school for well-off young ladies," Odessa explained, "But during World War II, the Army took possession of it to provide more bed space for patients. It's gone to pot over the years 'cause it costs too dang much to maintain. Other than its historical value, the Glen, as they call it, has basically been left unattended with no practical use. So, Darlin' nobody's gonna come looking for you out here."

As they walked through the dilapidated grounds, Renee gazed at the mishmash architecture representing Victorian-styled mansions, colonials, Swiss chalets, a blue-framed Dutch windmill, and even a Japanese pagoda—all in varying degrees of deterioration. Wildflowers added color around bronzed boxwoods and freeze damaged shrubs. Renee realized there was no use reasoning with Odessa. She'd already killed once. She had to catch her off guard and overpower her. Getting her to talk about the Seminary buildings seemed to distract her. With Renee's prodding questions, Odessa pointed out features and explained their significance.

Renee walked carefully along a tree-framed cliff and felt a surge of dizziness whenever she looked down. They approached a rickety boardwalk that was nothing but a wooden plank and rail. A ravine of greenish-gray water that ultimately funneled into Rock Creek swirled below. Renee stopped dead in her tracks. She feared Odessa planned to throw her over the bridge.

As if reading her victim's mind, Odessa sneered, "That's right, Dr. Hayes, by the time you hit the bottom of that 80 foot drop, the rocks should crush your skull so you'll be killed instantly and won't feel a thing. That's not a bad way to go, is it Sugar?" Odessa smiled wickedly, "I try to be humane. I'm sure Jerome was already dead from the smoke before he felt any fire."

Renee spotted a large piece of splintered wood next to her foot. She knew she had to act now. She bent down to pick up the log and flailed it at Odessa—missing her head by only a fraction. Odessa grasped her wrist and seized the log, tossing it to the ground. She pulled Renee's wrist back hard and twisted it. Renee screamed in pain and stumbled forward. Then Odessa backhanded her with hard knuckles. Renee clumped to the wet ground and felt drips of blood seep from her nose.

The left brow of Odessa's badly plucked, arched eyebrows lifted in surprise. "That wasn't too smart, Sugar. You've made me mad. Now, instead of a painless death, you'll feel it. March," she yelled and poked a fist in Renee's back.

"Where are you taking me?" she pleaded.

Odessa refused to answer. Instead she shoved her victim forward down a winding path lined with thicket and trees. Just up ahead, a rundown castle sat like a fortress amidst a stretch of shrubbery and juniper trees. Their branches extended towards the moss-covered castle walls like claws. Renee stopped walking and asked Odessa about the lofty structure made of blotchy-gray stone.

"That's the Beta Castle. It used to serve as a sorority house for the girls. And at one time there was even a drawbridge. But I don't see how this history lesson's gonna help you none, Doll."

Two circular wings topped with steep-pitched roofs buttressed each end and towered above the castle's central structure. Small leaded windows exposed faint bursts of light but wooden planks boarded all the larger windows. At that moment, Renee knew her best defense would be to flee. If she could outrun Odessa, which shouldn't be too difficult, she might hide in the castle long enough for someone to find her. Maybe not the best plan but the only one she came up with. She figured Odessa didn't have a real gun because if she did, she would have used it by now. And she had probably exhausted all the electrical currents in her stun gun.

Suddenly, Renee took off towards the castle. Odessa chased after her. Renee leaped across a broken step obscured by shrubs as Odessa struggled to keep up with her. However, Odessa tumbled backwards on the broken step and cried out. Renee pushed through the dense ticket and trees without looking back. A heap of plywood blocked the entrance to the castle. Renee lifted armfuls and threw them aside. She realized it was dangerous to go inside the castle because of the rotten flooring and loose steps but she ran inside the main salon anyway to get away from Odessa.

She stumbled around in the dark openness, stepping carefully on loose floorboards and dirt flooring. When her eyes adjusted to the darkness, she noticed the scattered columns, the asymmetrical design of the building's interior, and the grotto-type rooms. She needed a place to hide, quick. Renee turned around when she heard a distinct sound behind her. Odessa's shadow stood at the doorway. After a few moments getting used to the darkness, Odessa came towards her.

"So, there you are," said Odessa in a matter-of-fact tone and standing only a few feet away.

Renee inched backwards away from her and bumped against an iron grate with wrought-iron bars. The grate rested loosely against a crumbled, wood-burning furnace. Odessa pushed Renee aside and removed the old iron grate, revealing an ash pit and a 3-foot high pass-through.

Odessa smiled triumphantly and volunteered another history lesson. "At one time, this pass-through served as an access tunnel for supplying wood logs and kindling to the furnace. Now, it'll serve as your tomb. Don't worry, Dr. Hayes, you should be comfortable in there," Odessa belted out a psychotic-sounding laugh.

"Mrs. Dillon ... Odessa, please don't do this," Renee begged, "You've already taken one life and you won't get away with it for long. It's only a matter of time before Alonzo talks to someone. That's how he is and you know it. With two capital murder offenses against you, you'll definitely face the death penalty."

"Save your breath, Dr. Hayes. Don't worry 'bout little ol' me. You're facing the death penalty right now, Darlin'."

Being much bigger and stronger, Odessa shoved Renee face first towards the dark hole. She braced her fall on the bed of ashes that felt like soft cement and could offer no resistance to Odessa's forceful attack. A 6-foot black snake slithered out in front of Renee, obviously not welcoming intruders to its ash pit home. Renee reared back and screamed while jutting backwards from the hole and in the process kicked Odessa in the knee. In a split second, Renee picked up a rusted shovel that she noticed next to the wall. She managed to hold Odessa at bay only momentarily.

Odessa lunged towards Renee palms up. Renee grabbed Odessa's first two fingers and bent them back all the way until she heard her knuckles crack and saw Odessa's distorted look of pain. But Odessa broke free and chased Renee up a split-level staircase. The long staircase led to a narrow landing then continued upward to a balcony. After a struggle, Odessa overpowered her again. She grasped Renee by the arm and twisted it behind her back. Odessa hammered her prey into the balcony. Renee's torso leaned forward over the balcony and the blood rushed straight to her head. She felt her knees buckle and the room seemed to float around her. The balcony ledge jammed against her chest and knocked the wind out of her. She struggled to breathe.

Odessa's laughter echoed throughout the castle's high, vaulted ceilings. She bent down to clutch one of Renee's ankles and propelled her forward even more. Renee used her one free hand to grip the railing to prevent herself from tumbling over but felt her sweaty palm slipping. She looked at the floor below and estimated a 30-foot drop from the balcony. She knew if the fall didn't kill her, she'd be seriously injured. For once in her life, she had something to live for, a man who truly loved her and a precious baby who needed a mother. She prayed to God to save her. It couldn't end like this.

In one quick move, Renee lifted her free foot to land a swift, hard kick in Odessa's groin. Odessa jumped back to get out the way and in the process released her hold on Renee. Odessa lunged at Renee with outstretched arms and renewed anger. Odessa ran towards her. Instinctively, Renee moved out the way. While in pursuit, Odessa slipped on a loose floorboard and sailed over the banister. She landed with a thump.

Renee looked down at Odessa's curled up body lying motionless on the floor. She rushed downstairs to check to see how badly she was injured. When Renee checked her pulse, there was no sign of life. Odessa's eyes stared out in a transfixed state and blood drizzled from her mouth. Odessa Dillon was dead.

Renee staggered up a narrow, two-lane road and saw its street sign, Linden Lane. She walked in the middle of the road and waved her arms over her head to stop a passing car. When the motorist stopped, she explained what happened and used his car phone to dial 911.

CHAPTER 42

F or the next few nights after Renee's narrow escape from death,
Deek wouldn't let her out of his sight. He insisted that she stay
at his place for a couple of days. Not wanting to be alone all night, she
didn't put up any resistance. It was almost time for her to move into
her own Victorian townhouse on 24th and I Street, NW with her newly
adopted, infant daughter, Katia. There were many wonderful changes
to come in her life, but right now being with him in his familiar
surroundings felt safe. Her mind was a jumble of thoughts as she lay
stretched out on Deek's bed, only half watching a British film classic
called *Brief Encounter,* and waited for him to come home from the
station. The television was the only thing she could figure out how to
operate in this high-tech house full of gizmos and gadgetry. She sipped
from a glass of burgundy and its rich dry flavor warmed her insides.

Every now and then she caught more of the Noel Coward movie,
and at some point she began to relate to the heroine's overwhelming
feelings of love for a man that she could not share her life with because
they both already had ties and obligations to someone else. Renee did
not want to let in old doubts about her future with Deek and mar
her current happiness. Instead, she recalled that exact moment when
she realized that she wasn't going to die and had actually managed to
overpower Odessa without anyone coming to her rescue but God. She

thought, *"Maybe there is a purpose for me and a reason why my life was spared."* At this point she didn't know what that purpose was but there was still time to discover it. She reflected back to a few nights ago on the first evening they arrived at Deek's house, after surviving her ordeal with Odessa Dillon.

Deek unlocked the front door and stepped aside for her to enter first. All of a sudden Renee felt her vision turn blurry and her feet give away from under her. He caught her before she collapsed.

"I'll be okay," she said, "being out in the cold and battling with Odessa must have drained my strength."

"Would you like me to fix you something to eat?" he asked.

"No, thanks, Sweetheart. I think I'll just lie down for a while."

Without saying a word, he lifted her up in his arms. Renee clung to his muscled shoulders as he carried her upstairs to his bedroom. Deek gently laid her down on the bed's black, cotton-sateen sheets. She fixed her gaze on him as he removed his sports jacket and folded it neatly across a chair. He loosened and snatched off his tie, then unfastened his gun holster and the one strapped to his ankle and set the weapons aside. Deek nuzzled beside her on his queen-sized bed, both fully clothed. She fell asleep just like that, exhausted but feeling completely safe and protected.

The next night her minor bruises and scraps had pretty much heeled and she was more rested, having slept most of the day while he was at work. Once he arrived home that second night, he had barely managed to remove his tie and weapons before they started kissing. Erotic passion mingled with a strong, metaphysical force that could not be stopped by either of them even if they had wanted to stop.

Renee quickly pulled off her dress and stretched out on the bed before him in panties and a black lace bra. He, simultaneously, unzipped and removed his slacks. She helped him unbutton his shirt, which he took off. This time they lay side by side in each other's arms wearing nothing but their underwear. They kissed slowly and gently as if savoring every sensation. Deek's warm tongue wandered under and between her breasts until her nipples stood up and reached out to his kisses. His lips continued to roam downward as he discovered new pleasure points on her body that she didn't know existed.

Renee slid on top of him. Her fingertips caressed and tongue kissed his hard body. She touched the healed gunshot wound embedded on his lower abdomen, an injury he had sustained that summer while attempting to save her from a killer. She stroked every part of him. No words were spoken, only moans of pleasure. Longing to taste him, she eased downward until her mouth reached his rigid, throbbing flesh. She licked and tasted more of his sweet juices. He groaned and quivered in pleasure.

She moved upwards to face him and rubbed her anxious pelvis against his. If she felt faint or weak now it was only from her growing excitement. After donning a condom that he quickly retrieved from the nightstand, Deek grabbed her hips and arched his body forward into her and she willingly received him. She felt him enter, very gently at first.

From making love to her before, he knew she wasn't used to his size yet. Not wanting to hurt her, his movements started slow and gentle. But as her body relaxed more and blended into his, their pace and intensity increased.

They grabbed, pinched, and kissed each other frantically while making love. The movements felt wild and untamed. Suddenly, her body tensed and a million tiny nerves of pleasure washed over her. Renee kissed Deek's neck and licked inside his ear. He closed his eyes tightly. His body stiffened and quivered, followed by a burst of liquid that felt warm inside her. They trembled in ecstasy and clung to each other for several more minutes after that. Renee closed her eyes and rested her head on his neck as their breathing slowed down. They held on tight as if trying to prevent each other from falling off the bed. She hadn't realized they had both drifted off to sleep for a quick nap until some time later when her movements caused him to stir. Deek kissed the top of her head and smiled. He turned on his side, facing her and supported himself on a raised elbow. She glided her fingertips across his chest and shoulder.

"Tell me, what's the best part of your day?" she asked, breaking their silence.

"Well, that depends, Doc," he said, staring into her eyes, "Everyday is uncharted territory for a homicide detective but there's one thing I know for sure. Right now, this moment is the best part."

"And why is that?" she smiled, tickling his side playfully.

"Because ... ," he grabbed her hand forcefully then said with a serious look, "I can do something you'll never be able to do."

Renee frowned, "What can you do that I can't?"

"Look down and see your lovely face." He climbed on top of her, without relaxing his full body weight and smiled down at her.

"If you don't stop with all the flattery," she said, punching his biceps playfully, "I'm going to have to peg you as a hopeless romantic, Detective."

"I won't argue with that, Sweetheart," he said, and rolled back onto his side then touched her cheek, "You bring it out in me." His dark eyes caressed her with a loving look as he held her around the waist. Renee draped her arms around his shoulders then eased her body under his once more. They started making love all over again. Throughout the night, she lost count of how many times they made love. But each time Deek ripped open a new package of brightly colored latex condoms. She feared she might collapse from exhaustion but her stamina held out. Eventually, Renee and Deek fell asleep, entangled in each other's arms.

She realized the film had ended because something else was now playing on the TV. She clicked the remote to turn the television off. She had been so caught up in reliving the last few nights with Deek that she didn't know how the heroine's romance in *Brief Encounter* had worked out. It didn't really matter to her because that movie was fantasy. What she had now with Deek was real.

CHAPTER 43

Over the next four days after leaving Deek's house to return to her Foxhall Crescent Estates home, Renee busied herself by counseling a few patients, getting ready to move, and preparing for Katia's release from temporary foster care that Child Protective Custody had arranged. She still hadn't gotten used to thinking of herself as a mother even though she'd visited Katia daily at foster care, fed her, played with her, and held her until she fell asleep. It was much like her caretaker role of Baby Susannah this past summer, except a major difference was that Susannah had been seriously ill whereas Baby Katia was healthy and completely normal. Another major difference—Katia would be hers!

Seeing the towers of packed boxes pushed against the walls throughout the house that she had shared with her estranged husband, no longer bothered her. Until it was time to move she alternated her time between patients' therapy sessions and shopping for baby essentials with Brenda's help. Even Deek had managed to take off one day to meet her at the new house to assemble the crib and paint the nursery pale pink. Along the floor's edges of the nursery, he installed a wooden white-picket fence with painted on leaves and lilacs while Renee pasted up a lilac border to match the flowers. As Deek affixed the fence pieces to the wall, she realized that her notion of the 'white picket-fenced' perfect family had changed. She had adopted a baby without a husband by her side to help raise her. Yet, as time passed she grew more hopeful that Deek would be there to fulfill that role. Everything had been set in motion for Renee to take custody of her newly adopted baby daughter after she moved into her new place and got settled.

Tomorrow was moving day. She had finally accepted the fact that Bill could never express the depth of emotional attachment she craved in a relationship, no matter how much he may have wanted to. It wasn't anyone's fault but she knew she could no longer settle for less. This would be her last night at the Foxhall Crescent Estates residence. Though many changes and uncertainties awaited her, Renee finally felt brave enough to rip that phony, organized world of hers apart and enjoy each day as if it were her last. She decided that from now on she would not let fear of the unknown prevent her from accepting and giving back love.

Any pre-moving day trepidation had now been overshadowed by the baby shower that Brenda, Veda and Cha-Cha had planned for her. In addition to moving boxes scattered throughout the house, the living room was now decorated with multicolored balloons that floated towards the ceiling in hues of pastel pink, yellow, baby blue, and mint. A banner saying, "Welcome Baby Katia! Congratulations, Renee!" stretched across the entranceway of the living room.

Remy, the limo driver arrived early, wearing a 'jaw stretched' grin and carrying an armful of his favorite CDs. He immediately volunteered for the role of DJ. Deek's FBI task force partner, Ana Santos arrived early as well and brought a bowl of her aunt's famous *ceviche* with a side dish of *canchita*. Chizuko, Renee's housekeeper, received the steady stream of friends and other guests who came to share in the happy event. Chizuko placed their baby gifts in an adjacent room on top an accumulating heap of other presents. For those who brought dishes of food to share, Chizuko found an empty spot on the jam-packed dining room table.

Visitors filed into the living room to ahh over pictures of Katia that Renee had strewn about and to wish her well. It didn't take long for her to dispense with trying to formally introduce everyone. As the room filled up, the guests chatted amongst themselves, nibbled from the buffet table, and mingled while she divided her time between each cluster of guests and answered the same questions repeatedly. *When will you pick up Katia? How will you manage your practice and take care of her? Do you already have a babysitter? Or will you get a live-in Au Pair?* She answered them as best she could.

Remy dominated the selections with a pulsating blend of Cameroonian music until Ana Santos asked him to play some of her CDs flavored with a Latin-beat that she pulled from her oversized purse. Not only did Ana Santos, Cha-Cha, Veda, and Remy contribute their favorite music, they each had brought an assortment of ethnic food to compliment the catered menu. Thanks to Chizuko, a fresh bouquet of red-rimmed, pink Amaryllis adorned the dining room table as its centerpiece, and provided a nice garnish to the smorgasbord of international and traditional soul food dishes crowding the table. Between the music, laughter, and multi-ethnic blend of accents and voices, Renee felt exuberant. Brenda had brought her three-month old son, Justin and his eyes flickered about at all the activity. Amazingly, the noise didn't seem to disturb him because he didn't cry once.

Renee glanced around the living room at the smiling faces and jovial laughter. She was relieved to see that Ana Santos had brought a date and he was busy teaching Cha-Cha how to salsa. Brenda and Sasha, Luke's fiancée, had just met at the shower but talked as if they were old friends. Of course, Deek's brother Luke could not attend as he was still away in training. It was good that Brenda and Sasha had bonded. They chatted away like they had lots in common to talk about. Brenda appeared to be almost as excited about Sasha's upcoming wedding next February as the bride-to-be was and offered to help Sasha with the planning. Renee knew that would be a relief to Deek since he could then gracefully bow out of helping Sasha pick out china patterns in his brother's absence.

Renee beamed when her longtime friend and mentor, Dr. Helen Stone arrived. Helen said she couldn't stay long since she had afternoon appointments with patients but just dropped by to wish her well. Helen looked thrilled to find out that Renee's new office where she'd be seeing patients, wasn't too far from her own downtown office. They planned to meet in a few weeks over lunch.

After Helen left, once again Renee found herself seated alone on the loveseat. She looked about and saw Deek huddled nearby in a corner with his partners, Detective Melvin Bradford and Special Agent Ana Santos. The law enforcement trio engaged in their own private discussion, but Renee easily overheard their conversation without trying.

"So Bradford, any plans now that you've only got two months before retirement?" asked Agent Santos.

"Why the hell do I need plans? What's wrong with sitting on my ass all day?"

Santos rolled her eyes towards the ceiling, "Figures."

"I got an idea, Mel," Deek piped up, "Why don't you work with my brother Luke and me at one of MPD's volunteer learning centers for troubled kids?"

"Say what? Volunteer?"

"Yeah. The Metropolitan Police Boys and Girls Club run these learning centers. They're staffed with retired teachers, school counselors, and police officers who volunteer their time," Deek explained. "Luke and I can only put in a few hours once a week. But after you retire, I think you'll be able to really do the kids some good, Mel."

"Isn't that one of those places where students who get suspended for long periods of time go to keep up with their school work?" Santos asked Deek.

"Exactly, in addition to a lot of other mentoring activities."

"That's a good idea Bradford now that you're retiring. Why don't you check it out?" Santos agreed.

Bradford looked at them both incredulously as if they'd suggested he go through an 8 week stint on Survivor and swim through shark-infested waters with an open cut.

"Let's see now," he said, drawing his eyebrows together as if giving the matter serious consideration. "We got choice A where I sleep late, sit on my ass all day, and don't do a damn thing. Or choice B, get up early to go holler at a bunch of bad ass kids all day for free? Hum, that's a tough decision, Partners," he said, rubbing his chin. "But think I'm gonna pick the A vowel this time, guys."

"Why am I not surprised?" said Santos, shaking her head.

"Hey Santos, if I were you, I'd mind my own business. Looks like you'd better keep an eye on your date over there instead of worrying about me." Bradford pointed to Ana's boyfriend who grasped Veda around the waist and twirled her around on the dance floor. "He seems to be making the rounds," Bradford chuckled.

At that moment, Deek caught Renee's eye and his gaze settled on her instead of the dancing couple. Earlier that day he had asked her out to dinner on this last night before leaving there for good. What else could she say but yes. Renee did not have any intentions of ever again saying no to the man she loved. As they stared into each other's eyes, they both seemed to be able to read one another's thoughts—*how nice it'll be to spend time alone together later tonight.* Neither one bothered to eat much at the shower since they planned to go out.

Detective Bradford eyed the buffet table then went to fill up his plate with a second helping. As Brenda passed by to go check on Justin who was now asleep in the study, Bradford stopped her.

"No hard feelings, Mrs. Johnson?" he said between chews, "Nothing personal, I was just doing my job."

"I understand Detective Bradford, I forgive you. We all make mistakes," Brenda said warmly, "Please excuse me while I go check on my son."

Renee admired Brenda's capacity to forgive and not hold grudges against people who wronged her. As for Irene Adams, Brenda had paid off all her mother's credit card debt with the insurance money she received after Detective Bradford dropped the charges against her, once the hold on her claim had been lifted. Even though Brenda overlooked her mother's selfishness, Renee could not and was relieved when Mrs. Adams declined Brenda's invitation to the shower.

Deek wandered over and sat down on the sofa next to Renee while her cat, Angel slept at her feet.

"I'm sorry about Mel being here. He heard me talking to Ana about the party today. I didn't invite him but I should have guessed he'd show up when she mentioned the dish her aunt was making to add to your buffet," said Deek.

"It's okay, Sweetheart. I'm not going to let anything ruin this day, not even Detective Bradford," she said. "Besides, if Brenda can overlook the way he harassed her and her mother when he thought they were guilty, I should be able to overlook his many faults."

"I realize Mel may be lacking in social graces but he's been my partner for the past two years. I'd risk my life for him if it came to that."

Renee cringed. "Honey, I couldn't bare the thought of losing you to save Melvin Bradford."

"Well, I wouldn't hesitate for a moment and I know Mel would put his life on the line for me too. That's just the way we operate. But that doesn't mean I wanna spend all my free time with him," he said, showing his dimples when he smiled at her.

Renee noticed the music selection changed to a nice, mellow tune. Suddenly, Cha-Cha strolled over and sat down on the matching love seat facing them. She rested her plate of heavily frosted cake on top of the coffee table in the center of the two complimentary sofas.

"I had to threaten to break both Remy's knees if he didn't play my new Erykah Badu CD," said Cha-Cha, swaying her head to Miss Badu's soulful voice, "Now I can sit here and chill for a minute."

"Veda's daughter, Sherrelle just phoned from her cell phone," Cha-Cha told Renee, "She's on her way over with a gift for the new baby. She insisted on using her own money that she gets from helping out around the shop and would not let Veda put her name on the gift she brought. That girl is something else," said Cha-Cha, shaking her head. "I told her to bring some tunes that the kids are listening to these days. And, when she gets here she can permanently relieve Remy of his disc jock duties."

"That's sweet of Sherrelle," said Renee.

"Yeah, Veda lucked out with that little lady. Makes me almost wish I had settled down and had a kid or two of my own ... Almost," Cha-Cha winked and took a bite of cake.

"I have to admit Veda's been a great Mom to Sherrelle ever since they reunited," Cha-Cha added. "I'm really proud of my girl Veda. She's come a long way thanks to your help, Dr. Renee."

"That's what I love about being a psychologist—seeing people make healthy changes in their lives," said Renee, "I truly believe that people can change if they so desire. It's gratifying when I see people accomplish what they want to achieve the way Veda has." Renee looked at Veda out on the dance floor, having a great time with Ana's date. Cha-Cha followed her gaze and nodded.

"Detective Hamilton, I almost forgot to thank you for stopping by Good Looks last week and schooling me about that lowlife Ian Mathias," said Cha-Cha, wrinkling her nose as if smelling rotten meat at the mention of her former boyfriend. "Turns out you were right about him."

"I take it you heard the news bulletin that Agent Santos and I arrested Mathias on Monday, along with his boy, DL, and four other Jett Set crewmembers."

"Yeah, I read it in the papers and heard it on the news too. But I'd already dumped the thug long before that. I hope he gets the chair for lying to me the way he did."

"Don't worry, Cha-Cha, the U.S. attorney's office has built a solid case against Mathias and his crew," said Deek, "His hitman, DL took our bait and plea bargained in exchange for testifying against him."

"Good." She picked up her plate and took another bite of cake.

"Like I told you before, Dr. Renee," said Cha-Cha with a deep sigh, "when it comes to men, I always seem to lose out."

Mel Bradford squeezed next to Cha-Cha on the loveseat. Renee wondered how long he had been listening to their conversation. Bradford leaned closer to Cha-Cha and tilted his head before re-introducing himself but Cha-Cha told him she already knew who he was since he had questioned her about Jerome's murder.

"A beautiful lady like you. Those guys must be bums," he said, "Would you like me to get you something from the table, some more cake, another glass of wine?"

Renee stared at both Bradford and her hair stylist. Bradford openly displayed his lust for Cha-Cha in her black, leather mini-skirt and stretchy tight blouse. But what Renee couldn't understand was why instead of giving Bradford a look of disgust, Cha-Cha offered him a hint of a smile. She even crossed her legs and finger-curled a lock of hair behind her ear.

"You married?" she asked him.

"Not any more."

"Then another glass of Kendall Jackson Chardonnay would be nice, Mel," she said sweetly.

Bradford nearly tripped over his feet trying to rush to the kitchen to pour Cha-Cha some more wine.

After he left, Cha-Cha cooed seductively, "Your partner's as cute as a teddy bear with those sad, brown eyes, that round tummy, and those three little pieces of hair sticking up on top his head."

"If you say so, Cha-Cha. Somehow, I never pictured Mel in that regard but to each his own," Deek chuckled.

"So Detective Hamilton, is your partner telling the truth about his marital status?" she asked, "I've had enough of married men to last a lifetime."

"Um hum," Deek nodded, "His wife divorced him last year."

Renee thought about warning Cha-Cha about Detective Melvin Bradford then decided to mind her own business. Besides, who was she to give advice about love? She was just discovering the true meaning of love for herself. Knowing Bradford, it wouldn't take him long to show his real personality and completely turn Cha-Cha off. His single status couldn't help him there.

"Yeah, I think an older, more mature man like Mel might be just what I need right now."

Bradford returned with the wine and plopped back down beside Cha-Cha. She lifted her glass to Renee in a toast. Bradford followed suit with his glass of bourbon.

"Here's to Dr. Renee, a great therapist, now a new mother, and to top it all off, heroine of the day."

"That's right, Doc," said Bradford, "We gotta hand it to you for nailing Odessa Dillon the way you did. She was a big girl for you to handle all by yourself."

"I didn't do anything but try to get away from her. And thank God I did."

"I read where Odessa's accomplice confessed," said Cha-Cha, "It's hard to believe that dude was supposed to be Jerome's best friend. And, to top it off, turns out he was the same bigmouth old dude who came into the shop sometimes to get Whittni, one of the girl's in my beauty shop, to wash his hair. Unbelievable," said Cha-Cha, shaking her head.

"Yeah, Jerome Johnson had one friend too many," said Bradford, agreeing.

"I wonder if Jerome knew before he died that it was his best friend who betrayed him?" said Cha-Cha. "But then again, I guess it does happen," she said thoughtfully with a sad look.

"Hard to say. According to his confession, Alonzo Woods followed his boss's orders like a boot camp maggot," said Bradford, "and if that wasn't bad enough, the guy's own wife called the station to tip us off while Dr. Renee was out battling in the woods with the wildebeest."

"After Alonzo's wife called, we got a search warrant and found so much evidence at his home we didn't even need his confession."

"That's right, the uniforms found his black Coogi jacket in the closet with burn marks on it. Plus, the gas receipt for the gasoline he used in the arson was still in one of the pockets," Deek said.

"So you see Doc, Mel and I would have eventually caught the bad guys. There was no need for you to risk your life going after them," said Deek, with a serious tone.

"I'm just glad the people responsible for such a vicious act were caught and brought to justice," said Renee, "I hope that finding and convicting Jerome's murderer will give Brenda closure now." During their conversation, Renee didn't hear the doorbell ring but looked up when Chizuko suddenly came rushing towards her, visibly distressed.

"Miz H, Mr. H at front door!" she shrieked while waving her arms in the air.

"Calm down, Chizuko. I'll take care it," said Renee and got up to go talk to him but before she could reach the hallway to speak to him privately, he walked through the living room.

"I didn't know you were throwing a party, Hon. Guess my invitation got lost in the mail. Bill spotted Angel in the corner, licking her already clean, white fur even cleaner. He called her to come to him but Angel ignored him. "Looks like my cat belongs to you too now," he said with a pained expression on his face.

"She always did. You gave her to me, remember. Listen, Bill, just because I didn't get around to changing the locks, doesn't give you the right to barge in as if you still live here," she said. "Don't forget, we're now legally separated and you moved out."

"You know that was a mistake," he said, with a menacing stare at Deek.

"Bill, why are you here?" she placed her hand on his arm, and spoke gently in order to diffuse any possible conflict. She was close enough to detect the alcohol on his breath. "I'm glad everything worked out for you and the FBI believed your story. Now that Shaw has been arrested for his connections to that drug dealer isn't it time for you to make a new start and figure out what you want to do with your life?"

Bill turned serious. "I already know what I want. I wanna get back what I had. If it wasn't for me listening to Shaw I would've never given you those divorce papers. It was a mistake, Renee." He reached out to her and moved closer, but she backed away. He snatched her by the waist without warning.

Renee jerked free of him before he had a chance to kiss her. It was only one o'clock in the afternoon but the liquor was heavy on his breath. At that moment, Deek leaped up from the sofa and stood next to Renee but she waved him back.

"Let's go talk in the kitchen," she told Bill and grabbed his hand to lead him out of the room.

Once they were out of earshot of everyone, she spoke softly. "Bill, your things have already been packed and labeled with your current address. The movers will see to it that all the boxes get to where they're going," she said. "All you have to do is be home tomorrow between noon and five when they arrive. This is happening and there's nothing you can do to change it. I don't want us to be enemies."

"Looks like you've thought of everything, My Dear." He pulled out one of the kitchen chairs and sat down. "I don't want to be enemies either. In fact, I still love you," he said without being able to look at her.

"Bill, I really would appreciate it if you'd leave now. I don't want a scene with all these people here."

"Neither do I, Sweetheart. That's why I'm asking you nicely if we can get back together. I'll try harder this time."

"Renee asked you to leave," said Deek, suddenly appearing at the kitchen doorway. "I think you need to respect her wishes, don't you?"

"I think you need to mind your goddamn business, Hamilton," said Bill, jumping up from his chair and now only inches from Deek's face. Both men looked at each other with unblinking coldness then Bill spoke, calmly. "Renee and I may be temporarily separated but we're not divorced yet. Just so you know, I'm not giving up. I'm not scared of you, Hamilton—with or without your police-issued weapon."

"Look man, if you wanna discuss this outside, let's go now," Deek said, trying not to lose his temper, "But I'm not going to disrespect Renee and her guests by arguing with you in her home."

"Such a gentleman," said Bill, with a sarcastic undertone. "Let me make this perfectly clear, I intend to get my wife back."

"No, Bill, you won't," said Renee, gently pushing Deek to one side and stepping between the two men, "I no longer want what you thought you were giving me for the last fourteen years. Please leave quietly. There's nothing else to discuss."

Bill elbowed pass Renee and moved closer to confront Deek, his adversary, once again. At that moment, Bradford appeared in the kitchen and stepped up to Bill. He held out his shield and dangled a pair of handcuffs.

"Don't worry, Doc. No need to call law enforcement on your former husband 'cause there's enough of us already here," he said wearing a sarcastic grin. "Don't be stupid, asshole. Seems to me you've already stayed past your welcome."

Bill smiled weakly at Renee and started towards the door. "No need to show me out, Babe. I know my way." He turned back around and narrowed his dark eyes at Deek. "This isn't over, friend," said Bill, with a chilly smile. Then, he turned to look at Renee. "I will be back," he said and left through the front door.

CHAPTER 44

October 24,

Later that evening, Renee dressed for dinner, completely alone in the empty boxed up house. By the time Deek returned to the house to pick her up, Chizuko had gotten everything cleaned up and back to normal before she left to go home. Other than the unpleasant confrontation with Bill, the entire day had been wonderful. She anticipated an even better evening alone with Deek with the hope of many more evenings just like it to come. And, in just a few days after she moved into her new home, she would pick up her baby! She still couldn't get used to how unbelievable that sounded. She finally had what she thought would never be hers.

Renee clamped on the three-diamond necklace that Deek had given her for her birthday. It settled just above the crevice of her breasts and gleamed against her skin. She wore tiny, diamond drop earrings that matched the necklace perfectly and complimented her scoop necked, red chemise dress. She swept her shoulder-length, Egyptian-sable hair to the left side, revealing only one of the diamond earrings.

"You look absolutely gorgeous," said Deek when she opened the door.

Dressed for the evening, he looked as fine as any runway male model in black wool slacks, taupe jacket and black Stacy Adams shoes.

A glimpse of taupe, silk necktie paired nicely with the taupe vest over a black dress shirt. He stepped inside the foyer just long enough to hold out her coat. Folding his dark gray trench coat over one arm, he followed her out. Neither one seemed to be able to wipe the permanent smile from their faces as they walked hand-in-hand down the long driveway to his car.

"Where are you taking me tonight, Detective? Not that it really matters because all I need is to be with you."

"You'll just have to wait and see. Several weeks ago, I asked to take you to dinner and as I recall, you turned me down," he said, opening the passenger side door for her.

"That won't happen again," she smiled and leaned into his arms for a quick kiss before climbing in the car.

They headed downtown and when Deek approached 9th and Pennsylvania Avenue, NW, Renee suddenly feared that he planned to make a detour at the FBI Building. After all he was still assigned to the DC Joint SOS Task Force and might have something important to take care of before their evening together could begin. Her worries subsided when he parked at 10th and Pennsylvania in front of the Asian-inspired TenPenh Restaurant and got out to open her door.

They crossed the threshold that separated Washington's swarming nightlife from an exotic haven of diffused, romantic lighting, soft music, and tantalizing aromas of Asian-Pacific cuisine. A hostess dressed in a floor-length, embroidered, silk tunic greeted Deek as one of their frequent customers and led them to a semi-private dining area, secluded within an etched glass enclosure. Moments later a waiter brought the bottle of champagne that Deek had requested and poured their glasses. Against the backdrop of teak furniture, Asian silk and woven wall hangings, soothing instrumental music resonated pleasantly throughout the restaurant.

The waiter came over to take their order. Deek suggested they try the restaurant's signature dish of Chinese-style smoked lobster with fried spinach. After the waiter left, Deek grasped Renee's hand from across the table.

"Sweetheart, I'm sorry I wasn't there when Odessa Dillon tried to kill you. Can you forgive me, Baby?"

"If you can forgive me for playing detective and almost getting myself killed."

"Renee, promise me you'll stop chasing down criminals by yourself. That's my job, remember?"

"Yes, Darling. I promise."

"Good. I know I can be a bit overprotective at times," he said. "Even though I was born and raised in Chicago, my maternal grandparents immigrated from Martinique and brought my mother to the States when she was a girl. My grandparents kept their Martinican traditions, so I guess I inherited a touch of my grandfather's West Indian male chauvinism."

"I can tell. Just don't get too macho on me. I'm not some helpless female type, you know."

"I know and I'm glad you're not," he said. "Anyway, not to worry. I like strong, assertive women. I just want you to be careful, Baby, when I'm not there, okay?"

"I understand, Darling. And the next time I decide to go chasing criminals, I'll tell you first," she smiled and winked.

"I can see I'm going to have a difficult woman on my hands. Maybe, I should just talk to Chief Frye about assigning you a piece and a shield."

"I don't need that to be a PI," she said teasingly.

"I hope you're joking, Renee."

"Of course, I'm joking, Honey. You know very well, I'm not interested in becoming a private investigator … at least, not now," she said. "All I want is to be a good mother to Katia, help my patients, and keep you in my life."

Deek closed his eyes and leaned forward across the table to kiss her gently and accepted her return kiss. They ignored the stares of other diners.

"The last time I remember being this adored by someone was with my first boyfriend when I was only sixteen years old. I forgot what it felt like to be cherished," said Renee. She grew silent for a moment when thinking about the time she fell in love for the first time and got pregnant at sixteen.

"I intend to spend my entire life reminding you," he said.

It didn't take long for the waiter to return with their meal, served on pale yellow china plates. They pressed their hands in the steaming moist, terry hand towels that the waiter provided. The dish looked too good to destroy its artistic presentation by eating it, but neither had eaten all day and they were both starved. So after a few moments of admiring the chef's arrangement, they enjoyed the perfect blend of seasoned flavors. After the meal, the waiter returned to refilled their champagne glasses. Deek motioned for him and whispered something in his ear before the waiter removed the dishes.

"Sweetie, do you remember when I was in the hospital this summer and you broke up with me …"

Renee started to argue but he held up his hand.

"No. Honey, I'm not blaming you. What I'm saying is, I thought our love had died. And when you reconciled with Bill, I figured it was over between us for good."

Renee interrupted him and tried to explain. "Deek, as terrible as that experience was when you got shot trying to save me, I wasn't ready to accept the truth about how deeply I felt about you until I thought you were dying."

He smiled, exposing his dimples. "Like my Grann Katia used to say, sometimes love must die so it can live again. Now I think I understand what she meant. True love always reveals itself in time."

Just then the hostess returned. Renee covered her mouth in surprise when she saw her carrying an armful of a dozen, long-stemmed, red roses wrapped in shimmering, gold tissue. She held the flowers out to Renee as a few onlookers gaped at them. Renee sniffed their perfumed fragrance and raised her eyes to Deek.

"Compliments of the gentleman," said the smiling hostess and bowed.

"Deek, these flowers are lovely, Darling. They're from you?" she said, removing the card.

He nodded while Renee read the card that simply said *'Yours for Eternity, Deek.'* The hostess pulled up a vacant chair and gently placed the bouquet down next to her.

"The stems have a little vial of water so your flowers will be fine until you get home, Madam. I'll send over your waiter with our dessert menu," she said then quietly slipped away.

"Tell me now, Deek, are there any more surprises you plan to spring on me? Because I'm already quite overwhelmed and don't know if my heart can take it."

"As a matter of fact, I think I do have one more," he said and reached into his pants pocket.

Deek placed a small, black velvet box on the white clothed table. "Wh-what's this?"

"I'm getting tired of holding onto this thing, Sweetheart. Why don't you do me a favor and wear it for me?" he said in a playful tone and slid the box towards her.

Renee held her breath as she slowly flipped open the lid. A two-carat, emerald-cut diamond engagement ring in an antique platinum setting perched brilliantly inside the box. Renee sat speechless, unable to remove her eyes from the enormous ring.

"It's a family heirloom that my grandmother gave me before she died three years ago. I never could figure out why I inherited it instead of Luke since he's older than I am. My mother told me once that Grann Katia said I was the serious, patient one and she believed I'd cherish it more."

"Your grandmother was right," said Renee, "You're certainly one of the most serious and patient men I know."

"Mom told me that Grann Katia knew I wouldn't just give it away frivolously to some girl I was merely infatuated with. But I'd wait until I fell in love and give it to the woman I wanted to spend my life with."

"What are you saying?" She looked at him without moving a muscle.

"Renee, will you do me the honor of marrying me?" he asked, staring at her with sincere eyes.

Tears dribbled down her cheek. She was afraid to speak, afraid her voice would quiver. She touched his arm instead. Deek held her hands and caressed them within both of his.

"You don't have to say anything now if you're not ready to give me an answer yet."

He picked up the cloth napkin and dabbed her tears away.

"Deek, I love you and of course, I want to marry you. I know now this is how it's supposed to feel when two people really love each other."

"I love you too, Sweetheart. I've never wanted to be with anyone as much as I want you. And don't feel like you're stuck with my grandmother's ring as your engagement ring if you don't like it. It's merely a symbol of how I feel about you. When you're ready, you can pick out exactly what you want."

"Deek, this *is* exactly what I want. It's beautiful. I don't deserve to be so lucky—to find someone like you."

"I'm the one who's lucky, Renee. I thank God for bringing you into my life."

Suddenly, she looked worried. "My divorce won't be final for another year. Even with a no-fault, uncontested divorce, the waiting period in D. C is one year."

"I'm well aware of the District's statutes, but Baby, I'll wait for you no matter how long it takes."

"You heard Bill this afternoon. Deek, I don't think he's accepted that it's over between us. I don't want to hurt him. He's really a good man."

"Don't worry, Sweetheart, we'll be sensitive to his feelings to a certain extent. But I'm not going to let him take advantage of your kind heart. Hopefully, he'll realize that he can't own someone like you own an automobile. I'm not going to let Bill or anyone else hurt you," he said. "All I know is, a year from now I want to be your husband and Katia's father."

"I'm not worried about him hurting me. I don't think he would intentionally do that," she said, "I'm frightened of what he could do to you. I don't think he's behaving rationally these days. He's had a lot of disappointments and a year is a long time."

Deek stroked her cheek. "Sweetie, I can take care of myself and you too. Let's not talk about him anymore."

The waiter returned with the dessert menu. "Would you like to try one of our signature desserts with your coffee?" the waiter asked.

Deek gave Renee a questioning look to find out what she wanted. Without answering, she opened her small, black evening bag and removed a single gold key.

He frowned, looking somewhat puzzled. "What's that for?"

Renee's eyes met his before answering. "It's the key to my new house," she said with an enticingly smile, "We can have our own signature dessert at home, if you prefer."

Deek turned to the waiter, still standing by with the menus in his hand. "Check please."

THE END